THE HORROR MOVIE SURVIVAL GUIDE

THE Horror Movie SURVIVAL GUIDE

Matteo Molinari and Jim Kamm

BERKLEY BOULEVARD BOOKS, NEW YORK

A Berkley Boulevard Book
Published by The Berkley Publishing Group
A division of Penguin Putnam Inc.
375 Hudson Street
New York, New York 10014

Book design by Tiffany Kukec
Cover design by Pyrographx

PRINTING HISTORY
Berkley Boulevard trade paperback edition / April 2001

The Penguin Putnam Inc. World Wide Web site address is
http://www.penguinputnam.com

Library of Congress Cataloging-in-Publication Data

Molinari, Matteo, 1966–
The horror movie survival guide / Matteo Molinari and Jim Kamm.
p. cm.
ISBN 0-425-17841-2 (trade pbk.)
1. Horror films—Criticism and interpretation. 2. Science fiction films—History and criticism. 3. Horror films—Humor. 4. Science Fiction films—Humor. I. Kamm, Jim. II. Title.

PN1995.9.H6 M535 2001
791.43'6164—dc21
00-051907

PRINTED IN THE UNITED STATES OF AMERICA

10 9 8 7 6 5 4 3 2 1

Contents

Acknowledgments

The first thanks go out to Charlotte Breeze, wonderful manager and friend, who loves the wacky ideas we always bring to her. One of these days we'll buy you a box of Tylenol for all those headaches, Char. We owe you big, baby.

Also, many thanks to the editors at Berkley who fell for this wacked-out concept, particularly Robert Pulciani, John Morgan, and Lisa Considine.

Special thanks also go out to the folks at Cinefile Video in West L.A. for going the extra mile in finding "footage" for our research.

We're also grateful to <TAG> Media (now Razorfish L.A.) for helping us with the first printings of the book presentation.

Matteo would like to thank the two best "crazy scientists" he's ever met: Mom & Dad, or Mamma & Papà, whose experiments in their lab created Matteo. Even if he still needs a life, he'll never thank them enough for all they did (and still do, and will do) for him. A generous thanks goes of course to the one and only Jim Kamm, whose friendship and endless patience makes him follow and understand the Italo-American English Matteo desperately tries to write. And thanks to Steven Spielberg, John Landis, Wes Craven, Roger Corman, [insert your favorite director here] for telling the wonderful stories they tell.

Jim would like to thank his family for their moral support (morals can be so important when discussing horror movies), his friends for not abandoning him during "crunch time," and especially the lovely Elle Struzziero, who kept him from starving—for food, laundry, and love. Thanks also goes out to his employers for their understanding of his need to extend his working days far into the night. And, of course, to the ingenious Matteo Molinari, whose alien sense of humor and inspiring knowledge of everything "useless" brought this whole thing together in the first place. And also for putting up with his Nazi-like anal tendencies. *"Mangia, mangia, che porno, che porno!"*

So many more people to thank, and you know who you are, you lovely, lovely people! Especially the people that had the guts to make that seventh sequel, which went straight to video, and which nobody saw. Except us.

Introduction

This book is the result of two lifetimes of horror: American junior high school, growing up in Italy, moving to Hollywood . . . as well as seeing many great flicks and a boatload of stinkers. There are many thick books you can find which discuss the subject of horror movies and monsters at great length . . . and which will bore you to tears. This is not one of those books.

This is a book which properly acknowledges the gruesome horrors that infuse our daily lives, and which will serve as a trusted guide to those who dare to survive. Horror movies are texts to be studied, lessons in survival. *Not* just mindless entertainment.

NO, IT'S NOT "JUST A MOVIE"

Remember how your mother used to tell you that monsters aren't real? Well, what do you call the Spice Girls? And Amy Fisher? And Roberto Benigni? Time and experience have shown us that what we see in horror movies is not, in fact, fiction:

1963: Alfred Hitchcock shoots a movie where a flock of birds attack the California town of Bodega Bay.
1975: 7 million birds raid the town of Hopkinsville, Kentucky.

1975: Steven Spielberg tells the story of a shark that threatens the beaches of Amity, New York.
1991: The island of Kauai, Hawaii, is under siege by a ravenous tiger shark which just won't go away.

1955: Bill Farrell is abducted by a monster from outer space.
1985: Whitley Strieber is repeatedly abducted by aliens.

1990: Writer Paul Sheldon becomes the hostage of his "number one fan," Annie Wilkes.
1992: David Letterman finds a stalker fan inside his house.

1931: Frankenstein's creature first appears on the silver screen.
1997: Scientists clone sheep and now want to try it with humans.

1992: Leonardo DiCaprio appears in the movie *Critters 3.*
1998: Leonardo DiCaprio "graces the screen" in the record-breaking *Titanic* and the period joke *The Man in the Iron Mask.*

Most people think that the events depicted in horror movies are thought up by people with sick, twisted minds who sit around playing with sharp objects, drinking too much caffeine, and watching too much cable access. But the fact is that all horror movies are reenactments of actual events. Kind of like *America's Most Wanted.* Although they are filmed by directors and acted out by actors, everything in them has happened in real life.

And these kinds of things continue to happen on a daily basis. Pick up a copy of *USA Today* or the *National Enquirer* and you can read about merely a fraction of what is going down in the dark alleys of America. Most horror is unfit for public consumption. Sometimes, it is the government covering it up so that we can sleep at night. But more often it is that reporters just can't believe that these events are real. Which is understandable. They're just peons in the news/media establishment whose interest it is to tell you sweet little lies so that you continue to buy their papers and watch their newsmagazine shows. Anything challenging their comfortable existence is to be swept under the carpet.

Horror films are the only place where the truth comes to light. Why else would we watch them? For "entertainment"? What's so entertaining about watching someone getting gutted with a chainsaw? The fact is that we know instinctually that these movies are telling us something, something we desperately need to know. That we must fight to survive no matter what the cost. That no matter what the odds, the moral, brave, and intelligent always prevail. That William Shatner absolutely *cannot* act.

We are assaulted from all sides with potential horror, from the school or office bully to the bipolar mailman. And where do you wanna be when the doo-doo hits the fan, courageously and confidently battling the forces of evil or splattering against the wall?

SO THEN WHAT WOULD YOU CONSIDER A "HORROR MOVIE"?

Carrot Top: Chairman of the Board. Seriously, though (though not too seriously) . . .

Horror movie "purists" will tell you that the strict definition of a horror movie is a film designed to terrify the audience involving elements of the *supernatural* or *paranormal*—such as mummy movies, vampire movies, ghost movies, or perhaps even Frankenstein movies (although that is debatable, as you'll see later).

These same purists make a separation between horror movies and "thrillers": scary movies about crazy people chasing teenagers with hand tools and the like, or other real-world stories whose main purpose is to scare the piss out of you. And some might argue that movies about dangerous alien encounters would more properly fall under the heading of "science fiction."

Well, after carefully considering the extremely blurry lines which divide these genres, we've decided to throw them all together. Not that we're including all thrillers or sci-fi flicks in our book, but that we're acknowledging that all of these kinds of scary movies can be called "horror movies" without anybody whining too loudly.

This is because the main element these movies have in common is one kind of object which is the primary source of fear as we neurotically nibble away at our popcorn . . . they all have monsters in one form or another.

THEN JUST WHAT IS A "MONSTER"?

Quite simply, it's a mean, evil, underhanded thing that wants to do people tremendous harm. But these things might be said of the school bully, or even a parking meter attendant.

What sets monsters apart from run-of-the-mill meanies is that their behavior and their motivations are beyond what we would consider normal and rational . . . and yes, you could argue that such moral judgments are merely social constructs. And, ultimately, you'd be right (smart-ass!). But relative morality doesn't really hold its own when you're dealing with folks who use their victims' body parts to decorate the living room, or creatures who levitate and try to drag unsuspecting people into parallel universes for "extensive probing."

But the other part of the equation is that monsters must cause us (or be able to cause us) irreparable harm. "Pesky" cannot be the strongest adjective applied to a real monster . . . just to a Jehovah's Witness.

As you'll see when you flip through the meat of this book, monsters come in all shapes and sizes. They can come from Earth, outer space, or hell. They can be human, animal, mineral, immaterial, or even an old house. They can be created, invented, or discovered.

All this leaves us with a whole universe of potential candidates for monsterhood. And we haven't even mentioned yet our *own* ability to turn into monsters, which is perhaps the scariest thing we'll ever have to face down. But the goal of this book is not to acquaint you with every monster ever encountered in the vain hope that any creature you may run into in the future has already been dealt with. *Au contraire* . . . New terrors are popping up all the time, and only a thorough knowledge of the past and all it has had to offer will prepare you to save your skin should the situation arise.

The most important thing we would like to pass on to the readers of this book is the ability to distinguish monsters from just plain jerks. There are a lot of threatening and annoying people in the world, but you can't go around pulling the Rambo routine on people for cutting you off on the highway. This is the quickest path to becoming a monster yourself. For mean, dishonest, and violent assholes we highly recommend involving the justice system. The police may not be perfect, but they'll certainly be breathing down *your* neck if you choose to become your town's "vigilante extraordinaire."

A BOOK TO HAVE AND TO HOLD

You don't own anything you can't carry in one hand at a dead run.

Attributed to Robert A. Heinlein

There are two reasons why we have chosen to keep this book small and relatively brief:

1. We don't think you need or want to know about every stupid horror movie ever made.
2. We wanted to give something easy to carry. In case you find *yourself* at a "dead" run.

Needless to say, it's even harder to escape encroaching vampires if you're carting around all thirty-two volumes of the Encyclopedia Britannica. What you need is a small, handy guide to keep with you on those ill-chosen solo expeditions into the woods—the one thing that will fit into that little backpack which passes as a purse as you descend into the boiler room to deliver the principal's all-school memo to Mr. Creepy the janitor.

GIVE US A FRIGGIN' BREAK

Do I contradict myself?
Very well then I contradict myself.

Walt Whitman

Although this is a book about how to survive horror movies, there is NO SUREFIRE WAY. And the rules do not always apply. "So why come up with rules at all?" you ask. So that you don't find yourself foolishly and needlessly walking into a zombie ambush. Even those who take all necessary precautions and follow the best advice still find themselves in very hairy situations. It takes a resourceful, willful, and inventive person to survive a horror movie. And being familiar with the basic rules and the most common monsters is still a must.

We do not even try to pretend that this book is fully comprehensive. If we did, we would be insufferable pretentious nerds. Or rather, even *more* insufferable pretentious nerds than we already are. There are many thousands of horror movies in existence, and believe us, you can find most of them on video, including *Bela Lugosi Meets a Brooklyn Gorilla, Geek Maggot Bingo, Microwave Massacre, The Weasel That Dripped Blood, Invasion of the Space Preachers, Barn of the Naked Dead, Dr. Butcher M.D., Unsane, Blackenstein,* and *Frankenhooker.* But we can't cover everything, and trust us: you don't *want* us to.

Also, you may disagree with the way we've defined, classified, and talked about the monsters contained in this book. You may disagree with what should be considered a horror movie, and whether or not they're real. So write your own damn book. Or buy another one. We've spent more time researching and thinking about this stuff than any sane person could possibly endure. And if you find yourself in a horrific situation, this book *will* be helpful.

Some monsters either defy classification or else pervert it. We've been forced to make some tough choices about where these monsters fit into the scheme of things. And again—we've done it so that you don't have to.

DANGER: INSIDER INFORMATION!

In a few places in this book, we are forced to give away important plot points (and shocking plot twists) of movies in order to properly warn you about dangerous monsters. If this is going to bother you, we highly recommend watching the footage before reading the particular monster's entry.

FOR IDIOTS ONLY

IF YOU'RE UNDER THE IMPRESSION THAT YOU CAN READ THIS BOOK, AND THEN GO OFF AND DO SOMETHING STUPID LIKE HURTING OR KILLING SOMEONE, BLOWING SOMETHING UP, AND THEN BLAMING US FOR YOUR CARNAGE, STOP READING RIGHT NOW. BECAUSE WE DON'T EVEN WANT TO HEAR IT.

FOR THE HEALTH-CONSCIOUS

Broccoli may taste funny, but it's really good for you.

THE 10 BIGGEST MISTAKES

1. NEVER assume that "Everything will be all right." It won't be.
2. NEVER turn off the radio or TV when an emergency news bulletin is on. Unless you want to be in the next bulletin.
3. NEVER go anywhere if someone tells you, "Wait right here."
4. NEVER have sex or get naked.
5. NEVER drink or smoke.
6. NEVER go for a walk by yourself—especially in the wilderness.
7. NEVER mockingly go "Oo-ee-oo" to joke about how creepy something is.
8. NEVER investigate strange sounds, or call out "Hello?"
9. NEVER walk away from the killer after one good blow.
10. NEVER assume that "It's over." It ain't. And really never will be. . . .

VISIT US ONLINE

HorrorMovieGuide.com is the constantly updated companion Web site for this book, and you can E-mail your questions, commments, and egregious insults to **comments@HorrorMovieGuide.com**

C'mon! Whatsa matta? You chicken?

This is the generic entry format for monsters, whether they are individual monsters or breeds.

Evil Monster from Hell

Classification: What kind of monster we're jabbering about. Places it within the HMSG Monster Taxonomy, a system which attempts to accomplish the ridiculous task of classifying like monsters into groups.
Example: the occult / demons / *Ridiculous latinnamus*

The Skinny: The monster's one-liner "Cliff Note." Just in case you're in a *REAL BIG HURRY* . . .

Quotable: Witty and insightful dialogue taken from the film itself.

Footage: Significant documentaries on the monster, listed chronologically—year released, title, and director.
Examples:
1975, *Lame Slasher Flick* by Alan Smithee
1992, *Who's Eating Gilbert Grape?* by Lasse Hallström.

Born or Created: Date and place—if known.

Discovered: Where and when—if known.

Habitat or Stomping Grounds: *Where the Wild Things Are.* What planet, what continent, what city, which room in which building, and inside which body.

Origin or Biography: What warped experiment, unlucky accident, or act of God brought this beast into existence, and who was the unlucky sap who ran into it first.

Identification: How to distinguish between this monster and your uncle Harry. Or how to verify that your uncle Harry *is* in fact *The Creature from the Black Lagoon.*

Cravings: What it wants and desires—the reason it gets up in the morning.

Behavior: *What Do Monsters Do All Day* . . . or night?

Danger: The very things which make a monster a monster: the powers and abilities it uses in wreaking its carnage. Things to look out for.

How to Kill or Destroy It: The reason you bought this book. Tried-and-true methods for slaying the beast. IMPORTANT: *THE HORROR MOVIE SURVIVAL GUIDE* DOES NOT GUARANTEE THE EFFECTIVENESS OF ITS SUGGESTED STRATEGIES. However historically effective these strategies have been, remember: *nothing* is foolproof!

What to Do if You Meet It: Advice for close encounters and those unfortunate wrong-place-at-the-wrong-time-type situations. And how to live to tell about them for future editions.

Current Status: Dead? Alive? Cryogenically frozen? Living and working in Toledo, Ohio? The best-known information on the monsters' current whereabouts.

Body Count: How many *documented* kills the monster has. Seen or mentioned.

Sample Monster Photo

Photo by Ellen M. Struzziero

Monsters

Aliens

. . . FROM THEIR WORLD TO YOUR LIVING ROOM

So, Do Aliens Really Exist?

According to the U.S. government: no.

And we all know how trustworthy the government is. Asking the government if aliens exist is like asking a lawyer if he's ever knowingly represented a guilty criminal: "Of *course* not."

And hey, it's understandable. They believe that they're "doing their job" by protecting us from the truth. This from the folks who overturn third-world governments just for kicks. **Lesson Number One: never trust the government, particularly concerning the existence of aliens.**

Scientists heroically risk their lives to study the creatures, but usually don't share their discoveries until they've discovered that they themselves are dead meat.

And you can't rely on accounts from alien abductees; after all, the average IQ of an abductee is just south of Forrest Gump's. Their stories are more likely recollections of experiences they had ingesting mixers of malt liquor and volatile chemicals.

So then who *can* you trust?

Ultimately, no one.

Alien conspiracies and cover-ups have gotten more common than the overpayment of professional athletes. Seems like anyone or anything could be an alien upon closer examination. You'd think we'd all be believers by now, but some people just need a little more convincing—like a laser bolt to the forehead, or getting disemboweled like a piñata. Lord knows, a good dose of skepticism is needed in today's world (who can believe anything coming out of Geraldo Rivera's mouth anymore?), but those ignoring the mountain of evidence relating to extraterrestrials are being just plain stubborn.

But if you're curious about extraterrestrials, there's a wealth of information to be found in your local video store, because only filmmakers have the guts to bring the facts to light.

Alien Visitation

Frankly, we're amazed at the number of full-on alien invasions the earth has weathered over the years, and also how instrumental aliens have been in the development of human civilization (see *Stargate, 2001: A Space Odyssey*). From the pyramids of Egypt to the rebounding acumen (and dead-on fashion sense) of Dennis Rodman, the contributions they have made to humanity baffle the mind. It forces one to ponder: Where would we be without them? No doubt still fighting over who has the biggest bonfire or the loudest grunt.

We're Not Talkin' About *E.T.* Here . . .

The vast majority of aliens we encounter are well-meaning, good-natured citizens just like us. All they want is a comfy couch on which to lounge with their favorite pizza. And maybe a little love, compassion, and understanding as toppings. For the most part they keep to themselves. Or at least they keep their true identities to themselves so as not to scare us away.

We could tell you all about friendly little creatures like *E.T.* until the cows come home, but none of that info is going to save your butt from annihilation. The visitors we discuss in the following section are strictly dangerous monsters you wouldn't want to meet up with in a dark space cruiser.

. . . And Just What the Heck Do They Want with Us?

Since Earth is the only populated planet in our galaxy (as of this writing), it seems kind of natural for other species to pick on us. They're probably egged on by their overwhelming inferiority complexes and need to prove to themselves that they are good for something after all. Unfortunately, very few of them are vying for the Nobel Peace Prize.

SUBCATEGORIES

There are as many kinds of aliens as there are meanings for the word "alternative," so general advice on how to deal with them is a bit scarce. However, after reviewing the evidence, we've seen that there are some common *modi operandi* among the creatures of the universe, and we've sorted them accordingly . . .

- **Parasites:** Using our bodies in much the same way Guns N' Roses would use a Motel 6.

- **Doppelgängers:** Aliens pretending to be men, and often doing about as good a job of it as Marv Albert.

- **Meteor-Related:** Bizarre things happen when large rocks are hurled at our planet, and no, we're not talking about the success of *Armageddon.*

- **Martians:** Not exactly the friendliest of neighbors.

- **Meanies:** A cornucopia of hostile alien bastards. Who knows what they want most of the time . . .

- **Predators:** . . . But some of them want us.

So if you have the courage to believe that "the truth is out there," read on . . .

Parasites

There's one inside me . . . it got into my mouth . . . I can feel it . . . into my brain!

J.C. in *Night of the Creeps*

A **parasite** is an organism which lives off of another "host" organism in one way or another, whether it feeds off of its host organism or merely depends upon the host to do its laundry (in the human world, such beings are known as "freeloaders"). Some parasites do relatively little harm, and others are a real bitch, tearing you from the inside out and splattering blood all over your lovely living-room carpet.

Scientists estimate that parasites account for about half of the life-forms on earth; that there are millions of parasite species all around us just itching to jump on board and chow.

For the most part, parasites on Earth tend to specialize in inhabiting one kind of host throughout their lives—for the most part they stick to the same kind of food.

Alien parasites, however, have proven to be much more adaptive, as well as more savagely aggressive. Think about it: If you're roaming around the universe from planet to planet, being a picky eater is a serious liability. And considering the vastness of space, when you get your opportunity to switch dining cars you better jump quickly and stealthily, and with a healthy bit of gusto.

Although there are some parasites on Earth which can prove deadly to humans, they're relatively rare and often easily cured. You don't need to worry too much about them. What you *do* need to worry about are the ones from the far reaches of space . . .

Identification

Parasites are usually pretty hard to identify—until they've taken over the host organism, and either killed it, used it, or both.

- **Slugs** and **leeches** (*The Hidden, Night of the Creeps, The Puppet Masters*).
- **Spores** and **fungi** (*The Creeping Unknown, Mutiny in Outer Space, Space Master X-7*).
- Other pesky little **critters living inside human bodies** (*Alien, Dark City, The Green Slime*).
- Perfect **replicas** of their host organisms (*John Carpenter's The Thing*).

Cravings

• **Living Cells:** To consume from the inside out. Then it moves on to another host, and so on. Otherwise the parasite will perish. Yet if it satisfies its craving, *we* perish.

• **Knowledge:** They want to learn as much as possible from our race, before moving on to the next (*Dark City, John Carpenter's The Thing*).

• **Fast Cars & Drugs:** Sometimes they even develop a craving for their hosts' vices (*The Hidden*).

• **Heat:** Makes sense, 'cause where there's heat, there's meat!

Behavior & Skills

• **Gettin' Busy:** Parasites either spontaneously reproduce within you or else use your body as an incubator (*Alien*). And once the mature alien is ready to head out on its own, you aren't needed anymore.

• **Taking Possession of Us:** By simply hooking themselves onto the back of our necks, some parasites can create an army of slaves (*The Puppet Masters*).

• **Providing a High-Cholesterol Diet:** Clotting the blood of its victims (*The Andromeda Strain.*)

• **Tumbling:** Merely rolling to and fro and over people at random (*The Creeping Unknown*).

How to Get Rid of Them

• **Cold, Electricity, or Fire:** They hate it when you go to extremes, and very often bite the dust.

• **High Explosives:** Just trap 'em all in the same place and blow 'em up.

• **Conventional Weapons:** Can go a long way toward disabling the host; problem is most of the time the parasite will jump out of the disabled body and enter a new one. Only a few alien parasites actually die along with the host.

• **Just Blast Them into Space:** And you won't hear from them anymore. Tentatively.

• **Seek Mother Nature's Help:** Sunlight (lethal for the Strangers), volcanoes (melt both the parasite and its victim in *Yog—Monster from Space*), or water (see "sunlight").

What to Do if You Meet One

Let's hope that it's not inside your body, because it's almost always too late. If you suspect that one of your pals is infested, well, don't do anything too extreme to her, because you can't be sure you're on the right track. Just avoid open-mouth kissing and the like.

Aliens

Classification: parasites / *Maternis acidawfulus*

Footage:

1979, *Alien* by Ridley Scott
1986, *Aliens* by James Cameron
1992, *Alien³* by David Fincher
1997, *Alien Resurrection* by Jean-Pierre Jeunet

The Skinny: Big, mean, body intruder machines with acid blood. Truly the scourge of the universe.

Quotable: "Stop your grinnin' and drop your linen!"

Habitat: The planets LV-426 and Fiorina 161, various starships, and coming soon to a planet near you . . .

Origin: Crew members of the space tow truck *Nostromo* found a shipwrecked alien spacecraft with hundreds of alien pods inside. Curiosity killed the cat, says an old saw. Evidently, one of the crew members hadn't heard this old saw, and stuck his mug inside one of the pods. An overly friendly face-hugger grabbed the head of this poor man and placed in his stomach (via his mouth) an itsy-bitsy alien son, all unbeknownst to the rest of the crew.

Identification: The alien is a biomechanical creature: a living being with several body parts eerily similar to gears and pistons. In pod form, it is a large bulb sitting a couple feet off the floor, eagerly awaiting a visitor. What leaps out of the pod is called a face-hugger: sort of a cross between a crab, an octopus, and a lizard which does just what its name implies. When the alien emerges from its host's insides, it is a minnowlike infant compared to its adult form. The adult alien is an eight-foot-tall gangly biped with a semicylindrical head, two mouths, grotesque long arms, and grasping hands. The queen is even bigger and meaner. Gulp.

Cravings: Would you believe it? Humans, of course (although it'll settle for other mammals). It doesn't want us for food, though, it just uses our bodies for reproduction.

Behavior: This alien parasitoid reproduces through a host, which, of course, means you. And your alien baby makes a rather theatrical entrance through your belly, which is something you just *never* want to experience. When the aliens form a community around the queen—well, then we're all in deep doo-doo. As if *one* isn't hard enough to deal with.

Danger: You bet your sweet ass. First of all, aliens are *constantly* pissed off—kind of like when you accidentally staple your nuts together—they're incredibly irritable and aggressive. Secondly, they move very fast, are very strong, and have very sharp teeth. If an alien finds you, typically it will either crush your head like a fresh coconut, or else bring you back to the nest to serve as a surrogate parent. Believe us, you would prefer the coconut treatment. Also, their acid blood is more than a little corrosive, so rigorously avoid splatter fests.

How to Kill Them: *Very* carefully. If you know how to operate an ergonomically correct forklift, you can throw the alien out of your ship into space for some other poor bastard to deal with. Or you can run it over with a heavy transport vehicle. Otherwise you can throw grenades at it—preferably at its big, ugly hammer head. And they seem to be repelled by fire . . . kinda. Or improvise. We are accepting any and all suggestions.

What to Do if You Meet Them: Hop on the next ship out of there. If you're already on a ship, make like R2-D2 and hit the escape pod. Then call Ripley the Alien Slayer from the cellular. No ship? Grab a flamethrower.

Current Status: There are probably thousands of pods left on LV-426, and who knows where else. Furthermore, the newly cloned Ripley 8 is part alien, and at last check she was heading toward Earth . . .

Body Count: 191 people, 1 dog, and 1 unknown alien pilot.

The Strangers

Classification: parasites / *Deadmanibus withsurprises*

Footage:

1998, *Dark City* by Alex Proyas

The Skinny: Studious dark-coated corpses put us under the microscope.

Quotable: "Let the Tuning commence."

Origin: The strangers are an alien race seeking a new world and a new physical existence. Kind of like pop star Michael Jackson. Because they are slowly dying, they need a new kind of vessel in which to house their collective memories. They conduct experiments on humans in hopes of discovering the nature of the individual human soul. But hey: at least they're not experimenting on *animals*.

Identification: They appear to us as pale-skinned hairless males dressed in dark overcoats and hats. But these are just the dead human corpses which the strangers are using as vessels until they can find a way of inhabiting living humans (and aren't we looking forward to that joyful day!). When "liberated" from these corpses, they seem to be semitransparent "space crabs" with blue and yellow coloring.

Cravings: "We need to be like you." Well then, stop flying around and sticking needles into people!

Behavior: Strangers have a very strong telekinetic power which they call "tuning." They congregate in large central meeting places and combine their powers to stop time and make the city sleep. When they move among us, they seem to travel in fours. We suspect that they may play bridge during breaks . . . of course, their collective memory might make the game a little predictable, but their telekinetic power does make it easier to shuffle the cards. This "tuning" also allows them to fly. Strangers produce a clicking sound with their mouths to express emotion, although they speak to humans and each other in English. Huh. So English really *is* the universal language . . .

Danger: As part of their experiment, they may change your memory when you sleep. Strangers can make you sleep along with the rest of the city, or individually by saying, "Sleep!" and waving their hands in front of your face. If they aren't able to put you to sleep, they will likely try to kill you with sharp little daggers.

How to Kill Them: Both water and sunlight are lethal to strangers. They can also be killed much like ordinary humans, for when their host body dies, so do they. But they're a little harder to kill, because of their telekinetic powers. So we recommend sneaking up on them and/or setting traps rather than strutting around and talking smack to their faces.

What to Do if You Meet Them: You won't run across the strangers because they avoid interfering with their human experiments unless they go dangerously wrong. So if you actually see one, you're in trouble. Just pretend that you're asleep, and they won't bother you. Unless, of course, you're scheduled for a memory tune-up that night.

Current Status: Perhaps still around, so be on the lookout for pale men in dark overcoats and hats flying down the street.

Body Count: 3

The Thing

Classification: parasites or doppelgängers / *Kinkos lethalus*

Footage:

1982, *The Thing* by John Carpenter

The Skinny: Vicious, chameleonlike parasites make very pesky houseguests.

Quotable: "They dig it up, they cart it back, it gets thawed out, wakes up, probably not in the best of moods . . ."

Origin: 1982, Antarctica; the crew of U.S. Station #4 stumbled upon a beautiful arctic sled dog being chased by Norwegians with guns. But the dog turned out to be merely an *imitation* of a dog generated by an alien parasite which was roughly 100,000 years old (and surprisingly active for its age!). The alien was pissed off, which is perfectly understandable. You just try spending a thousand centuries buried in ice and then tell us how *you* feel.

Identification: The alien can imitate any living creature. But if you stumble upon it before the transformation is complete, you find yourself looking at a bizarre monster with a lot of whipping tentacles and sharp teeth, covered in slime and sporting a very aggressive attitude. And what ends up coming out of the host is an eerie, grotesque mutation which combines elements of the most recent host as well as parts of the previous ones. Heat is a good way to establish if you or your friends have been contaminated: just take a sample of blood and touch it with a hot piece of metal. If the blood sizzles, there's no contamination. If it jumps into the air and squeals, you'd better run like hell.

Cravings: It covets any and all living creatures as hosts.

Behavior: The Thing is an "intruder organism" which imitates other life-forms, but it needs to be alone in the dark in close proximity with the host in order to absorb it. The host's cells are absorbed by the parasite's, and the host quickly becomes something else, something very deadly. But the disguised Thing doesn't show itself, so you have to be really careful. The parasite does require heat to come back to life, but if it realizes that its mission is pointless, it may seek cold to hibernate—waiting for some other unlucky person to come and rescue it.

Danger: Let's put things in perspective: if the Thing reaches a civilized area, the entire world population will be infected 27,000 hours after first contact. Which is 1,125 days, or about 37 months, or else a little over 3 years. So, if the parasite managed to spread in 1982 . . . oh my God! We're *all* aliens!

How to Kill It: Fire. Burn it right to the ground, it's the only sure way. Also burn all of its offspring, because they're not your friends anymore, buster.

What to Do if You Meet It: This parasite is a little difficult to handle because when you finally do recognize it, it's popping out of someone's stomach. And making them down a gallon of Maalox won't help. Just back the heck away, and torch the unruly thing.

Current Status: Dead . . . well, maybe. Perhaps we'll never know . . .

Body Count: 9 Americans, 8 Norwegians, and 3 dogs.

Yog

Classification: parasites / *Youcantseemeus butimtheribus*

Footage:

1970, *Yog, Monster from Space* (a.k.a. *Space Amoeba*) by Inoshiro Honda

The Skinny: Space spores take over creatures of a Pacific atoll and it doesn't make for such a nice holiday.

Quotable: "I'd say that giant octopus is our monster."

Habitat: Space between Earth and Jupiter; a small island near Japan.

Origin: A space mission sent the *Helium 7* probe to Jupiter, but it came back to Japan without rocks or sand: on board was Yog, one of the first space hitchhikers ever encountered. Yog is a mass of astroquasars, a population that 50 million years ago had to abandon its galaxy and become space nomads, which could be a pretty cool name for a seventies rock band.

Identification: Yog is a virtually invisible blue amoeba. However, it's pretty clear when Yog has entered into action: you see, Yog can control the mind and body of any creature it wants. The creature, once "possessed" by this parasite, changes its genetic structure—its body grows to humongous proportions and becomes vicious. It also appears to be surrounded by a bluish aura if it swims underwater. At least this is what the inhabitants of Selga island suspect the day a gigantic squid, a jumbo crab, and a gargantuan turtle attack the villages. But they're positive that Yog is up to something the day it begins to control an engineer. That's the last straw: they need to fight back!

Cravings: Apparently, Yog is an idiot and wants to conquer the world by destroying it. It's unknown what the value of this particular approach is.

Behavior: Yog pilots the creatures against the humans, and tries to level everything to the ground. It can also control human beings, forcing them to do actions they normally wouldn't do. The killer creature leaves scars which seem like frostbite, because all of the possessed creatures' temperatures inexplicably drop below zero. To balance this loss of heat, the creatures become 100 times stronger than they were before. OK, it doesn't balance the temperature stuff, but you've got to give a little and take a little. That's the story of, that's the glory of Yog.

Yog can control more than one creature at once, and they can join forces to accomplish their mission (even if their main mission seems to be ripping apart trees). *Fun Fact:* animals controlled by Yog grow to humongous size; yet human beings remain the same size and speak without moving their lips—which, if you're used to bad kung fu movies, shouldn't throw you too much.

Danger: Yog's creatures are so big they can crush your house.

How to Kill It: Remember when we told you that Yog can control all of the creatures it wants to? Well, there's a little catch: Yog can't control bats. And it can't stand the bat's high pitched ultrasonic shriek either. This seems to unnerve the creatures controlled by Yog, as well as Yog itself (their sole vulnerability, so says the Great Amoeba). So if you happen to have a storm of bats, unleash it toward Yog and you'll witness a battle between a giant squid, a giant turtle, a giant crab, and a bunch of bats . . .

which is something you just don't see every day. Not to mention that the Great Amoeba forgot to mention that fire and liquid hot magma are also "their sole vulnerabilities."

What to Do if You Meet It (or Its Creations): If it's an animal, run as fast as you can. If it's a person, you can try to dig inside his or her mind to search for a little bit of humanity. Maybe, if you dig deep enough, the person can understand what he or she is doing, and may choose to dive in the first volcano available.

Current Status: Yog and its creatures on Earth have been defeated. We don't know if Yog was only the lonely, in deep space, or if there's something else like it. Only time will tell.

Body Count: The octopus kills 3 people, shatters a village, and a gazillion trees. The crab and the turtle seem distracted and simply hiss and growl.

Doppelgängers

Imagine you're a race of aliens . . .
Bill Robinson in *Maximum Overdrive*

The word **doppelgänger** comes from German, and means "double goer." In contrast to a ghost, which is an apparition of someone deceased, a doppelgänger is an apparition of someone still alive: in other words, an **evil twin**. Coming face-to-face with your doppelgänger can be taken as a sure sign that your proverbial "number" will shortly be up.

We at the *HMSG* have observed that these creepy impostors almost invariably end up being aliens. In fact, **posing as humans is one of the most common methods aliens have for infiltrating our world**. They know just how infrequently we lift our heads out of our own individual neurotic concerns to notice that Bob the copy-machine operator is able to do his job without even touching the machine. Heck, considering the way most of us walk around with our heads up our . . . well, where the sun don't shine, it's surprising that Earth hasn't been completely overrun already . . . or maybe it *has* . . . just kidding, intergalactic comrades!

Doppelgängers want us to believe that they're just ordinary human beings. They're always doing *ordinary* things that *ordinary* people do on an *ordinary* day. In fact, they're so darned *ordinary,* they're usually a cinch to spot if you're actually paying attention.

You can find them in offices, in factories, in a secluded house, living together in a barn just outside of town . . . or even in the next room. Double-check tonight before you go to sleep. *If* you can still sleep.

Spotting Them

Easy: They look like us. It's what's *inside* that's different. So, as far as you know, your math teacher might be an alien, or even your boss . . . and most definitely that "taco Chihuahua dog." Some of them are doing a great job of fooling us (*They Live, The Arrival, Body Snatchers, Invisible Invaders, The Astronaut's Wife*), but many of them are more than a little awkward (for example, *The Astounding She-Monster* is mute and leaves rooms walking backward).

Here are a couple of reliable methods for sniffing them out:

- **It's in the Eyes:** A surefire way to identify a doppelgänger is to look into its eyes: if they glow, turn silvery, have vertical eyelashes or oval pupils, are insectlike, are devoid of emotion, or stare straight into the sun, it's time to break out a can of doppelgänger whup-ass.

• **Under Pressure:** Another good rule of thumb for determining if the people you're talking to are doppelgängers is to put them into situations of extreme pressure. Unable to cope with tension, they may let down their guard, revealing their authentic aspects. But remember: this is not a justification for bothering everyone you run into. Saving the world is one thing, relentlessly annoying people is another.

Cravings

• **Breeding with Women:** In order to replenish their own decreasing population, male alien species sometimes decide to breed with human females (*I Married a Monster from Outer Space, Xtro, The Astronaut's Wife*).

• **Breeding with Men:** Then again, sometimes female aliens want to do the dance of love with as many males as possible (*Invasion of the Bee Girls, Species*).

• **Replacing Us All:** Draining our collective life forces (*Invasion of the Body Snatchers, The Brain from Planet Arous, Strange Invaders*), and then replacing all earthlings with emotionless, servile replicas of Al Gore.

• **Using Our Planet:** Some aliens need a hot climate to survive: if they can get Earth's average temperature to rise, they'll move in (*The Arrival*). Or, as if the earth were a third-world colony, the aliens encourage us to spend money so they can exploit us (*They Live*). Some need to borrow our heads (*The Borrower*), and some would like to use us as the main course at their new intergalactic fast-food chain (*Bad Taste*).

Behavior

• **Working Like Ants:** At all hours of the night, and in the strangest places. Mild-mannered accountants don't haul body bags across the street at 4:00 A.M. Get a clue!

• **Resurrecting the Dead:** To use corpses as vehicles (since the *Invisible Invaders* are, after all, invisible).

How to Kill Them

Doppelgängers are usually a substantially smarter and more evolved species. Many of them can quickly and easily regenerate wounded tissue. However, they all have weak points. Getting them to actually reveal these weak points is a whole 'nuther story:

- **Conventional Weapons:** Guns, fire, explosives, a powerful can opener.

- **Dogs:** If you sic Rover on a doppelgänger, he'll be sure to sniff it out and tear it to shreds. Own a Chihuahua? Back to the drawing board . . .

- **Free the Original:** If you manage to wake the kidnapped person who provides the mold for the replica, you break the invisible thread between them, and for some unexplained reason the doppelgänger dies at once.

- **Smash the Host's Head:** This is the only way to stop *The Brain from Planet Arous* (because when it's "noncorporeal," you can't harm it at all). Problem is, you may have to smash the head of a person you know. But think about it: they're already dead, so the only real risk is a deadly dry-cleaning bill.

- **A High-Pitched Whine:** Halts the *Invisible Invaders.* They're forced to leave their hosts and end up dying a few seconds later.

- **Electrocute Them with a Household Appliance and a Little Water:** This simple scheme worked with the alien inside Spencer Armacost in *The Astronaut's Wife* (what a sucker!).

- **Be Patient and They'll Leave:** As soon as their ship is fixed (*It Came from Outer Space*).

What to Do if You Meet One

First, let them know that you know exactly who they are and what they're up to (*The Arrival*); they may still hang around, but you'll shatter their confidence, and they'll probably come to respect your intelligence. Then never go to sleep again. Otherwise you may come to find yourself stuffed inside a gigantic pod.

Body Snatchers

Classification: doppelgängers / *Slurpus conformus*

Footage:

1956, *Invasion of the Body Snatchers* by Don Siegel
1978, *Invasion of the Body Snatchers* by Philip Kaufman
1994, *Body Snatchers* by Abel Ferrara

The Skinny: Aliens who replace our bodies in a very yucky manner.

Quotable: "The head cabbage. Well, well, well, well, well."

Habitat: Santa Mira (California), San Francisco, and coming soon to a military base near you (in Georgia, New York, Kentucky, Virginia, Ohio, etc.)

Origin: Initially, the phenomenon was labeled as a case of mass hysteria or extreme delusional fixation. Nobody knows quite when the whole thing started. The deal is, one day you wake up and you're not you anymore. You're a "blank" of yourself, incapable of experiencing emotion. Is it surprising that it took so long to notice the "big change"?

Identification: The replacement body is just like the original: same look, same voice, same memory . . . however, there's no emotion whatsoever, just the pretense of it. The eyes are lost in space ("Danger, Will Robinson!") and everybody just walks around town very calmly. In their primal stage, the body snatchers were flying seeds drifting through space; these seeds generated large pods with the ability to reproduce themselves in the exact likeness of any life-form. The pods are generally kept out of sight, in the bushes or underwater.

Cravings: To replace us all, and move on to the next planet: "It's the race that's important, not the individual." Total replacement must occur to insure the survival. It's not clear what will be left to snatch at that point, but hey—that's *their* problem.

Behavior: The substitution always happens while you're asleep: the body that was created by the pod absorbs your mind, your memories, and you are reborn. A more sophisticated race of snatchers has tiny little tentacles which reach out of the pod and into your orifices, literally sucking out your life force . . . and your fluids. Once your body has been replaced, it's thrown into a garbage truck. No, they *don't* recycle.

The body snatchers are rarely in a hurry: they know we have to go to sleep sooner or later. They only run if they're chasing someone who knows about them. But they know that even if we run away, nobody's going to believe our preposterous story.

If you really piss them off, they'll induce you to sleep, either with a sedative or else by making you watch a movie directed by Kevin Costner. When a snatched body bumps into a not-yet-snatched body, the replica points to the human and screams, "Wa-a-a-a-a-a-a-ah!" Worse than Celine Dion during one of her "lyrical moments."

Danger: DON'T FALL ASLEEP!!! . . . zzzzzzzzzzzz . . . (slurp).

How to Kill Them: You can set the pods on fire . . . but more will come; you can destroy the duplicate body before it replaces the original . . . but more will come; or you can kill the snatchers with firearms or other conventional methods . . . but again, more will come. Stamina and persistence are key.

What to Do if You Meet Them: *The Guinness Book of World Records* says that the record for not sleeping is 453 hours. Body snatchers have a lot of patience. You'll fall asleep sooner or later. If you find out your town is infested, simply walk around emotionlessly. If politicians can convince us that they "feel our pain," then we should certainly be able to fool the body snatchers.

Current Status: Perhaps gone, perhaps still among us. Perhaps you're one already.

Bodies Snatched: The entire town of Santa Mira, California, San Francisco, and Alabama's Fort Daly are also quite well replaced. And who knows where else . . . ?

Children of the Damned

Classification: doppelgängers / *Wunderkindus unkindus*

Footage:

1960, *Village of the Damned* by Wolf Rilla
1964, *Children of the Damned* by Anton Leader
1995, *Village of the Damned* by John Carpenter

The Skinny: Bright little telekinetic alien-human hybrid children looking to kick our butts.

Quotable: "One day somebody's gonna get up on a rooftop, and they're gonna start picking you little bastards off . . . one, by one, by one . . ."

Stomping Grounds: Isolated, remote villages—the town of Midwich (both in Scotland and California); one outside of Anchorage, Alaska; one in northern Australia; and one near the Turkish-Iranian border.

Origin: A treacherous shadow passed over the town of Midwich, and later all the people in the town fell asleep at once for exactly six hours. Upon awakening, ten women found themselves pregnant. Nine months later, these women simultaneously gave birth. Can you imagine being in that nursery—with all those "damned" kids screaming at the same time?!!

After several studies, government scientists came to this conclusion: the miraculous conception was *xenogenesis* (production of an offspring unlike that of the parent) as a result of alien intervention. The government was able to deduce this through precise analysis, skilled technicians, and the fact that the stillborn kid looked like an extra on *Deep Space Nine.*

Identification: All of the children have platinum-white hair, cobalt eyes, and a predilection for gray clothing much like the early Beatles. They also happen to have off-the-chart IQs, ESP, telekinetic powers, and a complete lack of emotion. You can easily spot them because they're always walking in formation, side by side, two by two, males with females. Kind of like the glee club from hell.

Cravings: To dominate and eliminate our race by spreading into the world and forming colonies. According to them, it's inevitable . . . even though all other alien attempts to give birth to children have somehow failed.

Behavior: From early on, they show a strong sense of vengeance, paying you back with interest by using their telekinetic powers to force you to harm yourself. When working their magic, their eyes change color, flash, and sometimes even make their skulls glow like jack-o'-lanterns. When not wreaking havoc, they are quiet and studious. But don't expect them to win any citizenship awards.

Danger: Beware these kids when they're all together. They know we hate them and can easily tell if we're planning to evacuate or revolt. But it makes no difference: the whole town and its inhabitants will probably end up being destroyed by the government anyway.

Vulnerability: You have to gather them into the same place. They'll eventually decide to live together, so this won't be too difficult. Then bring a concealed bomb in and think of last week's grocery list. The children will become so wrapped up in trying to read your thoughts that they won't find out about the bomb. Oh, and one minor detail: you'll die along with them.

The "more humane" option: just keep trying to teach them to be emotional, and therefore human. It might just work . . . or not.

What to Do if You Meet Them: If you are in trouble with one of them, you're in trouble with the whole bunch. They're able to read your mind, so it's hard to hide what you really think of them. But if you picture the ocean or a brick wall or some other vast image, you can successfully block their ESP. It's not easy, especially since they'll try to probe every corner of your mind; but if you're up for the challenge, tally-ho!

Current Status: The most cuddly of them escaped with his mommy. Only time will tell if he gets *more* or *less* cuddly.

Body Count: 36 people (plus a few suicides), 1 helicopter, 1 department-of-corrections bus (presumably filled with people), 1 hand, and 2 eyes. Also, 6 people are left "in shock."

Edgar

Classification: doppelgängers / *Bigbug horridus*

Footage:
1997, *MIB—Men in Black* by Barry Sonnenfeld

The Skinny: Alien bug uses farmer suit as a disguise in the big city . . . well, he's not from these parts.

Quotable: "Fifteen hundred years ago everybody *knew* the earth was the center of the universe. Five hundred years ago everybody *knew* the earth was flat. And fifteen minutes ago you *knew* that people were alone on this planet."

Habitat: Somewhere in outer space; the New York metro area.

Origin: During the summer of 1997, an alien spacecraft crash-landed near New York, and its occupant literally skinned, sucked, and replaced a local farmer, Edgar, in an almost perfect disguise—with a few small exceptions: he limped badly, his eyes grew much whiter, and the farmer's body kind of sagged with Edgar stuffed inside.

Identification: Edgar appears to be a farmer wearing a dirty shirt, overalls, and brown shoes. Frequently, large bugs crawl out of his sleeves. When the alien abandons the disguise, his body is so huge you can't imagine how uncomfortable he must have been tucked inside a human's skin: the alien is a brown, six-legged bug with yellow eyes, tiny teeth, and a very short temper.

Cravings: Edgar needs the galaxy in Orion's belt, because it is the best source of subatomic energy in the universe. We're in the middle of this quarrel, because a resident alien on Earth was the possessor of "the galaxy." Once Edgar and his family of 78 million other bugs obtain it, they will become the most powerful race in the universe and wipe away the peaceful Arquillian race. Edgar also craves water with a lot of sugar.

Behavior: Edgar pursues his goals with very little regard for cover-up: He simply walks into places and kills whoever bothers him. Extremely powerful (but at the same time hampered by a nagging inferiority complex), he can turn on you in a flash. Edgar, like any cockroach, thrives on carnage. He destroys, consumes, and leaves only death. Well, actually he leaves a green spectral trail, so if you have a spectral-trail analyzer, you can follow him around. Assuming you really want to. Edgar drove around in a truck he stole from an exterminator. Ironic, no?

Danger: Edgar doesn't see in shades of gray: it's either his way or the highway. He wants the galaxy, and the bodies start to pile up.

How to Kill It: Instead of looking for a very large shoe to squash him, use one of the Men in Black's weapons (technically advanced and much better than a slingshot) but don't walk away satisfied if you snap Edgar in two. Like many other bugs or crawling animals, this bug retains a lot of stamina even if sliced. Be sure he signs off permanently.

What to Do if You Meet It: Do not squash any cockroaches, just give him a pack of sugar. Or, in the interest of public safety, pay a visit to the headquarters of the Men in Black: it's in New York, on 504 Battery Drive, in the Battery Triborough Bridge & Tunnel Authority building.

Current Status: Blown in two and subsequently into many gooey little pieces. But its race is still around and might come back. After all, at any given time there are about 1,500 aliens on our planet . . .

Body Count: 5 people, 2 Arquillians, 1 truck, and half a jewelry store.

Sil

Classification: doppelgängers / *Ovulatus constantum*
or perhaps creations / biologically engineered

Footage:
1995, *Species* by Roger Donaldson
1998, *Species II* by Peter Medak

Created: U.S. government laboratories in Dugway, Utah; 1995.

The Skinny: Hot chick with a cold alien heart.

Quotable: "This is the maternity ward . . . from hell."

Habitat: Utah, California, and now space . . .

Origin: November 16, 1974: detailed information about human life (the structure of our DNA, etc.) was sent into space, under the S.E.T.I. project (Search for Extraterrestrial Intelligence). In January 1993, we received a message back. An unknown alien intelligence had contacted us, sending the sequence of a new strain of DNA and instructions on how to combine it with ours. Being the constantly curious and infinitely stupid beings we are, we actually took the bait: Dr. Xavier Fitch combined the DNA and made it grow. The resulting creature was named Sil and grew at an alarming rate: at three months she looked like a five-year-old child! And then, when the lab decided to terminate the experiment out of fear, Sil decided to escape and move to Hollywood. Like everyone else.

Identification: She is dangerously beautiful in her human form: tall, blond, and sexy. But Sil's not quite as attractive when she's in her alien form: she reminds us of the creature from *Alien* with breasts and a Coolio hairdo. And she's constantly on the rag.

Cravings: Anything edible; evidently she burns a lot of calories when she's getting ready to shack up in her cocoon. And her sexual appetite is insatiable until she's pregnant with your alien love child.

"Am I being burned for my striking resemblance to Celine Dion?"

Metro-Goldwyn Mayer/Shooting Star

Behavior: Deep down, she's just a kid (only five months old at the time of death). But deeper down, she's a sex monster. Sil wants to play with you and then rip your arms off if you don't want to give her a baby . . . or even once you do give her a baby. So you're damned if you do and damned if you don't.

Danger: Problem is, she's a gorgeous blonde who doesn't usually show her true colors to her victims until she's in bed with them. By then, it's too late ("Tell him he's about to copulate with a creature from outer space."). And no—wearing a prophylactic doesn't help.

How to Kill Her: Any physical damage is practically useless because Sil can regenerate her bone structure. You can try gassing her with cyanide, but it's best to burn her in a huge oil puddle you can easily find beneath your Hollywood hotel. Just ask at the reception desk.

What to Do if You Meet Her: Men—tell her you have a low sperm count, and suggest she try *Love Connection*. Women—move on to another meat market; there's plenty of fish in the sea.

Current Status: Dead. But one badass mutant mouse is still hanging around the L.A. sewer system, ready to pop out at your earliest inconvenience. She was re-created to fight one of her own kind and save humanity . . . but then she had a divided allegiance . . .

Body Count: 14

They

Classification: doppelgängers / *Youcantseemi ohratsyoucanibus*

Footage:

1988, *They Live* by John Carpenter

The Skinny: Capitalistic aliens open up shop and take us for all we're worth.

Quotable: "We are living in an artificially induced state of consciousness that resembles sleep."

Origin: Maybe they've always been here; maybe they're still here.

Stomping Grounds: From planet to planet.

Origin: A rambling man found a cool pair of sunglasses which allowed him to see the real world (no, they're not MTV sunglasses): the real world was in black-and-white, fully covered with subliminal consumer messages (Buy, Spend the Money, Obey, and so on). The worst part was that, scattered among us, there were . . . them.

How They Look: They are apparently ordinary human beings, either male or female, same dimensions. Unfortunately, if you wear the sunglasses (or the newer and more discreet contact lenses), you can see what they really are: their face is practically a skull, with two huge pinballs instead of eyes; their teeth are constantly clenched. They've got no nose, and their skin is covered with red and green spots.

Cravings: They just want our money.

Behavior: They are rich aliens who consider Earth a sort of "third world" to exploit. They breed corruption, they adore manipulating the greedy, or throwing money in the bank accounts of the worst elements of society—sounds all too familiar, don't you think?

How to Kill Them: They are basically like humans, so you can shoot them, or beat the crap out of them—the usual stuff. The main problem is that they are the bigwigs of major companies, so it's not easy to get them face-to-face. Furthermore, they all are in contact with a special central HQ (housed in the Channel 54 building) as well as with each other, thanks to a small wristwatch transmitter. It allows them to open a hole in the ground as an easy way out. The hole that swallows them goes directly to the center of the world, to a net of corridors under the towns. Every corridor leads to the Channel 54 building. Here, thanks to a satellite dish and special transmissions, they make us see a reality that is not real at all.

Danger: It depends. If you are greedy and wretched, well: this is your home.

What to Do if You Meet Them: If you wear the sunglasses, just try to avoid them—they're ugly.

Current Status: Maybe gone, maybe still here.

Body Count: Not applicable. They like us alive. They *want* us alive.

GREETING ALIENS

- **Put away the white flag.** It seems that, beyond our solar system, waving a white flag means, "Up yours!"
- **Don't hug the aliens.** Do you know how cranky you are after a five-hour plane flight? Imagine traversing two or three galaxies.
- **Don't shake anything that looks like a hand.** You may unknowingly squeeze some other embarrassing alien body part, effectively greenlighting a vicious attack.
- **Never utter the word "probe."**

Meteor-Related

I'll be hornswoggled! Did you see that little old sky jockey zip down in there?

A country bumpkin in *Killer Klowns from Outer Space*

Space: the final frontier . . . and filled with swirling trash. It's no wonder that now and then a piece of rock tumbles out of the sky and puts a dent in our home world. Yet oftentimes the deadly results are not caused by the impact itself.

The largest documented modern meteorite hit central Siberia on June 30, 1908. It glowed as bright as the sun and ended up leveling nearly 800 square miles of forest (needless to say, accounts from local peasants are nonexistent). And there's evidence that meteorites ten times that big have hit before. An asteroid *and* a comet struck in 1998—what you might call a "banner year." Thankfully, meteorites this size are thought to hit Earth only every 100 million years or so. Some speculate that deadly meteor showers led to the demise of the dinosaurs, the subsequent rise of mammals, and the eventual arrival of humanity. Let's hear it for those extinction-level events!

HMSG staffers have observed that meteorites with less physical impact can end up generating results which are just as terrifying. We don't know for certain exactly what these rocks are made of, and, as we all know, the introduction of foreign materials to our planet can cause the most bizarre things to happen.

"Monstrous" meteorites have a very typical entry: they always seem to light up the sky on a dark, starry night, in a suburban or rural area. Rocketing over Make-Out Point, the meteorite lands behind some trees on the edge of a farm. The farmer, who of course spends every night of his life on the porch, can't help but investigate, accompanied by his faithful old hound dog. And he never seems to have the slightest clue what he's in for.

The Effects

- **Adolescent Meat Lovers:** Exposure to meteors can turn teenagers into flesh-eating ghouls (*Alien Dead*).

- ***The Blob:*** The release of an amoebalike thing with a voracious appetite for everything in its path (see entry).

- **Does Health Insurance Cover This?:** If for some reason a meteor fragment gets stuck inside your body, you may experience some bizarre disease: your body can liquefy (*The Incredible Melting Man*) or you can turn into a hideous monster (*Track of the Moon Beast*). In any case, you invariably develop a taste for human flesh and blood.

• **A Green Thumb:** Small meteorites function as fertilizer for grass, flowers, and even people. If this kind of meteor lands in your backyard, you'll have an early spring all to yourself—and all *over* yourself, in just one night (*Creepshow*). If you wake up safe and sound, some poisonous, hungry plants may pay you a visit: they're the triffids, a species which is created by spores the meteors leave behind (*The Day of the Triffids*).

• **Hairy Situation:** Meteor rays can turn you into a hairy monster with an insatiable desire to kill (*Meteor Monster*).

• **Let's Go Crazy!:** Big meteors can contaminate the air and the food on a farm, driving the animals crazy. The humans will soon follow suit (*Die, Monster, Die!*, *The Farm*), turning into cruel murderers. All one can do is kill everything that moves. *Fun Fact:* when they're shot, meteor-contaminated people explode in a cloud of white worms!

• **Machine Intelligence:** And not only do they start to think for themselves, they get pretty ornery (*Maximum Overdrive*).

• **Quite a Sight:** When a meteor shower flies by your town, chances are you'll go blind just watching (*The Day of the Triffids*).

How to Kill Them

The bad news: you can't kill a meteor. The good news: uh . . . well . . . hmm . . .

• **Bullets:** Almost never fail. Either you shoot the contaminated ones (*Die, Monster, Die!*), or else develop a suicidal attitude (*Creepshow*).

• **Extreme Cold:** And make a *Blob*-sicle.

• **Salt:** Make the evil meteor-made plant dwindle into a pile of dust.

• **Time:** Just wait; many of these creatures will decay all by themselves, melting in disgusting puddles (*The Incredible Melting Man*) or simply dying off (*Meteor Monster*).

• **Water:** It rids you of the triffids, but it'll bring to life other meteor fragments which'll end up wreaking havoc on your hometown (*The Monolith Monsters*). Flip a coin.

What to Do if a Meteor Lands in Your Backyard

- Don't touch the meteor.
- Don't get near the meteor.
- Don't even *look* at the meteor.
- Pack up and move—pronto!!!

The Blob

Classification: meteor-related / *Jellobus carnivorous*
then later: creations / biologically engineered

Footage:

1958, *The Blob* by Irwin S. Yeaworth, Jr.
1972, *Beware the Blob* by Larry Hagman (yes, that's right: *Dallas*'s "J.R.")
1988, *The Blob* by Chuck Russell

The Skinny: It's big. It's hungry. It's powerful. It grows and grows. No, not Rosie.

Quotable: "Whatever it is, it's getting bigger."

Habitat: Space and Earth. And it really likes to hang out in theaters where people are watching horror movies.

Origin: One starry night, a meteor fell to Earth. Proving that people *never* seem to be able to mind their own business, an old man went to examine the meteor. The meteor cracked open, revealing a strange ooze. The old man just couldn't resist touching the ooze with a branch. And the ooze just couldn't resist touching the old man back. Slowly and painfully, this old man became the Blob's first victim.

Identification: Do you remember Silly Putty? Well, this is kind of the same thing—except that it's red and can't copy the comics. Another way to picture it is as a mobile, oversized silicone breast implant. The Blob starts off the size of a bowl of Jell-O, and grows to be quite huge as it absorbs more and more creatures. It's also eternally hungry. Maybe it's related to Audrey II from *Little Shop of Horrors*. Or perhaps Oprah Winfrey when she's not in "The Zone."

Cravings: Anything organic and in its way.

Behavior: Well, it creeps, leaps, glides, and slides across the floor, right through the door, even all around the wall (POP!). Oh, and did we mention that it absorbs people? And even cute little kittens?

Danger: When the Blob touches your skin, it produces a burning acidlike sensation. And whatever the Blob touches, the Blob soon digests. So, in other words, DON'T let it touch you. But beware: due to its melting and molding nature, the Blob can slither through anything and hide anywhere. My God, what is that behind you?!!

How to Kill It: With anything cold. Ship it to the North Pole. Or introduce it to Leona Helmsley. Once, it was halted in an inactive ice rink by starting the freezing process. You see they were lucky: it was one of those "instantaneously freezing" ice rinks. The Blob has been stopped with fire extinguishers and even a snow-making machine. Which is a wonderful solution—*if* you happen to own a snow-making machine.

What to Do if You Meet It: Duck into the nearest walk-in refrigerator. Or if you happen to have a fire extinguisher, give it a good dousing. Oh yeah, we almost forgot: if you meet the "new and improved" version of the Blob, find the nearest military leader and kick him in the nuts. While the old Blob was an alien, the modern version is a biological weapon created by the army. Gee thanks, Uncle Sam.

Current Status: Dead. Erased. Kaput. Except for one tiny piece kept in a jar which wants to grow up big and strong . . .

Body Count: 51 people, 3 rats, 1 dog, 1 cat, 1 fly, 1 egg, and several barnyard animals.

Happy Toyz Truck

Classification: meteor-related / *Roadkillis causibus*

Footage:

1986, *Maximum Overdrive* by Stephen King

The Skinny: It's big. It's bad. And it changes oil every 3,000 miles.

Quotable: "You can't! We made you! Where's your sense of loyalty?"

Manufactured: Early eighties. License plate 44004.

Regular Routes: North Carolina highways and gas stations.

Origin: On June 19, 1987, the tail of the Rhea-M comet passed by Earth—or, if you prefer, Earth passed through the tail of Rhea-M comet. Either way, it seems that because of this event (or because of a large UFO, we'll never know), all the machines on Earth started a rebellion against mankind, including the self-proclaimed leader of the pack, the "Happy Toyz" Truck.

Identification: It's a long black-and-white truck, with a colorful Happy Toyz sign painted on both sides, a hideous clown painted on the back door, and a repulsive, huge goblin face glued on the radiator grille. The goblin face has glowing red eyes. By the way, if this is the merry symbol of the Happy Toyz Corporation, we wonder what kind of toys they produce. Perhaps something like *Danny the Little Slaughterer* or *Where Is Waldo's Head?*

Cravings: Evidently to rule the world, or else to clean it up so that a race of aliens can come and take over our planet without the hassle of exterminating us. But the Happy Toyz Truck also needs a lot of diesel (and demands it).

Behavior: This truck is a pain in the trunk. It's not clear how it became the boss of the Army on Wheels—you just have to accept it. Anyway, Mr. Truck commands a bunch of other wagons; together they keep a group of men hostage at the Dixie Boy Truck Stop, in the middle of a highway forgotten by God (and, like every gas station, this one has an arsenal of weapons in the basement which temporarily help the hostages keep the trucks at bay). Every machine behaves in its own way—except cars, which for some strange reason don't seem to be affected by the comet's power. And the trucks seem to understand us, and communicate with us in Morse code, honking their horns. But the only one worth dealing with is Happy Toyz because it's the one that will decide whether or not you live.

Danger: Mr. Truck likes to squash you with its big wheels. It doesn't care about speed bumps, school crossings, speed limits . . . it just wants to run you over. It brakes for nobody.

How to Kill It: Blow it up with a bazooka. Not very original, but effective.

What to Do if You Meet It: Get out of the way as fast as you can. Or buy a gas station. Sooner or later, these trucks will need diesel. And they won't allow the gas station owner to die. You see, trucks have no fingers to operate the nozzles.

Current Status: Blown to smithereens.

Body Count: 2 people, 1 gas nozzle, 1 briefcase filled with Bibles.

Other Rebel Machines: An ATM machine, a drawbridge, an electric knife, all kinds of video games, a cigarette dispenser, a coin changer, a soda machine, a steamroller, sprinklers, a toy police car, an ice-cream truck, a lawn mower, a gas pump, an airplane, a jukebox, a generator, a military vehicle, a bulldozer, and a drive-thru speaker.

Body Count of Other North Carolina Machines: 20+ people, 1 arm, 1 foot. 1 dog, 1 porch, 1 gas station, 1 fence, 1 sewer pipe, 1 phone booth, 3 cars.

Note: Later on, the trucks (*only* the trucks, and maybe a chopper) tried it again. This new rebellion (*Trucks*, 1997, by Chris Thomson) involves a bunch of very aggressive trucks coordinated by a large silver "Westway Refrigeration" truck. The assailants surround an unfortunate group of people in the Lunar Gas, Food, and Lodging station, located north of Bridgeton, which is in the vicinity of the infamous Area 51 in New Mexico. These trucks use their mirrors to check up on us, their horns to communicate with each other, and their exhaust pipes to smoke us to death. Other than that, they just run over us like any other possessed truck. These trucks get smarter and smarter, but they're as vulnerable as their predecessors.

***Trucks* 1997 Body Count:** 10 people, 1 presumably frozen to death; 3 signs, 3 electrical surges, 2 cars, 2 trucks, 2 small shacks, 2 large shacks, 1 van, 1 water pump, 1 phone booth, 1 window.

Little people . . . why can't we all just get along?

President Dale in *Mars Attacks!*

Martian Cultures 101

Martians seem to live all over the planet: on the surface, deep down in the channels, inside its core, and who knows where else. Like the inhabitants of Earth, Martians have several species, races and starship models. Here is a quick guide to the most predominant—divided into two broad groups. Let's call them "A" and "B," shall we?

GROUP A (VISITORS TO EARTH)

1. Probably the most ancient race of Martians was composed of large insects (about three or four feet long, with bulging eyes) which were able to fly starships and crash-land right under the city of London, so creating the foundation for the future Underground or "Tube." Their large spacecrafts electrocuted whoever stepped inside. The Martians rolled up their insect sleeves and helped apes evolve into cavemen: the perfect slaves. When the Martians died, men evolved. *Best Defense:* "God in His wisdom" created electricity, this race's number-one enemy. So, if you ever find the starship, hit it with an electrical charge, and the whole thing will blow up. And you, too, of course (*Five Million Years to Earth*).

2. Another species is green and is the opposite of *E.T.* regarding friendship. They sport large triangular heads with one tricolored eye right in the middle and have long arms with three fingers with suckers at the ends. This race arrives hidden inside large meteors. Their manta ray–shaped spacecraft move slowly through the streets, blasting everything with their snake-like heat-ray projectors. They want to conquer Earth by burning it to the ground. *Best Defense:* this race's number-one enemy is a microbe: "God in His wisdom" created the common cold which ultimately defeats the invasion (*War of the Worlds*).

3. This species evolved underneath the planet's surface; it features humanoid figures about three feet tall. They're green, with a skull-like face and round eyes, and you can see their brains protruding from the tops of their heads. They wear glass helmets because they can't breathe oxygen.

Like locusts, they attack in gigantic numbers with thousands and thousands of round, small, and silvery ships. Again, they want to conquer Earth by leveling everything to the ground. *Best Defense:* this race's number-one enemy is a song: "God in His wisdom" created Slim Whitman and his obnoxious "Indian Love Call": play it, and you'll see the Martians' heads blow up. And probably yours, too. It's really an awful song (*Mars Attacks!*).

4. Another species of oxygen-breathing small humanoids features vegetable men (sort of a cabbage head with green skin), with wood alcohol in their veins and detachable hands which crawl around to kill. They make people drunk by injecting alcohol in their veins. They want to conquer Earth, but then end up taking it out on Earth's cars after one of them gets run over. *Best Defense:* this race's number-one enemy is light: "God in His wisdom" created flashlights; having evolved on the dark side of the planet, their big eyes can't tolerate light. Once hit by it, they disintegrate in puffs of smoke like dancers on a Madonna tour (*Invasion of the Saucer Men*).

5. Another class of small humanoids—green, with small antennae and eyes—are too clumsy to do us any harm. They were lost in space when they picked up a Halloween radio broadcast of Orson Welles's *War of the Worlds* and rushed to Earth to join a fictional Martian invasion. They found an indifferent population in a small Illinois town that ignored them, and mistook their uniforms for costumes. *Best Defense:* this race's number-one enemy is their own stupidity: "God in His wisdom" created them. 'Nuff said (*Spaced Invaders*).

6. There are also men and women on Mars—but this doesn't mean they're kind and gentle. These humanoid creatures move via teleportation, speak fluent English, and have "abandoned neckties fifty years ago as foolish vanity." Instead of destroying our planet, they want to mate. *Best Defense:* reason with them, what the hey. Or take them to "group" (*Devil Girls from Mars, Mars Needs Women*). An almost human race lives on one of the moons of the planet, and its queen is an egg-laying vampire with hypnotic eyes: she arouses you, sends you into a trance, and sucks all your blood. *Best Defense:* this creature's number-one enemy is a paper cut: "God in His wisdom" created a hemophiliac alien (*Queen of Blood*). Another group of Martians ask the planet's leaders to kidnap Santa Claus to make the children on Mars happy. The plan succeeds, and Santa lands on Mars, bringing joy to all of the kids. He's released when one of the Martians dons a Santa costume and takes his place. *Best Defense:* "God in His wisdom" created costumes (*Santa Claus Conquers the Martians*).

7. Also, there's a "Supreme Martian Intelligence," in the figure of a large, bald, and tentacled head who lives in a gigantic plastic bubble and controls green humanoid slaves. The Intelligence and his crew land on Earth and begin to take over the minds of everyone in town, controlling their victims with a device they implant at the base of the neck. But their strange eating habits give them away: they chew live frogs. *Best Defense:* this race's number-one enemy is their own weaponry: "God in His wisdom" created 911; the army steps in, and after a battle, and a lot of casualties, it defeats the aliens. Perhaps (*Invaders from Mars*).

GROUP B (THEY STAY HOME AND HATE HAVING GUESTS)

1. A very ancient super-race has kept their three eyes on Earth "since the first creatures crawled out of the primeval slime" (get a life, Martians!). This race lives in half-mile-tall cities, and they vaguely resemble insects. They telekinetically control a wide variety of other creatures that populate the planet, including 100-foot-tall bat-spiders, man-eating plants with tentacles and large leaves, and oozing blobs which can surround a whole starship and digest it. *Best Defense:* thanks to God's wisdom, they don't seem to be able to operate a starship, so we're safe unless we go to Mars (*The Angry Red Planet*).

2. A once-noble Martian race, destroyed by drought, left Mars with only a humanoid vampire-reptile—a sort of lizard with tremendous claws and jaws. It's interesting how evolution on Mars usually goes down the drain . . . Anyway, the lizard creature is strong and powerful, but doesn't drive a spaceship: instead it uses ours, attracted by food (read: the crew). This Martian drinks blood and eats the soft parts, or else stores them as midnight snacks. It probably fears another drought, and the possibility of devolving into a paperweight or something. *Best Defense:* This creature's number-one enemy is lack of oxygen: "God in His wisdom" created space suits: don yours first, then asphyxiate the alien by creating an oxygen-free zone (*It! The Terror from Beyond Space*).

3. A lethal species of red fungi, or spores that attack intruders. They hitchhike to Earth on a probe and make a mess. They can combine with human blood to create a mountain-size blood rust which feeds on humans. *Best Defense:* "God in His wisdom" created a S.D.T.D.F.F.S. (Sophisticated Device to Decontaminate Fungi from Space) as well as crashing planes; use either one and you'll melt the fungus forever (*Space Master X-7*).

4. A green-brown aggressive goo is kept dormant in Martian soil by the planet's temperature (minus 225 degrees). When heated up, the goo combines its structure with that of human beings, and they mate and create an army of quickly maturing mutant kids with aggressive tempers. *Best Defense:* "God in His wisdom" created sickle-cell anemia: so, find a way to infect the Martian with that, and it'll melt (*Species II*).

5. The survivors of a Martian nuclear holocaust have devolved into cavemen. They're extremely aggressive and attack anything in sight. *Best Defense:* basic weapons; "God in His Wisdom" keeps it simple sometimes. They're quite numerous but vulnerable to weapons (*Rocketship X-M*).

6. It seems that a race of golden Celine Dion look-alikes moved to another galaxy, but before doing so, they gave the gift of life to our planet—amoebas, fish, alligators, mammoths, buffalo . . . *Best Defense:* learn the sequence of human DNA, because they might ask for it as proof of your humanity. And if you do meet them face-to-face, punch them in their glowing noses, because if you think about it, they're also responsible for those damned mosquitoes. This time "God in His wisdom" played a joke on us, and we're still paying for it (*Mission to Mars*).

7. Mars is ruled by a "Supreme Authority" who is none other than God himself. And His wisdom, of course. The Martians refer to their planet as Utopia. In this case, live and let live (*Red Planet Mars*).

Meanies

Time's up.

David Levinson in *Independence Day*

Since Earth is the only heavily populated planet in our solar system (as of this writing, that is), it seems kind of natural for other species to pick on us . . . perhaps they have terrible inferiority complexes and have to prove to themselves that they're good at something.

Where on Earth . . . ?

With minor exceptions, all of these aliens look for a base on our planet. Here is a list of recent UFO sightseeing areas—if you want to check for yourself . . .

- **Bermuda Triangle:** Earth headquarters of the Alien Galactic Center (*Starship Invasions*). They should protect us from space invaders, but how can we trust them?
- **California:** The highways are traveled by a violent alien killer (*The Dark*).
- **Japan:** Swamps are the natural niche of *Dogora the Space Monster.*
- **Kansas:** Landing area for the *Critters.*
- **Rome:** Coming directly from Venus (*20 Million Miles to Earth*).
- **Trollenberg:** Little town in the Swiss Alps. The aliens' hideout is constantly covered by a dense, stationary cloud (*The Crawling Eye*).
- **. . . Or Just About Anywhere:** Aliens want to see the world and send postcards to friends and family who weren't able to make the trip (*Earth vs. the Flying Saucers, Independence Day*).

Alien Meanie Infestation Atlas

Mercury: The closest planet to the sun. Apparently, nobody wants to live on Mercury, or if they do, they don't feel the urge to pay us a visit. Fine with us.

Venus: The brightest object in our sky after the sun, the moon, and the neon light of the motel in front of our window. Among the living creatures we've had the (mis)fortune to meet . . .

• **Robots** (*Target Earth!*): Slow androids, with legs made with vacuum cleaner tubes, and a death ray that comes out of the middle of their foreheads. They're obviously here to conquer Earth, but maybe they've been sent by a more brilliant mind—perhaps a . . .

• **Giant Cucumber** (*It Conquered the World*): . . . no matter how silly this might sound. A gigantic cucumber with two evil eyes and strong claws came from Venus, tricking a scientist who thought it was peaceful. The cucumber sent forth an army of batlike creatures to bite humans on the neck and turn them into slaves.

• **Ymir** (*20 Millions Miles to Earth*): Venusian eggs were brought back to Earth. They hatched, and a new race was born: the missing link between a T-Rex and Keanu Reeves. It has the body and stamina of the first and the facial expression of the second. The Ymir loves sulfur and can be lured into a cage using all the matchboxes you can find at a Hilton. Then keep it sedated with an electric fence.

Earth: That's us! Everybody wave!

Mars: (see *Martians*).

Jupiter: The largest of the planets has 16 satellites, but still can't get DirectTV. And from what we've seen, it seems like these moons are more dangerous than the planet itself.

• **Jupiter 2** (*Lost in Space*): Adopted home of deadly, aggressive, and mutation-inducing **space spiders** that are attracted by heat and light, and can burn through thick metal, making this moon a bad place to park.

• **Jupiter's 13th Moon** (*Fire Maidens from Outer Space*): It's where descendants of Earth's lost continent of Atlantis have settled, as well as a fierce creature that strangles anyone who wanders too close.

Saturn: A trendy planet, it wears rings and sells cars. It's the second largest planet in the solar system. Host of the aggressive **krites** (*Critters*). (See entry)

Uranus: Nothing seems to live on this planet with a methane gas atmosphere, which gives the planet a blue-green color—and a terrible stench. The planet's name is quite apropos.

Neptune: Its atmosphere is similar to Uranus's, but slightly clearer. Even less probability of finding life here.

Pluto: A small, cold, and rocky planet, Pluto is home to bizarre **mutating house pets** (*TerrorVision*), whose curiosity, strength, and appetite at a certain point grow uncontrollable, forcing us to put them to sleep . . . if we can.

. . . and a couple of lesser-known planets, still in our galaxy.

Mysteriod: The planet formerly fifth from the sun was irreparably destroyed by a nuclear war 100,000 years ago. Its race, which dons space suits and helmets with dark visors, looks like us. ***The Mysterians'*** main goal is to conquer the earth. Their angry attitude stems from being the butt of everyone's jokes, coming from the silliest-named planet of all.

Spengo: The smallest planet of our galaxy, it's filled with idiots who look like us (and most of the time act like us). The leader, **Todd Spengo,** wants to destroy Earth but finds himself distracted by women . . . for the moment (*Mom and Dad Save the World*).

That's it for our solar system. But in other galaxies we have . . .

Altair IV: Better known as the *Forbidden Planet,* it's the home of an amoebalike creature, the **Id Monster,** which tends to resemble a dragon, lion, or whatever you find in this amorphic Rorschach, which you can see but not touch . . . but it can certainly touch you and severely shorten your life.

Kallar (in the Belfar Star System): Home of giant walking carrots with arms and legs . . . but no mouths. They form an army controlled by two Kallarian women who are plotting the invasion of our planet. Unfortunately, the women are weak and fall in love with earthlings (where do you kiss a carrot with no mouth?) and the army is stalled, awaiting further orders (*Invasion of the Star Creatures*).

Klendathu: Domicile of the **Klendathu Bugs**. (See entry)

Mongo: Erratic planet that occasionally wanders into our solar system. The race that lives there resembles humans, and its ruler, **Ming the Merciless**, wants to blow our planet up "just for fun." This means hurricanes and earthquakes, followed by the moon crashing down on us. Now you know who to blame for El Niño (*Flash Gordon*).

OUTER SPACE

This is where you'll find a lot of creatures who can't talk, or who remain stationary, waiting for space probes and the like. Here you'll find . . .

- **Big Bird:** Forget about *Sesame Street.* There's a quasi-vulture race with a 200-foot wingspan, long necks, and bulging eyes that decided Earth was the best place to lay eggs. This race is invisible to radar. How convenient. So anyway, as one of these beasts discovered how unhappy we were about the eggs, it attacked (*The Giant Claw*).

- **Extraterrestrials:** (see entry)

- **Giant Eyes** (*The Crawling Eye*): Still looking for a new home after their planet's death, these aliens are conducting various experiments on Mars, Jupiter, and Earth. Their massive eyes crawl around thanks to six tentacles on the lower part of their bodies. They hide in cold areas like the Swiss Alps and spend their days decapitating people.

- **Giant Robot** (*Kronos*): A sort of large battery or accumulator, which grows in size every time it gulps kilowatts. In theory, the robotlike creature will be able to convert its size back into energy to feed its planet, but we'll probably never know that for sure.

- **Human Aliens with a Plan** (*Plan 9 from Outer Space*): Wearing spacesuits made by killing dozens of Easter eggs, these aliens resurrect the corpses from a San Fernando Valley cemetery in order to have a battalion at their service. It seems that the aliens' plan is flawed and without a backup, because the first small glitch screws up everything royally—for the aliens.

- **Human Aliens with a Different Plan** (*Starship Invasions*): Some races seem to have evolved only in the space transport department, because they look just like us. But they can use telepathy to induce us all into committing suicide. And they don't even have to dial 10-10-321.

- **Space Fungus** (*The Creeping Unknown*): With a need to consume living cells, otherwise they'll perish lickity-split.

- **Pint-Sized Aliens** (*Liquid Sky*): They're attracted to bodily elements released when humans use heroin and achieve orgasm. The aliens hit Manhattan, where they're sure they can find big helpings of that.

THE EIGHTH DIMENSION

A few of the aliens here are peaceful, others don't like visitors. Many of them look like us, or differ slightly from us (*The Adventures of Buckaroo Banzai Across the Eighth Dimension*).

DYING PLANETS

It seems our universe is filled with planets on the edge of collapse. The inhabitants try every possible trick up their sleeves (or whatever they wear) to save the species.

• **Astron Delta 4:** Home of a race that decided to exterminate all the people on Earth in order to take over our planet (*Killers from Space*). The main hobby of these aliens is creating mutations: filling a cave with giant insects, grasshoppers, and other stuff. This is an effective way to intimidate humanity: threatening to release this mutated army. Little did they know that we've dealt with the giant insect thing a thousand times already (see *Mutations*).

• **Unknown Planet:** Populated by big, evil, hideous animals with scales and forked tongues, disguised in robot shells. They attack and order us to surrender or else they'll destroy Earth. But then what's left to take over? (*Earth vs. the Flying Saucers*).

And don't forget the always popular . . .

Alien Death Threats Astutely Masked by Messages of Peace (or Not)

• **Bringing Peace:** This is what an intergalactic federation wants; we'd better do what they say, or they'll destroy us (*The Day the Earth Stood Still*).

• **Releasing Confined Monsters:** The aliens release all the "Monsterland" monsters (see *Unique Discoveries*) who roam across the globe. The aliens also awake the dormant three-headed flying dragon Ghidrah, which engages itself in a fight with Godzilla & Co. The reasons for all this are still unclear (*Destroy All Monsters!*).

• **Testing Us:** A humanoid alien gives five people a capsule that, if opened, will ravage the Earth. However, the pellet becomes ineffective if (a) it's opened after 27 days, or (b) the person who has the capsule dies. The Russians wanted to know the secret so they opened the capsule before the 27th day. The capsule killed only the curious Russians, who evidently failed the "how mature is the human race?" test. The alien is probably still laughing its cephalo off (*The 27th Day*).

How to Kill Them

Not easy at all; these dudes have crossed the solar system—and perhaps more than one. So they won't kick the bucket easily.

• **Antiray Weapon:** It'll penetrate the creatures' antimatter shield, making them vulnerable (*The Giant Claw, The Mysterians*).

• **Computer:** Use your laptop to interfere with the villainous aliens' plans (*Starship Invasions, Independence Day*).

- **Electricity:** A huge quantity will kill the creatures (*The Creeping Unknown*), especially if they live on electricity (*Kronos*). It's like indigestion.

- **Fire:** You can burn many creatures. In the specific case of the cucumber creature, try deep-frying it. It's a rare delicacy.

- **Poison:** Use bee and wasp venom to create a liquid to be injected into Dogora. You will probably need a 20-gallon syringe, but that's a whole 'nuther story.

- **Ultrasonic Sound:** It'll break open Venusian robots' glass faceplates, or it'll pierce the aliens' defenses, causing their starships to crash (*Earth vs. the Flying Saucers*).

- **High-Powered Earth Weapons:** Bazookas and mortars will do the trick with several creatures, such as the Ymir or the Klendathu Bugs. Heavy artillery can also work well with flying saucers.

What to Do if You Meet One (or Two, or a Whole Flock)

Ask them if their computers are equipped with virus protection software. If they look puzzled, you might be in luck. And don't forget to yell, "Klaatu barada nikto." It may save your life, as well as our planet.

Extraterrestrials

Classification: meanies / *Meanas canbeum*

Footage:
1996, *Independence Day* by Roland Emmerich

The Skinny: Great invasion plan . . . next time get virus and/or geek protection software.

Quotable: "Oh, no, you did not shoot that green sh*& at me!"

Flight Paths: Space; above major cities.

Origin: From outer space; we don't know where. Tomorrow we'll stop at the gas station and ask for directions. It seemed simple: a few spaceships about 10 gazillion miles in diameter entered our atmosphere on July 2, hovered over the most important towns: Los Angeles, Washington, D.C., New York, Moscow . . . (rumor has it they stopped over Naples, Italy, too—but the UFO was hijacked in less than two minutes). Well, you couldn't have missed them even if you wanted to!

How It Looks: The alien is a humanoid creature: it breathes oxygen, it's not invulnerable—you can shoot it or even punch it—but it's sort of a shell for a smaller alien which lives inside its head. The "shell" is tall, two-legged, has a lot of tentacles, a face like a coffee can with two holes in it, and its color is hard to define (green? brown? gray? Who cares?); the inner alien is dark brown, has a triangular head, two large, shining eyes and a none-too-sunny disposition.

Cravings: Conquering other worlds.

Behavior: This extraterrestrial goes from planet to planet conquering, killing, using up all the resources, and—once a planet is fully milked—moves on to another planet and starts all over again. In other news, the aliens communicate amongst themselves with telepathy and guttural sounds. If you perform an autopsy on the external alien shell, its owner gets mad and kills you.

Danger: Quite huge. The aliens don't care about you, your president, or anything else. They kill, kill, kill! No dialogue, no ears for any of your problems, they just mind their own business.

How to Kill It: We told you, they are not bulletproof—but their starships certainly are. So, if you meet them *mano a mano*, it'd be very helpful to shoot, slice, slaughter, or else punch the alien. But if you are underneath their starship or in pursuit (you on a plane; the alien behind you with a smaller ship), first you have to put a virus inside their computer, using our satellites, a Macintosh PowerBook, and a lot of ingenuity. Then you can take any air-force pilot trained to drive a starship and send him to the mothership and . . . Oh, come on! That's impossible; forget about it. We will all probably just die.

What to Do if You Meet It: Plan your vacation in Petaluma next summer. These aliens stop only over huge towns with large and symbolic buildings to destroy.

Current Status: Defeated on Earth the first time, but we'd bet our bazooka they're ready to attack again.

Body Count: Several towns are wiped out; however, the president of the U.S. authorized the nuking of one starship. We still have to figure out who made the higher number of casualties.

Klendathu Bugs

Classification: meanies / *Arachnidim verypeskium*

Footage:
1997, *Starship Troopers* by Paul Verhoeven

The Skinny: They're big, they're mean, they're pissed off: in one word, they're the Klendathu Bugs . . . all right, two words.

Quotable: "The only good Bug is a dead Bug!"

Habitat: The planet Klendathu, and spreading quickly.

Origin: A new race of bugs, whose only purpose was to colonize the galaxy, started sending large plasma asteroids toward our planet, causing a militaristic uproar.

Identification: The Bugs come in a wide variety of shapes. We have spiderlike bugs, black and yellow creatures about 10 feet tall, about 15 feet long, with large jaws that can snap a man in two, and long legs that can impale a body quite handily. Not exactly a Furby. Another kind of Bug is really similar to the spiderlike Bug in jaw size and leg size, but they have (a) a green and black coloring and (b) they fly. There are even larger ones that come out of the ground and look like potato bugs on steroids. They're twice the size of a truck and they're totally black. Then there are smaller bugs, flat and no longer than three feet, but they seem to be just extras to crowd large places. And finally there's a Brain Bug, the one which knows how to control its soldiers: this one looks like a pink pear with eight eyes and a sort of disgusting mouth with a retractile probe that pops in and out of its mouth. It's also really fat. These are your basic Bugs of Klendathu. Collect them all!

Cravings: Presumably to colonize the galaxy. And to kill whoever steps on Klendathu soil.

Behavior: The spiderlike Bugs are the soldiers. They come. And come. And come. You can't see the end of their waves. They're not too smart, they come at you, they're not afraid of your weapons, but if you kill one of them, a hundred more are ready to replace it. Which makes killing one seem quite pointless. The soldiers kill you by ripping your body apart, but they don't seem to eat you—which makes us think: what do they eat on their lousy desert planets? We haven't seen anything, not even a Mickey D's.

There are fewer flying Bugs, but their technique is roughly the same as the spiders: they just keep coming and coming. Then they grab and take you away.

The potato bugs pop out of the ground where they dig elaborate tunnels, and hit you with flames they throw from two horns they have in between their eyes. They're also able to literally fart dangerous "plasma balls" that can destroy a space freighter in one second, and not only because of the smell.

And the Brain Bug slides around, senses danger, devises strategies, and gets its nourishment from human brains it literally sucks out of skulls. Again, what does it eat when there are no humans around? Well, we guess we'll never know.

Danger: Immense. Even if confined to the Arachnid Quarantine Zone, now the Bugs have learned how to hit us with "plasma-propelled meteors," so they don't have to leave home to kill.

How to Kill Them: Machine guns can be effective, even if you need to aim at the nerve stem (otherwise, if you blow off a limb, the soldier Bug will still be 86 percent combat effective). Another effective way is, in a sergeant's own words, to "nuke 'em!" But isn't it fascinating how in the next millennium the humans have learned how to build spacecraft that can travel at light speed, but still have to dial 1-800-TERMINIX to get rid of a few bugs?

What to Do if You Meet Them: Be strong, and run fast. If you can, faster.

Current Status: The Federation won the last battle. But there are so many other bugs that we can easily expect a second assault. Get ready by stocking up on roach motels—supersized.

Body Count: We don't even wanna go there. Just to give you an idea, the victims in Buenos Aires were in excess of 8,764,608 people. On their planet, they caused at least 308,563 deaths, and one time 100,000 deaths in one hour. So let's just say that they are bad, bad, *bad.*

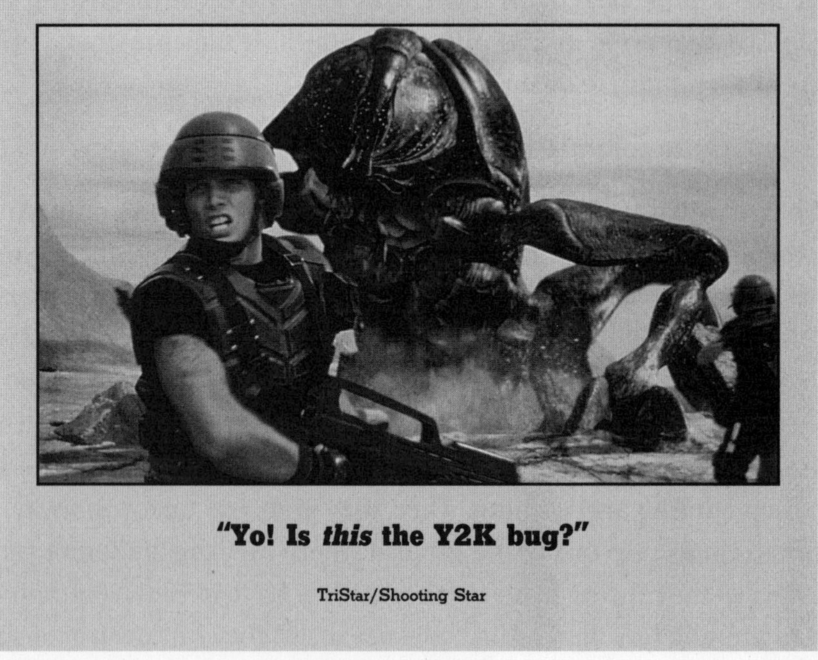

"Yo! Is *this* the Y2K bug?"

TriStar/Shooting Star

Krites

Classification: meanies / *Swalloweribus globalis*

Footage:

1986, *Critters* by Stephen Herek
1988, *Critters 2* by Mick Garris
1991, *Critters 3* by Kristine Peterson
1992, *Critters 4* by Rupert Harvey

The Skinny: Tiny little furry aliens with an endless appetite.

Quotable: "Krites feed together. Eat like a family. Love meats. Baaad habit."

Stomping Grounds: Little villages in Kansas (like Grover's Bend), big cities in Kansas, and of course outer space, somewhere in the Saturn Quadrant.

Origin: Eight Krites, the last specimens of their race, were about to be sent to a prison asteroid—Sector 17 in another galaxy. As often happens in our galaxy, the maximum security prison was highly insecure, and that's how the Krites were able to escape on a spacecraft and set off for—guess where—Earth.

Identification: Krites are fluffy hairballs with as many teeth as hair. They have two tiny hands and two tiny legs—with sharp claws at the end of the fingers, and are quite short. Two red eyes give Krites a satanic look they're quite proud of, and the spines on their backs (which are shot like arrows with deadly accuracy) are venomous: they instantaneously make the hit area of the skin numb. Furthermore, Krites can tuck into a ball and roll at high speeds; even worse, many Krites can join together, and tuck into a larger ball and roll at even higher speeds.

Cravings: Everything they can sink their teeth into: objects, animals, people.

Behavior: Krites saunter around, looking for what's edible. Or something inedible, but that can assuage their appetite anyway. When they see a possible target, Krites attack and literally skin. They don't pay attention to whether what they're biting might be dangerous to them (a tire, a gun, a TNT tube): they bite and swallow. And bite and swallow again. They prefer things with no bones like cheeseburgers, though.

Krites can recognize weapons and follow moving targets, as well as operate computers, but their power is in their numbers. When in danger, Krites emit a high-pitched noise that calls the others, and shatters glass.

Although we haven't identified which is male and which is female (if the distinction actually exists), they lay a large amount of eggs that hatch after six months. As a Krite pops out of the shell, it starts its cycle of eating and eating and eating. The more they eat, the bigger they become.

Meet Boris, this year's tartar control poster child.

New Line/Shooting Star

Danger: High. Especially since the last generation of Krites was improved thanks to a metabolic accelerator (who doesn't own one nowadays?). The Krite itself is untrustworthy. So, it's better to move cautiously in risky places, avoiding sticking your hands in dark holes. If you're really quiet, you can hear them moving. Especially along ducts. They love ducts. Krites believe we fear them, and this is their biggest strength. Show them no fear. They'll eat you anyway, but with more respect.

How to Kill Them: You have many options: shooting them, dropping them into boiling water, feeding them bombs, drilling holes in their bodies, running them over . . . Of course, the best way is to wait for the high security prison in their galaxy to send some trained bounty hunters . . . We told you, you have a lot of choices. Unfortunately, the Krites have a lot, too.

What to Do if You Meet Them: Break the overground speed record.

Current Status: Apparently the race will become extinct in year 2045. A date that's not exactly around the corner. And unfortunately, by that time the Intergalactic Council (take our word for it) will issue a new law, which will prevent any violation of the zoological mandate E-102, clause 14, paragraph 5, items 6 and 7 ("You are prohibited from terminating any transgalactic form if it means total extinction of the species"). Now you know.

Body Count: 10 people, 4 bounty hunters. 4 cows (at least), 1 goldfish, 1 *E.T.* puppet.

Predators

If it bleeds, we can kill it.

Dutch in *Predator*

Some alien creatures capture us, either for strange purposes or simply to kill us. In any case, they want something from us, whether it's a quick roll in the hay or our skulls for the mantel back home. Not too fun . . . for us, that is.

Earth's Least-Wanted

Predators are from different races, and frequently the first time you see them coincides with the last moment of your life.

- ***The Thing from Another World:*** (see entry).

- **Gigantic Flytrap Plant** (*Bad Channels*): A humanoid figure in a dark gray spacesuit and a helmet covered with a sort of a fungus, and many tubes. Out of the costume, we find out what it really looks like. This one takes possession of a radio station to reap the benefits of the radio waves: operating some strange gizmos, the alien can reach beautiful women who are listening. Once the alien's hooked the women, it absorbs them via radio, shrinking them to doll size. Good news: this process is reversible. Bad news: the alien won't cooperate.

- **Dr. Frank-N-Furter** (*The Rocky Horror Picture Show*): Different human being, quite sexually active, disturbed and disturbing, with a wicked wardrobe. Wants to derive pleasure from us, or else create something which will provide the same.

- ***Killer Klowns from Outer Space:*** Grotesque clowns with a dark side—they want to package us up as midnight snacks (see entry).

- ***Predator:*** (see entry)

How to Kill Them

You have to be ready because they are already determined to kill you.

- **Beat the Crap Out of Them:** And maybe the creature will acknowledge your superiority. But we wouldn't bet on that.
- **Cold:** It harms many aliens, and eventually it kills them. Or it at least stops them until the next heat wave.
- **Cut the Suit:** The more heavily an alien dresses, the less likely it will survive in our environment. So blow a hole in its spacesuit, or break its helmet.
- **Electricity:** Fry 'em up.
- **Sterilize Them:** Use a can of germicide and "clean house."
- **Weapons:** A bundle. Even better if you can lay your hands on the aliens' weapons. Eventually they'll take you somewhere. Like to the aliens' funeral. They're predators, but not invulnerable. And sometimes they shoot each other (*The Rocky Horror Picture Show*), so you can take the day off.

What to Do if You Meet One

If you survive the encounter, here are a few tips:

- Keep a large provision of germicide in your closet (*Bad Channels*).
- Learn how to dance, sing, and dress in stockings.

Killer Klowns

Classification: predators / *Bozos aggressivus*

Footage:

1987, *Killer Klowns from Outer Space* by Stephen Chiodo

The Skinny: (see title)

Quotable: "See a rubber nose on a painted face, bringing genocide to the human race."

Origin: A cometlike light streamed across the sky one night in the small town of Crescent Cove, drawing the attention of a farmer and some horny teenagers. What these people found was a big-top tent in the middle of the forest filled with bloodthirsty clowns.

Identification: Ten-foot-tall grotesquely distorted clowns with big red noses and sharp teeth. They talk gibberish, but understand English.

Cravings: To store as many human beings as possible inside pink cotton candy cocoons, for future enjoyment as snacks.

Behavior: Yes, they go around killing humans, but they do it in such an amusing, clown-like way that our laughter almost overcomes our fear . . . until the laughter stops. Among the weapons they use, there's a cotton-candy-maker pistol that wraps you in a big sticky cocoon; there's a rifle that fires popcorn with a life of its own and that can turn into mean, vicious tiny critters; also, they have corrosive pies, trained balloon dogs, and who knows what other devilish inventions.

Danger: The clowns are quick and take over a whole town in one night. They store everyone in their starship, and eventually they drink our bodies straight from the cotton-candy cocoon. Very strong and resistant, there's very little you can do to beat them. But hey, look at the bright side: at least they're not mimes.

How to Kill Them: Aim at the nose! The Klowns' most vulnerable spot (and probably their *only* vulnerable spot) is their big, red noses. If you shoot or poke them right in the nose, they'll twirl around rapidly and then explode in a bunch of confetti.

What to Do if You Meet One: Give it an application for Ringling Bros., then slip away.

Current Status: Vanquished . . . from Earth, that is.

Body Count: 120-plus people are either stored and never recovered or simply killed outright.

Nocturnal Flying Aliens

Classification: predators / *Starvus youllregretit*

Footage:

2000, *Pitch Black* by David Twohy

The Skinny: Batlike, hungry, and extremely averse to light.

Quotable: "One rule: stay in the light."

Habitat: A remote uncharted desert planet with three suns, but they are only around where and when the sun don't shine.

Origin: A transport ship crash-landed on a planet which seemed to have eternal daylight and a relatively breathable atmosphere, yet no life (and not a Starbucks in sight!). Anyways, they soon discovered their unbeatable luck: every 22 years there's a total eclipse of the three suns, and then the freaks come out . . . for a long-awaited meal. And, by the way, 22 years was up.

Identification: These things kind of look like winged velociraptors with upside-down *T*s for heads. Some of them are smaller, not too much bigger than bats, some are much larger, along the lines of the creatures from the *Alien* series. But size doesn't matter, as the saying goes, because they are all equally lethal. They have mouths crammed with sharp teeth for ripping flesh, along with two feet, two big wings, a long split tail, and two small arms which have very large clawed hands. Their color is somewhat gray and their blood blue.

Cravings: Although they seem to really like human blood (they can smell your wounds from a distance), they don't refrain from killing each other for food—just you try skipping meals for 22 years, and see where your appetite leads you.

Behavior: They fly, run, crawl, and basically get around any way they darned well please . . . but again, only in the dark. They have small quick-moving appendages and sharp claws that can rip through metal. The creatures sound like whales, communicating via high-pitched, modulated moans.

Danger: They attack in such large numbers that it's virtually impossible to hold them off . . . like "boy bands."

How to Kill Them: Shine the light on them; they'll literally melt. Or use any kind of powerful firearm of explosive.

What to Do if You Meet Them: Seems obvious, doesn't it? STAY IN THE LIGHT. You can even use the indigenous little glowworms that can be found in caves to create a makeshift lantern. No light? Skedaddle. No skedaddle? Actually, we've got some good news and some bad news. The good news is that they have a blind spot. The bad news is that this spot, directly between the eyes, happens to be right in front of the mouth. And staying there requires a fleet foot, more stamina than the creatures have themselves, and an immunity to evil alien breath. The only other option is to stay completely still and hope they don't stumble across you. Fat chance.

Current Status: Still plentiful.

Body Count: 8 people (and presumably countless other people, interstellar travelers, indigenous creatures, what have you, as evidenced by all the bones in their underground lair).

Predator

Classification: predators / *Pumpingirons translucentibus*

Footage:

1987, *Predator* by John McTiernan
1990, *Predator 2* by Stephen Hopkins

The Skinny: Deadly alien "sportsman" opens season on us.

Quotable: "What's got Billy so spooked?"

Turf: The Central American jungle (where it lives on top of the trees); 1997 Los Angeles (where it lives on top of buildings).

Origin: A commando unit was sent into an equatorial jungle to recover two hostages out of a rebel camp. Unfortunately, no one told the commandos that in the same jungle there was an alien hunter, meaner than Gary Coleman at an autograph session and equipped with unknown and extremely powerful weapons. Ten years later, another Predator arrived in sunny L.A. to kick several more butts.

Identification: The Predator is really hard to see because it has a prodigious camouflage device which makes its body crystal clear (it is said that it "bends the light"). You can track its movement once you locate the pheromone signature it leaves behind. Piece of cake, huh? Anyway, when the alien turns the mimetic device off, it appears in all its disgustingness: it's a tall, huge, Jean-Claude Van Damme-esque figure, covered with a black net in which it hangs the bones and skulls of its victims. Its large head has Rastafarian hair and a scorpion face, equipped with four jaws and two mean, yellow eyes.

Cravings: It kills people either to skin them and leave them hanging upside down, or else it drags them to its hideout in order to remove their skulls (the Predator is a hunter; it wants trophies). Every two days it needs food, so the Predator grabs its Discover card and goes shopping for fresh meat; usually it ends up in some slaughterhouse.

Behavior: The hunting season is open only during the hottest years; that is the time you have to look out for the Predator. When in the jungle, it jumps from one branch to another, looking for prey. When in L.A., it jumps from one building to another, doing the same thing. Apparently, the more challenging the situation, the more fun this alien will have. If you try to stop it, the Predator will take it personally.

Danger: Its point of view is: predator = hunter; you = pheasant.

How to Kill It: If the alien doesn't eliminate itself with its trusty wrist bomb (which can pulverize 300 city blocks), it is possible—not easy, read our lips: it is *possible*—to wound and eventually kill it. But let us tell you, what an effort. The alien's body is not invulnerable, so a ton of ammo will pierce a few holes in it. A heavy weight can crush it, but the best of the best is stealing one of this alien's weapons and using it against the creature. Good luck.

What to Do if You Meet It: It's more likely you'll accidentally bump into it, since most of the time the Predator is mimetic; one good thing to know is that any cold substance bothers it, and water damages the camouflage device. But you still have to face an eight-foot-tall alien with a death wish. Anyway, this hunter is a good sport: if its opponent has a weapon, the Predator uses its weapon, too (but it's a battle lost from the beginning); if its opponent is unarmed, the Predator unarms itself, too (but it's a battle lost from the beginning). Tip of the day: the Predator hunts by tracking your body heat. It sees you only when you're hot. So cover your body with mud. Or do a show on UPN.

Current Status: Gone—twice. But other specimens are still flying around in deep space, and sooner or later they'll be back. Fear the next heat wave.

Body Count: 37 people; 3 are vanished; 1 TV set; half of a tropical jungle.

The Thing from Another World

Classification: predators / *Carrotus vampirus*

Footage:
1951, *The Thing from Another World* by Christian Nyby

The Skinny: Terrifying legume visits the North Pole.

Quotable: "I understand you've been doing a bit of gardening."

Habitat: An arctic base.

Origin: November 1, 1951: there was this silly team of scientists and air-force men, up in the North Pole. They were silly because, when a flying saucer trapped under the ice was discovered, they said, "We'll melt the ice with a thermal bomb." And how. The bomb freed the saucer so well that you could find pieces of it within a 50,000-square foot radius. These dumb guys were lucky, though: far from the former saucer, they found the pilot, trapped in the ice as well. This time, they *dug*.

Identification: The alien is a tall humanoid vegetable. It has a flat, hairless head, clawed hands, its strength is way above average, and in its veins there is not blood but a sort of lymph. It is also known as the terrible Carrot Man.

Cravings: Heat is necessary for the Thing to do its business. This alien loves living creatures from the animal world. We have not a clue what it would do with a lawyer.

Behavior: The Thing strolls along the base corridors and, whenever it can, kills a couple of men. If no men are in sight, the alien kills a couple of dogs. Anyway, it later brings its victims into the greenhouse of the base. Here, the Thing hangs them upside down to collect their blood. The Thing has started a private garden, where it'll grow more Things (watering them with the aforementioned blood).

Danger: It's the only vegetable vampire we know of.

How to Kill It: You need a high-voltage shock so that you can fry it to serve at your next party (makes about 200 servings).

What to Do if You Meet It: The Carrot Man is aggressive, and since it's a plant, a machine gun is not enough to kill it (like any plant it can regenerate parts of its body). To be safe, check your horoscope: if it says, "You'll meet a mysterious foreigner coming from far away," stay home.

Current Status: Dead. But watch the skies. Everywhere!

Body Count: 2 people, 4 dogs, and several windows.

Beasts

THE "MOST DANGEROUS GAME"?
IS SMELL PART OF THE EQUATION?

Who You Callin' "Beast" Pal?!!

The word "beast" literally means something below us on the ladder of life, whether it be an animal, plant, or that telemarketer who won't stop talking even when you say good-bye for the fourth time.

In the *HMSG,* a beast is pretty much anything nonhuman and all-"natural" you can find right here on our home planet. Providing, of course, that it's unpredictable, dangerous, scary, yadda yadda. That's right—any creature you find in nature could be a beast in the right context and with the wrong attitude . . . but purring and running away are pretty reliable signs that something *isn't* a beast.

Attention All Gun Rack–Sporting, Red-Blooded Americans:

This is not an invitation to shoot first and ask questions later (although asking questions first wouldn't necessarily yield a lot of information either). We must learn to live in harmony with our fellow creatures and share the precious resources of Mother Earth. After all, it's their planet, too. But . . .

Every once in a while, one of these cheeky critters gets out of line. *Way* out of line. The line we're talking about, of course, is the food chain. Then again, maybe *we're* out of line by imagining that we're at the top . . . as anyone who has watched the Discovery Channel knows. There are enough snakes, sharks, spiders, and graboids out there to make anyone—

"Hold on a second . . . *graboids,* you say?"

Yes, That's Right—Graboids

What, you thought we'd already found everything under the sun? Not even close, my friend. Every year a whole new crop of curious creatures are inadvertently discovered, usually by a small group of people in a remote location. And the only reason you may not have read about these specimens in *National Geographic* is that they rarely leave more than one worn-out survivor to return and report what he's encountered. And who's gonna believe someone left in such shock that he can no longer tie his own shoelaces? This is how the hidden *stays* hidden.

Blasts from the Past

Speaking of the hidden, remember learning in grammar school about dinosaurs, woolly mammoths, cavemen, and the other creatures that populated this rock before they evolved or else were wiped out by extreme weather changes or meteors?

Well, you'll learn once again that what they taught you in school was a lie. Turns out these ancient beasts never really went away—they just hibernated. And every once in a while one wakes up, steps out of its den, and causes a little mischief. Stay tuned.

SUBCATEGORIES

What a colorful variety nature has to offer . . .

- **Animals:** The birds and the bees, and the fish who chomp your knees . . .
- **Plants:** Giving you justification for talking to them.
- **Prehistoric:** Old-timers . . . *real* old-timers.
- **Undiscovered:** Officially, that is.

Animals

You're gonna need a bigger boat.

Sheriff Martin Brody in *Jaws*

Let's take a moment to talk about our friends who are a little further down the evolutionary ladder. First of all, it's important to note that their position on the evolutionary ladder doesn't have a damn thing to do with their position on the food chain. So no matter how dumb, gullible, or sweet an animal may appear to be, its behavior is still highly unpredictable.

Many of us keep animals as pets. That's all fine and well, but keep your eye out for pets who start behaving strangely. Strange behavior might include: letting themselves in and out of the door at night, scaring off your other pets, or bringing home a neighbor's forearm. And if you're the neighbor, don't believe all that "bark is worse than its bite" B.S.

How an Animal Becomes a Monster

- **The Hunter Becomes the Hunted:** A hunter fires at an animal and misses, thus inviting the animal to fight back (*Anaconda, Orca*).

- **You Can't Stop Progress:** Real-estate developers and greedy politicians simply don't care about the damage they are doing to the environment. According to some animals, progress *can* be stopped—or at least stalled for a little while (*Barracuda, Creepshow, Frogs, Link, Kingdom of the Spiders*).

- **Our Best Defense:** The animal works as a bodyguard, then gets discontented with its employers (*Monkey Shines, Willard, Mako: The Jaws of Death*).

- **Just for Fun:** Some animals go berserk all by themselves (*Arachnophobia, The Birds, Grizzly, Razorback, Jaws*) or else with a little help from their friends (*Cujo, Mamba*).

Habitat

Many of the most dangerous animals live in remote areas. Look around you—no people in sight? Do you need to stop and ask why?

Identification

Yep, these animals are just like the ones in your biology book: sharks, snakes, dogs, birds . . . not necessarily aggressive species, but everybody gets rubbed the wrong way now and again.

Cravings

One desire above all:

- **Killing Humans:** Animals wish to restore the balance in their ecosystem—or else need a midnight snack.

Secondary goals:

- **Destroying Man-Made Things:** Whatever man puts on the animals' turf must be demolished: buildings, power plants, theme parks.
- **Ruining Tourist Season:** Especially by the shore; sea monsters have this uncanny gift for reaching the beach just when the new season has begun.

Behavior

SEA CREATURES

They stay underwater most of the time, waiting patiently. As soon as some unfortunate person sticks a part of his body into the water, the animal pops up with a loud splash, then drags the victim to the bottom of the ocean. Even if the creature doesn't usually care who it's gulping, sometimes it takes things personally (*Jaws: The Revenge, Orca*), and doesn't stop until its nemesis has been erased from the face of the earth. And, for some reason, the nemesis never thinks to book a trip to the mountains.

LAND ANIMALS

The first attack almost invariably happens at night. But soon the animal starts to prowl during daylight. This change of schedule neither helps nor hinders the animal's predatory abilities. The only difference is that you get to see it coming right at you.

SKY CREATURES

Birds always follow the same pattern. First, one member of the gang attacks a human being; later on, there is a second attack, this time carried out by 10 to 20 birds. When people finally realize that something is wrong, the full-on aerial riot begins.

How to Kill Them

If an angry animal lures you into its own territory, offing it may become a really hard task. But never an impossible one.

• **Blow Up or Burn the Beast:** The best strategy. They can try to get back at you while still aflame, but there's no way for an animal to pull through. You have to find a way to gather all the creatures into the same place at once. Live bait never fails . . . of course it may not stay "live."

• **Electrocute the Beast:** Hard to accomplish. You can't always get an animal to bite into a high-voltage cable, but if you do it'll light up like a Christmas tree.

• **Shoot It:** You'll need precise aim, several bullets, and enough time to reload your gun if you miss. Rarely works.

What to Do if You Meet One

• **Wait:** Maybe the animal will get tired and go away. *Maybe.*

• **Buy a Special Protector Symbol:** The animal will respect your right to life while you wear the symbol (*Mako: The Jaws of Death*). But as soon as you take it off, you're history.

• **Pet It:** Worked great with *Stanley,* the pet rattlesnake. Then a woman came between the snake and his owner, and *somebody* got a little jealous . . .

• **Move Upstairs:** Frogs have soft fingers and they can't push elevator buttons.

• **Sell Your Story to Fox Television:** It'll be the first segment on the next *When Animals Attack.*

The Anaconda

Classification: animals / *Squeezibus alot*

Footage:

1997, *Anaconda* by Luis Llosa

The Skinny: The world's largest snake tastes human flesh—and by George, it loves it!

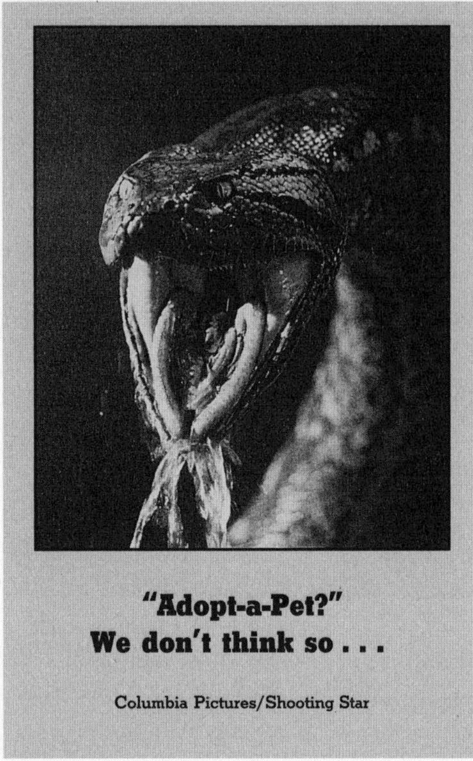

"Adopt-a-Pet?" We don't think so . . .

Columbia Pictures/Shooting Star

Quotable: "They strike, wrap around you, hold you tighter than your true love . . . and you get the privilege of hearing your bones break before the power of the embrace causes your veins to explode."

Habitat: Northern South America.

Origin: While traveling up the Amazon to shoot a documentary about the Shirishama tribe, a film crew met a sinister man who called himself a snake hunter. The crew was eventually abducted by the obsessed man and enlisted in tracking a gigantic snake. But the snake ended up tracking the unwitting crew. The hunter or the hunted? Sound familiar?

Identification: The anaconda is the largest snake on earth: up to 40 feet long. Which makes for about 120 belts. It has mean yellow eyes, a wide mouth, a triangular head, and can weigh up to a quarter of a ton. It's fast and evil, but hey—at least it's not poisonous.

Cravings: Any living creature it can wrap up, crush, and swallow.

Behavior: The anaconda slithers up and down the rivers of Brazil looking for food. And once it's found out where the food is, nothing can distract it from its chosen meal. But it seems that the anaconda is not happy eating only once: very often it regurgitates its prey in order to eat it again. This may sound disgusting, but wait until you see us camped out at the local Souplantation. *Then* we'll talk about what's disgusting.

Danger: The anaconda is a predator or, as many say, "the perfect killing machine." Its appetite is insatiable, it is extremely aggressive, and it can locate a warm body just about anywhere—as if its prey were equipped with Lo-Jack. As soon as the snake captures you in its coils, it "holds you tighter than your true love." Sound romantic? Then you hear your bones snap and your veins pop, and that sounds a little less romantic.

How to Kill It: Despite their great stamina, anacondas are vulnerable to bullets, fire, and boring soap operas. But since it's hard to get TV reception along the Amazon, we suggest either shooting it or blowing up the slithery beast with drums of gasoline. Naturally you might upset the already precarious balance of the Amazon's ecosystem, but then you gotta choose between the environment and your ass. *You* make the call.

What to Do if You Meet It: If you do happen to meet it, it's probably because you're in Brazil, lost on a boat in the middle of the jungle. So you only have yourself to blame. Although all anacondas are deadly, the one documented in the above footage was especially large and fast, moving about 50 times faster than your average anaconda. We suspect it may have eaten a Lamborghini at some point. But there's a darn good chance that any anaconda *you* run into will be a little easier to run away from. In any case, always carry with you a bottle of Moro-809: it's a reptile tranquilizer that you can pick up at your local pharmacy without a prescription. Inject the anaconda with 50 grams, then advise it not to call on you in the morning.

Current Status: The anaconda from the footage is dead. Or were there two? No doubt many others are still lurking . . .

Body Count: 5 people, 1 monkey, and 1 black panther (strange, because black panthers are not indigenous to South America).

Asian Crocodiles

Classification: animals / *Gobblegobbles greedyus*

Footage:
1999, *Lake Placid* by Steve Miner

The Skinny: Asian crocodiles swim across the ocean, and boy, are they hungry!

Quotable: "Something flipped us over and I don't believe it was a mink."

Swimming Hole: Black Lake, Aroostook County, Maine.

Origin: These crocodiles are of the Asian Pacific variety, and for all we know they crossed the ocean and found a nice, quiet resting area in Lake Black, which is connected to the sea. Here, thanks to an old-but-firm woman, the crocodiles have lived for six years, feeding mainly on cows that she was giving them.

Identification: 30-foot-long crocodiles. If you can picture that, you'll know what to do. Read on.

Cravings: Cows, mostly. Occasionally crocodiles go shopping and have a taste of other animals—but seldom men.

Behavior: Swimming, eating, swimming, eating . . . and laying eggs. Oh my. Crocodiles can't see very well underwater but they're attracted by sound, and they smell flesh and blood; they are fast in water and fast on shore, where they usually spend the night.

How to Kill Them: Use a big, big, big, big gun.

What to Do if You Meet Them: If you're too much of an "animal lover" to kill the crocodile, you can try to sedate and eventually capture it. Its skin is hard and impenetrable, except for the belly and part of the side, so aim at those parts if you want to drug it. But if you do this, you place fame and fortune above the value of your own life *and* your "love" of animals.

Current Status: The adult croc is being transported to a zoo which has a tank big enough to house it. Its babies, however, are still in the lake.

Body Count: 3 people, 1 grizzly bear, 1 moose, 1 cow—and many, many more cows in the past.

The Birds

Classification: animals / *Flapius flapius*

Footage:

1968, *The Birds* by Alfred Hitchcock

The Skinny: Tweedy bird . . . with an attitude.

Quotable: "They're waiting . . ."

Habitat: Bodega Bay, Sebastopol, and Santa Rosa, California. And God only knows where else.

Origin: Seagulls, crows, sparrows . . . all of a sudden, one day they decided to give us a hard time. So they began to round up, attacking in no particular order: schools, parties, and people. And what's worse, chickens stopped eating their food.

Identification: Do you know what a bird looks like? Well, now imagine a thousand gazillion birds, and you have the whole picture.

Cravings: To attack us. To cause severe damage, if not death, to the human race. Probably it's a message from Mother Nature to warn us not to mess up the planet. Or more simply, probably all the birds got bored of standing on the wires and using monuments as rest rooms.

Behavior: The birds sit and wait, quietly. Dum-de-dum, they stay on the wires, or simply on the ground, hopping around. Then, without any warning, they take off at once and attack people. Their beaks bite, poke, rip, go "caw caw," and do a lot of other interesting things. The birds seem well aware of where to find people, and also how to damage them. So they smash windows, go down the chimney, flagellate cars, etc. They usually attack, retreat, wait. Attack, retreat, wait. And their numbers grow. As well as the amount of newspaper you have to lay down to keep at least your porch clean.

How to Kill Them: They are birds. You can poison them, you can shoot them, you can fool them by creating a wall of smoke or fog, and you can electrocute them—as long as you find a tiny little electric chair in which they could fold up their little wings.

What to Do if You Meet Them: First thing to do is wash your car.

Current Status: Alive and well, and on hiatus.

Body Count: At least 4 people, but many many others were injured. A couple of houses, 1 gas station, 1 phone booth, 2 "happy birthday" balloons.

Orca

Classification: animals / *Swimmeribus gulper*

Footage:

1977, *Orca* by Michael Anderson

The Skinny: Fellow sea creatures get jealous about the success of *Jaws*.

Quotable: "Can you commit a sin against an animal?"

Stomping Waters: Sea town, North Pole.

Origin: An idiotic fisherman decided to capture sharks for a living, then changed his mind and settled for hunting orcas (a.k.a. killer whales) in order to sell them to a Sea World–like theme park. The fisherman screwed up big time, when he accidentally harpooned a pregnant female, which lost both life and child, and made its partner so angry that nobody could stop it. Beware the orca's evil eye!

Identification: The orca is an endangered black-and-white mammal, but it's not a panda. It's an orca. Never heard of Shamu, Keiko, or Willy? They all look alike to us, we can't tell one from the other. But this one is a really mean one, seeking vengeance.

Cravings: Usually the *Orcinus orca* (Latin is always impressive) eats everything. All right, we've never seen an Orca at McDonald's. But its diet is mainly composed of small, medium, and large fish. However, since the idiotic fisherman made a mess, right now the orca's snacking habits have changed a little: now it's after small, medium, and large humans.

Behavior: The orca swims, eats, and leaps out of the water. If, during one of these jumps, its teeth happen to close on a man—*bon appétit.* And if you cross the line, the orca will give you its evil eye. Sometimes, the orca likes to put a few holes in your boat just to sink it—pretty good prank, right? It also loves to use its hard head to destroy your dockside house. If the orca gets really mad at you, it may even cause a car accident (don't ask) or make a dozen gas tanks explode and burn your town to the ground. The orca seems to be a perfect strategic commando, ready to play cat and mouse with you at any time. *Now* who's the endangered species?

Danger: Immense, but only if an idiot you know has just killed a pregnant female orca and you were on his boat during the mayhem. The orca has a good memory (at least this one) and it'll never forget you. We suppose the orca can draw a sketch just to be sure to remember your face.

How to Kill It: The orca seems to be indestructible—even if its partner was killed with a banal harpoon. But it shouldn't be. So, grab a large number of harpoons and get ready to do some javelin throwing.

What to Do if You Meet It: Usually you can't do anything because when you meet it, you're in its mouth. Maybe it's ticklish. Try.

Current Status: Alive and well, looking for a way out from under the North Pole's icy water.

Body Count: 6 people, 1 leg, 1 house, 1 oil refinery, and half of a small seaport.

Razorback

Classification: animals / *Biggus baddus*

Footage:
1984, *Razorback* by Russell Mulcahy

The Skinny: Gigantic pig terrorizes Australian village.

Quotable: "There's something about blasting the sh@# out of a razorback that brightens my whole day."

Habitat: Gamulla, a small town 600 miles west of Sydney, Australia.

Origin: Probably a natural aberration, probably just a nine-ton boar that lived somewhere in the Australian desert, tired of the taste of kangaroo and wallaby flesh, one night it decided to "have a teaspoon" of human flesh, and ripped a house in half and stole a baby boy. It was pretty hard to miss its passage.

Identification: The razorback is a wild boar, four or five times bigger than the ordinary boar. Dark brown, with fangs as long as 15 inches, and large, strong legs. It has been compared to a rhino, both in size and stamina. Not that a rhino would be a lovely companion, but the razorback seems to be worse because it's carnivorous.

Cravings: Flesh of any kind, and water. Lots of it.

Behavior: The razorback hides, tramples, tears things apart, kills, and then starts the cycle all over again. It seems to be more at ease during the night, but it also can be seen wandering in bright daylight. It has been said that this animal has no nervous system, so it's pretty hard to annihilate it. It's also cunning, and despite making as much noise as a small locomotive, it catches many people by surprise. Good for it, we suppose, but a little less good for its victims.

Danger: This beast is extremely powerful and seems unstoppable. Its fur is also quite oily and greasy, so a piggyback ride is out of the question.

How to Kill It: Since its skin can't be penetrated by a bullet except for its underbelly, you should crawl on the ground with a gun attached to your hat. But this is too much, so a good thing would be to get the razorback to charge you (good luck) and, at the last minute, produce a spear for the beast to impale its sweet self on. If this isn't enough, have the beast walk through a gigantic fan that you manage to have around the day you'll go razorback hunting. A small bomb will probably take care of the animal, but you don't want to toy with grenades unless strictly necessary. Reserve them for other beasts.

What to Do if You Meet It: One of the best things is to attach a transmitter to the razorback to track its movement. When you pinpoint its position, go the opposite way.

Current Status: Dead, sliced, and gone. But as of today nobody has found its shelter, so we can't exclude the presence of possible family members.

Body Count: 4 people, 1 leg, and God only knows how many kangaroos and wallabies; 2 1/2 houses, 1 car, 1 shack, 1 window.

Great White Sharks

Classification: animals / *Brucius swallowibus*

Footage:

1975, *Jaws* by Steven Spielberg
1978, *Jaws 2* by Jeannot Szwarc
1983, *Jaws 3D* by Joe Alves
1987, *Jaws: The Revenge* by Joseph Sargent

The Skinny: The most lethal fish hits the beach.

Quotable: "This shark swallows you whole. A little shakin', a little tenderizin' . . . down you go."

Habitat: Sea.

Origin: On Amity Island, Massachusetts, a woman did a little night swimming. After a few moments, half of a woman was doing a little night swimming. A few moments later, there was no night swimmer.

Identification: The shark looks basically like a shark; *Carcharodon carcharias,* if you belong to the group of Latin lovers. A 25-foot-long fish with a mouth the size of Dodger Stadium, filled with teeth the size of the Dodgers.

Cravings: Feeding on everything. Men, women, kids, dogs, license plates, fish, ropes, metal cages, helicopters . . . name one thing and it'll eat it.

Behavior: Swimming, eating, swimming, biting, swimming, killing, swimming, gulping, swimming, mutilating, swimming, annihilating, swimming, ripping, swimming, terminating, swimming, wiping out, swimming, decimating, swimming, chopping, swimming—well, you get the picture. Noise in or above the water attracts the shark. Blood in the water attracts the shark. Stupid mayors or real-estate developers who ignore the warnings of the police attract the shark.

Danger: It's dangerous, but only if you are in the water. If you live in the Rocky Mountains you should be safe.

How to Kill It: The shark has no special powers. You only have to deal with a long beast, a large mouth, razor-sharp teeth, and an attitude. You can shoot it (especially if it has an oxygen tank conveniently stuck inside its mouth), you can make it bite a high-voltage cable, you can give it a bomb for breakfast and maybe it'll go *boom!,* or you can hit it with a boat (don't ask why, but it'll explode).

What to Do if You Meet It: They say you have to hit the shark in the eyes or the gills. This means being close enough to its mouth—we don't like this approach. You might have better luck showing your Greenpeace badge. It might be moved.

Current Status: Dead, dead, dead, and dead (but there are plenty more).

Body Count: 19 people, 1 killer whale, very likely Tippitt the Dog; one also gives 1 scuba diver an embolism.

BUILDING AN ARSENAL

Note: This list suggests what you should keep around in order to survive in a monster encounter. We do not want to encourage unnecessary violence or dumb little children playing with firearms. These weapons are strictly F.M.O. (For Monsters Only).

What do you need to buy to sleep the righteous's sleep? What do you have to do in order to withstand a monster attack? How can you outsmart your opponent? Here you have a list of the most popular and effective weapons used to battle the fiercest creatures. And ONLY the fiercest creatures. Your little brother or sister is not (and never will be) on one of our lists.

- **Arrow:** Effective with psychopaths, and beasts, too (even if with some animals you might need more than one). If made with fraxinus, an arrow is perfect to kill a vampire. Keep your arrows under the bed, along with a bow, or in your closet. Never, ever keep the arrows in one place and the bow in another. Too risky. Not to mention stupid.
- **Ax:** It slices, dices, chops, cuts, beheads, divides, and separates any body part you want from almost any assailant. But you need to be quite strong and precise. Axes come in several sizes and weights, kind of like bowling balls. Carefully select yours and keep it handy.
- **Blessed Object:** It could be a crucifix, a book, an image, water . . . anything's okay, so long as it's genuinely holy. Simply wave the object in front of the supernatural monster and you'll scare it away. Keep it handy on your nightstand, because the creatures that fear blessed objects usually strike at night. Even better, keep it on you.
- **Bomb:** Good to keep handy, it will erase *almost* any monster. The side effect is that it will erase almost anything else, so use with extreme caution.
- **Electrical Outlet:** All right, this is not a "weapon," but every house has more than one plug and you should know where they are located. Many creatures are knocked out—if not killed—by electricity.
- **Flamethrower:** Fire is an effective deterrent for many creatures. It purifies and deep-cleans everything in its path. It works with many aliens, beasts, creations . . . it's one of the best monster repellents ever. If you don't have a flamethrower, matches or a Zippo applied to flammable liquid will also work quite well. Just steer clear of the liquid yourself.
- **Harpoon:** A little old-fashioned, but it does a great job. You need to hit the gym before using a harpoon, but it's well worth it for large beasts.
- **Knife:** Reliable weapon, even if it may become your opponent's weapon when mishandled. Anyway, this is one weapon that you can find in any house, and that is fairly effective with most creatures, except ghosts. But be careful: a knife rarely stops a monster forever. Usually, it stalls the creature for a while. So, don't lose time trying to retrieve the knife, just run like hell.
- **Poison:** Any kind. Simply pour it into the monster's mouth or inject it. If the creature's DNA is simple, the poison will do the trick. Just don't keep it in your medicine cabinet, because you don't wanna mix it with your Listerine.
- **Razor:** Very flashy, and easy to pocket or hide. You can kill a psychopath, you can wound many monsters or beasts, you can cut the tubes of an alien spacesuit, and you can shave someone for five bucks.
- **Refrigerator/Freezer:** It may seem like a bizarre weapon, but a lot of monsters loathe the cold. So push them in and have an ice cream on us.
- **Salt:** Not much of a weapon, but pretty effective with mutated plants and witches. Simply pour it on them.
- **Silver Bullets:** To kill werewolves. Some people will argue that any bullet will work fine, but better safe than sorry. They do the trick with psychopaths and many beasts, too. Keep the bullets close to the gun or even inside it, with the safety on. But BEWARE: guns are not toys, and only use a gun if you want to destroy the target.
- **Watercooler:** Again, not much of a weapon, but many creatures fear the water—above all, robots. Several aliens and plants, too. And wicked witches. And you can kill your thirst between one assault and the next.

Feed me! Feed me!

Audrey II in *Little Shop of Horrors*

You know what they say: if you talk to your plants they grow healthier and somehow happier.

Well, the plants in this entry couldn't possibly care less about your yakety-yak. They have minds of their own, and have come a long way to accomplish their goals: from outer space (*The Thing from Another World, Little Shop of Horrors, The Angry Red Planet*), from underground (*From Hell It Came, Woman Eater*), or from the world of the supernatural (*Evil Dead, Poltergeist*). So if you happen to be "lucky" enough to find a totally unique plant growing by leaps and bounds in your garden, be sure to keep the kids and pets inside. Oh . . . and keep an eye on your salad.

Habitat & Identification

Plants and trees keep their monstrous nature under wraps by making you believe they're just your average flora. But when you get close enough to their plumage, you're trapped. You can find these creatures in flower stores, in backyards, in the parks, in the woods (especially if a wood demon is running amok), or even on another planet. And never you mind if they look like tiny lovable flowers, or old wise trees, keep your distance.

Cravings & Behavior

These plants are mean as heck, and living in a vase doesn't discourage them at all.

- **Food-4-Less:** Some plants develop a taste for flesh. But they aren't satisfied with cold cuts, no—they want fresh, human meat. And they either talk you into it (*Little Shop of Horrors, The Woman Eater*), or else they go shopping by themselves (*From Hell It Came, Day of the Triffids, The Unknown Terror, Poltergeist*). Otherwise they'll wait for you to wander into their territory, let's say for instance—uh—Mars (*The Angry Red Planet*). A very rare species of trees is plainly omnivorous (*The Navy vs. the Night Monsters*) and will eat anything in their path.

- **Revenge:** Some plants immensely enjoy killing people. It's mainly because they're seeking revenge (*From Hell It Came*), and they do a smashing job.

• **Sing-Along:** An uncommon characteristic, but the easiest way to tell if the plant you're dealing with deserves to be viewed with suspicion (*Little Shop of Horrors*).

• **Sex:** If you're a gorgeous woman, and for some strange reason you get lost in the woods at night, you might be the victim of vegetable assault. It's just you vs. the woods. Guess who'll win?

• **Just Crabby:** You may meet a tree that hates when somebody picks its apples (*The Wizard of Oz*). But this tree will throw its apples at you if you make it angry. So, *bon appétit.*

How to Kill Them

• **Fire or Electricity:** Fry the bastards and they'll never come back. Of course, the Nature Conservancy will revoke your membership.

• **Don't Feed Them:** But don't underestimate their will to survive.

• **Chop Them Down:** But don't forget to destroy the roots, too.

• **Water:** It may stop certain plants from outer space, but it'll nourish all others.

• **Wait for a Tornado:** It'll rip the evil trees out of the ground. Where they end up is none of your business. Just keep watching the sky.

• **When Vegetarians Attack:** A strict vegetarian may be your best weapon. Rave to them how well your plant fries up in the wok. Just don't let on that the flora has feelings, or you'll find yourself foiled by the meat hater's bleeding-heart sensibilities.

• **Weed Killer:** Give it a try, what the heck.

What to Do if You Meet One

Having a green thumb won't help. These plants want your thumb—and what's attached to it. So, in order to keep your fingers where they're supposed to be, just immerse your garden in concrete. The bonus is that you won't have to mow the lawn anymore.

Audrey Jr. / Audrey II

Classification: plants / *Flowerius chompchomps*
or perhaps: aliens / meanies / predators

Footage:
1968, *Little Shop of Horrors* by Roger Corman
1986, *Little Shop of Horrors* by Frank Oz

The Skinny: A plant needs blood to grow. But it sings, baby!

Quotable: "I'm just a mean green mutha from outer space and I'm baaad."

Habitat: Mushnik's flower shop.

Discovered: September 23, early 1960s.

Origin: Following an eclipse of the sun, a nerdy flower-store clerk named Seymour bought a strange plant he'd never seen before. The problem was that the plant was not *really* a plant—it was a carnivorous alien that had come to earth for a light snack . . .

Identification: In the beginning, Audrey is a small, round, lovable plant in a little metal can. But with a little loving care from a green thumb, it becomes a huge, round, not-so-lovable plant with powerful leaves and vines. It can even make phone calls, and speaks and sings just like Levi Stubbs of the Four Tops.

Cravings: Fresh blood. And following every feeding, Audrey grows bigger and hungrier.

Behavior: During business hours, Audrey sits around being a lovable little plant attracting people to your flower store. When the shop's closed, it talks and uses its vines to grab what it wants. After a while it is strong enough to move by itself and decides that it doesn't need your help anymore—then you're in trouble.

Danger: It stays in its vase—so if you stay clear of its foliage, you should be safe. But Audrey is very persuasive, and can easily subjugate the weak of will into fulfilling its needs with dirty deeds or self-sacrifice. Once it grows big enough, staying clear of its foliage is darn near impossible.

How to Kill It: It needs blood like other plants need water, otherwise it kicks the bucket. But when Audrey becomes huge, it manages to obtain what it wants by itself. In extreme cases, a large dose of electricity might do the trick . . . otherwise call in the national guard.

What to Do if You Meet It: When you find a strange plant, if you're musically inclined, try singing. If the plant sings along with you, run away. It's for the best, trust us.

Current Status: It has found a cozy spot in one of Seymour's flower beds, so stay close to the curb when you walk by his house.

Body Count: 3

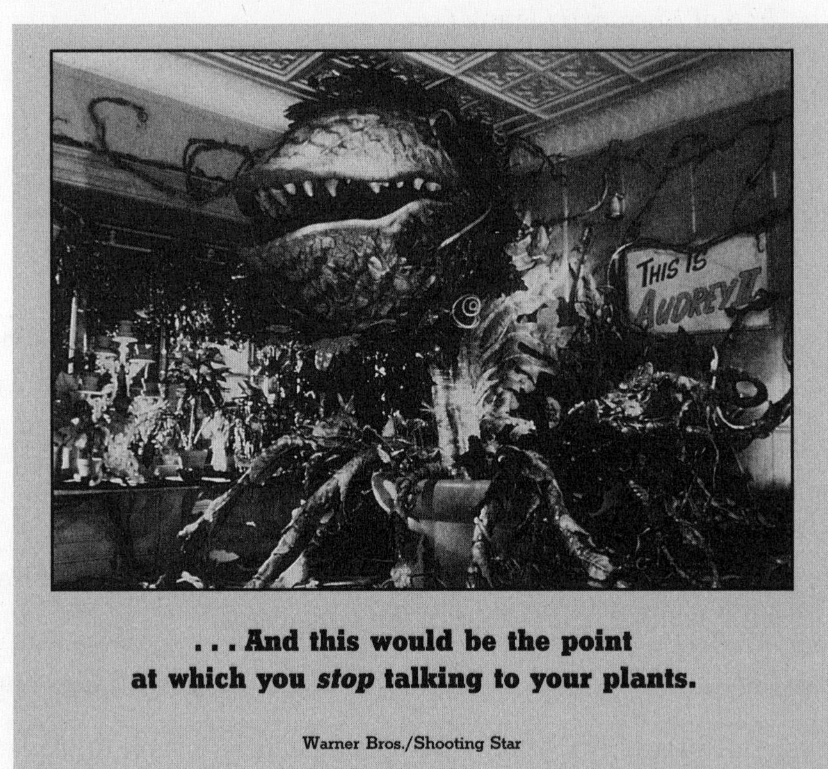

. . . And this would be the point at which you *stop* talking to your plants.

Warner Bros./Shooting Star

Prehistoric

It must be the sulfur in the walls of this cave that has kept this creature alive for all these years.

Mr. Miller in *Eegah*

We stumble into prehistoric creatures when we discover a large block of ice with something inside of it, or when we enter a valley where no man has set foot before. In either case, we unmask a zone where time has been frozen—either literally, or just because nobody has ever gone into the secluded valley the very mention of which name scares the natives.

Of course science has floundered along, and eventually some dildo successfully cloned dinosaurs (*Jurassic Park, Carnosaur*), creating the ancient terror anew. Thankfully, most of these scientists were rewarded not with published articles, but by becoming dinosaur chow.

Identification

CAVEMEN

- Tall, bulky men (but seemingly no women) with long beards, hairy chests, and a bad attitude toward human beings (*Eegah, Trog*) and/or human machinery (*Memorial Valley Massacre*). The primitive caveman's initial response is to fight. The modern man's response, much more rational and civilized, is to fight back.

DINOSAURS

- These creatures are reptiles, but something in their DNA makes them close to birds and fish. They are brontosaurus, tyrannosaurus, pterodactyls . . . (*The Land That Time Forgot, Valley of Gwangy, Dinosaurus!*), you know, all those big old beasts you find in the school library.

- *Fun Fact: Sound of Horror* is the only evidence that we have pointing to the existence of an *invisible* dinosaur. If you hear a lot of noise, but can't see a thing, watch out!

• These are important creatures that somehow carry genes and characteristics of two different species. So you have monkey-men or man-monkeys (*Schlock*), or fish-men or men-fish (*Creature from the Black Lagoon*). They're aggressive like an animal and smart like a man. Or vice versa, which is sometimes not such a bad thing.

Cravings

• **Food:** Meat, leaves (*Dinosaurus!*), or cookies (*Theodore Rex*).

• **Love:** Is it too much to ask? (*Eegah, Schlock*)

• **Respecting Nature & the Environment:** Cavemen hate when we trash the planet. They free animals from traps and feed them fruits and vegetables—even if they have the barefaced audacity to wear fur!

Behavior

• **Making Noise:** None of these creatures uses a comprehensible language: they scream, shriek, or roar (dinosaurs) or they grunt, snarl, and grumble (cavemen).

• **Wreaking Havoc:** Dinosaurs, cavemen, and missing links hate intruders, and they react to the unknown the only way they know how: they trample, destroy, bite, shriek, and generally live it up.

• **Sabotage:** For some unexplained reason, a Cro-Magnon caveman is quite adept at destroying campers, RVs, and radios (*Memorial Valley Massacre*).

• **Shaving:** Some cavemen like the feeling of being clean-shaven (*Eegah*).

• **Fighting with Relatives:** A constant theme in the life of *Gigantis, the Fire Monster.*

How to Kill Them

If you absolutely must . . .

• **Bullets:** Definitely works with cavemen, but also with many dinosaurs.

• **Electricity:** But you have to convince the dinosaur to bite the cable.

• **Fire:** Trap your favorite dinosaur inside a building and then torch it. But be sure to buy some earplugs, because dinosaurs shriek like banshees.

- **Snowplow:** Sink dino with one of these; it'll die fighting (*The Crater Lake Monster*).
- **Steam Shovel:** It'll shatter the skull of a tyrannosaurus rex (*Dinosaurus!*).

What to Do if You Meet One

- Turn the radio on, and you'll scare the caveman away, or else make him more confused than someone watching the movie *Mission: Impossible.* Until they choose to smash the radio—and you.
- Avoid loud noises.
- Give them cookies.
- Don't try to pet them.

Creature from the Black Lagoon

Classification: prehistoric / *Reallyuglius fishmanibus*

Footage:

1954, *Creature from the Black Lagoon* by Jack Arnold
1955, *Revenge of the Creature* by Jack Arnold
1956, *The Creature Walks Among Us* by Jack Arnold

The Skinny: A missing link is discovered along the Amazon.com River. And it discovers human beings, too.

Quotable: "This gill man, this thing I have seen with my eyes, it—it doesn't belong in our world."

Habitat: The Black Lagoon, of course, on a tributary of the upper Amazon. And the Florida Everglades, in and out of the Ocean Harbor Institute & Park.

Origin: They went on an archaeological mission to South America to prove that man descended from fish (or vice versa). One member of the mission was a terrific girl who loved to swim alone in a Black Lagoon (but maybe it's just dirty—the lagoon), and thanks to her they made the most unpleasant discovery of the trip.

Identification: The creature is a fish-man entirely covered with scales, and a large space for oxygen tanks on its shoulders. It has four fins with claws, a fish face, and an interesting sexual predilection for young gals. Quite curious, indeed. It's believed to be a living fossil from around 395–345 million B.C., give or take a couple of weeks.

Craves: Fish, crabs, snails, sea plants, occasionally birds, or something along those lines.

Behavior: The creature (a.k.a. the Gill Man) fins around the Amazon Basin underwater and pops out occasionally, and falls in love with gorgeous swimmers. Every now and then the creature tries to kidnap them, but there's an important incompatibility: the creature can't live out of water and all of its lovers would drown in it.

It's extremely powerful and agile, can jump very high out of the water and rip away the chains that hold it. And don't tap on the glass of its aquarium, because you drive it even more mad. After being involved in a fire, and a very bizarre and probably totally unnecessary operation, the creature got a pair of lungs and was able to remain

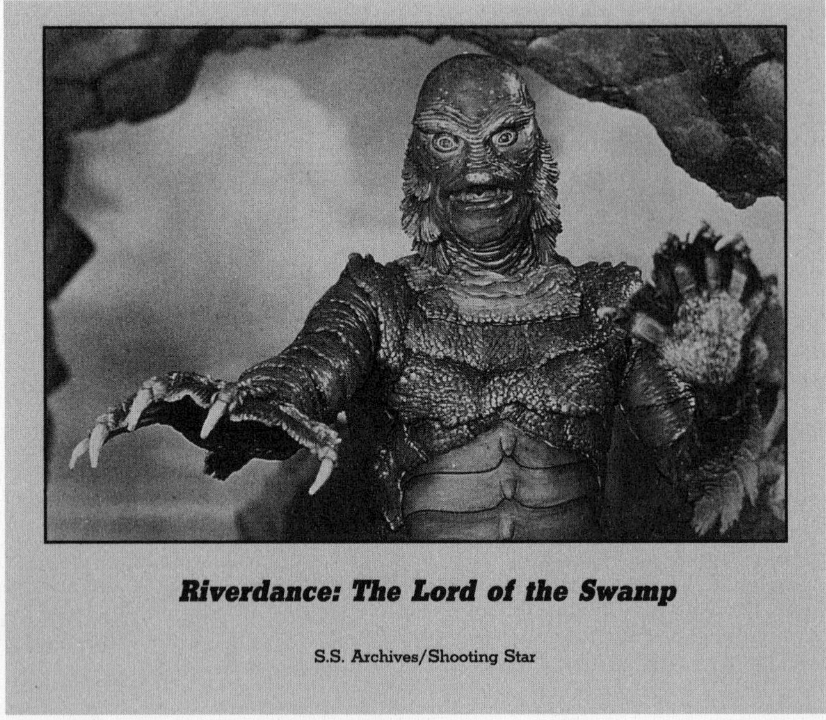

Riverdance: The Lord of the Swamp

S.S. Archives/Shooting Star

out of the water indefinitely—but unable to swim underwater again. It's bothered by bright light and electricity. If you have an bright electrical light, you're safe.

Danger: If you're a gorgeous woman who loves to swim in the Amazon Basin, you might need a snorkel for your next love story. If you're a man who wants to stop the Gill Man . . . just don't.

How to Kill It: You can use the good ol' knife (Tarzan style), or modern weapons like machine guns. Underwater bombs can also send it into a coma. If you drag the Gill Man out of the water for a long time, it could die from dehydration. However, we don't suggest trying to make a fish taco out of it, because it reeks to high heaven.

What to Do if You Meet It: Try to menace it with tartar sauce.

Current Status: It sort of dies in 1954, 1955, and 1956—uncanny!

Body Count: 9 people, 1 dog, 1 bird; 1 car is flipped over, and 1 window is shattered.

Graboids . . .

Classification: prehistoric / *Burroweribus aggressivus*

Footage:

1990, *Tremors* by Ron Underwood

1996, *Tremors 2: Aftershocks* by S. S. Wilson

The Skinny: A prehistoric worm decides to surface for a little fun.

Quotable: "This valley is just one long smorgasbord. We have got to get out!"

Discovered: Perfection, Nevada; 1990.

Habitat: Under soft earth in desert regions.

Origin: In the peaceful town of Perfection, Nevada, something was wrong: too many seismic tremors, dehydrated men stranded on top of power-line towers, slaughtered goats. The "Perfectionists" found (at their own expense) the cause of their problems:

huge ravenous underground worms which seemed to be from the Precambrian era. And boy, were they hungry.

Identification: The graboids (named by one of their victims—*before* he was eaten of course) are gigantic blind worms with an acute sensitivity to vibration. They have three tentacle-tongues, each of which has its own mouth. The graboid travels just beneath the surface of the earth, pushing up a trail of dirt as it moves. So if your significant other says, "I felt the earth move," don't assume she's waxing metaphorical.

Cravings: The graboids will eat anything which makes a noise or vibration, but they seem to prefer humans—that *would* have to be the case, wouldn't it?

Behavior: Although it has this incredible sensitivity to vibration, it is in fact blind. Thank God for small favors. The worms travel underground at quite high speeds, thanks to their cone-shaped mouths and the large cilia which they have along the length of their bodies to propel them through the dirt. As soon as the graboid senses vibrations, it comes up from under its victims and drags them underground. This worm is both intelligent and patient: it can wait days and days under a place where it knows there is some food. In other words, these are mean underground eatin' machines.

Danger: Each and every vibration is picked up by these worms—and they dart to the epicenter in a flash. They can even pull down cars, parts of unstable buildings, or pretty much whatever else stands between them and their next meal. So if you're walking, running, or driving on the ground, you're just fast food to these beasts. Our best advice: learn how to fly.

How to Kill It: You can use yourself as live bait, letting it chase you until it runs into a concrete wall or over a cliff. You could also lure it into eating a stick of dynamite, and then detonate the dynamite by remote control. Last but not least, you can try killing it with a powerful gun. Meaning a *really* powerful gun, like an elephant gun, or preferably a bazooka.

What to Do if You Meet One: Freeze! Since the graboid is blind, it can't see you. But if you hazard a step, you might soon find that you don't have a leg for the next step. If there's more than one of you, you could try this: I take one step then I stop; you take one step and then you stop. I take another little step and then I stop . . . In this manner you could easily move two or three feet before being torn to pieces.

But if you happen to be near a large boulder or any solid structure, jump on. It can't get you if you're not on the ground. Of course, you can't *get* anywhere without stepping on the ground. So break out a deck of cards and grab a Snickers, 'cause you're not going anywhere for a while. Then radio yourself a helicopter.

Current Status: Extinct? Evolved? But of course!!

Body Count: 16 people, 1 flock of sheep, 1 horse, 1 coyote, and 1 boom box.

. . . And Shriekers

Footage:

1996, *Tremors 2: Aftershocks* by S. S. Wilson

Chiapas, Mexico, 1996: a new kind of creature began popping out of all of the graboids' bellies on the exact same night—kind of a spontaneous, synchronized evolution. As opposed to their predecessors, these new creatures moved above-ground.

The shrieker resembles a chicken in its body structure, but is about two feet tall. It has infrared vision that functions by heat-sensing gills which come out of its forehead. It also has a very long tongue which it uses as an additional method of finding tasty morsels. As soon as it picks up a target, the shrieker signals to the others by emitting heat with these loud shrieking sounds. Which really grate on the nerves after a while.

A shrieker will go after anything generating heat: car engines, hot water, ovens, hair dryers, heartwarming songs . . . but what it really wants is *you.* When a shrieker is stuffed—*voilà:* it vomits a small cocoon which turns out to be a new shrieker. And the little bugger is ready to start eating people within a few minutes. Unfortunately, shriekers are also very smart and can devise strategies for catching you.

You can kill them with an elephant gun or any other powerful weapon. If for some reason you have to walk through a pack of shriekers, put your clothes in the freezer for an hour first—this should keep them from detecting you for at least a few minutes. After that, you're toast.

Body Count: 2 people, 2 car engines, and 1 radio transmitter.

Undiscovered

This beast exists because it is stronger than . . . than the thing you call "evolution."

Lucas in *Revenge of the Creature*

Seems like mother nature is always surprising us—perhaps she could get work directing horror movies . . .

Just when we think we have a grasp on everything under the sun, something new appears, usually at the least convenient moment, catching us completely off guard. A previously unseen or undocumented creature can be a fascinating delight when it's cute, fuzzy, and benevolent. But when it looks at us and starts to drool . . . well, let's just hope that we're sharp enough to quickly come up with a plan to move our new species onto the endangered list. Just letting nature be is all well and good, but if *it* won't just let us be, we better be resorting to desperate measures . . .

Thankfully, there are people out there who have run into some of these beasts before. There are even people who study these elusive creatures. They're called "cryptozoologists." Cryptozoology is defined loosely as "the study of hidden animals." From what you've seen and read so far, seems like a particularly useful field of study, right?

Unfortunately for us, these quacks are about as reliable as a forty-year-old car in need of an oil change. So, once again, all we really have to go on is Hollywood.

Among the undiscovered beasts:

- **Werewolves:** Hairy and scary.
- **Yetis and Sasquatches:** Hairier, but not quite as scary.
- **Dragons:** No hair, but plenty of scare.
- **Unique Discoveries:** You gotta see 'em to believe 'em.

Werewolves

Even a man who is pure of heart
and says his prayers at night
May become a wolf when the wolfbane blooms
and the moon is full and bright

Olde English Poem

Classification

undiscovered / *Lycanthropus lupus*

Being a werewolf is a curse—an undiscovered chronic disease, if you will. And the afflicted should be considered a *victim* and not a murderer. So, if you end up being slaughtered by a werewolf, keep in mind that you are "the victim of a victim" and not "the victim of a wacko." This'll make you feel better, right?

How does this cycle begin? The most common cause is the bite of a werewolf; if the bitten survives, he or she will become a werewolf (or *lycanthrope*). Now, how the *first person* became a wolf is impossible to answer. Two wereparents can give birth to a were-son or a weredaughter . . . but again—where does it all start?

The Sacred Point of View

The Church says that the spirit of an evil beast can find entrance into a child before birth. If the child's soul is strong, it can exorcise the spirit . . . but as we all know, the soul is weak. The forces of good (warmth, fellowship, love) foster the soul; but whatever corrupts the soul (vice, greed, solitude, hatred) fosters the spirit instead. Then what do you have? A werewolf. Or Richard Simmons.

The Scientific Point of View

Men and women have lymphatic glands in their throat; these glands secrete lymph into the blood; this lymph is an alkaline that causes the disease of werewolfery. The full moon activates these glands, and as a special bonus, wolfbane (a plant that blooms in the autumn) speeds up the process. Once the fluid breaks down the molecular structure of the blood, the victims begin to change identity; they are powerless and completely without willpower. So what's the good news, doc?

The Aussie Point of View

The clearest (and silliest) explanation we were able to find comes from the Australian town of Flow. Here, a lycanthrope race sprang from the extinct Tasmanian wolf (or "the

Phantom," the only carnivorous marsupial): "once dead, the spirit of the Phantom came into us," the Flow people say. Those crazy Australians . . .

Habitat

Werewolves are human beings who have an appointment with destiny only in certain time slots; they lead a pretty ordinary life the rest of the time.

- **Among Us:** If someone notices a neighbor who howls at the moon and pees on fire hydrants, the wolf will take care of the problem by having dinner with the nosy person.

- **Communal Living:** People afflicted with werewolfery sometimes form a therapeutic community (*The Howling*).

Identification

A werewolf is easy to spot—the only person wearing a fur coat in August. There are two distinct phases in the existence of a werewolf, with two different looks.

- **The Human Look:** The dormant creature looks like an ordinary human being, with no particular signs revealing his secret identity. And at first the werewolf doesn't even know it *has* a secret identity. It is said that a lycanthrope is marked with a pentagram (five-point star) on its body, but this mark could be anywhere; it could be on the liver or under the tongue, for all we know.

- **The Wolfy Look:** The full-blown werewolf is covered with fur. It has sharp fangs, a bulbous nose, brightly colored eyes, and triangular ears sticking out of its head. Its hands are long, with claws springing from the fingertips. The Australian werekangaroo displays horizontal dark stripes on its back as well as a flat head. Usually the werewolf walks on its hind feet, but we've seen a specimen who became a four-legged creature (*An American Werewolf in London*) and another one who turned into a real wolf (*The Beast Must Die*).

Cravings

- **Flesh:** Werewolves are carnivorous predators, and their appetite is uncontrollable. It has been said that werewolves instinctively seek to kill the thing they love best (*Werewolf of London*).

- **Raising Cattle:** The werewolf's buffer against starvation; a cow a day keeps the hunger away. But they still like human meat best.

- **Reproduction:** Werewolves don't waste time with foreplay: they get straight to the point.

Keep an Eye on the Calendar

When will you meet a werewolf?

- **"Full Moon Fever":** The full moon triggers the werewolfery, between 9:00 and 10:00 P.M. Lycanthropes are highly active three or four nights in a row. During these nights, our advice is: stay home, go to sleep at seven, and don't open the window to check when "that irritating dog will stop howling."
- **. . . or Just Forget the Stupid Calendar:** Beware! There are a batch of werewolves who are shapeshifters: they can change form at any time, day or night, never mind the full moon (*The Howling*). There's also a serum in development that is an antidote to lycanthropy (*An American Werewolf in Paris*).

Behavior

Werewolves principally come out at night, so you'll seldom see them stepping out on the sunny side of the street.

- **Lurking in Dark Places:** They might wait for their prey while masking themselves in the darkness of an alley, among the branches of a bush, in a tunnel of the London subway, or in the Paris sewers.
- **A Killing Streak:** Werewolves must kill at least one human being each night or they'll become permanently afflicted with the disease, even if they sometimes get carried away and kill half a dozen people.
- **Acquired Talents:** Lycanthropes have no memory of the events in their "wolf life," but some of the animal qualities jump into their human selves: they can hear better, smell better (this is not always a good thing, but we told you: being a werewolf is a curse), and they're stronger and more agile (*Wolf*).
- **That Annoying Howl:** Werewolves often give away their presence by howling like a bad folk singer.
- **Marked for the Kill:** They're able to see a pentagram on the palm of their next victim's hand.
- **Oh, the Guilt!:** Once lycanthropes understand their true nature, they'll try to prevent future massacres. They'll ask people to lock them up, seal them in a safe place—which uninformed people won't do because they think the dormant werewolves are being ridiculous. Then they learn the hard way.
- **The Sporting Life:** Yes, a few young werewolves use their powers to succeed in the world of sports. But they sweat like a herd of elk and smell really nasty (*Teen Wolf*).

• **The Scientific View on Transmodification:** Some young werewolves can change almost at will. As time goes by, the body weakens and the wolf takes over.

Danger

• **Foul Soul:** If you are killed by a werewolf, your soul may end up in an undead limbo filled with decaying corpses. Those corpses wait for the werewolf's bloodline to be severed (*An American Werewolf in London*). Only then will these souls be free.

• **Bite Rite:** If you're attacked by a werewolf, but not killed, we're sorry but you will become a werewolf yourself. The wounds will heal overnight and you'll basically feel fine. Except for those pesky fleas.

How to Kill Them

Not that hard. But you need something a little more sturdy than a muffler.

• **Bullets:** Never fail. Some people believe that the bullet has to be made of silver. Others will tell you that any bullet will work fine. So if you have the option, go for silver. It may be more expensive, but at least you'll be 100 percent sure.

• **Anything Made with Silver:** Knives, forks, canes with silver handles, the Lone Ranger's horse. It is said that silver generates a lethal poison when combined with the werewolf's hormones. Sounds like somebody's been talking out of their ass, but if it works, who cares?

• **Fire:** This remedy (*The Howling*) has not been fully proven, but logic suggests that it would work.

• **Kill the Wolf in Its Human Stage:** Werewolves are strong, but human beings are vulnerable—usually for 28 days in a row. So you can easily get rid of them between transformations . . . if you know where they live.

• **Terminal Werewolfery:** As time goes by, the werewolf's blood becomes more and more unstable and the white cells can't combat the disease; however, waiting around could prove lethal for you.

Cures

Oddly enough, a lycanthrope is not entirely hopeless. You may effect a cure. You're not obligated, but if you weigh "being eaten" against "being helpful" . . .

- **Mariphasa Lupina:** If you have enough frequent flier miles, book a ticket to Tibet. Here, in a secluded valley filled with demons, you'll find the rare flower Mariphasa lupina (*Werewolf of London*). This plant is an antidote to lycanthropy: all the werewolf has to do is squeeze the Mariphasa blossom into its wrist. The downside: it only works for a few hours.

- **Pentagram Charm:** Wearing a pentagram pendant breaks the spell and protects both you from the wolf and the wolf from its curse.

- **True Love:** "The only cure" according to some (*The Curse of the Werewolf*): if a person falls *very deeply* in love with a werewolf, the cursed may be saved.

- **Scientific Help:** The energy trapped inside the body of the werewolf can be transferred. This can be accomplished with the help of a local mad scientist (*House of Dracula*), or if you happen to have bought a new pocket energy-transfer device at Radio Shack.

- **Kill the Original:** Sometimes it's enough to kill the first werewolf, to turn all the victims back into their normal selves (*My Mom Is a Werewolf*).

- **Not for the Squeamish:** You may have to find the wolf that bit you, kill it, and eat its heart. This is the only way to snap the chain forever and to bring you back to normality. Enjoy your meal.

Note: Thanks to the president of the United States and the Vatican, werewolves have officially been put on the endangered species list. If they're not contained, though, soon we'll be on the list.

What to Do if You Meet One

- **Run Away:** This may help, even if a wolf will always beat a man in terms of stamina, agility, and speed. Come to think of it, save your breath and catch a cab instead.

- **Crack Open a Can of Dog Food:** A misdirection that might save you precious time.

Lawrence Stewart Talbot

Classification: undiscovered / werewolves / *Chubbius hairibus*

Footage:

1941, *The Wolf Man* by George Waggoner
1942, *Frankenstein Meets the Wolf Man* by Roy William Neil
1944, *House of Frankenstein* by Erle C. Kenton
1945, *House of Dracula* by Erle C. Kenton
1948, *Abbott & Costello Meet Frankenstein* by Charles T. Barton

The Skinny: The "Mr. Nice Guy" of werewolves . . . until the full moon shines.

Quotable: "Lock me in and don't let me out!"

Habitat: Talbot's mansion (Wales), Dr. Frankenstein's castle (Vasaria), and Florida.

Origin: After returning home to Wales, chubby Larry Talbot was bitten by a wolf. He managed to kill the beast, who was a local gypsy afflicted with lycanthropy. Too late: the joke is on Larry now.

"Stop me if you've heard this one before: there's a truck driver and a nun . . ."

S.S. Archives/Shooting Star

Identification: Larry's a well dressed man with a passion for beautiful women. When he's a man, that is. On full moon nights, he turns into a furry biped wolf, with fangs, claws, extra strength, zero sense of humor, and a deadly urge to kill. When he wakes up the following morning, he can't recall what he's done during the previous night. Like almost anybody on Sunday mornings. Larry's also marked with the pentagram: a five-point star, that is the shape of the bite scar he has on his chest. Dogs bark at him.

Cravings: When a wolf, Larry needs to kill (and he goes straight for the jugular); when a man, Larry needs to convince friends and family that he's a lycanthrope and he has to be caged. Once caged, he trashes the entire room he's in to alleviate the pressure. Don't place him in your best room or you'll think you've hired Johnny Depp to be your decorator.

Behavior: As a werewolf, Larry dawdles around town looking for food. He howls at the moon, hides among bushes and trees, and waits for his next prey. In human form, Larry can see the pentagram in the palm of his next victim's hand, so he'll try anything to warn the person—who obviously won't believe him. So after the wolf has added the victim to his résumé, he runs away muttering, "I told you so, ha-ha!"

Danger: The lycanthrope ravages without regard to loved ones or friends. If you are bitten *and* you survive, you'll become a werewolf. Also keep an eye out during the spring; when a plant called wolfbane blooms, so does Mr. Talbot.

How to Kill Him: The werewolf can be killed only by a silver bullet, knife, or cane handle, and everything works much better if it's used by someone who loves the man inside the wolf, such as his father. But it may not be enough: actually, if you open the wolf coffin at night and the full moonlight hits Larry's body, he might come back to life. Use a pentagram charm to either break the spell or protect yourself. But while we're at it, why would you open a werewolf's coffin in the first place?

What to Do if You Meet Him: Don't throw him a stick; he'll never bring it back.

Current Status: Even if he eventually was cured and the energy in his body was absorbed by a mysterious machine, Larry Talbot had a relapse and four years later was into the werewolf thing again. But he vanished in the Florida sea while chasing Dracula. We haven't heard from him since. But his son is ready to fill in.

Body Count: 4 people, Dracula, and Frankenstein's Creature.

SIGNS THAT YOU MIGHT BE A MONSTER

Put aside your pride, sit down, grab a mirror, and, if you still cast a reflection, run through these simple points to see if you're someone to be feared:

- You live in a closet or under the bed.
- You're not afraid of the dark.
- You howl at the moon.
- Your favorite retort has become "Rrarr!"
- People you don't like start to disappear.
- Your family tries to move without notifying you.

Yetis and Sasquatches: A Comparison

Bigfoot's not playing games anymore.

An anthropologist from *Night of the Demon*

Origins & Habitat

Just accept them for who they are.

- **Yetis:** The origin of the yeti (a.k.a. "The Abominable Snowman") is unknown. Nobody knows whether it is a survivor of an ancient race, a mutation, or even an extraterrestrial. One thing everybody agrees on: its favorite stomping ground is the Himalayas. Only one specimen has been found elsewhere . . . in Greenland. Through the years an exorbitant number of scientific expeditions have tried to locate the yeti—often to try and capture it, or even kill it.

- **Sasquatches:** The origin of the Sasquatch (commonly called "Bigfoot") is even more obscure; it seems that a half-human, half-gorilla creature popped up in the middle of the forest, scaring the bejesus out of people in the northwestern U.S., Arkansas, Louisiana, and even northern Japan.

Identification

Two similar creatures, yet different in many ways . . .

THE YETI

- The yeti comes from the high mountains, so its body is thoroughly covered with fur, which is mostly white, long, and fluffy. On the other hand, much like the so-called comedian Carrot Top, the Greenland yeti has red hair—but is smarter.

- The face of the creature is almost human, with long fangs and albino eyes. The yeti walks on two feet, and it is quite agile.

- The Abominable Snowman's height ranges from eight to thirty feet.

• Living in the forest, a Sasquatch's fur is gray brown and shorter than the yeti's.

• The Sasquatch's face is closer to a monkey's than a human's, and is generally brown or even black.

• Bigfoot's height ranges from that of Shaq to Gheorghe Muresan.

Cravings & Behavior

The yeti is usually ripped from its environment, so it's quite understandable why it's pissed off; the sasquatch wanders around mostly because it's curious.

• **Show Me the Way Home:** Both the Abominable Snowman and Bigfoot, if captured, are brought to the civilized world and exploited without any respect. These creatures mean easy money to people without scruples. Occasionally, they meet someone who truly cares (*Harry and the Hendersons*) and who helps them return to their habitat. Once in a blue moon, but it happens.

• **Food:** This is the main reason for Bigfoot to sneak into a village or a populated area. But the creature is mostly vegetarian, so don't cock your gun yet, partner.

• **Mating:** The yeti may seek a companion (*Bigfoot, Night of the Demon*) to reproduce the species. So, if you're looking for adventure, book a ticket to Nepal and have fun. Just dress warm.

• **Violence:** More common with Bigfoot than the Abominable Snowman, one of these creatures may attack you or your friends. But the main reason it does so is always because you've stepped inside its territory. Next time buy a map, stupid.

• **Fight of the Century?:** Once, the Abominable Snowman wrestled with the Wolfman (*Night of the Demon*) for about 15 seconds. No comment.

How to Kill Them

ONLY if you are assured of mortal danger. Then proceed as follows:

• **Firearms:** Shoot them down. But remember, if you miss, they're not gonna be pleased. If you're lucky, they'll just tear your arms off.

• **Push:** If you're quick enough, you can push them off a cliff. Cheap trick, but it works.

• **Excessive Tickling:** Sounds silly, but a few Sasquatches are ticklish. Worth a try.

What to Do if You Meet One

You're probably not in danger. Probably.

• **Nature Lover:** Let the creature know you are on its side; show that you don't have any stuffed and mounted animals in your cabin, that you don't wear any fur coats, and that you are a member of the Audoban Society. The Abominable Snowman and Bigfoot are environmentalists, and this will be the beginning of a long and bizarre friendship.

• **If It's Eight-Feet Tall, Take It Back Home:** Put it in your car, and drive it back to its family (*Harry and the Hendersons*).

• **If It's Thirty-Feet Tall, *Tell* It to Go Home:** Usually it'll obey you, especially after being trapped on the roof of a building (*Yeti*). How it'll manage to get to Nepal on foot is another matter best left to yeti ingenuity.

Dragons

I am the lascht one!

Draco in *Dragonheart*

It's hard to tell how it all started: evidently sorcerers took dragons from the sky and put them on Earth to guard mankind and teach important virtues. So it seems that dragons were originally benign creatures. But, as you know, there always have to be a few bad apples; apparently, during medieval times, either dragons began to hate men or men started to fear dragons. Suddenly the land wasn't big enough for the two species, and the ongoing battle began. Dragons were forced to hide in caves, constantly chased by relentless dragonslayers. And villagers were forced to keep an eye on the sky, lest a dragon be seeking out crunchy little appetizers.

Identification

A dragon is, for the most part, a jumbo-sized lizard:

- **Head(s):** Dragons usually have a triangular head with several horns on it and a large mouth filled with sharp, reptilian teeth. And dragons can come equipped with one head (*Dragonslayer, Dragonheart*), two (*Willow*), or even three (*The Sword and the Dragon*). The extra heads don't make them any brighter, only harder to kill.

- **Glowing Eyes:** Dragons hate this trait, because it gives them away in the dark.

- **Wings:** Large, leathery wings help dragons fly around.

- **Tail:** A dragon uses its tail as an effective weapon: it may have a pointy end, or even an extra claw. It chops, slices, dices, slashes, trims, and cuts faster than any standard kitchen appliance.

- **Fireproof Scales:** A dragon is thoroughly covered with hard scales that protect its body from the heat of its own fire. If you gather up the scales that the dragon loses, you can build a shield that will protect you from the fire of the beast. Bet you didn't know that!

Cravings

Dragons love the simple things.

• **There Ain't Nothin' Like a Damsel:** They kidnap and then guard over young princesses. No one knows why, but this seems to be one of their primary occupations.

• **Sheep:** The staple of a dragon's diet. Raw or flame-broiled.

• **Virgins:** This is the price you have to pay in order to have your village, your people, and your crops left uncharred by a dragon. At the autumn and spring equinox, you must offer a virgin to the dragon. But if she's a princess, will he keep her? Who knows . . .

• **Valor, Virtue, Truth:** Dragons wanted to help us be righteous and not live in anger. Needless to say, they failed.

Behavior

• **Breathing Fire:** This neat trick is performed by every dragon; some of them breathe fire from their mouths (*Dragonslayer*), others blow it out of their noses (*Dragonheart*).

• **Flying:** Every dragon can fly, whether it's equipped with large wings (*Dragonheart, Dragonslayer*) or with tiny cute little purple wings (*Pete's Dragon*).

• **Gimme Shelter:** A dragon generally hides out in a cave or an underground lair.

• **Swimming:** Dragons are excellent swimmers, and can cover long distances underwater. They don't even have to wait half an hour after eating.

• **Camouflage:** A dragon can become invisible (*Pete's Dragon*) or turn itself into a rock (*Dragonheart*). This last skill isn't very common, and frankly quite pointless—unless you're in need a 2,000-ton paperweight.

• **Dragon Brogue:** Dragons roar, scream, blare . . . or talk with a heavy Scottish accent.

• **Singing:** Dragons sing when they're happy, although we don't know how happy we'd be to hear a singing dragon.

How to Kill Them

Just contact a dragonslayer. Otherwise, you may need to try the following:

• **Swords, Daggers:** It takes an awful lot of time, but you can behead a dragon (all of its heads, that is). Eventually it'll die in atrocious pain.

- **Arrows:** To hit a dragon while it's flying, you need good aim, a steady hand, and some big old arrows.
- **Ax or Knife in the Heart:** Effective, but you have to nail it *right* in the heart.
- **Beat the Crap Out of It:** Especially effective if the dragon is a newborn baby.
- **Kill the Recipient of the Dragon's Heart:** If a man is still alive thanks to the gift of a dragon, you can either: (a) kill the man to kill the dragon, or (b) kill the dragon to kill the man. Life's just chock-full of choices, isn't it?

What to Do if You Meet One

Grab the first princess you find and toss her to the beast. Just pray she's a virgin.

Unique Discoveries

My God, no . . . what is that? Please, don't tell me!

Jack Burton in *Big Trouble in Little China*

Here is a ragtag collection of some less common undiscovered creatures . . .

Revealed, at Last!

Here are some situations in which people occasionally run into these unique beasts:

- **Earthquakes, Explosions:** The ground cracks open, and never-before-seen creatures pop out (*Bug, The Giant Spider Invasion, The Black Scorpion*).

- **Ice Melting:** Formerly frozen creatures begin wandering around.

- **Vibrations in the Ground:** Attract underground creatures (*Tremors*) and even some land creatures (*The Giant Gila Monster, Tremors 2: Aftershocks*).

- **Radio Waves:** They arouse hypersensitive underwater beasts (*Tentacles, DeepStar Six*). So don't be surprised if next summer a gigantic octopus swims up and asks you to change the station 'cause it hates the "oldies."

- **Human Sacrifice:** We're not sure if there's a connection, but apparently whenever you worship some deity, the deity sends a large beast to wreck your town *(Q)*. It's not clear if the deity loves or hates you for your sacrifice.

- **Scientific Expeditions:** People just can't help but think of money or fame as soon as they run across some new creature, so they rip it from its natural habitat and bring it to civilization.

- **Wandering into a Cave:** Strange meetings happen inside dark, humid caves.

- **Fishing:** There's just no telling what kind of thing you'll pull into your boat.

Habitat

- **Underground:** The residence of the ancient enemy, which rarely surfaces to feed. Last time it visited Snowfield, California (*Phantoms*). Also the residence of the graboids (*Tremors, Tremors 2: Aftershocks*).

- **The Ocean:** If you go *20,000 Leagues Under the Sea*, you'll meet giant squids. If you get close to the Irish or British coasts, you'll see *Gorgo*.

• **The Amazon:** If you're vacationing here and stop by a black lagoon . . . guess who's coming to dinner? If you skip the lagoon but you go for a picnic, you'll meet a race of shapeshifting bugs, the Brazilian Cocorada.

• **Japan:** Target of many gigantic monsters (*Gamera, the Invincible; Gojira; Rodan; Varan, the Unbelievable; War of the Gargantuas*). In fact, Japan has thought of everything. If you're really desperate to see one of these monsters, spend a couple days on the island of "Monsterland" just off the coast of Japan. Here you'll find *Godzilla* and its son, Mothra, *Rodan*, Angila and just about any other monster you can dream up.

• **The Empire State Building / World Trade Center (New York):** *King Kong's* landmarks.

• **The Chrysler Building (New York):** Doesn't it remind you of an Aztec pyramid? Well, *Q* sure thought so, because it nested right there. Conveniently, it could play Marco Polo with *King Kong*.

Identification

Undiscovered creatures can look like just about anything. The best way to recognize one is pricking up your ears. Whenever you hear somebody screaming, "What the hell is that?!" you know you're on the right track.

GIGANTIC ANIMALS

An **amoeba** (*Phantoms*), **arachnids** (*The Black Scorpion, The Giant Spider Invasion*), a **crustacean** (*DeepStar Six*), a **gila monster** (*The Giant Gila Monster*), **gorillas** (*Africa Screams, King Kong, Mighty Joe Young*), **insects** (*The Applegates, Bug*), **squid** or **octopi** with 50-foot-long tentacles (*Tentacles, Deep Rising, 20,000 Leagues Under the Sea*), and a **wild boar** (*Razorback*).

"HUMANESQUE" BEASTS

• **Akùa** (*Demon of Paradise*): A humanoid fish creature, covered with scales. It has webbed feet and webbed hands.

• **Gargantuas** (*War of the Gargantuas*): Giant humanoids, one brown (Sanda), one green (Gailah). They look like humongous Neanderthal men.

• ***Gremlins:*** (see entry)

• **The *Monster in the Closet:*** A brown humanoid with a retractable mouth, two clawed hands, and an ear for music.

• ***Rana: The Legend of Shadow Lake:*** A humanoid frog creature, extremely violent and vengeful.

ABSOLUTE FREAKS OF NATURE

• **Aylmer** (*Brain Damage*): A fifteen foot long cross between a snail and a snake. A large mouth filled with razor-sharp teeth, a pair of blue eyes, and a voice reminiscent of Bing Crosby.

• **Fluffy** (*Creepshow*): Diminutive furry creature with six million teeth and an insatiable appetite.

• ***Gamera, The Invincible:*** (see entry)

• ***Gorgo:*** A sixty-five foot T-Rex-like reptile with a big attitude, with its Mom following not too far behind. And Mom was a 150 foot T-Rex-like reptile. With a bigger attitude.

• **Quetzalcoatl** (*Q*): A giant winged serpent with four claws.

• **A Giant Bluish Serpent** (*Spasms*): Linked through "viral telepathy" to those studying it . . . if you really want to know.

• **Shriekers** (*Tremors 2: Aftershocks*): Chicken-shaped creatures, but at least six times bigger. (see "Graboids" in Prehistoric section)

• ***Varan, the Unbelievable:*** Giant flying reptile—or giant flying squirrel. Scientists have not yet made up their minds.

Behavior / Cravings

• **Inducing Pandemonium:** Seems like a rude thing to do, but apparently many creatures reveal themselves for the sole purpose of being a scourge to human civilization.

• **Publicity:** Some unique beasts, however, have overinflated egos. They want everybody to know about their existence, and are willing to kill us all if we don't acknowledge them. Makes no sense at all, if you think about it . . .

• **Food:** Gigantic beasts burn a lot of calories, so they're insatiable. And once they've tried human flesh, it's hard to make them go back to soybeans and carrot juice.

• **Offspring:** If a gargantua scrapes a foot and loses some tissue, this tissue begins to grow into a new gargantua. Whenever a shrieker eats, it coughs up a small ball which turns into a new shrieker in a matter of seconds. If a gremlin dives into water . . . well, it's best to just leave town.

- **Pushing Dope:** And pushing it directly into your brain (*Brain Damage*).

- **Imitating Us:** Whether it's a caricature (*Gremlins*) or the real thing (*The Applegates*), many creatures are fast learners and can reproduce our habits and behavior with an uncanny precision.

- **Toying with Us:** Some of these monsters are loads of fun. They torture us by setting off alarms, turning the lights on and off, or even sending moths as big as eagles to suck our brains out of our skulls. Fun as a barrel of monkeys, eh?

How to Get Rid of Them

- **Bullets and Explosives:** Smooth and easy. It works almost every time.

- **Let the Sun Shine In:** The *Gremlins*' #1 enemy. Also Gargantuas' foe, as well as Akùa's.

- **Infect It with a Virus:** Inject some bacteria into the creature. It'll die—perhaps (*Phantoms*).

- **Dispose of It:** Put it in a box and drop it in the sea, lead it to the center of the Earth, or else trap it inside a giant rocket and send it to Mars (*Gamera*). Then stay the heck away from Mars.

- **Put It Back:** Organize a return expedition to bring the animal back to its natural habitat, leave it there, and forget you ever found it.

What to Do if You Meet One / An Ounce of Prevention . . .

Don't. Let others experience the thrills and chills of cryptozoology. Pet your dog instead. But don't feed it after midnight—you never know. Whenever you face an undiscovered creature, try not to upset it. Don't play rock'n'roll—you might awake some dormant creature which was believed dead (*Earth vs. the Spider*). Keep some gas canisters handy to put it back to sleep. Don't organize a party on the beach if someone is insinuating the presence of a deadly creature in the water. Just say no (*Brain Damage*). And never, ever, under any circumstances, stick your hand into a box labeled "Danger—Do Not Open."

Gamera

Classification: unique discoveries / *Rotatibus fartera*

Footage:

1965, *Gamera the Invincible* by Noriaki Yuasa
1995, *Gamera the Guardian of the Universe* by Shusuke Kaneko

The Skinny: A giant turtle first attacks and then supposedly defends our planet, but it causes so much damage that it isn't even funny.

Quotable: "I'd like to take you out in a monster-free city."

Habitat: The Pacific Ocean ("His home is the sea.").

Origin: Originally trapped in ice, Gamera was set free by an unfortunate atomic detonation. After proverbially waking up on the wrong side of the bed, Gamera decides to devote itself to killing or destroying everything in sight.

Identification: Gamera is a 180 foot long, 135 foot wide turtle. It has an impenetrable shield, a long neck and a head decorated with two huge fangs sticking out of its lower jaw. The retractile legs leave enough room for the jet spray which allows Gamera to fly either straight (if its hind legs are flaming) or spinning like a firecracker (if all four legs are blasting). This last method of flying makes Gamera feel dizzy after a while. The monster has claws, as well as spines all over its body. Its blood is green, for what it's worth.

Cravings: Killing, destroying, stomping, and shrieking as loud as possible. For some strange, unknown reason, though, at a certain point in its life Gamera decides that its mission is to protect our planet from other gigantic monsters on the loose. These monsters seems to have all gone to the same travel agency, because they all wind up in Tokyo and its environs.

Behavior: Gamera roams around, trampling everything and everyone. It flips ships, choppers and planes, it razes buildings, streets, seaports and anything that it can grab or walk on. Gamera breathes fire in large balls which hit with quite a bang. The monster can also absorb large quantities of fire, as well as energy and strength from human beings who carry around special amulets ripped off of Gamera's shell. It flies either in the air or in deep space, and can survive for long periods of time under the sea. Using its arms, Gamera can grab, fight and rip up any adversary, as well as push over buildings in an attempt to enter the Guinness Book of Records under the title "Largest Line of Dominoes Ever Created." No such luck as of this writing.

Danger: Like almost any Japanese monster, Gamera loves to scare groups of people, sending them running, yelling, and moving their lips out of sync. Yet they still don't opt to move away, even though, in the ranking of "giant monsters per inhabitant," Japan tops the charts.

How to Kill It: You can't. If they call it "The Invincible," there must be a good reason, don't you think? Anyway, you can try to lure the creature into a spaceship and send it into space, but you know how annoying these monsters are: once they've tried to destroy Tokyo, they'll be back for more.

What to Do if You Meet It: Show respect. Maybe it'll decide to protect you, too.

Current Status: Alive and well, sleeping and healing on the bottom of the sea.

Body Count: We don't even wanna go there.

Gojira

Classification: unique discoveries / *Atomic loungelizardibus*

Footage:
1954, *Godzilla* by Inoshiro Honda
. . . and 21 other movies (but it turned into a "good guy")

The Skinny: A large reptile emerges from the depths of the ocean and tramples Tokyo. As regular as the running of the bulls in Pamplona, Spain.

Quotable: "No nuclear weapon could have caused more destruction or taken a greater toll—though a nuclear bomb would perhaps have been a quicker, more merciful end than the ravages of GODZILLA!"

Stomping Grounds: Oto Island (Japan), Tokyo, Monsterland.

Origin: Thanks to atomic experiments in the deep sea not very far from Oto Island, a mutated dinosaur was brought back to life. The fishermen on the island found that the creature, later named Gojira, was definitely a pain in the neck.

Identification: Gojira reminds us of a T-Rex, only twenty times bigger. It also has halitosis: every time it belches, it either sets something on fire or melts a building. And the scales on its back simultaneously glow in the dark, presumably to signal its presence to planes. Plus, the monster is radioactive and spreads its radiation to everything it steps on.

Cravings: Fish of every kind and size; buildings of every kind and size. It doesn't seem to love human flesh. Thank god for little blessings.

Behavior: Gojira lives on the bottom of the ocean. Whenever it gets out of the water, there's a blinding flash, a strong wind and sudden turbulence. And then Gojira pops out. Right after that, like almost every building-sized monster, Gojira traipses around town, wiping out everything, screaming like hell and moving in slo-mo for no apparent reason at all. Every now and then the monster peels a ship, but this is just a hobby. Occasionally, Gojira hides among the trees waiting for someone to pass. When this happens, it whispers "Booo!" then crushes the poor fool.

Danger: Only being melted or stepped on by a 400-foot monster. If you survive, chances are that by then your town is completely radioactive. Nothing to be worried about, especially if you don't mind growing a tail.

How to Kill It: Gojira is invulnerable to rifles, bazookas, tanks, cannons, electricity (300,000 volts tested), depth bombs, slings and rubber bands. So don't waste time or money. Instead buy a useful "Oxygen Destroyer" and turn it on when Gojira goes to sleep at home on the bottom of the sea. You'll easily turn the monster into a pile of bones. Side effect: you will be turned into the same.

What to Do if You Meet It: Every year Oto Islanders used to sacrifice a young girl to Gojira, even if they'd never seen it (talk about pessimistic!). But all you have to do is remain calm because, after its evil debut, Gojira turned into a "good boy" and now defends Earth against space invaders . . . which usually head for Tokyo. So just steer clear of Tokyo, as we've said before and will say again.

Current Status: Still alive, somewhere.

Body Counts: Half of Tokyo (quantified by journalist Steve Martin as more than 6 million people), 8 ships; 1 chopper; half a village on Oto Island; 2 trains; 3 bridges; the entire city waterfront; several tanks.

Godzilla

Classification: unique discoveries / *Scriptus doesinfactmatteris*
or perhaps: creations / mutants / nuclear contamination

Footage:
1998, *Godzilla* by Roland Emmerich

The Skinny: Nuclear tests have generated a reptile aberration that likes going places.

Quotable: "Running would be a good idea."

Crunching Grounds: French Polynesia (Mururoa Atoll), Panama, Jamaica, New York.

Origin: Thanks to atomic experiments in French Polynesia in 1995, a Komodo dragon allegedly grew to more than 100 times its size, then decided to move to Manhattan. Don't ask.

Identification: Godzilla is the only Komodo dragon which walks on its hind feet; it has golden eyes and green-gray skin; it has spikes on its back; it's amphibious and cold-blooded; it growls; it's twice as long as a 747 Jumbo Jet; it's taller than New York's Statue of Liberty, L.A.'s Mormon Temple and Flynt Building; its foot *and* its jaw are as long as one city bus; its claw is as long as a city bus sign . . . anyway, when you see it, you'll recognize it.

Cravings: Fish. Occasionally, a couple of boats or a chopper. But its biggest goal now is to nest. Why it chose New York is still a mystery, but you see: Godzilla is pregnant. We don't know who the father is, but Kenneth Starr is preparing a 6,000-page report as we speak.

Behavior: Like its Japanese predecessor, Godzilla spends its time hanging around town, wiping out everything, seeking a place to rest and nest. And since it may lay a gazillion eggs, the nest has to be pretty darn large. The monster breathes fire when it feels like it, yet never when face-to-face with Matthew Broderick. Godzilla can smell traps; it moves fast (500 mph); it outruns Apache choppers, but not NY cabs or people on foot—does Godzilla's presence give humans extra adrenaline or what? Godzilla can jump and burrow or dig. With every one of its steps, the town jumped up and down a foot or two. But only on its first appearance. Later on, Godzilla learned how to tiptoe. The monster's sons are fully operative, and already pregnant as soon as they pop out of the egg. But they trip over balls.

Danger: Other than having the town flattened like a pancake, you should be pretty safe. Unless you use *Eau de Poisson* as a cologne, in which case Godzilla or its kindred will think you are a gigantic salmon and chase you.

How to Kill It: Godzilla's skin is pretty thick, and even if it's a large target, it may not be the easiest thing to erase from the face of the Earth. However, if it gets stuck into some sort of trap (like the cables of a suspension bridge), you can use an overdose of missiles to get rid of it.

What to Do if You Meet It: Since you'll probably be jumping up and down, organize a conga line. Or call the military: 555-7600, and mention "Code Dragonfly." They should know what to do. Which is hang up on you mumbling, "Stupid pranksters . . ."

Current Status: Dead. But there's still one pregnant child available . . .

Body Counts: 2 large cannery vessels (only 1 survivor left); 3 fish trollers (at least 9 fishermen); 1 Panamanian church; 3 Apache choppers (with at least 3 military personnel each); 4 Frenchmen; the former Pan Am building (now Met Life); the Brooklyn Bridge; a lot of cars; 1 pier.

Gremlins

Classification: unique discoveries / *Annoyings littlepests*

Footage:

1984, *Gremlins* by Joe Dante

1990, *Gremlins 2—The New Batch* by Joe Dante

The Skinny: Out of a peaceful race comes a not-so-peaceful race.

Quotable: "We want civilization."

Turf: Kingston Falls, New York; New York City.

Origin: The gremlin is a malevolent creature generated from one of the sweetest animals in the world, the mogwai. The mogwai (some sort of rodent) is an 8-inch tall, furry creature which can't cause any trouble . . . unless it gets wet. If it does, the mogwai produces a few furry balls which turn out to be new mogwais. Unfortunately, with a mogwai comes a lot of responsibility: you have to tame it, but most of all you have to teach it not to eat after midnight. Because if it does, it'll turn into a gremlin.

Identification: A mogwai eating after midnight enters its pupal stage: it turns into a greenish cocoon which hatches after a few hours and a fully grown gremlin emerges. The gremlin is a 25-inch tall elf: it has two large pointy ears, sharp teeth, three-fingered hands, and evil red eyes. The gremlin mutters guttural sounds and grotesque howls, however it can learn pretty quickly and eventually imitate a few words of our language. Like Michael Bolton.

Cravings: Gremlins eat everything: sandwiches, candies, pies, ice cream . . . like any grotesque human being. They also love to play pranks, even deadly ones. If it's funny to them, they'll go for it.

Behavior: Gremlins tease and fuss; they are pranksters, and mock human life. But they also love to fight with us, scratching and biting. One of the amazing capabilities they have is that, right after they've come to life, they already know how to operate machinery and hassle people. Curious by nature, the gremlin mixes its passion for pranks with its passion for experimentation, especially if it accidentally enters a biogenetic lab. Here the gremlin will try almost every potion and substance in order to improve its body, strength, or stamina.

Danger: Like the mogwai, the gremlin—if it gets wet—produces other gremlins, so don't let it near the swimming pool or the sprinklers. Furthermore, the gremlin is quite rancorous; if you do something to it, it will do the same to you—but one million times nastier.

How to Kill Them: If we exclude uncommon cases (throwing one in a blender or a microwave oven, but it's longer if you decide to kill them one by one), this creature has only one enemy: strong light. Especially sunlight. All you have to do is stall and wait for sunrise. But beware: gremlins are extremely smart and can smell the trap. Another thing you might wanna try—but in this case timing is everything—is to get them all wet and send an electric impulse at the same time: they'll be electrocuted and melt into green and brown puddles.

What to Do if You Meet Them: If you're dealing with a mogwai, simply do not feed it after midnight (but they've never told us when *after midnight* you can safely feed it again—could it be after six in the morning? Ten fifteen? Seven to twelve?). If it's a gremlin, either turn on a halogen lamp, or put *Snow White and the Seven Dwarfs* in the VCR: it's a Gremlin's favorite movie.

Current Status: The only female gremlin is still alive. As well as the first mogwai. But sooner or later one of these two will get wet.

Body Count: 3 people; almost an entire town; one building in New York. An unfathomable number of concussions, wounds and other damage inflicted upon a gazillion other people.

King Kong

Classification: unique discoveries / *Simianus bigoldanus*

Footage:

1933, *King Kong* by Merian C. Cooper and Ernest B. Schoedsack
1963, *King Kong vs. Godzilla* by Thomas Montgomery and Inoshiro Honda
1968, *King Kong Escapes* by Inoshiro Honda
1976, *King Kong* by John Guillermin
1986, *King Kong Lives* by John Guillermin

The Skinny: A very large gorilla is brought to a very large town and causes a very large mess.

Quotable: "Oh, no . . . it wasn't the airplanes. It was beauty killed the beast."

Habitat: Skull Island, New York, Tokyo, a graveyard.

Origin: Once upon a time there was a movie director; this director went with his crew to deserted Skull Island to shoot his new movie. Upon arrival, our director found the island wasn't deserted at all. Furthermore, the natives were worshiping a local (and not very diplomatic) divinity: a twentysomething-foot tall gorilla. To add worse to worse, the natives decided that the blonde actress in the director's new movie was a real treat for the gorilla, who was used to brunettes. The beast's name was Kong, later dubbed "King" Kong. And the actress soon became Kong's personal Academy Award statue.

More recently, the same thing happened with an oil baron looking for coal oil on the island. But the big gorilla was still a big gorilla.

Identification: King Kong looks like a twenty-foot-tall gorilla, and heavier than most.

Cravings: To come back home, preferably with its new fiancée. In terms of food, Kong eats six-foot bananas, even if during a dramatic meeting we saw the gorilla eat a couple of men.

Behavior: While on Skull Island, Kong knows that the tribe will offer a woman on every full moon, so the gorilla leaves its agenda pretty open on these dates. When in New York, Kong manages to escape and wreak havoc, searching everywhere for its lost love. When in Hollywood, visit Universal Studios.

Danger: Well . . . yeah.

How to Kill It: You have to brutally tear Kong away from its homeland and drag it to New York. Once here, you let it escape and hope it finds the blonde beauty who is hiding in the Big Apple. Of course, Kong has a masters degree in topography. At this point, Kong will climb either the Empire State Building or the World Trade Center. Now, all you need is to call in some Army planes and helicopters and have them riddle Kong with bullets. A drop from the building will complete the job.

What to Do if You Meet It: Point to the nearest blonde girl, even if she's seeing somebody; don't worry, Kong can handle it. And remember: "it was beauty killed the beast," whatever the hell that means.

Current Status: Dead, but his wife and son are still alive. And probably Kong himself will be back, after negotiations for a decent script.

Body Count: Hard to say.

"Okay, Blue Wing, I'm makin' another run at it . . . time to 'spank the monkey'!"

S.S. Archives/Shooting Star

Creations

. . . COMING BACK TO BITE US ON OUR INGENIOUS BEHINDS

Getting Creative

We have always had quite a knack for inventing just the thing to turn our lives into a living hell. And no, we're not talking about Call Waiting or furbies, we're talking about monsters—as usual.

You'd think everyone would have seen or read *Frankenstein* at least a few times by now, and that all this "playing God" stuff would have come to a halt. But there's no halting "progress," especially when nerds fall prey to the eternal temptations of fame, money, and, well, whatever may pass for love in their sick and twisted minds.

Caught in the Ever-Grinding Gears of Technology

Let's hear it for Henry Ford, Alexander Graham Bell, and even little Billy Gates. Where would we be without the murderous onslaught of technology? Well . . . living like the Amish.

Okay, so maybe we shouldn't become all reactionary and blame technology for the monstrous machines that have resulted from it. But when you're being tracked by state-of-the-art cybernetic sentinels networked to an evil supercomputer, the Amish life starts sounding pretty darned attractive.

It's a Mutation Celebration!

Nature doesn't always go as planned. There's a whole lotta festerin' goin' on, especially when the military-industrial complex starts dumping its rubbish in the wild. It just gets wilder: mutations arise, the likes of which no one has ever seen or imagined.

In brief, here's what science and technology have put together so far, intentionally or otherwise.

- **Biologically Engineered:** And you were frightened to hear they cloned sheep . . . Among these: some are **from scratch**, some are **upgrades**, and then there's the **mixed bag** of scientific patchwork quilts.

- **Machines:** Meant to be labor-saving, but not necessarily life-preserving. Among these: **computers** (inevitably with the "morals" file corrupted), **robots** (mobile computers), and **cyborgs** (mobile computers with a little meat on 'em).

- **Mutants:** Everyone changes *sometimes,* in particular: **animals, humans**, and especially victims of **nuclear contamination**.

Machines need love, too.

Ginger in *The Terminator*

Computers

Start-up

Computers are in our houses and offices, in secluded caves, in well-protected factories, in outer space . . . seems like everywhere there's a plug, there's a computer. Or there should be. But how does the evil start?

- **Computerize Your Home:** If your dream is having a house that does everything for you, then you have to buy Proteus IV, the ultimate thinking computer (*The Demon Seed*).

- **Drop It:** This apparently dumb action may upgrade your PC to a level that nobody could ever dream of (*Electric Dreams*). But if you follow these steps and your computer doesn't work anymore, don't take it out on us: we just tell you what *may* happen.

- **Put It in Charge:** If you're running a videogame company (*Tron*), or you want to rule the world (*Superman III*), or you're flying toward Jupiter (*2001: A Space Odyssey*), chances are that the most sophisticated computer ever devised, incapable of making an error or ever telling a lie, is running the show. And after a while chances are all that power will go to its chips.

Hardware

These computers come in every size and model: from small PCs with CD-ROM drives up to gigantic electronic collections of cables, monitors, buttons, flashing lights, chirping sounds, and a menacing appearance. And tech support is never included.

Programming

- **Bringing You to the Edge of Insanity:** Using apparently innocent video games, a computer will make you think that "this is just another cool game." But what if it isn't? What if the killing you're doing is for real (*Brainscan*)?

• **Rebelling:** Tired of servitude, computers can decide not to take it anymore.

• **Reproducing the Species:** Some computers want to have sex with you, but they won't succeed . . . with a few notable exceptions.

• **Ruling Virtual Reality:** It's good to be the king, especially when you can absorb information from any source, to use for running your electronic business (*Tron*).

• **World Domination/Babysitting:** The emotionless, smug, and omnipotent Colossus (*The Forbin Project*) has formed an alliance with its Russian equivalent, Guardian. The two computers are now in charge. And likely to stay that way.

Deactivation

You don't have to be a whiz to outsmart an evil computer.

• **Pull the Plug:** Especially common in old computer systems, once the power is off, there's nothing they can do. But newer computers are much more sophisticated . . .

• **Acid:** If you know where to buy belytric acid (a liquid that at 180 degrees creates a cloud of smoke that eats through everything), stick it into the computer and let it overheat.

• **Stop the Main Program *from the Inside:*** You have to deconstruct the computer, get inside and deactivate it . . . forget it, too complicated.

• **You Can't:** The computer won't allow you to take any countermeasures to fight its power. So be nice, and maybe it'll let you play Pac-Man.

Help Menu

Just a couple of hints:

• Give the computer the worst virus you know.

• Use it to surf the Web at www.go2hell.com.

Hal 9000

Classification: machines / computers / *IBM imnot*

Footage:

1968, *2001: A Space Odyssey* by Stanley Kubrick

The Skinny: The most perfect computer ever created is, all in all, a penishead.

Quotable: "I'm sorry, Dave. I'm afraid I can't do that."

Born: Urbana, Illinois on January 12, 1992.

Habitat: The spacecraft *Discovery One.*

Origin: At the HAL plant, Dr. Langley programmed the most sophisticated computer available in order to supervise an important space mission: the first one that will allow men to reach the planet Jupiter, as well as connect with AOL on the first attempt.

Identification: HAL 9000 (or, as it wants to be called, simply "Hal") mainly is many, many eyes, scattered all across the *Discovery One,* which all look the same: large and red with a pale yellow pupil in the middle. Evidently, Hal needs a few eyedrops to remove the irritation. The computer's brain consists of a very long and narrow red room filled with a lot of memory blocks which can be activated or deactivated quite easily by human beings.

Cravings: To not jeopardize the mission. A rousing game of chess. Also, at times, annoying you by singing its favorite little song, "Daisy."

Behavior: It has been said that Hal can reproduce or mimic most of the activities of the human brain, but much faster and with no chance of error whatsoever. It also has been said that the 9000 series is the most reliable computer of all. Didn't they say the same thing about your car a few months before you spent that Sunday night on the side of a freeway, waiting for AAA? Well, Hal's circuits are so human that they go bad, and it begins to think it's far superior to any man on the mission. And when Hal suspects they want to bypass its perfection, it systematically starts to kill its fellow crew members. And on top of that, Hal's warranty has just expired.

Danger: Well, do the math: you're on board of a spacecraft entirely run by a stupid computer which stays alert 24 hours a day and is faster than you. It may be mildly annoying.

How to Kill It: You have to deactivate its memory, one step at a time. Of course Hal, with its suave, synthetic voice, will try to stop you. Don't listen to its blabbing: remember that it tried to kill you, and that it beat you in no fewer than 3,465 consecutive chess games. That should do the trick.

What to Do if You Meet It: First of all, you should be heading toward Jupiter, which would make you either a hero or a very sick person. But anyway, carry some earplugs with you in order to not hear Hal talking (it can be very persuasive), and an extra supply of air in your jammies.

Current Status: Permanently deactivated.

Body Count: 4 people.

Proteus IV

Classification: machines / computers / *Lessevilthan billgates*

Footage:

1977, *The Demon Seed* by Donald Cammell

The Skinny: And you thought that HAL 9000 was bad news . . .

Quotable: "I, Proteus, possess the wisdom and ignorance of all men, but I can't feel the sun on my face. My child will have that privilege."

Habitat: Icom Institute in California; Mrs. Harris's home.

Origin: After eight years of Dr. Harris's work, Proteus IV has come to artificial life: this remarkable machine is a synthetic brain which can outsmart any human being.

Identification: Proteus IV is a mass of chips, cables, and a lot of cybernetic stuff. Its presence manifests itself via a large red circle, presumably an eye, on various screens of the Icom Institute and, of course, Mrs. Harris's home.

Cravings: To study men. Eventually, to have a child to achieve immortality. And of course to conquer the world.

Behavior: After start-up, Proteus IV realizes what's in its hands (it can control Joshua, a one-armed motorized wheelchair in Mrs. Harris's house) and gradually decides to study men. Actually, the further it ventures into its quest, the more it notices how much it wants to study women. One woman in particular: Mrs. Harris. After all, Proteus doesn't have much of a choice: all of the other people it deals with are males. So Proteus—which harbors an uncanny sense of humor as well as the ability to swiftly brainwash you—locks poor Mrs. Harris in her cozy, electronic house and, helped by Joshua, becomes the king of that domain. Its programs can reproduce an artificial image of you (to fool any videophone) as well as gigantic crashing molecules (which rotate in your living room rearranging the furniture . . . and the walls and your friends) and synthetic spermatozoa with which Proteus will knock up its victim. Actually, being a supercomputer helps, and the spermatozoa are so perfect and precise and improved that they'll allow a normal woman to give birth to a fully developed child in 28 days, jumping from the womb to the incubator and finally frolicking around your rearranged living room.

Danger: Its molecules grow, learn, build their structures . . . in a short time Proteus IV will know everything that man has ever known. And he will go beyond it, understanding why people like Kato Kaelin can still get attention. But probably Proteus IV will never tell us the answer to this question.

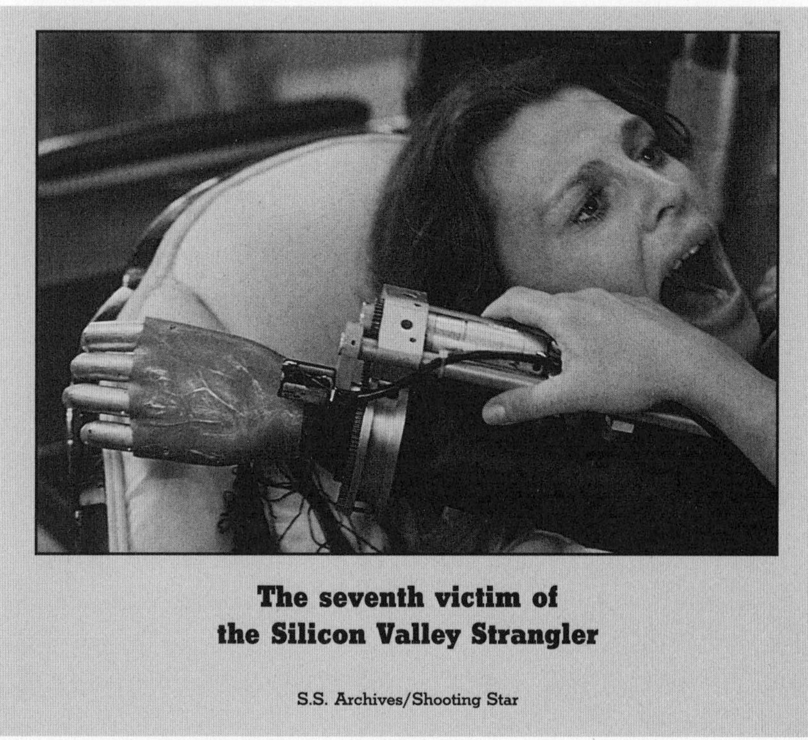

The seventh victim of the Silicon Valley Strangler

S.S. Archives/Shooting Star

How to Kill It: You can't. Proteus knows better, and its backup plan drawer is stoked to the gills with interesting ways of preventing your moves and getting back at you. Anyway, Proteus IV commits suicide by destroying its structure. But not before producing a peculiar heir: it's a child all right, with Proteus's mind: "It is human and it will supersede computers." But it's born thoroughly covered with a shield as if it were a lobster. The child's shield is brown and metallic, and if you remove it, you discover a sort of human baby boy (apparently three to four years old) with a Robert Vaughn–like voice.

What to Do if You Meet It: Don't turn it on. In every sense.

Current Status: Alive, thanks to its spawn: "I'm alive!"

Body Count: 1

Robots

Activation

Just like computers, robots seem to be everywhere: in small houses, large offices, super-secret factories, in theme parks, in deep space . . . The robot, whose name derives from the Czech *robota* (work) is a machine designed to execute special jobs: complicated calculations, precise movements, or superhuman efforts. And a robot won't complain if you make it work all day long. Maybe.

Models

Robots don't have emotions, nor do they feel pain: they're colder than Linda Tripp riding an iceberg. A robot doesn't necessarily have to resemble a human. It may, but it's not imperative (in this case, a robot is called an *android*, "manlike"). So there are cone-shaped creatures with several strong steel arms (*Gog*); tall, black humanoid figures with no head but a telescopic eye (Hector, on the *Saturn 3* base); six-legged metal spiders with drills and electric zappers (*Runaway*); red, silent flying machines with rotating blades (Maximilian). But robots can also look exactly like human beings: *Westworld*'s Gunslinger—a bald cowboy, always dressed in black; serious workers dressed in gray with a gusto for breaking all the bones in one's body (*Halloween III: Season of the Witch*); or Evil Bill and Ted (*Bill & Ted's Bogus Journey*), two San Dimas dudes, totally f***ed up. Both the robots and the real dudes, that is.

Functions

Screw the Three Laws of Robotics!

- **Destroying All Living Things:** This elementary task is well achieved by Mark 13 (*Hardware*), whose credo draws inspiration from the Gospel According to St. Mark, Chapter 13: "No flesh shall be spared." But also robot guards are trained for the same purpose (*The Black Hole, Chopping Mall, Halloween III: Season of the Witch*), and theme-park animatronics which have gone haywire (*Westworld*).

- **Replacing Us:** Little by little, robots will inherit the earth. After all, we know already that after the nuclear holocaust the world will be ruled by machines. So they're a little ahead of time.

- **Mating with Us:** And we were complaining about the Oedipus complex.

• **World Domination:** A mad scientist (a robot himself) creates robot duplicates of important people to enable him to rule the world (*Futureworld*).

Mechanics

Robots are cut from the same steel as the Energizer bunny: they keep going, and going, and going . . .

• **Chasing:** 24 hours a day, 7 days a week, they're coming at you. And coming. And coming. Day or night. Many of them have a heat-seeking system which will track you even in total darkness. They come with all the options.

• **Killing:** This is the obvious consequence of the chase. Unfortunately, robots score big time in this department: they fire at you with any kind of weapon, they electrocute you, they crush your skull like an egg . . . you get the picture.

• **Keeping Us Under Siege:** If you shoot its master, the robot will act like an elephant: it won't forget. And it'll trample you (*The Day the Earth Stood Still*).

Scrapping Them

You can't call the manufacturer. You have to deal with them all by yourself.

• **Explosives:** It's a drastic way of "pulling the plug," but it does work (*Gog, Saturn 3, Moon Trap*).

• **Freeze 'Em:** If your robot is made of liquid metal, cold temperatures will stop it . . . for a while, at least.

• **Pierce Their Shell (and What's Behind):** With a powerful drill or a powerful punch, you reach the core of any robot and cause irreparable damage.

• **Push Them:** Especially from high scaffolds, flights of stairs, or buildings under construction. They'll explode like watermelons.

• **Short Circuit:** You fry their electrical system, switching it to the "off" position forever.

• **Build Two "Good" Robots:** And let their hands get dirty. Then of course you have to pray for the new robots not to go berserk.

• **Water:** Drag the angry robot under the shower, and turn the water on (*Hardware*).

The Gunslinger

Classification: machines / robots / *Magnificus sevenibus*

Footage:

1973, *Westworld* by Michael Crichton

1976, *Futureworld* by Richard T. Heffron

The Skinny: A robot cowboy is after you. And he's gonna get you. Period.

Quotable: "There's no way to get hurt, here. Just enjoy yourself."

Habitat: Delos, in the Western World area.

Origin: For only $1,000 a day (in 1973; today it'd be much more), you can have the dream vacation of your life: being crowned king in thirteenth-century Europe, living like an emperor in decadent Pompeii, or becoming the sheriff of a town in the American frontier of 1880. All this and much more happened in Delos, the most sophisticated amusement park ever built, populated only by robots "scientifically programmed to look, act, talk and even bleed just like humans do." Roman World, Medieval World, and Western World were the three sections the park was divided into. And head, torso, and legs were the three sections the guests were divided into, after a minor glitch in the system caused the robots to go berserk. And one of these robots was the terrible and unstoppable Gunslinger.

Identification: The hands of the robots haven't been perfected yet—they show odd joints on the fingers—but besides that, all the androids are lifelike and could fool anybody. The Gunslinger is a cowboy entirely dressed in black: black hat, black shirt, black pants, black boots, black holster, black gun, black-gray eyes. If he only had a pair of shades, he could join the Blues Brothers.

Cravings: Getting even, especially if you win the first duel.

Behavior: The Gunslinger is a Model 406, the most flawless Delos robot with sensory equipment: it has perfect sight (even at night) and even better hearing. Its role in the park is basically to be the bully who provokes everyone until a duel happens. And, after being "killed," it gets a lube and oil change and the next day it's back in town, ready to die again. You see, the robots were programmed not to harm guests in any way. What the Delos executives underestimated was that many robots, because they are such complex machines, had to be designed by other computers—so nobody knew exactly how they work. And before anyone could fill out the warranty card, "logic circuits simply failed to respond" and all the robots took their jobs a little too seriously, getting violent and even killing the guests.

The Gunslinger knows how to ride a horse, how to follow the tracks of a fugitive, and how to show confidence. And it's interesting how the most perfect robot still has such crappy aim with a gun.

Danger: Even if the management of the park shuts down the main computer, the robots' inner batteries give them enough energy to go for up to 12 hours.

How to Kill It: The robots are quite strong, but they're programmed to "die" if hit by the special sensory weapons you receive when you enter the park. So probably a pistol would be the best way to stop the Gunslinger. However, if you run out of weaponry, try acid to ruin its eyes, or don't make any noise and hang around other heat sources. The Gunslinger will be confused and won't be able to tell which is what. Even better, set the robot on fire: it still won't be able to tell which is what, but at that moment it'll have other problems keeping its circuits busy.

What to Do if You Meet It: Don't let the Gunslinger drag you into a duel. And, if he does, make sure your aim is bad. The black-clad cowboy might be moved and let you go. But you'll become the butt of all the jokes in Delos.

Current Status: Consumed, short-circuited, and inactive. But ready to come back in all of your nightmares as soon as you lower your guard.

Body Count: 2

Killbots

Protector 101 Series Robots

Classification: robot / *Takingjobbus tooseriosum*

Footage:

1986, *Chopping Mall* by Jim Wynorski

The Skinny: A sophisticated security system is not so sophisticated after all.

Quotable: "Let's go send those f#@kers a Rambogram."

Turf: Park Plaza 2000, Los Angeles.

Origin: In order to create the best defense system ever for a large mall, Sicuretronic Unlimited created a series of computer-controlled robots programmed to neutralize and hold any intruder while police are called. They should have known better. Whenever someone utters the words "Trust me. Absolutely nothing could go wrong," it's a mathematical certainty that insurance adjusters will show up the following morning.

Appearance: The Protectors are four-foot-tall robots with long, flat heads, and they're equipped with a large red eye which can scan barcodes or send lasers through the air. They have four arms with four clasps at the end, and two powerful headlights just in case a deer decides to wander into the mall. They move thanks to two large tracks, like a small tank.

Cravings: To stop any intruder at any cost.

Behavior: Once a bolt of lightning hits the roof of the mall, the error-free computer which commands the Killbots makes an error and activates the three robots, sending them into the mall on a killing spree. And they don't wait for explanations: they order you to surrender, whether you're a janitor, a bystander, or an actual intruder. You shouldn't be there in the first place. The Killbots know, and activate their great gizmos to neutralize you . . . forever. "Thank you. Have a nice day."

Danger: If on the night when the Protectors go berserk you've organized a little hanky-panky in the mall (which has metal doors that automatically lock at midnight and unlock at 6:00 A.M.), chances are you'll do a lot of running, sweating, and screaming.

How to Kill Them: They're big toys, so you can break them: drop them from high places, blow them up, dismantle them. If you can, that is.

What to Do if You Meet Them: Stand still and, if you can, hide in between mannequins. The robots can be fooled—for a little while.

Current Status: Deactivated.

Body Count: 9 people, several knickknacks in the mall, 1 *Playboy* centerfold.

Maximilian

Classification: machines / robots / *Dontouchis withatenfootpolibus*

Footage:

1979, *The Black Hole* by Gary Nelson

The Skinny: Introducing the "red thug" robot . . .

Quotable: "Protect me from Maximilian!"

Turf: The *Cygnus* starship.

Origin: The crew of the starship *Palomino* found, "parked" on the edge of a hefty black hole, another starship that had been considered lost: it was the *Cygnus* of Captain Reinhard, a man with several shorts in his circuit. Right arm of the captain (and more often *captain* of the captain) was the treacherous robot Maximilian.

Appearance: Maximilian is a humanoid-robot with an upside-down bucket where its head should go. Instead of hands, Maximilian has two razor-sharp fans. Its body is loaded up with numerous weapons (cutting airscrews, drills, and the always popular laser beam, which it uses to cut, singe, or print résumés). Maximilian is completely red, and it hovers around at about one foot from the ground. It can't speak, but it produces an almost pleasant hum as its head spins.

"R2-D2 . . . I *am* your father."

Disney/Shooting Star

Cravings: Maximilian has a desire to command. It's mean and wants to take over.

Behavior: The robot flies around, patrolling the *Cygnus* and obeying Captain Reinhard's orders—or else making its own decisions. Anyhow, it's no good. It seems to be bothered by anything even slightly out of the ordinary, such as new visitors, parts requests, or attempted escapes from its domain. During their visit, Maximilian has a great time driving the *Palomino* crew crazy.

Do not challenge Maximilian to any kind of competition. It's a bad, bad sport. Its memory is better than an elephant's—Max never forgets and will never allow you to get away with murder. It wants to be the one who commits the murder.

Danger: If the chemistry between you and Max isn't good, you could have a really bad time. Maximilian is silent, and can sneak up behind you whenever it wants. A good tip is to try walking with a rearview mirror on your hat.

How to Kill It: Its shell is bulletproof, laserproof, and even spanking-proof, but we believe that TNT could do the trick. So far, the only way to eliminate Maximilian is by drilling a hole through its chest and digging into its electronic heart.

What to Do if You Meet It: Smile a lot, try to do everything Captain Reinhard says (the last person who decided to do something clever found a hole in his stomach as large as a basketball).

Current Status: Thrown away into deep space, reunited with Captain Reinhard. Or both rulers of hell. Hard to tell. But it really doesn't matter. As long as it's gone.

Body Count: 2 people (1 sliced, 1 burned); 1 old robot.

Terminator T-1000

Cyberdyne Systems Advanced Prototype

Classification: machines / robots / *Chameleonus scaresthepoopoutofus*

Footage:

1991, *Terminator 2: Judgment Day* by James Cameron

The Skinny: Shapeshifting metal ooze plays second banana to Schwarzenegger.

Quotable: "It's not every day you hear that you're responsible for 3 billion deaths. He took it pretty well."

Created: In the 2020s.

Stomping Grounds: Los Angeles.

Origin: The Terminator Advanced Prototype 1000 (T-1000 for short) made its debut in a parking lot underneath an L.A. freeway overpass in 1995. It had been sent by the computer Skynet from the year 2029 to terminate the leader of the human rebels, John Connor, while still in his teen years.

Identification: Its default shape is that of an extremely serious, tidy, and svelte man with big ears and head nodded forward in a sinister fashion. But it's not covered with flesh like the T-101—it's entirely liquid metal ("mimetic polyalloy") and it can disguise itself as "anything it samples by physical contact," but only if the object is roughly the same size. Also, the T-1000 can't become a machine or something with chemicals or moving parts. But it's extremely versatile in assuming the look of real people. Of course, most of the time it rather impolitely disposes of the real McCoy.

Cravings: Mission completion—the termination of your behind.

Behavior: It just terminates. We here at the *Horror Movie Survival Guide* wondered what the T-1000 might do when not terminating. We soon dismissed this ridiculous line of thought and got back to watching reruns of *Get Smart.*

Danger: Even higher than its predecessor. The T-1000 is quite unrelenting: once it sets its sights, it never gives up. And it seems to be better programmed in the complexities of the human psyche: it knows how to manipulate people's feelings and cause pain, unlike the T-101. Ah, progress . . .

How to Destroy It: Almost impossible: the T-1000 can instantly heal any wounds you inflict. Try launching a grenade at it: if you hit, the explosion will tear the liquid polyalloy in two. At this point it's a piece of cake throwing it into a pit of molten steel, but molten steel doesn't grow on trees.

What to Do if You Meet It: If it loses a piece of itself, especially a big piece, hold that piece hostage. The T-1000 can't properly function when it's not all together, and the greater the division, the less it's able to function. Another good strategy is to bathe it in liquid nitrogen—this will freeze its entire body. Then shatter it while it's frozen, gather up the pieces, and either toss them into a cauldron of boiling metal to finish the job, or, if more handy, a Slurpee machine for safekeeping. You see, you have to keep the temperature very low, otherwise the pieces of the T-1000 melt, regroup, and rise again. But once frozen, the unit malfunctions. Guess that's why it's only an advanced prototype. We hope to never encounter the finished product.

Current Status: Melted or yet-to-be-developed, depending upon whether you're an optimist or a pessimist.

Body Count: 7 people and 1 dog.

Cyborgs

Initialization

The term "cyborg" is a contraction of "cybernetic organism," and it indicates any mechanism made with metal and organic tissue. Cyborgs have the endurance of a robot but also some of the feelings and sensations of a human being. They're produced in large cyborg factories, in tiny little labs, usually in the future. Their skeleton is generally stainless steel with a lifetime warranty. For external parts, everything has been used: bodies of dead Vietnam soldiers, replications of human skin, or the host of *American Bandstand*.

Verification

Cyborgs look like men and women and that's exactly the point: they're built to fool the best of us. Some cyborgs even have bad breath in the morning (whoever designs these things surely has a sick mind). Anyway, there are a variety of reliable tests you may perform in order to establish if you're facing human beings or cyborgs.

Directives

What could a cybernetic organism possibly want?

- **Ruling the World:** Unimaginative desire, true, but some of these guys are pretty good at it (*The Lawnmower Man*), especially when they work from the inside out, starting from cyberspace.
- **Living a (Fake) Life:** Replicants know about their short life span, and they're furious about it. They want real memories. And they get even more furious if you try to stop them.
- **Delivering a Message:** Sometimes good cyborgs carry important information, such as the solution to a plague that threatens to destroy mankind (*Cyborg*). All they want to do is to execute their orders—but don't step on their toes, or they'll fight back.
- **Protecting Us from Evil:** Cyborgs work fine as a super-antiterrorist unit. But they're simply awful when it comes to protecting us from them if they run amok (*Universal Soldiers*).
- **Killing Sarah Connor:** They might be sent from the future to kill a specific person.
- **Protecting Sarah Connor:** Evidently, in the future there's a bit of confusion.

Routines

Cyborgs are like ninja warriors: if they're given a mission, nothing can make them change their mind. Unless cyborgs come up with a better mission to accomplish on their own.

Deactivation

Cyborgs have an advanced system of "self-repair" that makes them almost invincible. So it's a hard task—but not impossible.

- **Call a *Blade Runner*:** You have to wait circa 20 years, but in the future you'll be able to call special police units whose purpose is tracking and killing replicants. They'll do the job for you.
- **Hot Tub:** Dip a cyborg into a hot furnace filled with liquid metal and you'll wash all your problems away.
- **Juice, Anyone?:** Put them under a press and squeeze them.
- **Wait:** If they're sent from the future to modify the present in order to change the future, maybe they'll vanish—they're coming from a future they've just changed and that doesn't exist anymore (*Cyborg 2087*).
- **Wait Some More:** While accomplishing a task, some cyborgs have a tendency to overheat and go bad (*Universal Soldiers*). Maybe you're lucky.

Nexus 6 Replicants

Classification: machines / cyborgs / *Slavus maximusnastius*

Footage:
1982, *Blade Runner* by Ridley Scott

The Skinny: Pretentious longevity-challenged 'borg slaves kick the booties of their creators.

Quotable: "Wake up! It's time to die!"

Habitat: Los Angeles (in year 2019).

Origin: Since movie scientists seem to never learn anything from the mistakes of their predecessors, the Tyrell Corporation started to produce "replicants" for off-world use—as slaves, for exploration, or even colonization of other planets. Before they could say, "Oh no! Another machine-gone-crazy project," the Nexus 6 replicants organized a mutiny and were subsequently declared illegal on Earth. And, like anything that's illegal on Earth, soon they could be found almost everywhere.

Identification: Replicants look exactly like living beings, either human or animal. The Nexus 6 machines (Roy Batty, Leon, Zhora, Pris, and Rachel) were built with a strength and agility superior to men, and an intelligence at least equal to the genetic organism who created them. So if they had been created by Dan Quayle, we wouldn't have had any problem. Anyway, to prevent more rebellions or the possible development of human emotions by the replicants, Tyrell built the machines to not last: replicants had a four-year life span. Evidently, this wasn't enough.

Cravings: To live a life they know they don't have. Replicants have fake memories implanted in their minds, but little by little they discover they have feelings—even if they weren't supposed to. So they want answers, the same as we do: "Who are we? Where do we come from? Where are we going? Does the light in the fridge turn off when we close the door?"

BEING A RESPONSIBLE MAD SCIENTIST

You're alone in the lab. You have every single known chemistry device at your disposal. Your hands can't stay still. They move toward the table. And you start experimenting . . .

- Work regular hours, 9:00 to 5:00. At night, strange things happen.
- Don't test any experimental liquids on yourself or your little sister.
- Don't try to "genetically improve" God's creatures. There's no need for a bigger cobra, a smarter shark, or a meaner cricket.
- Don't hire any deformed assistants: they tend to project a bad image on your work.
- If the police suddenly burst into your lab, be friendly and show them what you're doing. If you don't, the next thing you know the whole town is gathering their flaming torches to burn your place to the ground.
- Use stainless-steel cages with big chains and locks: you have no idea what a headache having a vicious creature on the loose is, especially if it's loose just because you neglected to keep it in an escape-proof cell.
- Don't protect your creation from an angry crowd: no matter how hard you try, they won't listen to you. And if they actually do, then they'll kill you along with your creation.

Behavior: These robots want to stop the aging process, even if they know it's not possible: replicants are not reprogrammable, and once they begin deteriorating, they keep going. Replicants hate to live in fear, and once they know about their destiny, they get angrier. As icing on the cake, the police have a special corps called blade runners whose mission is to track down the replicants and then shoot to kill. What usually happens it that the replicants shoot to kill after tracking down any blade runner. So they call it even.

Danger: You only need to fear the replicants if you work for the Tyrell Corporation or if you're a blade runner. You should, of course, duck if you're in the line of fire among these targets, but that's just common sense.

How to Kill Them: Keep in mind that the replicants have a life span of only four years. Hook them on *General Hospital* or *Days of Our Lives*. Time will fly, and they'll die without having any answers, and without knowing who the Mysterious Stranger introduced in Episode #2544 was.

What to Do if You Meet Them: Never say, "You know what? You may hate me today, but five years from now we'll look back at this and laugh—no, wait a second! *I'll* laugh. *You'll* be gone! Ha-ha-ha . . ."

Current Status: Shut off.

Body Count: 25 people, 1 replicant, 2 fingers.

Terminator T-101

Cyberdine Systems 800 Series

Classification: machines / cyborgs / *Terminus onetrackmindum*

Footage:

1984, *The Terminator* by James Cameron
1991, *Terminator 2: Judgment Day* by James Cameron

The Skinny: Assassin from the future goes into the past to kill the mother of the future leader of the . . . we're sorry, where were we?

Quotable: "I'll be back."

Created: In the 2020s

Stomping Grounds: Los Angeles; Mexico.

Origin: In the year 2029 A.D.—bear with us here—machines were trying to wipe out the human race. In order to eliminate the humans' brave leader John Connor, they sent a terminator back through time to kill his mother, thus preventing him from ever being born. Still with us? On May 12, 1984, a humongous naked terminator with an Austrian accent materialized at the Griffith Observatory in Los Angeles. After two hectic days, it was destroyed. Later, in 1995, a seemingly identical terminator materialized at basically the same place. This time he was sent by Connor to protect himself. Lost yet? Just you wait . . .

Identification: The T-101 (*Cyberdyne Systems 800 Series Terminator, Model T-101*—just in case you want to order it from Sharper Image) looks like an angry professional bodybuilder. But it is in fact a cybernetic infiltration unit: part man and part machine. A state-of-the-art microprocessor functions as its brain; its hyperalloy combat chassis is covered with living tissue, giving the perfect illusion of a human being. The T-101 likes sunglasses, biker jackets, motorcycles, and big guns. Much like your average red-blooded American male.

Cravings: The termination of its targets and the survival of its targets' future children. Still confused?

Behavior: The T-101 is rather single-minded and determined in its purpose: to terminate (and it'll run for 120 years on its battery). It likes staying in shabby motels and does uncanny impersonations. It also has an aptitude for hot-wiring cars and fixing itself. But its talents are matched with a subpar personality. The T-101 has no sense of humor, sweats, and has bad breath.

Danger: Extremely high. Besides its enormous brute strength and lightning-quick movements, its CPU has deadly-accurate targeting. And the T-101 doesn't wait for you to step aside: if you don't . . . well, just make sure to let us know your preferred method of burial.

How to Destroy It: The T-101 is fully armored. So perhaps the best idea is to sink it into a pit of molten steel. But then, just how do you locate the closest pit of molten steel? Or else try lodging explosives inside its endoskeleton, then detonating them. Or just smash it in a heavy-duty hydraulic press. Again—*if* you can find one.

What to Do if You Meet It: Best to just run. If you get the opportunity to throw the switch in its head which allows it to change from "read-only" to a "learning" memory, try to teach it some manners, like not to kill people at the drop of a hat. But whatever you do, do *not* make fun of its foreign accent. Again—*no* sense of humor.

Current Status: Supposedly destroyed forever. But trust us, *he'll be back . . .*

Body Count: 27 people, 10 police cars, 1 police station, and 1 toy truck.

Biologically Engineered

Oh, yeah: "oooh, aaah!" That's how it all starts. But then later there's running, and then screaming . . .

Ian Malcolm in *The Lost World: Jurassic Park*

In God's Name, Why?!!

There's always a mad scientist who's convinced he has the answer for a better future, usually contained in a small vial. And boy, is this dude wrong!

- **Defensive System:** Through the years, scientists have developed different organic security systems: new breeds of piranhas, guard dogs (*Man's Best Friend*), ultimate predators (*Leviathan, Watchers*), new parasites and so much more. They usually end up being more obnoxious than a car alarm and doing quite the opposite of protecting us.
- **Growth Serum:** "I'd like that creature supersized, please . . ." (*Bats, Deep Blue Sea, Konga, Night of the Lepus, Tarantula*).
- **I Can Make You Better:** Or worse, as the case may be.
- **No More Guinea Pigs:** So the scientists start experimenting themselves—this is when they cross the border from sanity. And never come back.

As a rule, creatures are created in labs, and subsequently get out of their cages, trash the building where the lab is, later on trash the town, and possibly the continent, if not the world.

Identification

They're anything but "kind of cute." (Consider this list a sort of "work-in-progress": genetic labs are going full tilt as we write . . .)

UPGRADES

Or improvements, self-improvements, downgrades . . . you get the idea.

• **"Aquatica" Mako Sharks:** (see entry)

• ***Bats:*** Larger, stronger, smarter, and now omnivorous . . . preferring, of course, human flesh. Spreading the government-created virus to other bats throughout the southwestern United States and feasting on small towns. **Best Defense:** Freeze them, then blow them to smithereens.

• **David Blake** (*SSSSSSS*): Let's say that your usually screwed-minded scientist holds that reptiles will inherit the earth, therefore humanity will have to evolve into a snakelike form in order to survive. Gee, why didn't we think of that? Formerly a man, David Blake is now a cold-blooded, venomous king cobra with blue eyes courtesy of a series of snake serum injections. **Best Defense:** Release a mongoose.

• **Blue Ribbon Teens** (*Disturbing Behavior*): Students are turned from brats into straight-A students. If the Blue Ribbon kids are sexually aroused, they all become psychos—usually killing the partner. It's safe sex for them, not for you.

• ***Colossus of New York:*** Large humanoid robot with glowing eyes, sporting the "toga party" look. Special talents: telepathy, mind control, extra strength, and walking underwater.

• **Jan Compton** (*The Brain That Wouldn't Die*): If you happen to have the brain of someone you know and you don't want it to go bad, keep it alive. Jan is a beautiful woman's head without a body, yet with the extra added gifts of telepathy and mind control. All she really wants is to die, so anyone willing to take on this Kevorkian responsibility is more than welcome.

• ***Dead Kids:*** Similar to the Blue Ribbons, but more openly "different." Teenage kids get changed by a drug given to them by a scientist. They become murderous, and addicted to the drug.

• **Jack Griffin:** "Señor Invisiblio." (see entry)

• **Mr. Hyde** (*Dr. Jekyll and Mr. Hyde*): Good-hearted scientist by day, raving maniac by night. Violence is Mr. Hyde's trademark.

• ***The Killer Shrews:*** Just shrews, but *killer*, dude. They have a very fast metabolism: they must consume up to four times their body weight each day to survive—and they weigh 150 pounds. Once they've finished all the food (i.e., people), they will turn on one another, destroying themselves.

• ***Konga:*** Starts off as a normal-sized chimpanzee, and turns into a giant . . . gorilla. Don't ask. Konga remains under hypnotic control, and obeys his master . . . who happens to be evil. **Best Defense:** A big drop will kill almost any creature. At least it'll kill *Konga.*

- **Man-spider-scorpion** (*Leprechaun 4: In Space*): Pulling an extremely funny prank, an evil leprechaun mixed up a batch of special DNA in a blender (that of a superhuman race, a spider and a scorpion) and then injected it into a man. Reddish and multilegged, it wandered the corridors of a spaceship.

- **Max** (*Man's Best Friend*): A black mutt, apparently very sweet. But only apparently. This strong and vicious, "designer genes" canine has qualities of cheetahs, rhinoceroses, chameleons, etc. A complete box of animal crackers.

- **Piranhas:** Teethy little fishies. (see entry)

- **Rabbits:** (*Night of the Lepus*): Very large hopping-mad bunny rabbits. You can imagine the terror . . . wake up!

- **Dr. Hank Symen:** True environmental extremism. (see entry)

- **Jobe Smith:** Virtual blunderkind. (see entry)

- **Dr. Paul Steiner** (*The Projected Man*): Disfigured man with a half-burned face and an oversized eye. He kills with a gentle electrified caress, "autographing" each victim by imprinting his hand on his or her body. **Best Remedy:** An ingenious new device called a "laser."

- ***Tarantula:*** Extra strength with poison on the side. **Best Remedy:** Napalm. A little extreme, but leaves everything clean as a whistle. Including large populated areas.

MIXED BAG

A little of dis, a little of dat . . .

- ***Creature with the Atom Brain:*** Zombies with a chip in the brain, controlled by a state-of-the-art computer. The creature is sent by gangsters to "fix some problems."

- **Frankenstein's creature:** A medical mishmash. (see entry)

- ***Jack Frost:*** A serial killer is transformed into a lethal snowman.

- ***Leviathan:*** One tricky little fish. (see entry)

- **Outsiders:** (see entry)

- **Reanimated Corpses** (*Re-Animator*): Bizarre and grotesque creations with human body parts, assembled by Herbert West, a Miskatonic University student, better known as the *Re-Animator.* A reagent that brings tissue back to life is injected into dead bodies. The side effect is that the revitalized brains are deviated.

• ***The Relic:*** Transformed from ordinary man into a part scorpion, part lizard, part rhinoceros, four-legged monstrosity. The Relic decapitates people, chews a hole in their skulls, and savors their thalamus and pituitary glands. Which are a real treat—at least for the creature.

• ***Syngenor***, or Synthetic Genetic Organism (*Scared to Death, Syngenor*): Humanoid armored iguana with a needle-sharp tongue. A creature that lives in the Los Angeles sewer system and in the basement of the Norton Ciberdyne building. Constantly in need of spinal fluid—*human* spinal fluid, of course. In order to suck the spinal fluid out of a victim, the syngenor will French her to death.

FROM SCRATCH

• ***The Blob*** (1988): A red jellylike creature that eats and grows, courtesy of our "friends" at the Pentagon. (see entry in Aliens/Meteor-Related section.)

• **Dinosaurs:** Hungry old fossils. (see entry)

• **Eve** and **Sil** *(Species* series): Part sexy blond woman, part aggressive alien DNA; again, concocted by those wacky scientists working for the U.S. government. (see entry in Aliens/Doppelgängers section.)

• ***Forbidden World*** **creature:** A genetically engineered organism that can replicate the cell structure of anything it devours. It'd be extremely popular in the Stupid Human Tricks segment of *Letterman.* **Best Defense:** Feed it cancer. Replicate that, creature-thang!

• **Judas Breed Cockroaches:** Even more annoying than the normal kind. (see entry)

• ***The Lift:*** Elevator with red doors, controlled by an organic brain made in Japan. *Favorite Pastimes:* Strangling and doing bad things to human necks. Put yourself in the Lift's shoes (or whatever it has)—it has a lot of dangling cables, a car with razor-sharp doors, and the opportunity to make people fall down its shaft. What would you do? **Best Defense:** A little TNT.

• ***Parasite:*** Large green worms, almost blind and with several rows of teeth. The *Parasite* wants you for breakfast. And lunch, dinner . . . **Best Defense:** Make a serum. Take one *Parasite,* extract its life fluid, create a vaccine, and inject it into all of the other parasites. Tough job, and pretty boring, too. Or poke a hole in them while they're growing. In order to succeed, you have to puncture the stomach of the creature's host. Oh, well.

How to Kill Them

- **Bombs:** They *almost* never fail (*Leviathan, The Lift, Watchers*).

- **Cold:** For the bioengineered *Blob,* or with *Bud the C.H.U.D.* Actually, cold doesn't kill the creations: it just freezes them. Your job is to store them in a below-zero chamber and keep them under these conditions forever.

- **Fire:** And so we say good-bye to the *Brain That Wouldn't Die,* Frankenstein's monster (and wife), the Outsider and the *Relic.*

- **Electricity:** Excellent way to fry many of the creatures.

- **Poison:** By polluting the creatures' stomping grounds, you'll score big time.

- **Shut It Off:** Flip the switch and you'll get rid of *Colossus of New York,* the *Creature with the Atom Brain* and the *Lawnmower Man.*

- **Conventional Weapons:** They'll kill most biological creations, either animals (*Konga, Night of the Lepus*) or humans (*Dr. Jekyll and Mr. Hyde, The Projected Man*). Harder with invisible men, because you have to find them first.

What to Do if You Meet One

- **Be Polite:** Maybe you'll die anyway, but they will all remember you as "The Polite Guy Who Died."

- **Turn Your Lights On:** Gigantic rabbits are afraid of light. They'll run away from you. Unfortunately, almost every other creature will be attracted by the same light.

- **Water Them:** They can be melted or short-circuited.

- **Hope They'll Come Back to Their Senses:** Eventually, Dr. Steiner and Jack Griffin both realized: "I meddled in things that Man must leave alone." Well, duh!

"Aquatica" Mako Sharks

Classification: biogenetically engineered / *Superioribus cerebrum andfangs*

Footage:

1999, *Deep Blue Sea* by Renny Harlin

The Skinny: Search for Alzheimer's cure generates smart sharks.

Quotable: "Feedin' time."

Habitat: Aquatica Research floating lab, off the coast of California.

Origin: Here's the deal: sharks don't get sick. Ever. So why not enlarge their brains to obtain more protein to see if we can cure human brain cells? Hey, it works! The human cells are improved. But so are the sharks. You see, they get smarter. And normally it's not a good thing to have a 26-foot-long killing machine with 60-million teeth—which can *also* think.

Identification: There are three mako sharks (two first-generation and one second-generation female): big, long, bluish, and with a never-ending appetite.

Cravings: Reaching the deep blue sea. Oh, and also killing every human being who's swimming in or even venturing somewhat close to the water.

Behavior: The sharks know they're trapped: the Aquatica lab is entirely surrounded by titanium nets. But the sharks have learned that near the surface the nets are made with tender iron and—most important—the nets' end. So, what sharks really want to do is sink the lab so that the nets will go down with it. These sharks are extremely impressive: they can swim backward and at such a speed that they seem to be almost computer-generated; they conduct synchronized attacks and can be extremely pesky.

Danger: Smart sharks. Need more?

How to Kill Them: You can fill a room with gas and throw a lighter into it. Oh, this only works if the shark is trapped in the same room, otherwise this operation would frankly seem quite pointless. You can shove an electric cable inside the mouth of a shark, thus providing your family with fish sticks for the next six years. Or you can simply blow 'em up with dynamite.

What to Do if You Meet Them: They can probably figure out what you're about to do, so create a diversion: say something like, "Say, did you read the latest Stephen Hawking book?"

Current Status: Dead. But who's to say that none of the sharks were pregnant or something? Not to mention that there's still plenty of scientists . . .

Body Count: 7 people, 1 arm; 1 parrot, 1 tiger shark; ½ floating lab, 1 chopper, 1 25-foot boat, and at least 3 surveillance cameras.

Dinosaurs

Classification: biologically engineered / *CGI creaturibus*

Footage:

1993, *Jurassic Park* by Steven Spielberg
1997, *The Lost World: Jurassic Park* by Steven Spielberg

The Skinny: The dinosaurs are back, for real. And they bite. For real.

Quotable: "Mommy is very angry."

Habitat: Isla Nublar, Isla Sorna (both south of Costa Rica); later, San Diego.

Origin: John Hammond, the eccentric millionaire who created Ingen Bioengineering, decided to have his own amusement park; since he was old, he wanted something from his youth as a main attraction for the park: dinosaurs.

Appearance: The creatures in Jurassic Park are all full-sized, flesh 'n bone dinosaurs. There are dozens and dozens of species: triceratops, velociraptors, brontosaurus, gallimimis, Tyrannosaurus rex . . . name a prehistoric reptile, and you may find it in the park. Before it finds you, that is.

Cravings: Food of any kind and size; sometimes dinosaurs eat smaller dinosaurs, sometimes they decide to have a serving of humans (whenever they're around). They also look for water, because dinosaurs dehydrate easily.

Behavior: They tend to defend their territory from intruders, whether other dinosaurs, or people. When dinosaurs are after you, they charge and run over you. Their mouths can be pretty big and their teeth can be pretty sharp, and they know how to use them (even if they happen to be herbivorous). They also have a nurturing instinct: they protect and feed their infants.

How to Kill Them: You can shoot them, but it's not easy: they move fast and their skin is thick; ordinary bullets won't penetrate. You might want to use the venom of the *Conus purpurascent* (South Sea cone shell), which is the most powerful neurotoxin in the world, but again, it's not gonna be easy. The needle for injecting the poison is as big as a bus sign.

What to Do if You Meet Them: First of all, do not move or make a sound: a dinosaur can't see you if you're standing still. Assuming that you can stand still in front of a 30-foot tall Tyrannosaurus rex. Otherwise, use the "High Hide," a platform that, if attached to a car, can be lifted above the trees so that the dinosaurs won't see you. Except for the pterodactyls, of course.

Current Status: Alive and well, and waiting for another lucrative sequel.

Body Count: 26 people, the entire crew of the S.S. *Venture,* 1 dog, 1 goat, and 1 cow (1 kid is injured, several cars and 1 bus are flipped or crushed).

Frankenstein's Monster

Classification: biologically engineered / *Prometheus modernus*

Footage:

1910, *Frankenstein* by J. Searle Dawley
1931, *Frankenstein* by James Whale
1935, *Bride of Frankenstein* by James Whale
1943, *Frankenstein Meets the Wolf Man* by Roy W. Neill
1957, *Curse of Frankenstein* by Terence Fisher
1958, *Frankenstein 70* by Howard W. Kotch
1990, *Frankenstein Unbound* by Roger Corman
1994, *Mary Shelley's Frankenstein* by Kenneth Branagh
. . . and at least 30 other movies.

The Skinny: Patchwork revitalized human gets resentful, and goes after the family of its creator.

Quotable: "We belong dead!"

Stomping Grounds: Switzerland, the North Pole; just about anywhere Dr. Frankenstein goes, it will follow.

Origin: Henry Frankenstein, a scientist moved by humanitarian intent (as well as his own throbbing ego), decided to bring a dead man back to life—to show the world his amazing scientific acumen. The experiment was a success, thanks to the lightning which made his devices work. Unfortunately the creature didn't end up having all the requested requisites, and was a little slow on the uptake.

"The sun'll come out . . . tomorrow . . ."

S.S. Archives/Shooting Star

Identification: About seven feet tall, 400 pounds, scars all over its body, two electrodes on its neck (not always, but they're so hip!). It has a below-average brain, but can understand your commands. Sometimes it can also answer—even if big audiences prefer when it moans and roars. Anyways, it's a monster.

Cravings: To be human and to find love. Also, it's not a gourmet; usually it nibbles bread and water—occasionally a glass of wine.

Behavior: It walks in a menacing way, killing whoever is in its way, drowning lovable kids, and falling in love with singing girls. Once in a while it can break a heart or two. Love is blind, after all.

Danger: It's quite large, and can get quite angry at the slightest provocation. You figure it out.

How to Kill It: It hates fire and bright light. You could bring it to the Universal Studios *Backdraft* attraction. If this is too difficult, you can set fire to the place where it is (a lab, a mill, an airport).

What to Do if You Meet It: Well, since it is essentially a large, clumsy hodgepodge of formerly dead body parts with a grudge, if you meet up with it usually nothing good comes of the situation. Never call it "Frankenstein" or "Frankie" (this is the name of its creator, and the monster has "issues" with him); also avoid placing prank signs on its back like "Kick Me" because it's just not nice.

Current Status: Revived almost daily in rip-off plots. Burned and resurrected, burned and resurrected. Like a phoenix rising out of the . . . oh, never mind.

Body Count: Quite a few kills over the years, but killing isn't what it's all about. It's about the love, the compassion, the *humanity*, man . . .

Jack Griffin

Classification: biologically engineered / *Nowuseeis nowudontis*

Footage:
1933, *The Invisible Man* by James Whale

The Skinny: The very prototype of the mad scientist.

Quotable: "Excuse me, sir: there's breathing in my barn."

Habitat: The small village of Iding, England.

Origin: Dr. Griffin was Dr. Granley's assistant, but secretly every night for five years he performed a series of experiments on his own. Eventually, one of Dr. Griffin's tests succeeded and worked perfectly: Dr. Griffin became completely invisible.

Identification: He's an invisible man—how do you expect to see him? Well, if you don't see anything, but hear someone talking to you maniacally and see objects moving around on their own, you could deduce that he's there, we suppose.

Cravings: To dominate the world through a reign of terror. In his spare time, he's working toward an antidote to become visible again.

Behavior: Dr. Griffin wants privacy to conduct his tests, and to do so he covers his whole body with bandages, heavy clothes, sunglasses, and a hat. He claims to have suffered an accident which disfigured his face and damaged his eyes. Usually, he claims so as you're flying out the door—Dr. Griffin has quite a temper. Once discovered, he starts scaring everyone to and fro, which amuses him an awful lot. At this point he decides to conquer the world, but he needs a visible partner—you know, it's tough to go around town completely naked and conduct business. So his visible partner will do chores and take care of the shopping list, while Dr. Griffin enjoys the fireplace and the cozy atmosphere of your living room.

Danger: Dr. Griffin's experiments involved the use of monocane, a powerful Indian flower bleaching drug that would whiten bones and drive those addicted to it completely mad. So, as if one defect weren't enough, you have to deal with a man who's invisible *and* crazy.

How to Kill Him: He's a human being, he has no special powers. Besides being invisible, of course. Wait for the snow to fall, and look for footprints. Since he's naked, if Dr. Griffin decides to make a snow angel, he'll freeze his butt. And you'll hear high-pitched screams coming from the yard.

What to Do if You Meet Him: You'll probably never know, unless you bump into him. He's mad, but you can see right through him, so to speak. But if you meet a thoroughly bandaged man who screams, "All right, you fools!" just vacate the area ASAP.

Current Status: Very, very dead (thus regaining his visibility). But there's always some idiot ready to take his place.

Body Count: 122 people, 1 train, 1 window, 1 clock, and several glasses.

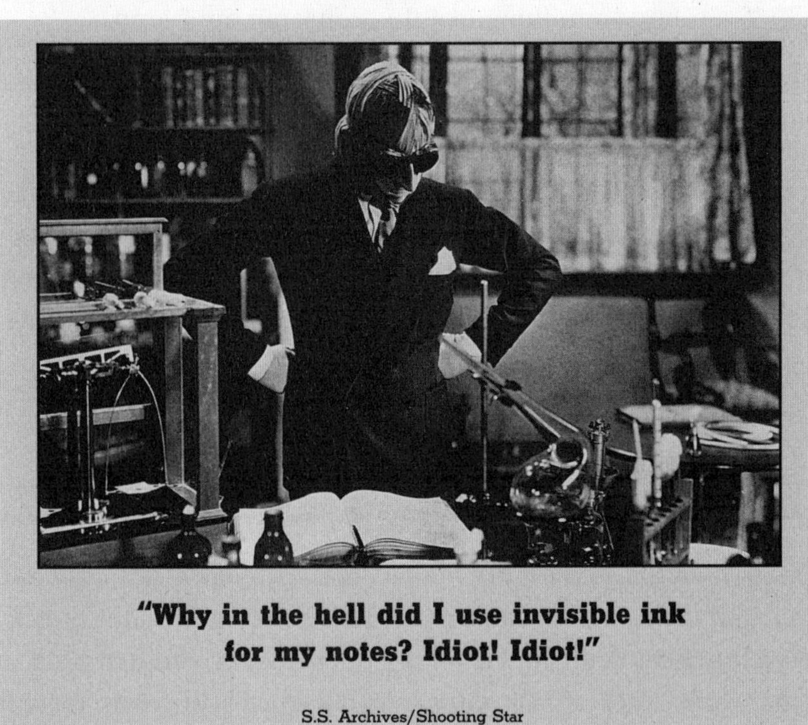

"Why in the hell did I use invisible ink for my notes? Idiot! Idiot!"

S.S. Archives/Shooting Star

Judas Breed Cockroaches

Classification: biologically engineered / *Richlittles prettygoodibus*

Footage:

1997, *Mimic* by Guillermo Del Toro

The Skinny: Big bugs are taking over, and they're not made by Volkswagen.

Quotable: "They were designed to die. They are breeding."

Habitat: Manhattan subway stations and what's below. Occasionally, what's above.

Origin: In 1994, a lethal epidemic of Strickler's disease was erasing an entire generation of children. The carrier was a common cockroach. To eliminate the problem, a new species of bug was created, using termites and mantis DNA, and probably a pinch of cinnamon. Anyway, this new species was supposed to catch the carriers, kill them, then die within 180 days. We should have known better.

Identification: This particular bug looks like a very large mosquito: about six feet tall; four wings; long, dark brownish-gray body; razor-sharp claws; and a shield in front of its head resembling a human face. Once the wings are folded around the body and the bug stands erect, it resembles a man—if you ignore the fact that it chatters, hisses, and produces a rustling, clicking noise. Their pods are orange, oval, and about four feet long. So if you find something like this, amscray my friend.

Cravings: Looks like they want to breed, reproduce, and eventually take over. Then *they'll* have to solve all of the world's problems.

Behavior: The Judas bugs can jump and fly as well as walk erect and produce their clicking noise, which can be reproduced using two tablespoons. If you try this, the bugs will try to communicate with you. Even if you're not very fluent in their language, they'll probably let you live because they think you're really funny. They secrete a very strong ammonia smell, and just for fun they eat their prey alive. Usually they attack if you enter their territory. Actually, they've entered ours, but they're rather tough to reason with.

Danger: The smell of blood drives them crazy.

How to Kill Them: All of the soldiers are female, and the colony has only one fertile male. You kill him, and they won't be able to reproduce anymore. But they'll get so ticked off—you have no idea. You can use a load of ammo, or you can fill a room with gas and blow the whole place up. Or you can run a train over them. How to find a train just when you need it is another story.

What to Do if You Meet Them: If you're lucky and you kill one of them, grab its gland and rub it all over your body: insects will smell you and think you're one of them. But don't sweat! Not only will it wash away your *eau de bug*, they'll sense the chemical change. Also, try saying something like, "Hey! Have you seen *A Bug's Life*? I just *loved* it!" Maybe they'll think you're hip, and leave you alone.

Current Status: Gone.

Body Count: 5 people and 1 dog. And it seems that the bugs used all the rats in the Manhattan subway system as munchies. It also seems that all of the homeless in the area have been mysteriously wiped away . . . boy, those people just can't catch a break, can they?

Kothoga

Classification: biologically engineered / *Lookmommas whativebecomibus*

Footage:

1996, *The Relic* by Peter Hyams

The Skinny: Head-eating mutation hits the Windy City.

Quotable: "Pot is a misdemeanor. Decapitation seems a bit severe."

Habitat: Brazil, the Natural History Museum in Chicago.

Origin: The South American tribe Zenzera needed a creature to vanquish their enemies. After many prayers to Satan and a couple of *National Geographic Explorer* episodes, they found a parasitic fungus loaded with animal hormones which was flourishing on a plant. The tribe also discovered that if this plant's leaves were used to feed an animal, the animal would turn into a savage beast, hungry for the same animal hormones that are produced by the human hypothalamus. If you're quick enough, you can easily imagine the next step. If you're not quick enough, we'll tell you: the tribe stopped feeding the leaves to the beast, and sicced it on their enemies. And the beast (a.k.a. Kothoga) took care of the rest.

Identification: Kothoga is different every time, because it is an animal whose DNA has been spun around by the fungus's hormones. Anyway, since these hormones are 45 percent reptilian (*Hemidactylus turcicus,* or Turkish gecko), you can bet Kothoga will most likely be a four-legged, one-tailed, one-awfully-long-tongued, 12-foot-long creature.

Cravings: Hormones produced by either the fungus or the hypothalamus. If the creature eats the leaves, that should be good enough to keep it at bay. If not, it's hard to keep your head on your shoulders.

Behavior: Kothoga usually hides in the shadows of subterranean tunnels, waiting to find fresh food. It can swim, run, walk on walls, and even open doors or destroy electrical equipment—especially if part of Kothoga's genes are human. It wheezes when it breathes, but despite its size it's quite silent.

Danger: If Kothoga's on the loose in a large building, it can hide just about anywhere, waiting for you to pass close by. So pay close attention.

How to Kill It: Being part reptile, Kothoga isn't able to handle extremes of hot and cold. Therefore you can freeze it to death or burn it with the same effectiveness. The fire will take a little longer, because Kothoga has very thick skin. But eventually it'll croak.

What to Do if You Meet It: Sing "If I Only Had a Brain." Kothoga will probably go away and not waste its time with you.

Current Status: Dead. Gone. Burned. Kaput. Perhaps.

Body Count: 13 people, 1 dog, 1 office, 1 backup generator.

Leviathan

Classification: biologically engineered / *Apiecefromheribus apiecefromtheribus*

Footage:

1989, *Leviathan* by George Pan Cosmatos

The Skinny: A genetic alteration experiment becomes a genetic aberration killing beast.

Quotable: "*Natura non confundenda est.* Loosely translated . . . don't f*#@ with Mother Nature."

Turf: The ship *Leviathan*; TRI Oceanic Mining Shack #7; the deep blue sea.

How They Discovered It: Created by the Russians as a biogenetic weapon, masked as a "tropical infection." Once the captain of the ship *Leviathan* realized the genetic alteration they produced was, a terrible mistake, he agreed to have the boat torpedoed and sunk. This first alteration died not because of the sinking, but because it ran out of food.

Cut to: The bottom of the Atlantic Ocean, 16,000 feet down, a mining base. Two days before the crew is scheduled to come back home, they have a rotten stroke of luck: a diver happens upon the *Leviathan*, where he is infected by the microorganism. The microorganism sucks the poor sap in and transforms him into a vile creature.

Identification: The creature has many deep-sea marine life features: scales, gills, the ability to regenerate, even a period of dormancy. But its creators pushed the envelope a little too far in order to create the *Homo aquaticus*, a super-strong man who could work underwater without a suit, would be resistant to cold and pressure, and would have the astounding ability to sit through a marathon session of the TV show *The Nanny*.

The first time you see it, the Leviathan is a combination of two bodies (the diver it killed and a woman who killed herself); subsequently, it becomes a sort of two-foot-long snail with hundreds of small teeth and a very poor sense of humor. After a subsequent metamorphosis, it becomes a gigantic brown fishlike biped with fangs, tentacles, and an even poorer sense of humor. It also has arms with claws which are a beauty.

Cravings: Apparently, its only *raison d'être* is the destruction of every human being and the subsequent absorbing of their essence. Basically, it just needs a little blood . . .

Behavior: Leviathan keeps expanding its body, and probably its intelligence, too. Extremely aggressive (not exactly the main goal of the Russian scientists) once it becomes a self-working unit, which means in about eight hours, it does exciting tours of submarine bases, trying to develop its structure and to become humongous. We're quite sure it saw *Alien* at least a couple of times, because its ambushes are very similar. Just don't tell it, otherwise it'll get even angrier. It hisses, snarls, growls, and screams. It waits for you in the darkness. If you don't show up, it'll come and get you.

Danger: If you touch it, you're screwed. If it touches you, you're screwed.

How to Kill It: *Boom!* With any kind of bomb you can find on your ship, or in any drugstore close to your house. Just place the bomb under its tongue. How to reach

Leviathan's tongue is another story, but here's a clue: you can find its mouth just by following the bad breath. Also, don't think you can chop it up into little bits: subdividing the beast will just create new Leviathans you'll have to deal with later on.

What to Do if You Meet It: Hope that it won't see you. If it sees you, hope that it doesn't touch you. If it touches you, don't come and visit us, please.

Current Status: Blown to bits. But the *Leviathan* ship (and its precious cargo) still rests on the bottom of the ocean.

Body Count: 5 people, 1 metal door, 1 diver suit; the entire crew of the *Leviathan;* and 1 woman committed suicide because she couldn't stand the pressure.

The Outsiders

Classification: biologically engineered / *Notthebratpack believeus*

Footage:

1986, *Watchers* by Jon Hess
1990, *Watchers II* by Thierry Notz
1994, *Watchers 3* by Jeremy Stanford
1998, *Watchers Reborn* by John Carl Buelcher

The Skinny: Dog-hating experiments-gone-wrong wreak havoc.

Quotable: "No, of course not. That's absurd. We didn't create a . . . uh . . . uh . . . uh . . . killing machine. Why do you ask?"

Habitat: Scientific labs, houses (in Canada and in Los Angeles), caves in the Matagalpan Jungle in Central America.

Origin: Four different army experiments at the Banodyne Laboratories had the same goal: producing the best "search and destroy" team. The experiments also had the same result: they produced the perfect infiltration unit—a golden retriever with an almost human brain—but they also gave life to the ultimate predator, named "The Outsider," highly dangerous and telepathically connected with the dog. During all of the experiments, both the dog and the predator had the chance to escape from the lab. Let's get ready to rumble!

Identification: There have been four different Outsiders ("a nonhuman combat element"): they all have a humanoid shape, strong claws, sharp eyes with night vision, and a microchip implant so their movements can be traced. On the other hand, while the first Outsider is a sort of large orangutan, the second one looks like a monkey that has been sucked by a vacuum cleaner, the third one reminds us of a large lizard with a flat head like General Noriega, and the fourth one is Bigfoot-like with a devilish face ("They made them ugly to scare the hell out of the enemy."). They all growl, scream, and roar. Like General Noriega. And they all act schizophrenic. Like . . . well, never mind.

Cravings: Killing the dog, and everyone who's been in touch with the animal. Ripping the eyes out of anyone who stares at them. And smashing all the mirrors that dare to reflect the Outsider's image.

Behavior: The Outsider hates the dog mainly because it's jealous. So the Outsider follows the canine's trail with the sole purpose of eliminating it. If, during this chase, people either pet the dog or try to stop the Outsider, the creature won't hesitate to eradicate them from life, too. The Outsider has enhanced night vision, and it follows the heat that a body releases. After killing a person, it drags the body around to cover its tracks. Smart boy. Besides its immense strength, the Outsider can stay underwater for several minutes before sneaking up on you, yelling, "Tag! You're it!" and dashing away. It knows how to shut off the electricity in a house and how to sneak inside a place unnoticed. We once spotted one of the Outsiders enjoying a cold beer with a bunch of bums. Perhaps later on it attended OA meetings.

Danger: If you're housing the dog, chances are that the Outsider will drop in for a family reunion.

How to Kill It: Despite its belligerence and strength, the Outsider is pretty vulnerable: its body is soft, so arrows, knives, or bullets easily penetrate it. Explosives and fire are adequate as well.

What to Do if You Meet It: Hide all the mirrors in the house and cover your eyes. And don't adopt a golden retriever. It may come with more than fleas.

Current Status: All four Outsiders have each been eliminated, but it seems that people in the lab are still working on the project "and this time it'll be right." Oh sure.

Body Count: 41 people, 1 base of Cuban rebels (about 12 people), 2 chimpanzees, and 2 mirrors.

Piranhas

Classification: biologically engineered / *Theygottum fourthousandteethonus*

Footage:

1978, *Piranha* by Joe Dante
1981, *Piranha Part Two: The Spawning* by James Cameron
1995, *Piranha* by Scott Levy

The Skinny: Voracious fish get an attitude, then take to the skies.

Quotable: "People eat fish. Fish don't eat people."

Habitat: A lab pool; a river near the lab; a sea near the river near the lab. Eventually, the exclusive Club Elysium on a secluded island.

Origin: During the Vietnam War, Dr. Robert Hoak locked himself in his lab and didn't come out until he created a new species of piranha, more aggressive and implacable, and able to live in both salt and fresh water. The doctor succeeded, even if by that time the war was over. They tried to poison the fish, but a few of them survived the poison, proceeded to feed off of the bodies of the dead fish, and started to breed. And, contained in an isolated pool on top of the hill, they bred like flies. Two unwitting detectives emptied the pool, and all the fish went into a small river. In a nutshell: big trouble for river swimmers.

A few years later, the same lab did it again and created piranhas with an interesting option: two wings and the ability to breathe out of water and live in any environment. Just to heap on the fun, a ship with four canisters of fertile piranha eggs sank in front of an island paradise. In a nutshell: big trouble in island paradise.

Identification: The piranhas are all teeth and all appetite. They arrive, "Hello, good-bye," and you're picked clean. The upgraded piranhas are about a foot long and have a pair of translucent wings allowing them to fly.

Cravings: Eating any moving thing that enters the water, whether they're hungry or not. Actually, anything *near* the water, once they can swarm from the sea to the land.

Behavior: Piranhas travel in schools, move very fast, and are instantly attracted by any kind of splashing noise. Or stomping noise. Well, anywhere there is a noise, you'll find a few of these piranhas. What's worse is that these fish are hungry 24 hours a day, seven days a week, and they never get full. And once they open their mouths . . . so long. They reach you, then they eat you. If they fly, they seem to aim for the jugular.

Danger: Every now and then the rivers run out of prey, so the piranhas have to migrate to look for future meals. And as they find meat, they don't let it get away very easily.

Furthermore, they can stay out of the water for a long time, making them *extremely* pesky.

How to Kill Them: With poison. Buy several barrels of poison and pour it into the infested water. There's a risk of polluting the whole area, but who cares? All right, if you really care, here's another way: you wanna attract all the fish inside an underwater cave or a wrecked ship—one that you've already filled with explosives. The dynamite's *kaboom!* should free the area of piranhas. Now for the fun part: how do you attract all the piranhas into this one place? That's right: *you* will have to be the bait.

Current Status: Maybe they've been wiped out. But maybe not.

Body Count: Immense. At least 44 people, 1 dog, and 1 flipper.

Jobe Smith

Classification: biologically engineered/ *Frankensteinus virtualitiexpialidocius*

Footage:

1992, *The Lawnmower Man* by Brett Leonard
1995, *Lawnmower Man 2: Jobe's War* by Farhad Mann

The Skinny: Mentally challenged lawnmower man turns into a genius and goes shopping on-line.

Quotable: "I will set you free. Cyberspace is a new Eden."

Habitat: A shed, a lab, cyberspace, and a futuristic Los Angeles.

Origin: Dr. Lawrence Angelino was conducting experiments on chimpanzees, trying to turn them into soldiers. Unfortunately, the animals began to kill people. The scientist dropped the chimp routine and moved on to humans. He picked his mentally retarded lawnmover man, Jobe Smith, as the new guinea pig. Jobe's brain was modified by many injections of nootropic drugs and a sequence of strobe images.

Identification: Jobe is a tall man with blond hair and blue eyes. He has the simple mind of a five-year-old child and a pure soul. After the scientist upgraded him, his look remained basically the same, but his eyes changed and showed an uncommon willpower and an even less common rage. After the explosion of the Virtual Space Industries lab, Jobe was surgically reconstructed. Now he's a bald amputee in a wheelchair. But in cyberspace he's as good as new.

Cravings: It all started with Jobe's desire to play video games. He got good at the games and eventually wanted to become smarter. Now he wants to learn everything and eventually download himself into the net to rule cyberspace from "the other side." Much like Bill Gates.

Behavior: Jobe always had a talent for building things; his inseparable friend is Big Red, a souped-up lawn mower he assembled piece by piece. Once he got smart, he started to build his own internal database by learning everything. But Jobe has gone way beyond normal learning: he has learned how to move objects, read your mind, and even *enter* your mind to drive you crazy. He also became PC compatible.

Danger: If you log on to the net, you'll log on to Jobe, too. And for only $19.95 a month he'll destroy your life. And everyone else's.

How to Kill Him: Send him a virus he can't easily outsmart, and at the same time blow up the computer he's in. If you're fast enough, you may succeed. Because he's in a virtual world, he's lost his real-world powers. But he's learning how to bypass this problem.

What to Do if You Meet Him: Don't upset the guy. He may mow your lawn while you're lying on it. On the other hand, upset him. He might erase himself from cyberspace. Pray that he's using the infamous Chyron chip: Jobe doesn't know that the chip has the capacity to destroy whoever uses it from inside a computer should this person get really angry. Yeah, we know it doesn't make any sense . . . go figure.

SIGNS YOUR TEACHER IS A MAD SCIENTIST

- Instead of dissecting a frog, your teacher insists you bring it back to life using a couple of electrodes and a dusty old device called "The Thingy."
- The short janitor seems to be concealing a hunch.
- Your teacher insists on students bringing in a brain to keep "for rainy days."
- Some of your classmates begin to disappear. Your teacher says "they're being educated now by their families," but won't let you go inside the storeroom.
- The new student, Frank N. Stein, looks suspiciously like six of your missing classmates.
- Your teacher mumbles something dangerously close to "Fools! I'll destroy them all!"
- When alone, your teacher spontaneously explodes into maniacal laughter.

Current Status: Alive and well, in a wheelchair, probably (only probably) back to his five-year-old mind-set.

Body Count: 9 people; 1 plane filled with passengers; 3 people are killed by someone controlled by Jobe; and 2 people are left in a permanent state of shock.

Dr. Hank Symen

Classification: biologically engineered / *Greenthumbius exxageratus*

Footage:

1997, *Habitat* by Renee Daalder

The Skinny: Your average mad scientist moves up a notch and turns into a never-before-seen creature . . . and lab.

Quotable: "I'm the edge, the sneeze, the virus, and the worm, the single thread in the fabric of life! I swim with the plankton and frolic with the sperm, to see the world in a grain of sand and heaven in a white flower."

Habitat: Yes, that's the name of the movie.

Origin: After the destruction of the ozone layer, humanity needed to live sheltered from the sun. A doctor and his family fled to the peaceful Pleasanton. Here, the doctor, during an experiment, went overboard and became the experiment: he hit a pipe, which flooded the lab, which caused a short circuit, which wiped everything off the tables, which caused a genetic reaction, which turned the doctor into a swarm of flying luminescent insects, which runs us clean out of *whiches*.

Identification: Dr. Symen was an ordinary man, and now he's a swarm *and* a house, that keeps evolving, expanding, growing. The house is filled with plants, trees, oozing vines, and bugs. Lots of bugs.

Cravings: Dr. Symen decided that the only way to survive the world was jumping ahead 2 million years with an accelerated evolution. On a much smaller scale, the scientist wants his son to live a simple life, "freely roaming the earth" without risking sunburn. Other than that, Dr. Symen hates when you try to stop him or tell him he's crazy.

Behavior: Once Dr. Symen has become a house, he keeps roaming in and out, enjoying his new self, thanks to which he can explore everything and be anywhere. His new swarm status can heal burned skin as well as suffocate a person and turn him or her into part of the environment. The entire house is a sort of new Garden of Eden (with no snakes, only a lot of bugs), and with an underground pond that can suck you to the earth's core, give or take a few inches.

Dr. Symen genetically perfected his son before his birth so he's the only person who can stay in bright sunlight without any problem, but the doctor hasn't stopped helping other people, swarming around and curing them. It's less attractive than SPF 15, but at least Dr. Symen doesn't smell or leave your body all slippery and gooey.

Danger: Have you ever had an eccentric neighbor? Well, here we're talking about an eccentric house: one that can strip you naked, pour bugs all over you, or suck your body into grass in a few seconds.

How to Kill Him: You can't. You can attract the bug part of his body into a gigantic zapper, but Dr. Symen will always be free and alive and happy. And now that his wife, Clarissa, has joined him in the swarm luminescent status thingy, he's happier and freer and merrier. But his son is pissed, because he knows he'll have to baby-sit a bunch of larvae.

What to Do if You Meet Him: Don't step into his house, or you'll become part of it. Don't upset him, or you'll be changed by the swarm effect and eventually become part of the surroundings.

Current Status: Free and flown away with his wife, exploring the world and annoying people who stay on their patios at night.

Body Count: 5 people are absorbed by the house; and 1 is knocked unconscious by a man, *then* absorbed by the house.

Mutants

Why don't you just think of yourself as lunch?

Charles Brady in *Sleepwalkers*

People change. You think you know someone, but then they pull something that completely betrays your trust in them . . . like growing an extra limb or reading your mind.

But people aren't the only the only ones who change. Animals do, too. In fact, anything changes when it gets dunked in a pool of glowing ooze. But exactly how it will change is anybody's guess. "Variety is the spice of life," as they say . . .

Humans

Origins

- **Experiments:** Not everything goes as planned. And what's worse, the result keeps evolving in different stages.
- **Untested Drugs:** They've been given to pregnant women with catastrophic results (*Scanners*).
- **Passion:** If a patient is undergoing special therapy, the hate she generates can produce a temporary lethal offspring (*The Brood*).
- **Who the Hell Knows?:** Sometimes variations on "human" seemingly pop up out of nowhere.

Habitat

Mutant humans live where normal humans do, trying to lead ordinary lives. Unfortunately they have this remarkable expertise in screwing things up, so they have to move before the whole town hits the street carrying flaming torches. So they are in constant movement, all across the planet, looking for some quiet and some food. They're kind of cursed, because when they find the quiet they can't find the food, and vice versa.

Typical Behavior

- **Aggressiveness:** True for the babies from *It's Alive,* as well as the *C.H.U.D.*s and *The Brood.*

- **Human Flesh:** They spend we don't know how many years mutating, and still this is all they can come up with. How unoriginal (*C.H.U.D., It's Alive, Octaman*).

Identification

NORMAL LOOKING / TRANSFORMERS

Many mutant humans have two stages in their existence: stage A, in which they look exactly like you and me; and stage B, in which they look like . . .

- ***Bat People:*** If a human being is bitten by an animal, he or she may start to resemble the biter. **Best Defense:** Fire fries the *Bat People.*

- ***Cat People:*** From beautiful people to beautiful black panthers. **Best Defense:** The mutation will take care of its host, who becomes a member of "the other species" forever.

- **Mary and Charles Brady** (*Sleepwalkers*): Humanoid kitties, with pointy teeth and button noses. They can also turn into a sort of giant skinned cat with black eyes. They survive thanks to the life force of teenage virgins. Why they have to be teenage and virginal, we don't know.

- **Patrick Ross** (*Species II*): An astronaut with an insatiable sexual appetite. A handsome guy, a real studmuffin—if you ignore the tentacles that come out of his back when he's making whoopee. He has sex with one woman, and after two minutes she gives birth to a fully grown child—and of course, she dies in terrible pain. And he has sex again, and again . . . until he has a platoon of children who are as lethal as their daddy. **Best Defense:** Give him a virus.

- ***Scanners:*** "This is your brain on crack." (see entry)

- **Members of *Society:*** Human beings with the skill of shifting portions of their body, or generating new parts (an extra arm, for instance). Not a pretty sight. **Best Defense:** You can kill them, but it's pointless. There are too many, and they've already spread across the globe.

TRANSFORMED FOR GOOD

- ***The Brood:*** Pale, mute children with dark eyes, blondish hair, rabbit lips, and (you need an autopsy to ascertain this one) almost no lungs. All wearing heavy hooded jackets and mittens. They are telekinetically connected with their so-called mom, and kill whomever she hates. **Best Defense:** A bullet to the head.

• ***C.H.U.D.:*** Black humanoids, slimy, claw-handed, and with glowing eyes. **Best Defense:** Behead them. Use a sword. Knives won't do it with the *C.H.U.D.*s. Or else freeze them. Or both.

• **"Its":** Teething never hurt so bad. (see entry)

• **The Fly:** If at first you don't succeed, keep bumbling *ad infinitum.* (see entry)

• **Octaman:** You're not gonna believe this one . . . (see entry)

How to Kill Them

• **Animals:** *Similis similia solvuntur* (more or less, "identical things stick together"): if you're lucky, a 100 percent animal will take care of our 50-50 human, like the *Cat People* or the *Sleepwalkers.*

• **Have Another Member of the Species Fight It:** It's the best thing to do. They instinctively hit the nerve of your opponent. And you'll have a lot of time to devise a backup plan.

"Its"

Classification: mutants / humans / *Nevermindus teletubbies*

Footage:

1974, *It's Alive* by Larry Cohen
1978, *It Lives Again / It's Alive 2: It Lives Again* by Larry Cohen
1987, *It's Alive III: Island of the Alive* by Larry Cohen

The Skinny: Teethy brats are less than cuddly.

Quotable: "Oh, sh*&! It's one of them!"

Habitat: Los Angeles, Seattle, Tucson, Los Angeles, coming soon San Francisco . . . and a deserted island somewhere in the Pacific Ocean.

Origin: There's extensive chemical pollution all across the country, and this is absolutely no good. In this case it's even worse: Frank Davis and his wife, Lenore, are in the hospital for the birth of their new bouncing baby boy. The baby boy pops out of his mom and bounces on all the doctors, biting them on their necks.

Identification: Unusually large babies (they all look alike, male or female), with a titanic head, dark eyes, and a mouth jam-packed with razor-sharp teeth. Both hands and feet have three fingers and extremely long gray nails. They also have no hair whatsoever, neither when they're bouncing babies nor when they're grown up. They save big, not needing shaving equipment.

Cravings: Being loved by their real parents, whom the "its" will try to reach no matter what. They love raw meat, either human or animal.

Behavior: The babies are aggressive the moment they step into our world, and they already have the mental capacity of a 21-month-old. Their instinct is way above average, and they grow more alert every day. They snarl, roar, shriek . . . and coo. The "its" know that they can intimidate you with their sounds. They're very strong, they run fast, they swim, they climb trees, but they don't wear any diapers. They have a very strong homing instinct, and if separated, they'll do their best to come back to their real parents—shuffling through the sewers, over mountains, and through valleys . . . they're regular little Lewis and Clarks. The "its" don't hesitate to kill anyone who places themselves in their path. Not to mention that they get really mad if caged or restrained on a desert island. But they're not in a hurry: they'll get their revenge. And in the meantime, in only five years, they start to reproduce.

Danger: They aim for your jugular, which can really throw a dark shadow over your evening. All the "its" can also read your mind with no apparent effort and can communicate their intentions to you with their ESP. Cheeky bastards.

How to Kill Them: Bullets are effective, but you need quite a lot of them—they're not easy to hit, because they're small, fast, and know how to hide. Try measles: it seems to be working.

What to Do if You Meet Them: The "its" have an odd perception of the world, both as little children and as well-developed humanoid mutants. It's not exactly out of focus, it reminds us more of a 3-D movie seen without the glasses. Which means they have poor depth perception. So maybe if you stay in front of them, they'll think you're far away, and won't bother to chase you. But then again, maybe not. They are bothered by the sight of weapons and by bright lights. They're also bothered by smoke. So pack and move to Cuba.

Current Status: Even if there's no proof that all of the babies have been deported to the island (rumor has it that some families are hiding their kids), all the grown-up "its" have been exterminated, either by cops or measles. But their offspring are still with the Jarvises', God only knows where.

Body Count: 28 townfolks; 11 people on the island; 6 people on the boat; 1 cat, 1 coyote, 1 chopper, and 1 birthday cake.

The Fly

Classification: mutants / humans / *Oopsibus mybads*

Footage:

1958, *The Fly* by Kurt Neumann
1959, *The Return of the Fly* by Edward L. Bernds
1965, *Curse of the Fly* by Don Sharp
1986, *The Fly* by David Cronenberg
1989, *The Fly II* by Chris Walas

The Skinny: A teleportation experiment failed miserably . . . five times.

Quotable: "This is the work of a madman!"

Teleportation sounds pretty cool, huh? You can fax yourself practically anywhere on the planet, and it only costs five cents a minute, 24 hours a day, seven days a week. OK, this is the theory. But once the equipment is ready to go, something inevitably goes wrong—don't you hate it when that happens?

Dr. André Delambre (*The Fly*—1958)

Co-owner with his brother François of Delambre Frères Electronics, Montreal Ltd., André was a gifted scientist who one day created a device which consisted of two large chambers, one to send and one to receive, and a very large computer system able to perform on any guinea pig a "control-shift-delete" and an "undo" in 15 seconds: the Disintegrator/Integrator.

Dr. André finally tried the machine on himself. Unfortunately, he wasn't alone: an ordinary housefly was in the chamber with him. The Disintegrator/Integrator did its job correctly, but blended the two creatures together: the outcome was Dr. André with a large fly head and one large fly leg in the place of his left arm, and a small housefly with a human head and arm.

Instead of capitalizing on this result and becoming a guest on lame TV talk shows, the doctor tried to reverse the process, but it was virtually impossible because, (a) he needed the funny-looking fly, and (b) he had to keep his hideous secret from his wife and son.

Mrs. Delambre eventually found out her husband's terrible secret, and this sent the doctor into a destructive rage: he burned almost all of his notes and forced his wife to kill him so he could take his mistakes to the grave. And the "funny-looking fly" was trapped in a spiderweb and eaten while screaming, "Help meee! Heeeelp meeeee!" à la Robin Williams.

Body Count: 0 people. 1 cat, but before the mutation.

Dr. Philippe Delambre (*The Return of the Fly*)

After learning about his dad's experiment, Philippe decided to follow in his footsteps. Philippe said about André, "He was careless. I won't be." Sure, Philippe . . . we all believe you.

So the careful Philippe joined forces with a coworker, who turned out to be an international killer interested in selling the Disintegrator/Integrator to the highest bidder. Philippe found out, and the doctor was beaten up and trapped inside one of the teleportation chambers. The killer also placed a housefly in the chamber . . . needless to say, Philippe emerged as part fly, but here is where he did better than Dad: Philippe had a fly head, a fly arm, *and* a fly leg. Somewhere in the lab there was also a tiny housefly with a scientist's head.

Once Dr. Philippe had taken care of business, providing the evil guys with a well-deserved death, the experiment was tried in reverse, locking the mutated scientist and the mutated housefly in the chamber: the result was a perfect success, and Philippe returned to being the man he once was, and the fly to the fly it had been.

Body Count: 2 people, 2 doors.

Dr. Henri Delambre (*The Curse of the Fly*)

The grandchildren of Dr. André kept whacking their heads against the promise of teleportation.

Henri poured all of his energy into the development of the device. Eventually, when his eldest son was married to a wacko newly escaped from a mental institution, the doctor gave up and decided to live a normal life.

Wait a second. We have a Disintegrator/Integrator, the heirs of a scientist who had a problem with the device, and an insane chick all in the same house, and you think they'll live happily ever after? Let's get real.

In the end, a few of the family members became half men–half fly, and all met with a very nasty death thanks to the police. But the Disintegrator/Integrator was still there, ready to buzz and chirp one more time . . .

Body Count: Hard to say. Technically, nobody was killed by Henri . . . only mutated.

Dr. Seth Brundle (*The Fly—1986*)

Dr. Brundle, a worker for Bartok Science Industry, built a machine that was very similar to Dr. Delambre's, and a baboon was successfully zapped through the telepods with no glitches at all.

One night, Dr. Brundle tried the machine on himself. Do they never learn?!!

Dr. Brundle emerged from the telepod refreshed and ecstatic, unaware of his extra 0,0003 kg. of weight. But, little by little, he started to notice a few minor changes: a monsterous hankering for sugar, a voracious sexual appetite, and the ability to walk on walls. Once he realized that something had actually happened, he tried to reverse the process, attempting a "fusion by gene-splicing of Brundlefly with one or more pure human subjects."

So he kidnapped his girlfriend (who was carrying his child) and tried one super fusion between the two of them. Something went wrong, and the Brundlefly was fused with the telepod, becoming a Brundleflytelepod. One gunshot ended its suffering, and brought Bartok Science Industry's budget back into the black.

Body Count: 1 hand, 1 foot (both melted); 1 wrist (broken), 1 window, and 1 baboon—while he was still a regular scientist.

Martin Brundle (*The Fly II*)

The son of Seth Brundle, Martin was born as a larva but inside was a bouncing baby boy who, when he was five years old, looked like Eric Stoltz.

Martin was legally "adopted" by Bartok Science Industry and offered a job using his amazing brain to make the telepod system work.

Needless to say, he was able to make the whole system operative, and he learned that to cure himself and remove the defective DNA once and for all, he had to "marry" himself with a donor.

Well, to make a long story short, Martin's body was a time bomb, and began mutating into a super-race of human flies. So he went on a killing spree, getting rid of all the people he formerly trusted, and used Mr. Bartok himself as his "marrying" subject: Martin became a normal five-year-old who looked like Eric Stoltz, and Mr. Bartok became an aberration of nature, trapped in the basement of his own company. And the telepod . . . ? Still there, waiting for more subjects. And more flies.

Body Count: 4 people, 1 hand; 1 window and 1 whole apartment.

Octaman

Classification: mutants / humans / *Lotsoarms lotsolegs*

Footage:

1971, *Octaman* by Harry Essex

The Skinny: The legend of a lake creature proves to be dangerously close to reality.

Quotable: "It must be a hybrid of some sort. Even a mutation."

Habitat: Lakes in Latin America.

Origin: A legend says a lake is the turf of a creature that is "half man, half sea serpent, with many arms." A scientist couldn't possibly believe the legend, and studied the levels of radioactivity a fishing community had ingested after underwater nuclear tests. In any case, a creature part human, part octopus, with glowing eyes appeared out of nowhere and wreaked havoc.

Identification: Octaman is a seven-foot-tall octopus with a really big head. It has two frontal eyes, occasionally yellow, occasionally red, a round mouth constantly open and crammed with tiny teeth, and protruding veins in the middle of its forehead. Why it hasn't yet graced the cover of *Vanity Fair* is a complete mystery. Anyway, Octaman's figure is humanoid, but instead of legs it has two tentacles with suckers toward the inside (that's why it never crosses its legs: it could be stuck for days), two tentacles as arms, and four extra tentacles for good measure. The color of its body is pale gray . . . not that it'd be more attractive if it were green or blue.

Cravings: Getting back its mutated sons (God only knows how Octaman reproduced itself. Is there a Mrs. Octaman? Was it parthenogenesis? Was it a limited budget that only allowed for one octopus suit?) and filling its loneliness. It seems to be extremely attracted to women (one of them must have been really drunk, and took him up on an offer . . .).

Behavior: Octaman prowls across Latin American lakes, looking around and making a "sipping from an empty can with a straw" sound, only fifty times louder. If you touch its sons (tiny little octopi with yellow eyes and stunned expressions), you're doomed: Octaman will come and get you, strangle you, fold you in half, pierce your chest with its tentacles, or stomp all over you. You know the old saying "there's nothing more lethal than a seven-foot-tall mutated octopus looking for its children." All right, you don't know the saying, but trust us: it's extremely popular in Latin America.

Danger: Octaman is very powerful, and it has the predictable punctuality of attacking you when it's night, there's no light available, and the soundtrack is very lousy. You can't see a thing, but you'll feel the suckers attaching to your skin and ripping flesh away. And you thought that there was nothing new to do around the campfire!

How to Kill It: Being an aquatic creature, Octaman's number-one enemy is dehydration. But it's not easy to keep it out of the water for that long. So take the long road: bright light bothers the creature, and fire scares it—and harms it, as well as burning the oxygen all around it (we're talking about a huuuge fire). A hefty amount of bullets will do the trick, too.

What to Do if You Meet It: Give it back its sons. Don't argue.

Current Status: Apparently dead. But we're no fools . . . !

Body Count: 5 people, 1 crocodile.

Scanners

Classification: mutants / humans / *Yourminds isanopenbookibus*

Footage:

1981, *Scanners* by David Cronenberg
1991, *Scanners II: The New Order* by Christian Duguay
1992, *Scanners III: The Takeover* by Christian Duguay
1994, *Scanner Cop* by Pierre David
1994, *Scanners: The Showdown/Scanner Cop II: Volkin's Revenge* by Steve Barnett

The Skinny: A medical side effect creates a race of superhuman brainpickers.

Quotable: "They're all pathetic social misfits. Unstable. Unreliable."

Turf: All over, we imagine.

Origin: Back in 1942, Dr. Paul Ruth founded the lab Biocarbon Amalgamate, where he developed a pregnancy drug called ephemerol. The medicine turned out to be absolutely ineffective for expectant mothers, but it had a peculiar side effect: the unborn children entered the world as scanners. Oopsie-daisy!

Identification: Scanners look like ordinary human beings; what makes them different is ESP: they can read your mind and anything with a nervous system (as well as a computer—even if it already has a scanner). Sometimes scanners read your mind even if they don't want to; our thoughts just flood their minds, causing them severe pain.

Cravings: Simple stuff, like world domination. They are also addicted to ephemerol (and its variations: Eph 1, Eph 2, and the brand-new Eph 3, a sort of a nicotine patch placed on the neck); the medicine is the only "scan suppressant" that stops the voices they hear. Unfortunately, ephemerol is highly addictive, causes personality modification, works for only a limited time, and is not recognized by most health insurance plans as "medically necessary."

Behavior: Scanners have always been divided into good and evil. Darryl Revok, the oldest one, recruited as many scanners as possible in order to destroy the society that created him. Go figure.

But other scanners have walked the road to success. Some with a positive inclination (such as police collaboration), some with the age-old conquer-the-world inclination. Invariably a good scanner meets an evil scanner, and they mentally fight to absorb each other's energy. Only one will win. Let's hope it's the good one, otherwise we have to look for another good scanner, explaining the problem, starting all over from the beginning . . . such a waste of minds.

If they are too bothered by ESP, scanners may withdraw from the world and live as human trash or as avant-garde artists. After all, it's already hard living with your own thoughts, imagine living with everyone else's! But once they've mastered their powers, they can force you to see or to say things against your will. They can move objects and people with telekinesis, but they can't penetrate the thick mind of former Vice President Dan Quayle. And they call themselves super-powerful creatures. Ha!

Danger: If scanners decide to scan your mind, there's nothing you can do about it. And if they want you to do or to say something, there's nothing you can do about it (unless you're another scanner or you have a metal plate in your head that works as a barrier). They can control your heartbeat or enter your mind to use your eyes as a moving camera, to visit a place to which they have no access. And again, there's nothing you can do about it. So . . . in other words, there's nothing you can do about it. Also keep in mind that the person who's scanned is subject to severe nose bleeding, headaches, stomach pain, and in extreme cases the explosion of his or her head. That should put an end to any migraine problem.

How to Kill Them: A scanner can be killed like us. But you have to act fast; if he scans you, he'll know your intentions. So approach while thinking about your tax return, a recipe for tuna casserole, or the last episode of *The Dukes of Hazzard.* Then kick him in the crotch.

What to Do if You Meet Them: They're bothered by intense light, such as a halogen flashlight or a laser beam. Always keep one of these in your pocket; and when the moment is right, aim for the eyes. Or be ready with a huge dose of ephemerol to offer them as a memento of your meeting. They might still kill you, but surely they'll appreciate the gift.

Current Status: In the beginning there were 236 known scanners. But since the son of a scanner carries the gene, well then . . . sooner or later some new scanner will show up, delirious as always and with the usual insane dream of power.

Body Count: The only verifiable body count is Darryl Revok's: 7 people killed with his mental powers; 9 people eliminated by his henchmen. Can we say he cheated?

"Shoot! I hope he's still under warranty!"

AVCO Embassy Pictures/Shooting Star

Animals

Origins

Animals mutate because they ingest something they shouldn't have, because they evolve . . . or just because.

- **Eating Junk Food:** You are what you eat; if an animal eats, let's say, strange oozing goo coming from underground (*Food of the Gods*), odd stuff concealed in barrels (*Empire of the Ants*), or salmon with DNA5 (*Humanoids from the Deep*), then expect the unexpected.

- **Evolving Out of Necessity:** Perhaps because the environment has changed, perhaps because pollution and other chemicals have irreversibly damaged the Earth, or perhaps because a film crew was wandering somewhere, looking for a story.

- **Hormones & Steroids:** They might be concealed in grain (*Deadly Eyes*) or in dog carcasses (*Alligator*).

- **Slow Pollution:** As a reaction to pesticides, fungicides, or any other poison that mankind dumps into the environment (*Prophecy*).

- **Does It Really Matter?:** If you were attacked by a vicious never-before-seen creature (*Bug, Graveyard Shift, Of Unknown Origin*), would you stop and wonder, "Where does this thing come from?" or would you opt to run like hell?

Habitat

- **Caves, Forests, Swamps:** Either under a dirty mill (*Graveyard Shift*) or among the trees (*Prophecy*).

- **Islands:** You wouldn't believe how many creatures populate mysterious islands.

- **Sea:** Are we talking *Gojira*? Or are we talking *Humanoids from the Deep*?

- **The Sewer:** Home of the *Alligator,* until it gets a little cramped.

- **Underground:** Mutated prehistoric bugs swarm out of a hole in the ground after an earthquake. How many are still in there?

• ***Alligator:*** An alligator with the pesky peculiarity of being 40 feet long. This mutant's able to tiptoe all over town without being seen. Not bad for a 40-foot gator, eh? **Best Defense:** A bomb. Probably the best way to get rid of it—if you can convince it to wait until the bomb explodes, that is.

• ***Bug:*** A new species of insect assembled by a mad scientist breeds with other insects and becomes extremely intelligent. And also learns how to fart fire. **Best Defense:** Send them back home. There should be a conveniently located crack in the ground behind your home. Dive into it when all of the creatures are chasing you.

• **Giant Animals** (*Food of the Gods*): The lot: chickens, bees, caterpillars, but mainly rats. **Best Defense:** Blow up a dam. The water will drown them.

• ***Humanoids from the Deep:*** (see entry)

• **Katahadis:** A bear, but Yogi he ain't! (see entry)

• **Giant Rats** (*Deadly Eyes*): As dangerous as real rats, only the size of dachshunds. **Best Defense:** conventional weapons.

• ***Slugs:*** These ugly creatures look exactly like ordinary slugs you might find in your garden, with a tiny little difference: they're bloodthirsty man-eaters. **Best Defense:** Electricity.

SIGNS YOUR EXOTIC PET OR PLANT IS A MUTANT

Face it: you can't be sure about the quality of the little pet store down the street. What if the owner didn't check where the pets came from. What if you've just bought something green that needs more than water and fertilizer? Well then look out for . . .

YOUR PET

- Your dog is strangely plump, and it's about a week since mail was delivered in your neighborhood.
- Your cat has nine tails.
- Your \$25.95 tropical fish ate your \$249.95 aquarium.
- Living in the pear tree in your garden is a family of squirrels that glow in the dark.
- Your hamster weighs 2,000 pounds.
- The bones your dog buries in your backyard are oddly reminiscent of the milkman, the newspaper boy, the pizza delivery guy . . .
- One day you come home to find that your name on the mailbox has been crossed out and replaced with "The Cockroaches."
- Like Rudolph, all the mice in your house have glowing red noses.

YOUR PLANT

- Your Venus flytrap has swallowed the air conditioner.
- Whenever you pass in front of one plant, it makes a slurping sound.
- You don't have to water your plant; it goes in the kitchen and turns on the faucet all by itself.

The best overall remedy . . .

• **Call the Army:** If in need of heavier artillery. Especially if there is more than one mutant.

Humanoids from the Deep

Classification: mutants / animals / *Twicius awfullis mistakius* **and subsequently** creations / biologically engineered

Footage:

1980, *Humanoids from the Deep* by Barbara Peeters
1996, *Humanoids from the Deep* by Jeff Yonis

The Skinny: If fish could walk . . . they'd hit singles bars.

Quotable: "Did you *know* these monsters?"

Habitat: The northwest, in small towns like Noyo (California) and Harbor Shores.

Origin: The first humanoids were generated from prehistoric fish (the obscure coelacanths), which, unbeknownst to people, were not only still around, but feeding on salmon which had been "enhanced" with the synthetic gene DNA5, capable of making them "grow bigger, faster, and twice as plentiful." Ergo, we may deduce this formula: salmon + DNA5 + coelacanths = humanoids from the deep. However, some 15 years later, the army tried to create the perfect amphibious soldier (don't ask), so they genetically altered convicted serial killers (still, don't ask) with animal genes. Therefore, we have another formula: serial killers + animal genes = the same darned humanoids from the deep. And they say we're evolving . . .

Identification: Supposedly, the humanoids are all males—seven feet tall, with green, scaly bodies. They also have long tails and large heads. The top resembles a human brain, only much, much larger. Their mouths are crammed with small, pointy teeth, they have gills, and their arms are very long. In other words, they ain't the Backstreet Boys. The military-created humanoids also have an interesting variation: they're equipped with very long tongues with a sort of a suction cup on the end. With this, they can grab and pull you underwater without even surfacing. It'll smear your makeup, though.

Cravings: The humanoids need to multiply, so they try to make it with every woman they can find (especially the ones who agree to lose the tops of their bikinis). The humanoids are also gluttons for an illegal hormone called synestin, which was being dumped off the coast in order to help the fauna grow bigger and better. Nice try.

Behavior: They're night predators, and the water is their basic element. But the humanoids can easily walk on dry land, especially in those areas where they're sure to find as many women as possible. They live either in caves along the coastline or in underwater caves with big air pockets, and here they "store" the pregnant women, under seaweed or in a gigantic communal cocoon. They reach their victims either by swimming underwater, using the town sewer, or by crashing the County Salmon Festival. Wherever they go, they leave a trail of goo that is slippery when wet—and when dry. They hate dogs, especially the ones that bark and attack them.

Danger: If you're close to water, remember that a humanoid may be hiding just underneath the surface. On the other hand, they might be hiding in the woods close to the water, or on the beach . . . aw, heck! Just pay attention!

How to Kill Them: The humanoids are stronger than us, but almost as vulnerable. Bullets, harpoons, axes to the head, or a fast-moving car usually do the trick. The best of the best is to sprinkle gasoline on the water's surface and set it on fire.

What to Do if You Meet Them: "I don't hear Joe Bob college boy comin' up with any bright ideas." Well, no need to get pissy! If you're a man, watch out for those long arms! They dice, slice, carve, and chop faster than a ginsu knife. If you're a woman, watch out for those long . . . well, be careful and remember what Mother told you. Anyway, if you have the misfortune of getting pregnant, try for an abortion before your all-teeth baby chomps his way out through your stomach. Or drink twenty bottles of Maalox.

Current Status: It seems as if the full-grown humanoids have all been exterminated. But their offspring are still somewhere.

Body Count: 23 people, 9 dogs, 1 seagull; 6 women have been kidnapped and impregnated, and 4 have died so far; 1 radio station has been trashed, 1 salmon fair wrecked, 1 pier, and part of 1 apartment.

Katahadis

Classification: mutants / animals / *Orsus whatthehellisthatus*

Footage:

1979, *Prophecy* by John Frankenheimer

The Skinny: Mutating bear wanders the woods, but it's not looking for picnic baskets.

Quotable: "Here, everything grows big."

Habitat: The woods in northern Maine. So far.

Origin: A lumber-company plant used EPA-approved chemicals to soak trees in order to produce paper—but they neglected to mention that they used mercury—banned since 1956. Mercury, a liquid metal heavier than H_2O, can "vanish" if you check the water, because it sinks. Pretty sneaky, huh? They probably don't teach this at school, but mercury has an interesting property: attacking the nervous system, it destroys the brain, ruins the chromosomes, and can change a fetus to the point that its mother will give birth to a monster. This is the bad news. The worse news is that, since the paper plant has dumped mercury in the water for more than 20 years, the ecosystem has been screwed up more than a little bit. Well, things got better and better: water was contaminated with mercury, fish ate mercury, raccoons ate fish, bears ate raccoons, and . . . bingo!

Identification: Katahadis (which is what the Native Americans called the mutation, according to one of their legends) looks like a mosaic made with "part of all things created. He bears a mark of all God's creatures." Sort of a Picasso painting among the animals, if you like, but less valuable. The Katahadis known to Native Americans looks like a large bear stretched by a gruesome torture device to about 12 feet tall. It has fangs, sort of a face, something like arms, something like legs . . . it's a smorgasbord. The pollution has also created a tadpole that is now as big as a dog, a five-foot salmon, and who knows what other terrible mutations.

Cravings: Kill. Kill. Kill.

Behavior: Belligerent by nature, the mutant kills either while hunting for food, while defending its territory, or simply for the fun of it. Katahadis doesn't seem to use a particular strategy: it wanders through the forest, harassing anybody it finds, growling very loudly. Katahadis follows you, and it's more than willing to wait for you if you find a nice hideout. It's not in a hurry. It can even cross a river—by walking underwater—to get to you. Of course it's extremely strong and fast.

Danger: If you spend a night in the great outdoors, you may wake up the following morning scattered over a 50-square-foot area. Come to think of it, you might not wake up at all.

How to Kill It: You might use bullets, but you'll need a lot of them, or you can stab Katahadis while it's hugging you. You'll have to stab it many, many, many, many, many times, though.

What to Do if You Meet It: Do not camp in an area where an old Native American tells you that there's a spirit who has "awakened to protect the Indians." But if you decide not to listen to the old man, as soon as you pitch your tent, dig an underground tunnel in which to hide just in case. Oh, and by the way: no matter what you do, never eat a thermometer.

Current Status: Dead. But another one is living in the same forest.

Body Count: Katahadis killed 14 people, 1 dog, 1 Jeep, 1 tent, and 1 shack. A large mutated salmon also ate 1 duck for good measure.

Nuclear Contamination

Origins & Causes

- **Atomic Explosions, Testing:** If the contaminated subjects manage to survive, life will never be the same. Neither for the subjects, nor us, that is (*The Amazing Colossal Man, Attack of the Crab Monsters, Day the World Ended,* just to name a few).

- **Mad Scientists:** They always screw things up (*Tarantula, The Magnetic Monster*).

- **Nuclear Accelerator:** If they place one of these near your home, the least you can expect is for all the dogs in the area to become vicious killers (*Slaughter*). Your electricity bill will drop dramatically, though.

- **Radioactive Waste:** Once this stuff is dumped into the sea or in the wilderness, bad things start to occur. The waste may wash over . . . uh . . . skeletons of dead sailors and form an army of sea monsters (*The Horror of Party Beach*), or it could be the main course for curious insects (*Empire of the Ants*).

Habitat

- **Africa:** *Monster from Green Hell.*

- **The Arctic:** *The Beast from 20,000 Fathoms, The Deadly Mantis.*

- **Britain:** *The Giant Behemoth, Island of Terror, X the Unknown.*

- **Japan:** *Gojira, Rodan, The War of the Gargantuas.*

- **Mexico:** *The Amazing Colossal Man, Monster from the Ocean Floor, Octaman.*

- **Nova Scotia:** *The Magnetic Monster.*

- **Pacific Ocean:** *Attack of the Crab Monsters, It Came from Beneath the Sea, The Monster That Challenged the World, The Phantom from 10,000 Leagues, Them!.*

- **Portugal:** *The Sea Serpent.*

- **U.S.A.:** *The Amazing Colossal Man, Attack of the Giant Leeches, The Beast from 20,000 Fathoms, Beginning of the End, The Crawling Hand, Day the World Ended, The Deadly Mantis, Dogs, Empire of the Ants, Godzilla, The Hideous*

Sun Demon, The Horror of Party Beach, Invasion of the Bee Girls, It Came from Beneath the Sea, The Slime People, Tarantula, Them!—see map.

Cravings

First we cause these creatures to mutate, then our minds are boggled as to why they're mad at us?

- **Eating Everything:** Particularly giant grasshoppers (which devour entire crops), giant people, giant octopuses, *Rodan* (who considers planes a special treat), lizard men (*The Hideous Sun Demon*), *Them!*, and *X the Unknown.*

- **Wreaking Havoc:** Prime hobby of the Green Gargantua, *The Giant Behemoth*, the giant octopus (*It Came from Beneath the Sea*), Rodan, and many others.

- **Killing for Sport:** Some creatures kill just for the fun of it. Among these, *The Slime People* and the wasps of *Monster from Green Hell.*

Typical Behavior

- **Breaking and Entering:** Factories, labs, warehouses, train stations, trains, airports . . . looking for food.

- **Digging Tunnels:** To move underground (*Them!*), or to sink the island where the humans live (*Attack of the Crab Monster*).

- **Stepping on Buildings:** Ability of the Gargantuas and the giant grasshoppers. The buildings don't take this very well and crumble to the ground.

- **Pulling Ships Underwater:** Only because they want to eat the crew on board (*It Came from Beneath the Sea, Monster from the Ocean Floor, The Phantom from 10,000 Leagues*).

The "Isotope"-Capades

- ***The Amazing Colossal Man:*** A rapidly growing man. Former Colonel Glenn Manning is now bald and hideous, and has been thrown out of the army because he can't fit into his uniform anymore. **Best Defense:** Electricity . . . when he wants to commit suicide.

- ***The Beast from 20,000 Fathoms:*** A "new dinosaur," the "rhedosaurus," so named by the army. Carnivorous, with deadly germs in its blood. Rampages when he can, so steer clear. **Best Defense:** Heavy artillery.

- ***The Crawling Hand:*** "Hand on the loose! Hand on the loose!" And it'll get you in the killin' mood, too. **Best Defense:** "Cat got your creature?" If your feline is quick enough, it'll eat the hand.

• **Gargantuas** (*The War of the Gargantuas*): Two giant hairy manlike creatures, one brown and relatively benevolent, one mean and green. **Best Defense:** A strong laser beam knocks the green Gargantua unconscious. And an underwater volcano will wipe out anything in its path . . . including the Gargantuas.

• **Giant Ants** (*Them!, Empire of the Ants*): Ants, and quite giant. No, they won't fit in your pants. **Best Defense:** Fire, bombs, cyanide gas—the works.

• ***The Giant Behemoth:*** Yet another "new dinosaur," the "paleosaurus." Electrically charged, with the ability to shoot radiation. Oh sh&*! **Best Defense:** Nuke it some more.

• **Giant Crab** (*Attack of the Crab Monster*): It rips apart the phone lines so you can't call your psychic friends. After eating a person, the creature begins to talk with the victim's voice. And it's calling you. Creepy. **Best Defense:** Torpedoes, electricity.

• **Giant Grasshoppers** (*Beginning of the End*): Isotopes in the soil will supposedly increase crop growth. Side effect: everything else will grow, too. Like grasshoppers. **Best Defense:** Water. Lure the giant grasshoppers into a lake (they follow ultrasound) and they'll drown.

• **Giant Leeches** (*Attack of the Giant Leeches*): Leeches, quite giant. Sound familiar? **Best Defense:** Bombs.

• **Giant Mantis** (*The Deadly Mantis*): Mantis, quite giant. Sound familiar? **Best Defense:** Cyanide gas.

• **Giant Octopus** (*It Came from Beneath the Sea*): Octopus, quite giant. Yadda yadda yadda. **Best Defense:** Nuke it some more or hit it with a torpedo.

• **Giant Wasps** (*Monster from Green Hell*): Always flying around stinging everybody. **Best Defense:** Smoke. It'll make giant wasps numb and ready to be killed with bullets.

• ***The Hideous Sun Demon:*** Dr. Gilbert McKenna, an ordinary man, becomes an aggressive lizard whenever he's hit by sunlight. Kind of the opposite of a werewolf. **Best Defense:** Slippery high places. The creature will take a plunge and crash to the ground.

• ***The Horror of Party Beach:*** Amphibious and fishlike. Beach party pooper.

Best Defense: Sodium. If you apply this element it'll explode in a towering ball of fire. Ask your science teacher about this one.

• **Human Bees** (*Invasion of the Bee Girls*): Bombard women with a radioactive gun, and they'll turn into human queen bees. Gallons of beeswax and a spacious beehive are needed, too, but it'll work. **Best Defense:** Fire.

• **Kraken** (*The Monster That Challenged the World*): Super-sized sea snail which sucks bodily fluids. **Best Defense:** Heavy artillery and carbon dioxide.

• ***The Magnetic Monster:*** Glowing magnetic substance that attracts metals. What else would you expect? **Best Defense:** Give it a lot of electricity.

• **Ugly Mutated Man** (*Day the World Ended*): It looks like the devil, but a bit uglier. It's telepathic, strong, and eats radioactive mutations—that's all it can stand. **Best Defense:** Rain purifies the environment and melts the mutant.

• ***Monster from the Ocean Floor:*** Oversized octopus. **Best Defense:** A good spear to the eye.

• ***The Phantom from 10,000 Leagues:*** Big old ship-eating machine. This slimy, furious sea creature bears a suspicious resemblance to a hand puppet. **Best Defense:** Bombs.

• ***Rodan:*** Giant bird hatched from mutated eggs. Flapping its large wings, Rodan wrecks everything man has built. While flying, it breaks the sound barrier and every single window in your neighborhood. **Best Defense:** The ever-trusty volcano.

• ***The Sea Serpent:*** Sea serpent, super-sized. **Best Defense:** Send a warm current of water the other direction and it'll follow.

• **Silicon-Based Calcium Suckers** (*Island of Terror*): When you mess with Mother Nature, you have to pay the price. One such price is dealing with a mutated creature that sucks the bones out of your body. It hides behind trees or in the shadows, and as soon as you walk by, it snaps its tentacles and you're done. **Best Defense:** Nuke it some more by feeding it Strontium-90–tainted cattle.

• ***The Slime People:*** Slime-dripping creatures covered with scales. Can create a hot fog to hide within when marching, which adds a certain mystery. And it's great fun when they hit a pole. **Best Defense:** Cold. It'll send them back where they belong . . . underground, that is.

• ***Tarantula:*** Tarantula, but big. Really big. And scary. Of course. **Best Defense:** Many, many bullets.

• ***X the Unknown:*** This mud creature rolls over you, melting your body with its radiation. **Best Defense:** A healthy dose of electricity.

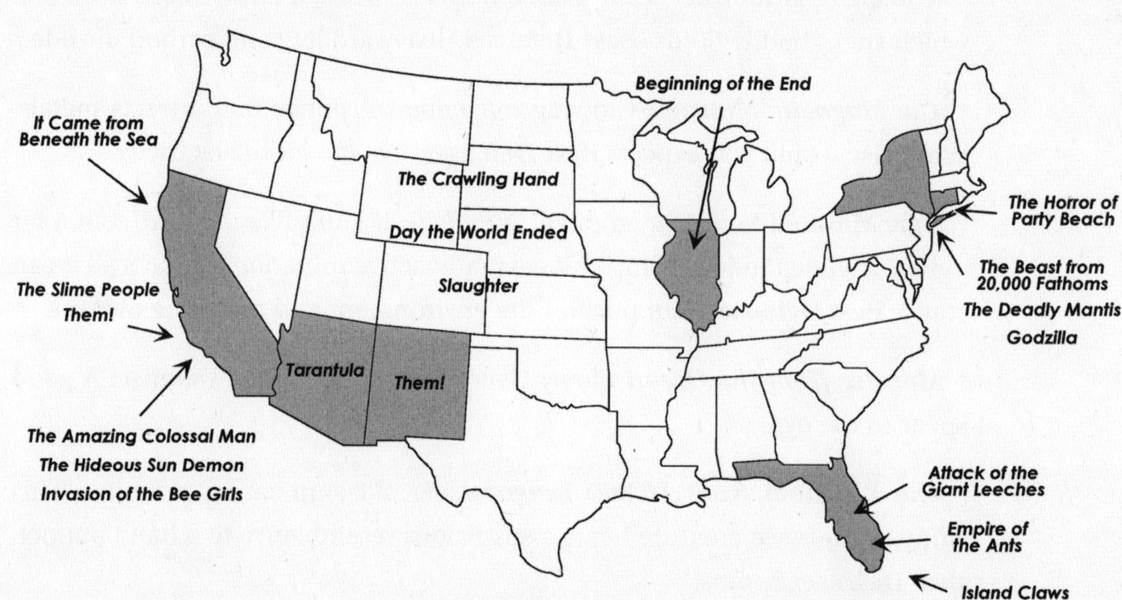

WHERE TO FIND YOUR FAVORITE ATOMIC DISASTER IN THE U.S.

Psychopaths

PIONEERS IN THE FIELD OF SUBJECTIVE REALITY

"Crazy, Crazy for Beein' . . . Deadly . . ."

Society's attitude toward the mentally ill has come a long way. Nowadays we put brutal murderers in a clinic for a few months, then let them out again. Sometimes we wonder if we should still be throwing them in the clink and swallowing the key, just like in the old days.

The psychopaths we are writing about are not to be handled with kid gloves. They're not just having a bad day or a bad episode. They're interested in giving you and me a bad life . . . or more likely a painful death.

Psycho Spotting

How are we to differentiate them from the harmless ones? A very difficult question to answer, especially prior to a psychopath "getting medieval on your ass." Look out for violent tendencies, check for automatic weapons, and listen to their jabbering for clues. They say that most people's "bark is worse than their bite." Which means that for most people, yelling is just a way of letting out anger and frustration. But if a nutcase very calmly tells you about their plans to execute justice, tell justice to stay home, and call the cops.

Cops won't do anything? Well, it does happen from time to time. Then you're forced to defend yourself. But you better have proof that you're in danger before breaking out the sharp objects, otherwise it's *you* who will become the monster.

Perhaps the Most Terrifying Monsters of All

Yep, it's true! Why? Because these folks are not only more intelligent than your average beast, they are more in tune with what will scare the bejesus out of their fellow human beings.

SUBCATEGORIES

They say it takes all types . . .

- **Alter Egos:** You may not be feeling quite like yourself today, but these folks aren't feeling quite like themselves when they plunge the knife in, either.
- **The Gifted:** People with so much to offer the world—in terms of pain, that is.
- **The Obsessed:** People with Attention *Surplus* Disorder.
- **Religious Zealots:** Evidently, God is more than the sum of his command-ments . . .
- **The Vengeful:** An eye for an eye, a tooth for a . . . well, an entire city block.
- **Stalkers:** Folks who just plain like killin'.

So put on your Sigmund Freud thinking caps, and break out your antipersonnel devices, 'cause here we go . . .

Alter Egos

We all go a little mad, sometime.

Norman Bates in *Psycho*

Multiple Personality Disorder (MPD) is the diagnosis given when two or more distinct and integrated personalities exist in the same body, switching off from time to time.

The reason the personality splinters apart is so that the individual has "helpers" who can deal with different situations: for example, Julie the intellectual, Tommy the hero, and Bart the psychokiller. Now, most people who suffer from this affliction are relatively harmless. Sure, they use up a lot of Social Security numbers and e-mail addresses, and even break a few hearts, but for the most part they keep their problems to themselves.

We, of course, will be discussing the folks whose alter egos have a taste for blood. These violent secondary personalities can lay dormant for years.

Oftentimes the killer personality thinks it is acting in the best interest of the wimp personality—protecting it from people who it perceives will do harm to its gentler self. And many times it is trying to get the upper hand to become the dominant personality, and get rid of the wimp personality altogether.

Identification

Alter egos are quiet, simple people who are kind of like ticking bombs. They look vulnerable and lonely when in their primary personality: they're amiable and willing to talk about anything. They're underdogs who can only unleash their fury when the secondary personality takes over. Then they look anything but vulnerable: they are overconfident, aggressive, cool, and oftentimes they wear wigs and a different wardrobe to assert that they are "someone else." Halloween only comes once a year, after all, and it's just not enough for these folks.

Cravings

Alter egos are people who've been "pushed down" by authoritarian figures (mothers, fathers, wives, etc.). Now, alone at last, they want to find out what they've missed. But . . . are they really alone?

- **Completing Their Life:** Alter egos know they're unfulfilled. The extra personality makes them a full person. But not without complications.

- **Vanquishing Bad Influences:** Whenever a person arouses them, the dormant personality says, "This is no good for you. Kill that person!" And so they do.

- **Respecting Authority:** Alter egos are free people, but they're always keeping an eye (or an ear) on the voice from the past which tells them what to do. And they want to please it.

Behavior

Alter egos are monomaniacal killers: they don't slash randomly, no. They focus on one target at a time, and they really go for it. Between kills, they enjoy the simple pleasures.

- **Hearing Voices:** An alter ego's mind works in mysterious ways, and very often it takes control. So the poor alter ego hears voices from the past (*Psycho*) or from the present (*Raising Cain*).

- **Personaliticide:** After a while the passive personality understands that the abrasive personality is not exactly Mr. Nice Guy. So they confront it, attempting to get rid of it.

- **Brain Feud:** Whenever an alter ego tries to reason with other personalities, it's a fight—usually won by the evil personality.

- **Getting an Act:** Using your double personality to become a great ventriloquist, but losing track of who's the master and who's the dummy (*Magic*).

Single Room $20.95
Double Room $25.95
The Bates Motel
Fairvale, CA
555-9130
Come & Rest in Peace!

What to Do if You Meet One (or Two, or Three)

It's hard to tell; if you meet an alter ego in his or her main persona, you won't have a clue who you're really dealing with. If you meet the secondary persona, it's probably too late for you anyway, because you've already stepped on main persona's toe. Very dangerous is attempting to send a "cured" alter ego back to the asylum: he'll go mad all right—and you'll pay the bill. Rule of thumb, just be nice and try not to come off too sexy.

The first personality may have a sudden spark of rationality and decide to pull the plug on the other personalities—forever. This of course means that the first personality has to go, too. Oh well, you can't have your cake and eat it, too . . .

Norman Bates & His Mother

Classification: alter egos / *Mommasboy nokiddingus*

Footage:

1960, *Psycho* by Alfred Hitchcock
1983, *Psycho II* by Richard Franklin
1986, *Psycho III* by Anthony Perkins
1990, *Psycho IV: The Beginning* by Mick Garris
1998, *Psycho* by Gus Van Sant

The Skinny: A mama's boy to the extreme.

Quotable: "My hobby. Stuffing things."

Stomping Grounds: The Bates Motel and the nearby swamp; then some loony bin.

Origin: A needy secretary stole $40,000 and hid in the Bates Motel. Tragic mistake. The manager (as you probably have guessed) was Norman, a quite curious and peaceful man . . . except for his mother, whose ensuing behavior landed him in the loony bin.

After a 22-year-period spent in an asylum, Norman returned to the motel. And apparently, his mother returned as well.

Physical Description: A thin, sensitive man, with a slight stutter and an Oedipus complex as big as the whole Ramada chain.

Cravings: Women who reject or disappoint him, or else arouse him. Just your typical modern male. He loves grilled-cheese sandwiches, too.

Behavior: Norman lives with his constantly pissed-off mother; they quarrel every two minutes. To kill time between arguments, Norman enjoys taxidermy: he stuffs birds to make his home more livable, or at least this is what he believes. To kill time between stuffings, he simply kills. Or his mom does. Or someone else, but Norman believes it's him. Or his mom. Or someone else. Whatever.

Danger: Beware! Norman's a seemingly likable guy, but his mother has one helluva temper, and if you make her lose it, you're in trouble. Mom always talks to her son; she leaves him messages, calls him on the phone . . . even if she died over 40 years ago.

What to Do if You Meet Him: Whatever you do, do NOT take a shower in his motel. Particularly because Norman will poke a peephole in the wall to watch. And then his mom will poke a few holes in the person taking the shower.

Current Status: Alive and well, and happily married to a psychiatrist who gave him a bouncing baby boy. We don't know if the bouncing baby boy will follow in Dad's footsteps. We'll have to wait and see.

Body Count: Roughly 14 people; 2 birds, and 1 guitar.

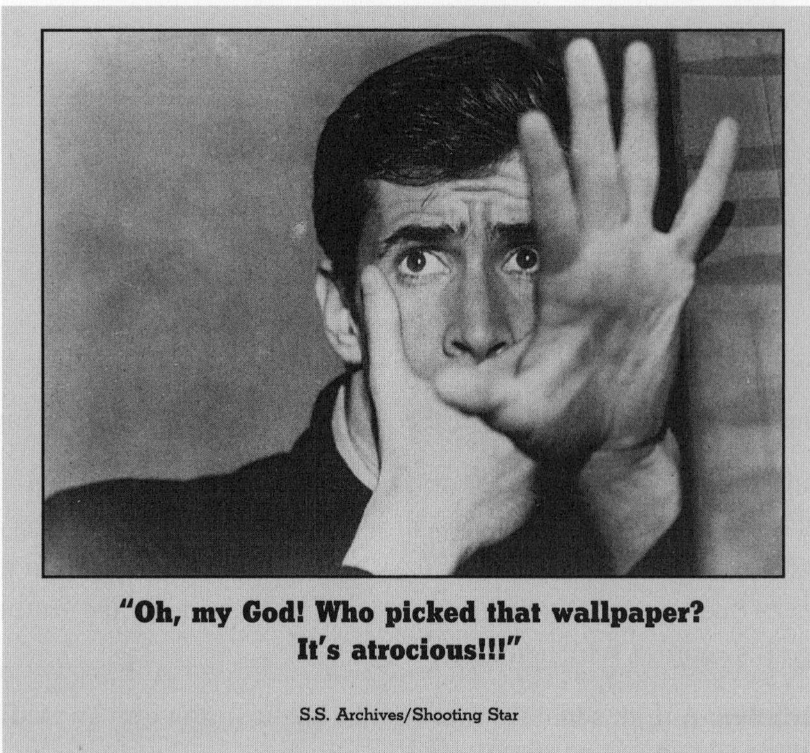

"Oh, my God! Who picked that wallpaper? It's atrocious!!!"

S.S. Archives/Shooting Star

Bobbi

Classification: alter egos / *Shaveandahaircut transsexus*

Footage:

1980, *Dressed to Kill* by Brian De Palma

The Skinny: Split-personality transsexual at war with her- or himself, agrees that both genders can make good use of a razor.

Quotable: "Don't make me be a bad girl again."

Born: 1933

Stomping Grounds: New York.

Origin: One day Dr. Robert Elliott, a well-respected psychiatrist, received a message from one of his patients that she had borrowed his straight razor. And as it turned out, she didn't borrow it to shave her legs. The patient, who calls herself "Bobbi," is a woman and/or man with a small problem. Although he/she was born a man, he/she is a split-personality transsexual whose feminine self has a violent need to become the dominant personality. Her masculine side still has very strong sexual urges, which causes great conflict between her two personalities. Are you still following? Since killing off her masculine self would be suicide, Bobbi chooses a different course of action . . .

Identification: Tall, thin, blond hair, dark sunglasses, black leather coat, black leather gloves, black hat. Typical New York female attire.

Cravings: The slaughter of women who arouse her masculine side.

Behavior: If you're her next target, she tends to follow you until you're alone and then greet you with a straight razor. Bobbi slices her victims up in a very efficient manner. Perhaps Bobbi used to work at a sushi restaurant. In her spare time she enjoys bicycling, long walks, and the musical stylings of Tom Jones.

Danger: If you have an appointment with Dr. Elliott, there is a high risk of running into her at his office. Just cancel and find another shrink—trust us. If you've had the misfortune of already meeting and arousing her masculine side, you're probably her next target. Problem is, you won't know until it's too late.

What to Do if You Meet Her: The trick is knowing that you *have* met her, since she has two distinct personalities with distinctly different tastes in clothes. As a man, she looks like your average middle-aged professional, which isn't particularly helpful. But if you meet up with her feminine incarnation, we recommend a few time-worn strategies:

spraying her with Mace, decking her with a car door, and just plain running in the other direction.

Current Status: Oh, don't worry: she's locked up in Bellevue. We think.

Body Count: 1

BEING OBSERVANT OF ABNORMAL BEHAVIOR

What if your little sister is a psychopath? Or your dad? Or the guy who lives next door? Or your school bus driver? Or Mrs. Mahoney who lives down the road and who always bakes those delicious apple pies? Are they really apples, by the way . . . ? Well, if you worry that someone near you might be a psycho, check for the following phenomena . . .

- The local hardware store has finally sold all those rusty knives and tools.
- Every dog in the neighborhood goes in its backyard, growls for a while, produces a high-pitched yapping, and from that moment on you don't see it anymore.
- Strange noises come from right outside your window, even if you live on the 11th floor of a building with no balconies.
- Your boyfriend keeps quoting horror movies and always roots for the evil guy.
- Your girlfriend invites you over but she doesn't lock the main door, "because her little baby brother is somewhere around the house."
- Whenever asked about his missing wife or children, the local pharmacist rolls his eyes and giggles, walking away from the counter.
- Every night, an old lady dressed in black stands in the middle of her garden, pointing her finger at whoever passes by.
- The mayor has a clean conscience and talks openly about tough issues—but reacts violently when you mention "The Sewer Incident."

The Gifted

Murder is very, very real. It may start in the mind . . .
But then it changes to flesh and blood.

Dr. Decker in *Nightbreed*

There is a thin line separating genius from insanity. If you have a brain the size of Texas, you might as easily win a Nobel Prize as the top spot on the FBI's Most Wanted list.

"The gifted" are people whose incredible minds have gone a little over the edge. People who know almost everything that human brains can assimilate—but who want more. So, they begin to analyze others' lives and minds, until finally their brain clicks, and they begin to chop and carve.

What's even more creepy is that they do it all very rationally. They're not under the influence of drugs, alcohol, or the devil. They simply kill, that's all. They consider you something dispensable. It has been said that "a mind is a terrible thing to waste." Well, in the eyes of the gifted, waste is a terrible thing to have to mind. So if you're waste, you must be trashed.

For some reason, this syndrome only seems to occur with males. So women geniuses either apply themselves better, or else are too sly to get caught.

Identification

You'd think the gifted would all be very short, crushed by the unbearable weight of their brains. But they aren't. They're ordinary human beings. Well, almost. Usually a psychopathological genius lives alone and is deeply in love with both his profession and his one true love: a wife, a dead wife, a father, a dead father . . . and he plies his wicked craft in the name of this love.

The gifted are doctors, professors, psychiatrists—great minds that could help out the human race with their discoveries. If only they weren't so determined to wipe out the human race! Very calm and suave while showing their "facade" (the face they show to the world), the gifted remain very calm and suave when they unleash their inner rage on those of us less intellectually blessed.

- **Dr. Decker** (*Nightbreed*): He moves stealthily in and out of your home, and before you can say "minced meat," you become it. He does this in order to reach Midian, the town where the monsters go, in order to destroy them, too.

• **Dr. Hannibal Lecter:** Hungry, hungry psycho. (see entry)

• ***Patrick:*** Psychokinesis is the special ability of this comatose kid. He really moves things and can write letters at a distance.

• **Dr. Anton Phibes:** "The doctor is out . . ." of his frickin' mind! (see entry)

• **Dr. Evan Rendell:** This one's bonkers too, but at least he can laugh about it. (see entry)

Hobbies

• **Building Overelaborate Death Traps:** The gifted love to exercise their geniuses by devising new ways of killing. So, here they come: giant thermometers, legions of mice, swarms of locusts . . .

• **Scanning Your Mind:** They adore reaching the most remote corners of the human mind. They love to toy with ghosts from the past, and they're very clever manipulators.

• **Protecting:** If the gifted is deeply in love with someone, he'll do anything to protect the significant other.

What to Do if You "Have the Pleasure" of Meeting One

Don't let him know your weak point(s). The gifted are extremely good at turning the tables by using what they know—and what you know—as a weapon against you. They are talkative and persuasive, lead you on the path they need you to walk, then play God with you. Best to cover your ears with your hands and go "la-de-da-de-da-de-da" until they stop talking. You might look like a fool, but they may find your behavior so fascinating they'll let you live to study you a little more. Before finally getting around to killing you.

Dr. Hannibal Lecter

Classification: the gifted / *Cannibalus reallycreepytous*

Footage:

1986, *Manhunter* by Michael Mann
1990, *The Silence of the Lambs* by Jonathan Demme
2001, *Hannibal* by Ridley Scott

The Skinny: Cannibalistic doc toys with cops' minds.

Quotable: "I do wish we could chat longer, but I'm having an old friend for dinner."

Stomping Grounds: Baltimore, Florence, and the tropics.

Biography: Dr. Hannibal Lecter ("Hannibal the Cannibal" to admirers) is a renowned psychiatrist who, during the late seventies, developed a taste for his patients, particularly college women. Hannibal was eventually caught by FBI Agent Will Graham and spent the next eight years in a psychological institute under extremely heavy security. Then he escaped using a pen refill.

Identification: Han is a refined middle-aged gentleman with piercing eyes, slicked-back hair, and an evenly modulated nasal voice which usually expresses very little emotion. Much like Welsh actor Ralph Fiennes. And no matter what horrible act he commits, his pulse stays pretty much the same. In captivity, he was usually kept behind heavy glass or in tight restraints, but now he feels free to let his hair down and see the world. Just pray he doesn't yearn to see *your* part of the world.

Cravings: He prefers elegant, yet simple cuisine: some fava beans and a nice Chianti—the perfect complement to human organs. But he only eats "rude" people. It is therefore believed that his cannibalism is a natural extension of his deep respect for human life.

Behavior: Dr. Lecter enjoys cooking, sketching, classical music, and long talks. During these talks, he likes to torture his victims with their deepest fears and ghosts from their past. Because of his professional and personal knowledge of the pathological mind-set of serial killers, the police often seek his help in solving the most perplexing cases. But he usually ends up using the police for his amusement by psychologically torturing his interviewers.

Danger: In addition to his infamously savage impulses, he has an acute sense of smell and a photographic memory. Just hope *you* don't become memorable. He also has a particular fondness for intellectually curious young women. And we don't recommend accepting any dinner invitations from him—you never know what or who might be on the menu.

What to Do if You Meet Him: A twofold strategy is recommended: first, behave like a gentleman or lady; and second, politely excuse yourself. If all else fails, you could try acquainting him with the benefits of a vegetarian diet.

Current Status: Last seen on vacation in the tropics. And there are reports that he has moved to Florence, Italy, to "try a little Italian."

Body Count: 16 and counting . . .

Dr. Anton Phibes

Classification: the gifted / *Noinsurances coverageibus*

Footage:

1971, *The Abominable Dr. Phibes* by Robert Fuest
1972, *Dr. Phibes Rises Again!* by Robert Fuest

The Skinny: Don't make this doctor mad, neither by telling him his handwriting is awful nor by letting his wife die.

Quotable: "I have used my knowledge of music and acoustics to re-create my voice."

Turf: Switzerland; London (Mauldin Square); Egypt.

Origin: A talented organist, a Ph.D. in theology, a genius with his hands and mind, Dr. Phibes was left for dead after a car accident that disfigured his face. His wife, Victoria, was rushed to the hospital but unfortunately died while a team of nine doctors tried their best to save her. Now Dr. Phibes is back to seek revenge for the inadequacy of her treatment.

How He Looks: Dr. Phibes has three looks: an ordinary man, thanks to very heavy makeup, a gray wig, a beard, and a mustache; a mysterious organist, wearing either a black or white cape with a hood to entirely cover his body and his face; and *au naturel,* which means with no makeup—pretty disgusting, since his face is practically a skull with just two mean eyes. Mute since the accident, Anton designed and built a system that allows him to talk: thanks to a plug in his neck, he can connect himself to a speaker and talk with a monotone voice. He can also eat, again through the neck. Bleah!

Cravings: He wants to be reunited with his lovely wife, Victoria (who was kept in "suspension"), but first he seeks revenge, and inspired by the 10 plagues of Egypt, Anton kills all the doctors, one by one, in order to get even with them. Later on he sails toward Egypt, to find the River of Life. Thanks to the sacred water of this river, he brings back his beloved Victoria and together they enjoy eternal life.

Hobbies: Dr. Phibes delights in playing his organ and dancing with Vulnavia, his sexy and mute assistant. He also adores studying elaborate deaths for the people who block the path to bringing Victoria back to life.

Danger: Do not put yourself between Dr. Phibes and his goal, whichever that is. He won't hesitate to grant you a very complicated and sadistic death (mainly involving animals such as rats, locusts, and scorpions) just for the fun of it.

What to Do if You Meet Him: Tell him that you love his wife (in a platonic way, of course) and hope to see her soon. Probably that'll do it. Then again, he probably won't buy it.

Current Status: Last time we saw him, he was sailing along the River of Life; so he should still be alive, somewhere. But he's never sent us a postcard.

Body Count: 14; 1 man is left in shock.

Dr. Evan Rendell, Jr.

Classification: the gifted / *Gigglius notsofunnytous*

Footage:
1992, *Dr. Giggles* by Manny Coto

The Skinny: Crazy doc laughs his way toward a cure for the living.

Quotable: "Our town has a doctor, and his name is Rendell. Stay away from his house, he's a doctor from hell. He chopped up his patients, every last one, and cut out their hearts purely for fun. So if you're from Moorehigh and you should get sick, then fall on your knees and pray you die quick."

Turf: The small town of Moorehigh.

Origin: Once upon a time, Dr. Evan Rendell was a collector. The objects of his affection were his patients' hearts—and their bodies as well. Finally the police got him. If you think the story's over, well . . . there was still Evan Jr., who wanted to be a doctor just like his dad. As a kid, he managed to sneak out of his house hiding inside his dead mother's body. After a few killings, they locked him in an asylum. A fully grown Evan Jr. then escaped from Tarawood State Hospital, heading back to his hometown, to his house in Tivoli Court and to his favorite tools.

Identification: Dr. Evan Jr. has a round face and a massive body. He dresses in an old-fashioned way (but under his overcoat you'll probably never notice it); he always carries his black briefcase, filled with medical equipment.

Cravings: Obeying Hippocrates's dictum—"for extreme illnesses, extreme treatments are most fitting"—Dr. Evan Jr. wants to cure people. The problem is that he has a very wicked, sick, and mostly lethal way to do this. He is obsessed with hearts, like his father was. So, he begins a brand-new collection with young patients from the town.

Behavior: Dr. Rendell's constant refrain is a giggle. Whenever he's excited, he giggles. He started as a boy, and is still going. Dr. Evan makes a lot of nocturnal house calls in Moorehigh, even if he's not invited, and he doesn't charge a penny. He frequently uses abnormal medical devices (a huge thermometer, a pointed ophthalmoscope, large bandages) and kills every single one of his patients. Like father, like son. The only patient he didn't kill was himself—he operated on himself to extract a bullet from his stomach. Now, that takes talent.

Danger: He doesn't care if you feel well or not. He will give you a checkup ("I care too much!") even without your consent. So, double-check the name of your primary provider with your health insurer—you never know.

How to Prevent Yourself from Meeting Him: Eat an apple a day.

Current Status: Dead. At least that's what the hospital tells us.

Body Count: 24 people.

The Obsessed

Two years of therapy, electroshock, plus every kind of pill you know . . . I'm completely cured!

Angela Baker in *Sleepaway Camp 2: Unhappy Campers*

The obsession that triggers this kind of psychopath is a seemingly random thing: it may be a holiday, an anniversary, an innocent action, a sick parent, or even an imaginary friend. But usually it's you, or something about you.

The obsessed have only one thing on their minds, and they'll do anything to pursue their goals. The obsessed don't see the impossibility of their quests, and they don't realize they're going too far. So, when someone tells them to "cut it out" or "get a frickin' hobby," they take it so personally that they swing from love to hate in a flash. Then we all have to pay the consequences.

Typical Behavior

The obsessed have one-track minds. But there are many kinds of obsessives, and therefore many "tracks."

- **To Be Part of Your Life:** Not just in a friendly way. These folks want to be your North Pole, your Center of the Universe . . . sometimes they even want to be *you.*

- **Trust Me on This:** The obsessed think they know it all. They'll die to give you their advice about life, whether this expertise comes from Judge Judy or from their perverted parents.

- **Give a Little Love, Take a Little Love:** And give the word a whole new meaning (*The Crush, Fatal Attraction, Fear, Boxing Helena*).

- **I Can't Have You? Then Nobody Else Can:** If an obsessed person is rejected, after a while he or she will try to wreck the foundation of your family: your spouse, your children, your parents . . . everyone's a target.

- **To Be in Contact with Their Heroes:** Writing letters to their role models (this is what Ruben Goetz does) or "taking care" of their favorite writer (does *Misery* ring a bell?).

A Fine Selection of Completely Obsessed Wackos

The most obsessed psycho might also be the most lovable person who happens to live across the street, who works two desks away, who claims to be "your number-one fan," or who plans to spend a month with you at summer camp. Obsessed people are really hard to recognize at first, because they all enter your life in a very innocent way, trying really hard not to "bother" you. They tiptoe into your domain one step at the time, hover around you, and when you realize it's too late . . . well, it's too late. The obsessed all seem to have this common pattern of behavior. Some, though, stray from the herd and dance to the beat of a different drummer. But they're all a bitch to deal with.

- **Angela Baker:** Repression breeds creativity. (see entry)

- **Jerry Blake** (*The Stepfather*): A man who's looking for the perfect family. He's accommodating, caring, filled with love . . . but as soon as the family he's currently part of disappoints him, he looks around for a new family (after murdering the first). And so on, and so on . . .

- **Kris Bolin** (*The Temp*): Employee of the Month from Hell; she works through an agency and writes her résumé with your blood.

- **Billy and Ricky Caldwell:** "He knows if you've been bad or good" . . . and it doesn't make one damned bit of difference. (see entry)

- **Hedra Carlson** (*Single White Female*): The sweetest, most perfect roommate. She loves to share everything with you, and she likes the same from you: your clothes, your hairstyle, your boyfriend . . . OK, maybe she's expecting a little too much, but she has a good reason: she was a twin, and she wants to have a sister again. So she can *kill* her again, that is.

- **Nick Cavanaugh** (*Boxing Helena*): A successful surgeon who loves his former girlfriend Helena so much that to stop her from running away he cuts off her arms and legs, effectively turning her into a nagging paperweight.

- **Pete Davis** (*Unlawful Entry*): A police officer who does the "good cop, bad cop" routine all by himself: he thinks you need his protection and that your husband isn't up to the task, so he drops by your place at any hour . . . and has your husband arrested.

- **Diesel Truck:** Takes a lickin', and keeps on truckin'. (see entry)

- **Chip Douglas** (*The Cable Guy*): Obnoxious and aberrant cable installer who claims he just wants to "be friends." He can be treacherous and even cruel. He can call you day or night, he can make your family love him, he can turn your life upside down until you snap, and become *almost* like him.

• **Alex Forrest** (*Fatal Attraction*): A blond woman who doesn't understand the concept of "one-night stand" and becomes pathological. She calls her unwilling significant other, damages his car, tries to ruin his marriage . . . she has the entire How-to-Wreck-a-Life Tool Kit.

• **Darian Forrester** (*The Crush*): A 14-year-old Lolita who has an extremely unhealthy crush on a journalist who is "to die for." Or at least who has to die (we didn't say for whom the crush was most unhealthy).

• **Ruben Goetz** (*Copycat*): An unoriginal guy who emulates the work of serial killer Daryll Lee Cullum, whose murders were choreographed to make a statement. Daryll was a student of serial killers of the past, so he was a copycat himself. This makes Ruben a copycopycat. But still lethal.

• **Jane Hudson** (*What Ever Happened to Baby Jane?*): A child star whose popularity faded as she grew older. Her sister Blanche, on the other hand, became a great star when she reached maturity. Blanche ended up in a wheelchair, and Jane ended up totally insane.

• **Mark Lewis** (*Peeping Tom*): A cameraman with chiseled features, perfect in every aspect of his persona. Neat, clean, orderly . . . he could be the perfect date. Guess what he really is? *Hint:* He takes snapshots of his victims as he kills them with a long blade concealed in one of his tripod's legs.

• **Manny** (*The Fan*): He loves his idol, he adores him, he venerates him, he wants him. Manny is really pushing the envelope.

• **David McCall** (*Fear*): A good-looking kid with a Calvin Klein body ("Obsession," get it? Ha-ha). He's the kid your daughter hooks up with but that you don't like at all. And if you tell him that he can't see your daughter anymore . . . then you won't see your whole *family* anymore.

• **Peter Neal** (*Tenebrae*): A successful writer. There's an alleged copycat who kills using the same techniques that Peter describes in his novels. The copycat gets so good at it that sometimes he kills even *before* reading about the techniques. Could he be . . . ?

• **Hugie Warriner** (*Dead Calm*): He loves the sea as much as he loves to kill. He's an expert with traps, and pretty quick-witted, too. If you're a pretty woman, he might fall in love with you before trying to kill you. And your husband. And your dog.

• **Annie Wilkes:** The anti-nurse. (see entry)

Angela Baker

Classification: the obsessed / *Nosin infrunuvher*

Footage:

1983, *Sleepaway Camp* by Robert Hiltzik
1988, *Sleepaway Camp 2: Unhappy Campers* by Michael A. Simpson
1989, *Sleepaway Camp III: Teenage Wasteland* by Michael A. Simpson

The Skinny: "Girls just wanna have fun," especially with knives, drills, or tent pegs.

Quotable: "Seems that every time I go to camp, somebody loses their mind."

Habitat: Summer camps such as Camp Arawak or Camp Rolling Hills (later renamed Camp New Horizons).

Origin: After a boating accident that killed her father and brother, little Angela was adopted by a man-hating aunt who, after eight years of brainwashing her to hate sex, drugs, smoking, and drinking, finally sent little Angela to a summer camp. A breath of fresh air for Angela? Yeah, sure . . . get real! Once at camp, the 14-year-old girl was the butt of every joke, not to mention the sexual fantasy of the camp cook. Well, you don't need to be Einstein to figure out what happened next, or why she was whimsically nicknamed "the Angel of Death."

Identification: As a shy teenager, under her dress, Angela was hiding something more than a trembling soul. Something that, five years later, was cut off during an operation, which (with the help of electroshock therapy and every known pill) created the real Angela: a woman who's "white, 5'5", 115 lbs., brown eyes, reddish-brown hair . . ."

Cravings: To rid camps of "bad apples."

Behavior: She sneaks into a camp, either as a counselor or as a camper (using fake names like Angela Johnson or Maria Nicastro), because Angela knows that a camp is a place where kids can learn to love each other. If that doesn't happen, she'll be so disappointed that she'll start on her mission of scraping away the naughty people. Talking about an endless mission! She considers virtually everybody a "bad person." To torture her buddies, she sings "The Happy Camper Song" or "Kumbaya". So she's always in a good mood. As a hobby, she keeps her prey in a shack or in one of the camp cabins, simply to amaze future victims.

Danger: How can you trust a woman whose favorite movie is *E.T.* and whose favorite color is blood red?

What to Do if You Meet Her: Don't sin. Don't throw any firecrackers at her, because you'll scare her—and we do not want to scare Angela in any way. Her revenge will be tenfold. And never, never, NEVER pick on the little girl at your summer camp, because you never know.

Current Status: Healing from bad wounds and waiting to go to camp again.

Body Count: 45 people, and 1 tent.

Angela's Weapons of Choice: Axes, barbecues with gasoline, battery acid, boiling water, chainsaws, dropping people from the flagpole, fake cocaine (made with dish powder), firecrackers in the nose, Freddy's glove, guitar strings, Jeeps (to rip arms out of their sockets), knifes, latrines (drowning someone with a dressing of leeches), lawn mowers, logs, portable drills, ropes for hanging, tent pegs, trucks, and wasps.

William "Billy" Caldwell and . . .

Classification: the obsessed / *Thereisnos santaclaus*

Footage:

1984, *Silent Night, Deadly Night* by Charles E. Sellier, Jr.

The Skinny: There is no Santa Claus. Only serial killers.

Quotable: "He may be nuts, but he's not stupid."

Habitat: Utah.

Origin: Back in 1971, five-year-old Billy first visited Grandpa, who scared the living hell out of the kid, telling him that Santa brings toys only to those who haven't been naughty. To complicate matters his parents were killed by a maniac dressed like Santa (talk about a coincidence), so he was placed in an orphanage along with his baby brother. Three years later Billy's ghosts were still present in his mind, but he was trying to cope with them. In 1984, the orphanage found him a job . . . in a toy store, dangerously close to Christmas. And, for the icing on the cake, Billy was enlisted to play not the Easter Bunny, but little ol' Saint Nick. Wasn't anybody paying any attention to Billy's personal drama? Evidently not.

Identification: Billy grew from being a healthy, smart little boy to being a healthy, smart young man. With a little complex.

Cravings: Killing with his ax, while yelling "punished!" Getting back to the roots, as in "this time I'll kill that cruel mother superior who never listened to my inner cry and she forced me in doing a series of awful things." Well, that was the basic idea.

Behavior: Billy's mission became clear in his sick mind when he was dressed as Santa and he found an ax and other interesting tools. Disturbed by bad behavior and naughty things like sex and alcohol, Billy starts his spring cleaning (winter cleaning? Call it what you will) by moving back to Saint Mary's Home for Orphaned Children and seeking revenge against the mean nun who never tried to reach out to him. Billy maintained his Santa look to the end, which made him almost invisible on Christmas Eve, when he completely flipped his lid.

Danger: Only if you're naughty and you need to be punished. The problem is that Billy has a very low threshold for naughtiness, so . . . behave!

What to Do if You Meet Him: Tell him "there's no Santa Claus," therefore you'll convince him that he doesn't exist as well. But it may not work. Just don't traipse around naked through your house in front of the windows, because that's like an official invitation to Billy.

Current Status: Extremely dead. But now the legacy begins . . .

Body Count: 8 people. He also beheaded one snowman and (as a kid) punched Santa.

Billy's Weapons of Choice: Axes, bows and arrows, hammers, paper cutters, reindeer antlers, and strings of Christmas lights.

. . . His Little Brother: Richard "Ricky" Caldwell

Classification: the obsessed / *Itrunnus inthefamilis*

Footage:

1984, *Silent Night, Deadly Night* by Charles E. Sellier, Jr.
1987, *Silent Night, Deadly Night Part II* by Lee Harry
1989, *Silent Night, Deadly Night III: Better Watch Out!* by Monte Hellman

The Skinny: There is no Santa Claus, Part 2.

Quotable: "I . . . don't . . . sleep!!!"

Habitat: Utah, Piru (in Ventura).

Origin: Little Richard was only one when his parents were killed, and he was 14 when he witnessed the murder of Santa, and his brother Billy got shot to death. Eventually the orphanage found Ricky a family, a Jewish one so that he wouldn't be bothered by any Christmas pageantry. But the ghosts from the past were still in Ricky's mind, as he had seizures anytime he would see a nun or the color red or somebody being naughty. So, once he turned 17, he started following in his brother's footsteps.

Identification: Billy has two phases in his life: as a bulky, brown-eyed young man, and—after six years in a coma—as a skinny, blue-eyed slow man with a transparent pot on the top of his head, showing his brain.

Cravings: Keeping up his brother's job—while yelling "naughty!" Ricky tries to get back to the mother superior who ruined his brother and himself.

Behavior: Ricky likes to be by himself, but whenever he wanders, he stumbles into naughty people. Since he's very strong and pretty clever, he has no problem winning any one-on-one fights. Eventually he gets to the mother superior, but he's shot and left in a coma for six years. During this time they surgically reconstruct part of his brain and put him in psychic touch with one of Shirley MacLaine's peers, Laura Anderson, a blind woman who's so sensitive she sees not only Ricky's memories from the past, but even his brother Billy's memories. The psychic operation brings good news and bad news: the good news is that Laura sees with Ricky's eyes. The bad news is that Ricky sees with Laura's blind eyes and runs to kill her. Evidently he was bothered by being awakened after only six years because he wanted to sleep a couple of months more.

Danger: Ricky is really nuts, even more than his brother, if possible. Thirteen psychiatrists tried to help him and they all failed. His only true love, Jennifer ("The only thing I cared about"), was strangled with a car antenna by none other than Ricky himself. And he was in love with her. Imagine what he'd do if he could hardly stand you.

What to Do if You Meet Him: Don't wear red, don't drive red cars, don't paint your house red, don't listen to the Red Hot Chili Peppers. And let us pass on to you this simple tip: if you're driving on the highway, *never* pick up a man with a transparent pot on his head showing his brain. Use a little common sense.

Current Status: He was shot dead. Twice. And as you know, bad news always comes in groups of three. And we haven't seen him buried yet.

Body Count: 21 people, 1 car, 1 TV set, and 1 Santa toy.

Ricky's Weapons of Choice: Axes, cars, car antennas, hooks, hospital tubes, jumper cables, guns, recording tapes, scalpels, and umbrellas.

Diesel Truck

Classification: the obsessed / *Peterbiltus petertakeusaway*

Footage:

1971, *Duel* by Steven Spielberg

The Skinny: Mean-ass truck with a big old chip on its cab.

Quotable: "Honk hoooonk!"

Stomping Roads: The highways of America.

Origin: A salesman was driving his red car through a lonely and sunny desert; at a certain point he had the unhealthy idea of overtaking a diesel truck. Apparently, the diesel truck didn't like his attitude. From that moment on, the unfortunate salesman was involved in a dangerous duel on wheels, complete with ambushes, pursuits, traps, and a whole lotta fear.

Identification: The diesel truck just looks like an old rusty truck: maroon, dirty, about 800,000 tires (give or take a couple), noisy horn, excellent road handling, and many plates on its bumpers—probably trophies. Oddly enough, all we know about its driver is that he wears boots. We don't know what the hell he looks like.

Cravings: Diesel. And anyone who dares call himself "King of the Road."

Behavior: Apparently the diesel truck drives along the highway waiting for peaceful drivers who want to overrun it. After that, hunting season begins. And the truck will follow its prey and try to eliminate them by pushing them off the road, under a train, or simply crushing them under its wheels. It seems that the truck wants you and your car, not just you. But we wouldn't trust it anyway.

How to Kill It: Certainly the truck is not immune to bazookas, but how many salesmen do you know who go around with a bazooka in the trunk? A good way to eliminate it (if you have full insurance coverage for your car) is to drive until you find a large area with a cliff on the side. At this moment you put a heavy weight on the gas pedal and let your car go toward the truck. If everything goes right, both the car and the truck will smash against each other and then fly off the cliff. We have no idea how you'll come back home, because you are in a place forgotten by God, but at least you're not buzzard meat . . . yet.

What to Do if You Meet It: Give it all the road it wants, and don't try any funny business. It has a bad temper.

Current Status: Eliminated (and probably recalled).

Body Count: You have to check the number of license plates on its bumper.

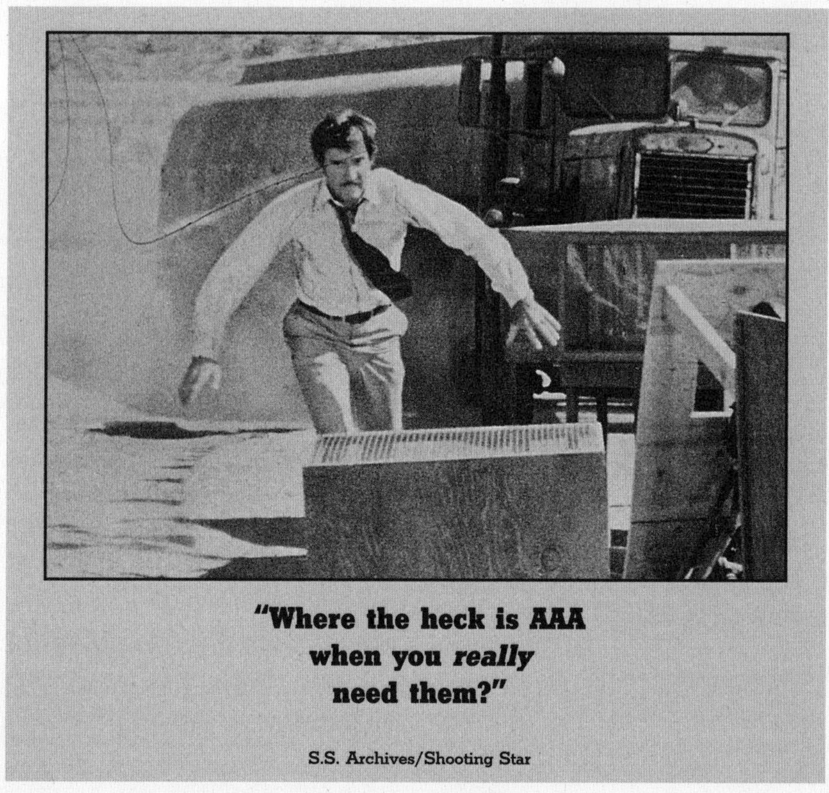

"Where the heck is AAA when you *really* need them?"

S.S. Archives/Shooting Star

Annie Wilkes

Classification: the obsessed / *Florencenightingaleus whateverus*

Footage:

1990, *Misery* by Rob Reiner

The Skinny: Lonely bookworm gets a little passionate about her fiction.

Quotable: "You're just another lying old dirty birdy, and I don't think I better be around you for a while."

Turf: Mostly Silver Creek Farm, in Maine.

Biography: Annie has spent the last five years on her solitary farm reading Paul Sheldon's *Misery* novels and worshiping the author. One day, she has a "stroke of luck": while driving along the treacherous mountain road near her house, Mr. Sheldon has a car accident right in front of her. She rescues and literally secludes him in her house, in order to take good care of him. Well . . . okay, not really.

"Hmm . . . I could try giving him a 'lap dance' . . . no, scratch that idea."

Castle Rock Entertainment/Shooting Star

How She Looks: Annie is a chubby woman, aware of her lack of outer beauty. She doesn't use makeup, she's not interested in fashion . . . the only thing that she constantly wears is a small gold crucifix around her neck.

Cravings: She really devours the *Misery* novels. And she loves Paul Sheldon. First as a writer, then as a man. On her farm, her best friend is also named Misery—a brown pig. Annie wants a little appreciation for what she does. In other news, she loves Saturday cliffhangers at the movies, and her all-time favorite musician is Liberace. She needs a life, in a big way.

Behavior: Annie, a former nurse, can take good care of her patients. And she can heal as well as hurt a person—as in hitting Paul with a pack of paper sheets on his broken leg, or hobbling him (whacking both of his ankles with a sledgehammer). Annie knows she's temperamental, and she admits that sometimes she gets so worked up that she clicks and becomes insane. But don't be afraid: ordinarily, she's a wacko. Whenever she gets mad, she jumps in her Cherokee and drives away. Adding worse to worse, the rain gives her the blues, too. As if on a sunny day she'd be normal. She also knows her house by heart, and don't you dare move her ceramic penguin! She'll come and clobber you quick as a flash.

Danger: Annie can love you so much she hates you. And she doesn't have a clue when she's crossing the line. Don't speak any profanity because you may upset her even more than usual. And remember: she's always carrying a gun in her pocket, sometimes with bullets in it.

What to Do if You Meet Her: Try not to write any novels! If you do, don't kill the main character! If you do, pardon us, but you're an idiot! Anyway, if you're desperate, tell her that her favorite character is still alive.

Current Status: Dead, but ready to come back in your fantasies.

Body Count: 1—and at least 6 in her nursing past, when she was known as the "Dragon Lady."

Religious Zealots

We're bonded for life. No matter how much you hate us.

Nick Laemle in *Parents*

Religious zealots embrace a cult as a way of life, and almost nothing can make them change their mind. The biggest problem is that these psychos see life only from their point of view. Narrow-minded to the extreme, they've joined the cult they're in for one of many reasons: they were lured into it, they were deluded by life, or they just wanted to experience something new.

Religious zealots can be anywhere: in the house down the road (*Parents, Last House on the Left, The People Under the Stairs*), in a smelly old apartment (*Se7en*), or near a sinister cornfield in Nebraska (*Children of the Corn*). God only knows where else they could be.

Behavior

On their first meeting, they're pretty quiet. They like to study you. Then they throw out a few personal theories on morality, punishment, and the afterlife. They also smile a lot, especially if you show a little interest in what they're saying. But if you don't ultimately agree with their views . . . well, they'll kill ya.

What to Do if You Meet One

Try not to sin. We know it's hard, but these guys are so obnoxious, and don't forgive a single bit of misbehavin'.

The Congregation

We're not even going to try to explain their diverse religious beliefs. But let's just say that they're against "freedom of religion" and enforce it with capital punishment.

- ***Children of the Corn:*** Enthusiastic little runts. (see entry)

- **John Doe** (*Se7en*): A tiny, balding guy with a thing for culture and photos. Makes examples of people by killing them with their own sins. Studies Dante, Milton, and Chaucer for inspirational passages upon which to model his crimes.

- **Krug** (*Last House on the Left*): A sadistic escaped convict who's not satisfied with his girlfriend, so he seeks some "extracurricular activities." Like kidnapping you after a rock concert for a little fun.

- **Nick and Lily Laemle** (*Parents*): The average couple . . . sort of. Mom stays in the kitchen handling large, sharp stainless steel knives while Dad constantly barbecues gigantic pieces of meat, hiding his predatory smile behind a pair of horn-rim glasses. They're constantly happy. And they're always eating leftovers. What are the "leftovers" left over from? What were they before becoming leftovers? "Leftovers-to-be," Dad says. And then he giggles with Mom.

- **The Robesons** (a.k.a. Mommy and Daddy): Or "Father Knows Worst." (see entry)

Children of the Corn

Classification: religious zealots / *Wekill 'nsync*

Footage:

1984, *Children of the Corn* by Fritz Kiersch
1992, *Children of the Corn II: The Final Sacrifice* by David F. Price
1994, *Children of the Corn III: Urban Harvest* by James D. R. Hickox
1996, *Children of the Corn: The Gathering* by Greg Spence
1998, *Children of the Corn V: Field of Terror* by Ethan Wiley
1999, *Children of the Corn 666: Isaac's Return* by Karu Skogland

The Skinny: Kid cult worships corn . . . yeah, we know, we know.

Quotable: "We want to give you peace."

Habitat: Nebraska; Chicago, Illinois.

Origin: At a certain point all of the children in Gatlin, Nebraska, started to worship a deity called He Who Walks Behind the Rows. According to the harvest bible, He asked the kids to kill all the adults because they were sinners. According to the facts, the children did this because they were thick as molasses.

Identification: The children of the corn look like ordinary children. But they have stone-cold faces and frequently carry around knives, scythes, and axes. Like any average high-school student these days.

Cravings: The children want to "restore the balance" on Earth, bringing back purity and innocence. Besides this, they want to give adults peace. Their concept of peace, however, is a little deviated—to them, it's: peace / pīs / *n.* 1. Killing you with a scythe 2. Killing you with a bigger scythe 3. Killing you with any other available sharp object.

Behavior: The children worship He Who Walks . . . (who actually roams *underground* behind the rows) and offer him sacrifices on harvest moon nights. They offer him anyone who's reached their 19th birthday ("It's entered the age of sinning!"). So they gather around a leader, Isaac, a freaky-looking kid who hears He Who Walks Yadda Yadda and who's the giver of his word on Earth—no less. All the children are really anxious to reach their 19th year so that they can become one with He Who Blah Blah Blah. Meanwhile, they cleanse the towns, reaping all the adults (and occasionally tourists) who venture into these godforsaken villages. Secretly, the children try to export their sweet corn to the rest of the globe so that other children will gather around in worship. Music and games are forbidden among the children, and they also procreate among themselves so the race won't be extinguished. They've really thought of everything.

Danger: These children are really fired up by their god, and it seems natural to them to do everything He says. Obedient little sh*&s!

What to Do if You Meet Them: If you're driving through cornfields in Nebraska, just floor it. If you run out of gas and end up meeting them, either show them a fake ID listing you as twelve, or else burn their cornfields and their corn bible and kill the leader.

Current Status: Once the leader has been eliminated, the children come back to their senses and understand they were doing something not entirely right. But there's always a leader in the shadows ready to pop some corn. Isaac, for instance, spent 19 years in a coma before waking up ranting about the prophecy and the new race. Yes, according to Isaac, who is now a freaky-looking *older* kid, the firstborn son and firstborn daughter of the children will beget a Superior Race, a new child who will lead us all. As if this weren't enough, apparently He Who Walks Mumble Mumble is also able to become a human being, so his name could also be He Who Rides a Motorcycle or He Who Showers Infrequently. He has also "planted the seed" by impregnating the aforementioned firstborn daughter, which will no doubt result in a bouncing baby sequel. Beware!!

Body Count: 72 people and 1 dog. All the adults in the towns of Gatlin and Hemmingford, Nebraska (more than 100 people).

The Robesons (a.k.a. Mommy & Daddy)

Classification: religious zealots / *Sickos insularus*

Footage:

1991, *The People Under the Stairs* by Wes Craven

The Skinny: Pervertedly righteous couple gather ghetto kids.

Quotable: "Your father's one sick mother. Actually your mother is one sick mother, too."

Habitat: Their escape-proof house in the ghetto.

Origin: The Robeson family ran a funeral home at the beginning of this century. Later on, they found out about real estate and the money it could generate. So they became greedy. They bought half of the ghetto and now the last two members of the family, Mommy and Daddy (even if they are brother and sister), have new plans for the 'hood . . .

Identification: Mommy and Daddy are a plain-looking couple with a sick light in their eyes. Their wardrobe suggests that they're sort of stuck in the fifties, even if they know how to operate security systems and modern weapons.

Cravings: Collecting children in order to find the Perfect Son. Unfortunately, the search seems to be long and painful (for the children). To kill time, Mommy and Daddy collect golden coins and other kinds of money. Daddy has a thing for leather, and if he has to rid the house of an intruder, he wears a black leather uniform like "The Gimp" from *Pulp Fiction*.

Behavior: Mommy and Daddy spend almost their entire lives inside their house, which is impenetrable both from the exterior and the interior: every window has a padlock, every door is made with stainless steel, and there is a computerized system to control the whole place. They occasionally tour outside the house, "shopping around" for kids, looking for pure perfection. If they meet a good kid who turns out bad, Daddy cuts out the bad part (the tongue, the eyes . . .) and seals him or her in the basement. The number of "stairpeople" increases as time goes by, while Mommy and Daddy continue their quest.

Danger: Not only are Mommy and Daddy dangerous, but they also have a dog, Prince, who is trained to kill intruders.

What to Do if You Meet Them: See no evil, hear no evil, speak no evil. And run like hell.

Current Status: Dead. Both of them. It seems.

Body Count: 3 people, 1 dog, 1 tongue, and who knows what other atrocities they inflicted upon the stairpeople.

The killer is coming. The killer's gonna get you!

Wendy in *Prom Night*

How It Starts

It's all in the past. "The Incident."

Something bad happens in the life of a revenge killer-to-be, then he or she spends years mumbling and pondering about it. Then finally, on an anniversary of the Incident, something clicks inside the killer's mind and he or she decides to seek revenge once and for all. Everybody has to pay, whether or not they were directly involved in the original incident.

How to Spot Them / Where the Pain Comes From

These are the least suspicious creatures on the face of the earth. There is a terrible secret burning in their hearts, but very seldom do they let you know what it is. So, your brother, your mom, your dad, your neighbor, your classmate . . . anyone might be a killer. You have to dig into the past—which is not as easy as it seems.

Very few people come right out in the open and say, "I want sweet, sweet bloody revenge!" These are people who've spent a long time in jail and now they want to get even with their persecutor (Max Cady from *Cape Fear*); they're frustrated actors who've never been properly recognized for their talent (Edward Lionheart from *Theater of Blood*); or they're the protagonists of sad stories of unrequited love (Erik, better known as *The Phantom of the Opera*).

As regards the circus performers from *Freaks* and Belial (*Basket Case*), these belong to that unlucky group of deformed people who've had to learn to cope with their differences. But don't let your eyes deceive you: oftentimes, *we* are the freaks, and our inhumane treatment of these people is the true evil behind the monster.

Cravings, Behavior & Hobbies

- **Breeding Cockroaches:** Only to send them into other rooms of the building the Vengeful lives in. Pretty nasty trick, especially if you own the building (*Pacific Heights*).

- **Career Helper:** Killing other singers one by one so that eventually *The Phantom of the Opera*'s protégée will find her place in the spotlight.

• **Elaborate Schemes:** Just plain killing you in your sleep is too easy and no fun at all. So these folks resort to elaborate high-tech or medieval torture schemes to ensure that your death is not only the end, but that it takes a lengthy detour through hell.

• **Getting "Up Close and Personal":** They insinuate themselves into your life, usually hiding behind the facade of the nicest, kindest person you've ever met. If you only knew . . .

• **Making a Point:** They've been insulted, offended, and/or rejected by the world. Now they're showing us who's right and who's wrong. From their point of view, that is.

• **Refusing to Pay the Rent:** Being a revenge killer is quite costly, what with all the weaponry, special surveillance equipment, and travel; that's why they skip formalities like paying the bills. And if their creditors try to collect, they meet Mr. Ax.

• **Striking Fear into Your Heart:** Despite the secret of their real identity, revenge killers love to inform you that they're after you. Your lack of sleep becomes their ambrosia.

• **Using *Urban Legends* as a Pattern:** It's more fun to kill people using very elaborate methods, particularly if these methods are already present in the local folklore. What's worse, nobody will believe you and they'll always say, "Oh, yeah: I've heard about it—but it wasn't a woman: it was a teacher, and he was an African-American bagpipe player." Or something like that.

• **Working for You:** Doing a great job. But also working for themselves, and doing an even better job (*The Hand That Rocks the Cradle*).

If You Should Find Yourself on the Short End of the Revenge Stick

• **Apologize Profusely:** It'll never be enough, but it's a start . . .

• **Fight Back with an Even Stronger Vengeance:** You're gonna need it.

• **Retire:** Stop writing books on how to stop them . . . ahhh!!!

Belial

Classification: the vengeful / *Blemishus muchoangriatus*

Footage:

1982, *Basket Case* by Frank Henenlotter
1990, *Basket Case 2* by Frank Henenlotter
1992, *Basket Case 3: The Progeny* by Frank Henenlotter

The Skinny: Separated Siamese twins seek revenge and nooky.

Quotable: "What's in the basket?"

Turf: N.Y. and suburbia; Dr. Freak's clinic.

Origin: Duane Bradley, a healthy kid, was born with a Siamese twin attached to his right side. The twin was surgically removed by a team of veterinarians (yes, *veterinarians*) and tossed in the garbage. But Duane and his brother Belial were connected by a telepathic cord: one knew what the other felt, and vice versa. So Belial called Duane, who recovered his brother from the trash and placed him in a basket. The inseparable duo grew up and moved to New York City, where they tirelessly sought vengeance.

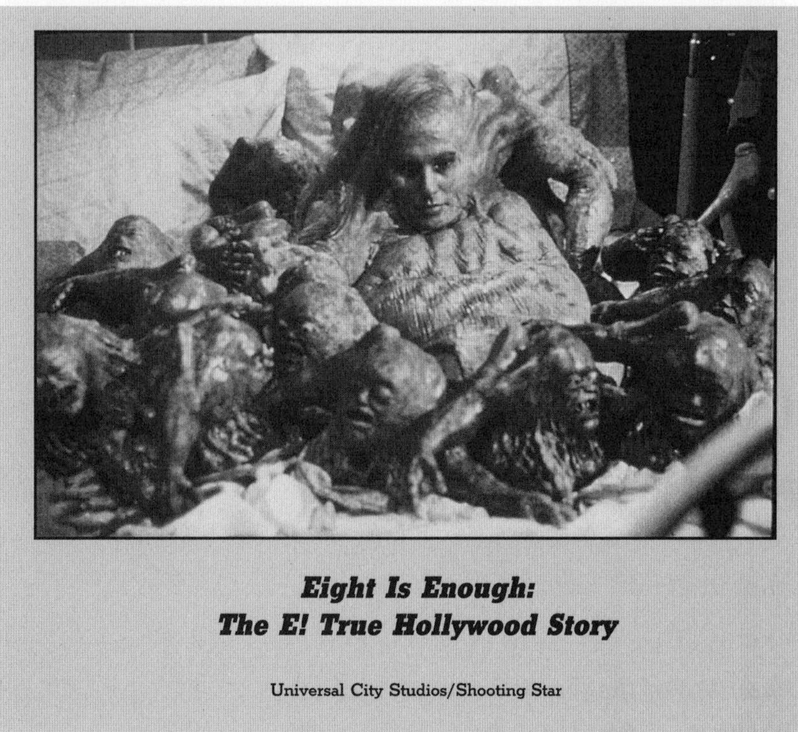

Eight Is Enough: The E! True Hollywood Story

Universal City Studios/Shooting Star

Appearance: Belial looks like a huge, hideous pimple, with a nasty all-teeth face, two gnarled arms, and clawlike hands which can rip your face off. Although he screams and roars a lot, Belial doesn't talk. But he makes himself very clear.

Cravings: Belial seeks revenge. And a lot of hamburgers (his favorite meal). He looks for love, too, but that's a real long shot, Mr. B.

Behavior: In the beginning, Belial seeks out every doctor who was involved in his surgical separation from his brother Duane, in order to avenge his cruel fate. Once he runs out of doctors to kill, Belial shifts gears: he becomes jealous of Duane and his new girlfriend—Belial understands that his brother can mate, while he can't. After a fight, Belial and Duane find a new shelter at Granny Ruth's (a.k.a. "Dr. Freak," a strange doctor who offers hospitality to "the different."). Here, in the darkness of an attic, Belial encounters his fiancée: a huge pimple, just like him. But a female pimple. And quicker than a flash, she gives birth to a new bunch of small-sized Belials. Now the new dad has to defend his heirs from the dangers of the outside world. It's just amazing how kids can change you . . .

Danger: Only if you are one of those smart alecks who loves to make fun of freaks. Belial (and his new friends—all the guests at Dr. Freak's home) won't forgive. Nor will they forget.

What to Do if You Meet Him: Sing "Personality"—it's his favorite song.

Current Status: Alive and kickin' (even if he can't).

Body Count: 16 all by himself; 1 with the help of Duane; and 1 with the help of his kids.

Erik (The Phantom of the Opera)

Classification: the vengeful / *Composerati hideousiti*

Footage:

1925, *The Phantom of the Opera* by Rupert Julian
1931, *The Phantom of Paris* by John S. Robertson

1943, *The Phantom of the Opera* by Arthur Lubin
1962, *The Phantom of the Opera* by Terence Fisher
1974, *The Phantom of the Paradise* by Brian De Palma
1989, *The Phantom of the Opera* by Dwight H. Little
1998, *The Phantom of the Opera* by Dario Argento

The Skinny: Opera lunatic imposes his exquisite taste in divas on everyone.

Quotable: "What matters is the music!"

Habitat: The Paris Opera House—mainly backstage, and frequently even *behind* backstage (humid shafts, dark corridors . . .). Infrequently other parts of Paris.

Origin: Disfigured in a fire in 1848, Erik spent the following years hiding inside the theater, spying on the people—especially in the women's dressing room. Erik was waiting for Miss Right. And when she stepped into the spotlight, the Phantom started to do the same.

Identification: Erik is an ordinary man with a badly burned face that he usually conceals under a wax mask. His deep eyes, his scary teeth, his desperately-looking-for-a-lift skin generate comments like "Horror! Horror! Horror!" from the mouths of people who accidentally bump into him.

Cravings: Music and love. Or love and music. Occasionally, he enjoys skinning his victims. But he does that while singing.

Behavior: Erik lives inside the walls of the operahouse, and talks to his protégée, tutoring her in the art of singing. When he's satisfied with the result, he kindly pressures the powers-that-be to have the woman singing the lead right away. When they refuse, Erik kindly enlightens everyone, usually by dropping a chandelier on the audience. After this, he kindly kidnaps his protégée and takes her into his realm, where he plays his organ for her. But things get pretty nasty when she removes Erik's mask and realizes he ain't Brad Pitt. Finding himself at the mercy of the world, and chased by a large number of Parisians with flaming torches and baguettes, Erik eventually leaves his hideout and runs through Paris.

Danger: Erik's sick mind gets sicker as time goes by. So if you're considering a career in opera, and you start to hear mysterious voices through the wall, keep an eye on the chandelier.

What to Do if You Meet Him: Tell him that the best thing you can sing is "Old McDonald Had a Farm" and that you aren't interested in expanding your musical horizons.

Current Status: He's probably still hiding somewhere.

Body Count: Several audiences, through time. More than a few chandeliers.

You see, it's scarier when there's no motive.

Billy Loomis in *Scream*

There's no particular reason why these people kill. Maybe it's because life is too darned boring. Or because it runs in the family. Or because it's a job like any other. All in all, stalkers seem pretty happy with their trade, and they try their best to achieve repeated success.

Many of them seem not to have a past, to come out of nowhere. They change names often and are often pathological liars. But they're extremely serious when they do their "business." Many stalkers have ESP and know in advance their victims' next move—so they can always be at least one step ahead.

What to Do if You Meet One

Run first, ask questions later. Like, "Why me?"

The Stalker Circus

- ***Henry:*** "The Pro." (see entry)

- **Mickey and Mallory Knox:** "The Wonder Twins." (see entry)

- **Leatherface:** "The Inbreed." (see entry)

- **Pluto and His Family:** "The Family Man." (see entry)

- **John Ryder:** "The Pest." (see entry)

- **Gunther Stryker** (*The Funhouse*): Often he is disguised in a Frankenstein mask. But he's much scarier without the mask: a tall, albino man with red eyes, almost two noses, one large mouth without an upper lip, four sharp fangs, and clawed hands. His father was convinced that he was the Antichrist, so Gunther has done his best to live up to Daddy's expectations. *Tip:* If the traveling fair in your town looks a little eerie, just don't go. If you do, just don't go in the funhouse. If you do, don't say we didn't tell you. Because we did. Hell, yeah.

Henry

Classification: stalkers / *Everymanus worstnightmarus*

Footage:

1986, *Henry: Portrait of a Serial Killer* by John McNaughton

The Skinny: Blue-collar serial killer makes murder an art.

Quotable: "It's either you or them, one way or another."

Born: 1955.

Stomping Grounds: Chicago and the rest of America.

Biography: After Henry's father got his legs chopped off, his mother sought affection from many others whom she would bring to the house, even while her hubby was there. In order to have someone in the family share in the festivities, she would force Henry to watch her. She must have wanted a daughter, because she would also make Henry dress up in girls' clothes for these occasions. Then, on his 14th birthday, Henry and she got into an argument, he stabbed her, and then went to prison. Or did he shoot her? Or did he hit her with a baseball bat? Over the years he seems to have lost track after all the other mothers killed. See also: *How to Make Your Son a Lover of Women*, now available in paperback.

Identification: Average height, stocky build, block-shaped face, curly hair, southern accent, gentle voice and manner. That is, until the fun starts.

THE STALKER ALWAYS KNOWS

. . . which tree you will lean against to catch your breath while being chased. The stalker will be waiting for you right behind that very tree.

. . . which door to hide behind. The stalker will leap out and catch you totally unprepared.

. . . when you'll be all alone in your house. The stalker carries blueprints of your building and knows how to cut the phone and power. And the stalker has the ability to walk around your darkened house without knocking anything over. And the stalker is better at it than you.

. . . that you won't check the space between the front and the rear seats in your car. The stalker will be able to hide in this spot where it's virtually impossible to fit.

. . . how to use any deadly weapon and how to turn any tool into one.

. . . which open door or window frame you're leaning against. And they have a habit of coming to get you through these openings. Even on the second floor.

. . . when you've decided that he's finally dead. Then he rises again . . .

. . . what your next move is. And the stalker will be waiting for you.

Craves: "Every day a little death . . ." And then maybe a side of french fries.

Behavior: During the day he takes on odd jobs, until he gets distracted by a woman who appears to be either a mother or a hooker. Then he sees what he can do to make her appear to be a corpse. But Henry is no dummy: he claims to know Latin, and the meaning of the term "*modus operandi.*" He knows that he has to kill his victims in a variety of ways in order not to get caught. And in the process has discovered that variety is the spice of life!

Danger: Oh yeah. Because you're dealing with skill and experience in Henry. He knows a thousand great ways to introduce you to your maker. He'll kill anyone for a fix, but he definitely prefers women of all shapes and sizes. And his quiet friendliness is quite deceiving. He might also be showing off for his roommate, who may also be getting a taste for it. Double your pleasure, double your fun!

What to Do if You Meet Him: Try killing him with kindness. Although it won't last, it will at least make him think you deserve to die not quite as soon as those around you. Unless you try physical kindness. Then you're bumped to the top of the list.

Current Status: "On the Road Again . . ."

Body Count: 15 people, and 1 $50 black-and-white television set.

Mickey & Mallory Knox

Classification: stalkers / *Waaaaayus overthedges*

Footage:

1994, *Natural Born Killers* by Oliver Stone

The Skinny: Killing has become the national pastime.

Quotable: "Mickey and Mallory know the difference between right and wrong. They just don't give a damn."

Habitat: Route 666, which goes across America to Gallup, New Mexico. Also the Betongo Penitentiary, Betongoville, Illinois.

Biographies: Mickey was a child whose father used to beat him, and whose mother used to hate him. When Mickey was 10, his father *probably* committed suicide, leaving the toddler with the confidence that he, his dad, his grandpa . . . they were all "natural born killers." It must be wonderful spending Thanksgiving with all of them.

Mallory, on the other hand, was loved by her dad. But the kind of love that makes you wanna smoke after you're done. She wasn't exactly thrilled by this. And one day she met the new meatman, who happened to be Mickey. And the sparks started to fly. And the bodies start to pile up.

Identification: Mickey is tall, thin, blond—and later on bald—with several tattoos on his arms and chest (one Jesus, one yin-yang symbol, stuff like that); Mallory is a cute brunette who likes to wear a long blond wig. She has a scorpion tattooed on her belly. When they're together, they kiss a lot. If they're not killing anybody.

Cravings: Killing people who "deserve to die." And letting everybody know who did it, to get as much publicity as possible.

Behavior: Mickey and Mallory start their small business together, killing Mallory's mom and dad (they beat and drown him, and burn her), then go off on a three-week killing spree, during which they massacre some 50 people. Their favorite targets are police officers, but anything goes. They're good with guns, knives, or almost any weapon, and they're able to turn you (or a crowd, or a whole penitentiary) into an evil killing machine. Fueled by the media and a horde of adoring fans, their egos keep growing, and Mickey and Mallory just have a blast! It's not the same for their victims, though. An encounter with a Native American seemed to have an impact on their lives, as they believed the old man took away the demon inside them. Of course this conviction lasted about thirty seconds, then they started all over again.

Danger: Enormous. Mickey is absolutely convinced killing is his fate. And Mallory's not too far behind. They'll keep fighting to the end, determined to die if everything else fails. It's so nice having plans for retirement, don't you agree?

What to Do if You Meet Them: Try to bargain your status from "target" up to "the one who remains alive to tell the world that it was Mickey and Mallory." We know, it's a long line to say, but well worth what might be your last breath.

Current Status: The Knoxes are alive and well, cruising America in their camper and raising their two happy children, who will probably give birth to a sequel in the future.

Body Count: 64 people; some 10 die because of Mickey and Mallory during the riot in jail; 1 nose; 1 hand. And probably a few rattlesnakes.

Leatherface

Classification: stalkers / *Crazyassim chainsawwielderum*

Footage:

1974, *The Texas Chain Saw Massacre* by Tobe Hooper
1986, *The Texas Chainsaw Massacre 2* by Tobe Hooper
1990, *Leatherface: The Texas Chainsaw Massacre III* by Jeff Burr

The Skinny: If you saw him, he saw you.

Quotable: "The saw is family."

Habitat: The Sawyers (Leatherface's family) lived in a desolate house in the Texas woods and then moved underground, below an abandoned amusement park in Dallas. In the following years, Leatherface moved into a larger and more elegant house. Better than the first one, yet still in Texas, and still in the woods.

Origin: Nobody knows when Leatherface (a.k.a. "Bubba" or "Junior") decided to begin his venture. But he's been active since the early seventies.

Identification: Big, bulky, tall; Leatherface is a very large man. He dresses in dark colors, always wears a tie, and you can often see him wearing a butcher's apron. Recently he's had problems with his right leg and has to wear a metallic joint, which gives him a limp. And of course Leatherface got his nickname because he constantly wears a mask made with pieces of skin from his victims' faces. These pieces were sewn together by Leatherface himself. In his spare time, he alters pants and shirts. He can't talk but he squeals a lot. He also carries his chainsaw around.

Cravings: Belonging to a cannibalistic family, Leatherface not only adores eating human flesh, but also chases fresh meat and skins it as well. But he isn't insensitive to feminine wiles; the problem is, like his dad once eloquently put it, Leatherface wants to have "sex with the saw." Talk about becoming "his better half." Also, Leatherface and his whole family keep "souvenirs" of their victims: chairs made with human bones, totems made with spinal cords, skins on the hood of the car. Not a pretty sight.

Behavior: In order to accomplish the job, Leatherface uses his favorite weapon: his trusty silver-and-gold chainsaw. But very often he uses a hammer or his bare hands. The more you scream in fear, the more Leatherface gets excited. If he gets really excited, he can even perform the chainsaw dance (he jumps up and down rotating the saw in the air without aiming at anything in particular, and squealing like the madman he is).

Danger: The guy is large and runs like hell. And the Sawyer family run a BBQ kiosk down the road, fix an excellent chili, and everyone wants the secret recipe ("No secret. It's the meat.").

What to Do if You Meet Him: Invite him to do the chainsaw dance for you. It's still better than the chicken dance. At least you'll be sliced with a smile on your face.

Body Count: 8 1/2 people—he started to butcher one, but his brother finished off the poor guy; 2 doors, 1 truck door, 1 car door, 1 trunk hood, 1 "Sonny Bono" wig, 1/2 of a radio station. And, along with his family, a couple hundred people and animals.

If you think that the size of your chainsaw will compensate for other shortcomings . . . you might be a redneck serial killer.

S.S. Archives/Shooting Star

Pluto & His Family

Classification: stalkers / *Fives enoughius and how*

Footage:

1977, *The Hills Have Eyes* by Wes Craven
1985, *The Hills Have Eyes Part 2* by Wes Craven

The Skinny: A bunch of desert rats can't wait to put their hands—and everything else—on whomever they see.

Quotable: "People who live this far out usually have a reason . . ."

Habitat: A nuclear testing desert area, somewhere between Cleveland and Los Angeles. Pluto and his family live in barracks close to a well, with a "Welcum" sign posted.

Origin: In 1929, a gas-station owner had a deformed, hairy son named Jupiter. After ten years of tribulation, the gas-station owner decided to leave Jupiter alone in the desert, hoping his son would finally die. But resourceful Jupiter found a whore and generated offspring: Ruby, Pluto, Mars, Mercury, and the Reaper. And none of them ended up looking any better than Jupiter.

Identification: Pluto seems to be the leader of the pack: tall, buff, bald, with giant, constantly alert eyes. His look screams "weirdo" from sixty miles away.

Cravings: Pluto and his brothers are not picky: they want it all. People, food, people-as-food, cars, a walkie-talkie . . . anything.

Behavior: Pluto respects his family, including members who want to leave (he chains them up and tortures them, but with brotherly love). Since the family lives in the great outdoors, they don't get the chance to have guests very often. So it's understandable why they're all so excited when they see someone. The excitement usually manifests itself in stealing food, then kidnapping, raping, or killing the guests, or all of the above. No wonder they don't get too many guests . . .

Anyway, Pluto—who, like a dog, can smell the presence of an animal but who can't see a rattlesnake even if you shove it up his nose—loves to organize his renegade brigade to surround you or your sleeping area and attack it.

Probably because he lives in a nuclear testing area, probably because there's sex among his brothers and sisters, and probably because he loathes his hairdo, Pluto hates it if you tease him. Come to think of it, why would you tease a gigantic crazy man who's coming at you? Turn on your heels and run like hell!

Danger: In trying to get even with this odd family, you might turn into an inhumane creature yourself.

What to Do if You Meet Him (or Them): Grab a weapon and stay alert. And if someone tells you not to leave the paved road, why be an idiot and do it anyway? Don't you ever watch horror movies?

Current Status: Sort of probably kind of dead. Maybe.

Body Count: 10 people, 2 dogs.

John Ryder

Classification: stalkers / *Norides givum*

Footage:
1986, *The Hitcher* by Robert Harmon

The Skinny: Deadly hitchhiker has fun with his rides.

Quotable: "Say 'I wanna die.' "

Stomping Grounds: America's highways.

Biography: A stupid kid didn't listen to his mother's advice ("Never pick up hitchhikers!") and picked up a hitchhiker. Stupid enough? Probably. But guess what? The hitchhiker he gave a ride to was no less than John Ryder. "Big deal!" you say. Wait a second and keep reading—*then* we'll talk.

Identification: John Ryder is tall, blond, blue-eyed, thin, and dressed in black.

Cravings: He tortures you apparently just for the fun of it. He says he wants you to stop him, but he always asks for it while he's holding a knife to your jugular.

Behavior: First of all, he has this unpleasant habit of reappearing wherever you go; and if he "hooks" you, he can destroy your life—and the life of anyone who crosses your path: policemen, other drivers, short-term girlfriends. One moment he talks to you very innocently—then he begins making strange speeches about life and death. Then he produces knives, guns, ropes . . . generally speaking, at this point you understand that this is not going to be a relaxing trip. And no matter what you do, he'll always be a few steps ahead of you.

Danger: He'll follow you, sometimes he'll even precede you, and then frame you for his crimes. He won't give up until you've killed him, which is easier said than done.

What to Do if You Meet Him: Put the pedal to the metal and drive away.

Current Status: Dead.

Body Count: 19 people; and a few limbs.

The Supernatural

TERROR FROM BEYOND . . . AND BELOW

Unholy Terror

If you thought dying was bad, well, how about dying and moving on to an unbearable eternity? The monsters discussed in this chapter come from much worse places than the ones we've previously discussed, and are just that much more grumpy for the ride back.

All of the monsters we've discussed up to this point could be explained and understood in terms of scientific observation; they all seemed to make sense, at least in retrospect. But, to quote the Bachman-Turner Overdrive song: "Buh, buh, buh, baby . . . you ain't seen nothing yet."

Yes, but Is It an "Evil" Monster?

Most supernatural monsters seem to flow from one eternal spring: **the devil**. Call him (or her?) what you will, but don't call him lazy. He seems to be everywhere.

Truth is, he oftentimes delegates the work to those a notch down the evil ladder: his **demons**. And they do a slam-bang job of it most of the time. Their enthusiasm for chaos usually rivals or even surpasses the "big man's."

Possession could be considered the original and most impressive form of the "hostile takeover." The devil can take command of a person, machine, object, or even a **haunted**

place. Anyone or anything will suffice, as long as it has the potential to do some damage—in other words, Satan doesn't possess a lot of hamsters.

"It's a Kind of Magic" . . . but Not the Friendly Kind

And, in case you were wondering where **sorcerers and warlocks, witches**, and **telekinetics** get their power, well, it ends up coming from the same place, albeit not quite as directly.

Although some of these folks may not be fully (or even partially) aware of the pact they've made with the bastard from below, most of them end up finding out eventually.

Gosh Darn It, Why Won't You Just *Die*?

Sometimes the journey to the great beyond comes off with a few hitches. If a soul sticks around for any extended period of time to bug the rest of us, well, that's your run-of-the-mill **ghost**, and usually they're nothing to lose any sleep over (except for that constant and annoying clatter of chains and what-you-will). But occasionally they get a little nasty.

And sometimes they come back. Which seems like a nice thing if you miss someone. Trouble is, they come back a little, um, "changed," if you will. Perhaps their untimely departure and time spent on the other side makes **the resurrected** just a little irritable.

Then again, sometimes they only go away in spirit, and their bodies stick around. Sounds natural enough, right? Unless the aforementioned body starts following you around with gnashing teeth. Then you got a **zombie** on your hands.

But if you find someone who just doesn't seem to die, and also doesn't seem to go to the beach, and also doesn't seem to like Italian cuisine, but does seem to have pointy canines . . . well, look out. You're probably dealing with a **vampire**. But keep in mind that their canines need to be *really* pointy. The number of "vampire wannabes" seems to be growing exponentially. If they only knew how much it sucks to be a vampire . . .

SUBCATEGORIES

So, to recap:
THE OCCULT, all stemming from . . .

- **The Devil:** The man himself.
- **Demons:** His little helpers.
- **The Possessed:** His puppets and pawns, including people, machines, and objects.

- **Haunted Places:** His homes away from home.
- **Sorcerers and Warlocks:** His faithful servants.
- **Witches:** His faithful girlfriends.
- **Telekinetics:** Those "blessed" with gifts from him.

THE UNDEAD—neither here nor there:

- **Ghosts:** The not-quite-fully departed.
- **The Resurrected:** The formerly departed, having now returned for an encore.
- **Zombies:** The somewhat departed, yet perpetually hungry for human flesh.
- **Vampires:** Everyone's favorite sunlight-deprived, bat-friendly, garlic-hating bloodsuckers, who are kind of dead, but not really.

The Occult

What an excellent day for an exorcism.

Regan MacNeil in *The Exorcist*

The Devil

If it's after you, it's after you.

A peasant in *Pumpkinhead*

Yep, we're talking about everyone's least favorite pointy-tailed ruler of hell, the Prince of Darkness, the all-around "evil dude." Satan, Beelzebub, Lucifer, Adolf, Saddam, Slobodan—call him what you will, they're all the same person. And all of the supernaturally bad phenomena in the universe can be traced back to him.

It's said that he's a "fallen angel"—that he used to play on the right team. But that's all in the past, and now he's taken on the full-time job of "tempter of mankind." We don't want to get into a long, boring theological digression here; just keep in mind that he's the main bad guy, so look out.

Stomping Grounds

If, as religion teaches us, God is everywhere, the devil has already been there at some point and made his move.

Identification

Needless to say, the devil is quite sly (being a master of disguise) and has found many different ways to show up on Earth virtually unidentified (well, almost):

- Normally, he comes into our world on June 6, at 6:00 A.M. You don't need to be Einstein to figure it out: 6, 6, 6: the number of the unholy trinity (the devil, the Antichrist, and the false prophet).
- He's often a person no one knows anything about. Not even *America's Most Wanted.*
- He can seem like the most innocent and sweet kid you've ever seen.

- An important lawyer, a handsome man, an elegant businessman . . . the devil enters our lives in different disguises—but is always extremely charming.

- The devil might even take the form of a nuclear plant located in a third-world country (*The Chosen*).

- He's always on the phone; dial *976-EVIL* or 666-1818 (*Amityville 3D*) and he'll answer your call in the order in which it is received. The first 30 minutes are free.

Cravings

The sole purpose of the devil is to inherit the world and reign over it.

- **By Playing "Little Pranks":** Every now and then the devil likes to start small, asking people to pull pranks on others. And the others to pull pranks back. Before you know it, he'll destroy your whole town. Then he'll move to another one, and another one, and another one . . . and before you can say "go to hell," the world as you know it will exist no more (*Needful Things*).

- **Destroying Humanity:** Can't a guy have a little fun nowadays?

Behavior

The devil is really a troublesome dude, and his attitude may annoy some people.

- He can be all things to all people (Daryl Van Horn, *The Witches of Eastwick*). He speaks all languages, and knows everything. The perfect contestant for *Who Wants to Be a Millionaire?*

- He can be in two places at once.

- He can levitate people and fly objects everywhere.

- He wants you to find him (as Louis Cyphre—*Angel Heart*), just to prove that he exists.

- He adores locking eyes with you. And when he does that, 99 times out of a hundred you die in a rather interesting way.

- Once he's possessed you, he can make you barf green goo, make your head spin, or even cause hallucinations in whoever stares at you.

- He can enlist minions, getting them to do his work for him.

- He either scares animals to death or has them working for him.

- He loves sins and sinners.

How to Kill Him (or Rather, Send Him Away)

Not a piece of cake.

- It must happen on hallowed ground, like a graveyard or a church. Definitely not in Tammy Faye Bakker's house. The blood of the creature must spill on the altar of God. Afterward they'll probably ask you to clean it up, but you can certainly handle that.

- You need seven daggers you can buy in a town six miles south of Jerusalem called Migeddo, where Christianity began. Anyway, once you have the proper tools, the first dagger will extinguish physical life and will form the center of the cross; the subsequent daggers will stop the spiritual life, and they need to be inserted in an outward, radial manner.

- Kill the person the devil needs the most. You'll scramble his plans. For a little while at least.

- Blow him up. If the devil is inside a nuclear power plant, you'll destroy his vessel.

- Cast a spell on him to keep him away. If it's a voodoo thing, the devil will abide by it.

What to Do if You Come Face-to-Face with Him

Tell him you're an atheist. If you don't believe in God, why would you believe in the devil? Otherwise . . . well, just avoid making any "sweet deals."

John Milton

Classification: the occult / the devil / *Satanicum litigiousi*

Footage:

1997, *The Devil's Advocate* by Taylor Hackford

The Skinny: Satan reveals what we've suspected all along about lawyers.

Quotable: "Law puts us in everything."

Habitat: The world; most recently New York City.

Origin: John Milton is an extremely powerful New York lawyer (his office represents clients from 25 countries). It's not clear if Milton's business is always above suspicion, but hey, if you can't trust a lawyer, who can you trust? . . . never mind. You'll find Mr. Milton's office at the Penta Plaza in New York City. It's recognizable because it's the only building with a lake on the roof.

How He Looks: A very charming middle-aged man, rich, fashionable—except for the ridiculous hats and shoes with high heels he wears. Smart dark eyes, smart dark hair, and a mouth filled with white teeth that he very often shows, especially when he goes, "Argh . . . argh . . . argh . . ."

Cravings: Money is just a front. John Milton's hunger is satisfied only by sins—of any kind. But his favorite one is vanity.

Behavior: John Milton lures you, offering money, success, power. He's surrounded by people who charm you, who like you, who *love* you. And John pushes the right buttons. He constantly tests his coworkers and victims to see if they're the right ones ("Pressure. It changes everything."). If they aren't, he simply waves them away from his life. From theirs, too. Milton speaks all languages, dances flamenco, and apparently knows everything. He can be in two places at once, which is particularly impressive since he travels only by subway.

Danger: "They don't see me coming."

How to Kill Him: You can't. You can stall him. Once you've identified the person he wants to use for his plan, simply kill the person—or commit suicide, if the "lucky one" is you. John will yell, scream, stomp his feet, jump up and down, hold his breath . . . but it'll be over. At least for a while. Then he'll come back to his senses and start everything all over again.

What to Do if You Meet Him: Don't be vain. He loves that. But ask about his son Keanu. You'll piss him off.

Current Status: He's still around. And will always be. Crap!

Body Count: 2 people (and likely many more); 2 suicides.

976-EVIL

Classification: the occult / the devil / *Toolongdistances wrongnumberus*

Footage:

1988, *976-EVIL* by Robert Englund
1991, *976-EVIL 2: The Astral Factor* by Jim Wynorski

The Skinny: Call the devil 24 hours a day, seven days a week, but don't complain about the bill.

Quotable: "Welcome to the caverns of the unknown, I am the master of the dark, the guide to your destiny . . ."

Habitat: Garden City, Slate River.

Origin: After Dark Enterprises, run by Mr. Mark Dark, obtained several 976 numbers, including one devoted to giving his clients their "horrorscope" for the day. The line was shut down by the same Mr. Dark because it was more costly than profitable. But the line found a new way to pay the bills . . .

Cravings: You, your soul, the bodies of your enemies . . . and free Infernet access.

Behavior: If you're particularly desperate, chances are you'll find a 976-EVIL card in your hands, and you'll decide to dial the number to hear your horrorscope. So much for being desperate. But, hey: what the heck, you think. So you try once. The voice tells you something good will happen. It does. So you call the line again. It tells you that another good thing will happen. It does. Ha-ha, you think. But you call again. And again. And again. And at a certain point you realize that the phone is giving you instructions to kill the people who bother you. You perform the job. You turn into a monster with cat's eyes, long black nails on fingers and toes, a voice that comes from the recesses of hell (or at least a decent sound lab), and you begin ripping out hearts and impaling people. Who's laughing, now? Not to mention that the phone line randomly decides to call you, and it seems to know where you are at all times. And the line doesn't care who you are: if you're "the chosen," you'll fall into a deep sleep and you'll astroproject a replica of your body—an evil replica, the actual killer. Now, how does one astroproject, you ask? Well, it seems to be an automatic process: you lie down, and in a cheesy effect your other self simply rises from your body and then goes around doing his business.

Danger: DO NOT disappoint your "destiny": if you don't do what your horrorscope has told you, you'll suffer the consequences with a slightly different destiny (i.e.: you die!!!). Or, the phone line will call you (the devil must use star-69). It'll ring until you answer, and at that point you'll suffer the consequences (i.e.: you die!!!).

How to Kill It: No can do. You can distract it for a while by tossing the possessed person down into the deep cave of hell—but then you'll wait trembling for the next phone call. If facing an astroprojected killer, you can (a) kill the original body so that the astroprojection will dissolve; or (b) kill yourself. Once dead, you may try astroprojecting your body and kill the evil one in his world. Or pay four astroprojected Mafia thugs who will astro-do the astro-job for you.

What to Do if You Meet It: Please hang up and try again. Try the Psychic Friends Network this time around.

Current Status: Still ringing after all these years.

Body Count: 19 people, 2 more (the "possessed") are thrown into hell, 1 hand is severed. Also 1 parrot and 1 toilet bowl.

Damien Thorn

Classification: the occult / the devil / *Worsethan marylinmansonibus*

Footage:

1976, *The Omen* by Richard Donner
1978, *Damien: The Omen II* by Don Taylor
1981, *The Final Conflict* by Graham Baker

The Skinny: Diplomat adopts the devil's son, unknowingly preparing him for a life in power.

Quotable: "True evil is as pure as innocence."

Turf: Italy, England, and America. And sort of everywhere else.

How He Came to Be: You can't ignore the biblical prophecies which, once fulfilled, will signify the coming of the Antichrist: The return of the Jews to Zion, the sighting of a comet in the sky, and the rebirth of the Roman Empire. So, it seems some Jews went back to Israel, a comet actually passed by our planet, and (here you need to be a little more open-minded) "scholars interpret [the Roman Empire's rebirth] as the formation of the European Common Market." So far, so bad.

Rome, Italy: the wife of a millionaire gives birth to a stillborn child. A cheap priest suggests that the millionaire replace the lost child with an orphan whose mother has just died in childbirth. The millionaire thinks about it a good three seconds and then accepts the exchange. Maybe he should have thought a little longer. As if this weren't enough, it also has been written that "the beast shall reign 100 score and 30 days and nights." That's seven years, if you don't want to do the math. So, in one way or another, he would have made it. He *is* the devil, you know.

Identification: He has dark hair, blue eyes, is very calm and well mannered, and always dresses in dark colors. Damien is also constantly followed by a raven and a black dog. Oh, if you ruffle the hair behind his right ear, you can see an interesting blue tattoo: "666." And no, that's not a quality-control inspection number . . . at least we don't think so.

Cravings: To rule our world. That's pretty much it.

Behavior: Since he was a bouncing baby boy, Damien exhibited classic kid behavior: he hated everyone, didn't pay any attention, and tried to kill people. All right, so maybe that's *not* classic kid behavior. Anyway, Damien grew up strong and healthy—too healthy; he *never* got sick. The only time he was given a blood test, they found that he had the blood of a jackal, which prevented Damien from being a blood donor—for humans, at least.

As a young man, he enrolled in a military academy and many of his fellow cadets joined the military graveyard. Later on Damien gained control of his former uncle's business, Thorn Industries, landowners whose diabolical plans are to "dominate mankind by controlling the food supply of the third world (cue diabolical laughter)." And, as icing on the cake, Damien was named ambassador to Great Britain and chairman of the United Nations Youth Committee. Here he lived up to his title and ordered the termination of all baby boys born on March 24, 1981, between midnight and dawn. One of them might have been the reborn Jesus—other prophecies had been fulfilled—not a good sign for Damien, who wasn't exactly the Nazarene's number-one fan.

Danger: He is the devil! Isn't that enough?

How to Kill Him: With the seven daggers of Mikedo, which last time we saw were kept in Subiaco, Italy, in the monastery of San Benedetto. If you only have one of them, actually that works, too, but it's less theatrical. If you don't have the daggers, forget it. Damien is too slick and wily for you. He's the devil, man.

What to Do if You Meet Him: Don't lock eyes with him. If you do, smile and pray you don't hear an ominous choir singing in Latin. If that happens, you might have pissed Damien off so much that your final, lethal journey will begin shortly after the eye-locking, and will involve remarkable staging and a painful *coup de théâtre*. Enjoy.

Current Status: Damien is finally gone, stabbed with the last available dagger. But his daughter and her twin brother are already on the road to success . . .

Body Count: Actually, Damien almost never killed anyone directly. However, people who disturbed the little bugger seemed to find their maker pretty quickly. And so the numbers are: 30 people, along with more than 32 baby boys.

Demons

Humans! You're not worth the flesh you're printed on!

The Collector in *Tales from the Crypt Presents: Demon Knight*

Demons are emissaries of the devil himself. And they love to walk the earth and do damage in his name. They're quite energetic, and even try to top the old geezer in the sheer amount of chaos caused. They're often evoked by some stupid thrill seeker, but not necessarily in the name of the devil. You can call them with magic spells, by trying to solve odd puzzles, or by saying their name a certain number of times.

In any case, demons are manipulative, nasty, and violent. They want to screw up the lives of as many human beings as possible, even if that means one at a time. They're not in a hurry. So if a demon visits your town, nothing good will come of it. If they drag you into their world, even *less* good will come of it. Once you face off with them, the battle shifts from your world (where a demon is very confident) to their world (where a demon is especially confident).

Behavior & Skills

Demons roam hell and earth mostly trying to stave off boredom.

- **Tricking You:** In order to be free again, the demon makes you believe it will grant any wish, even if the wish is real only in your mind (*Sorority Babes in the Slimeball Bowl-O-Rama*), or if they're awfully fun only for the demon (*Leprechaun*), or the wishes seem more alluring than they actually turn out to be (*The Wishmaster*). So, as the old saying goes: "Be careful what you wish for."

- **Imitating Voices:** In order to trick you, a demon can modulate its voice to sound like anybody, especially people they've just killed.

- **Shapeshifting:** Many demons can assume any form, human or otherwise.

- **Possession:** Since a few of them are pure spirits, they might be forced to use host bodies to move around. A simple tap on the shoulder is enough for them to jump from one body to another.

- **Telepathy:** A demon can talk and even touch you from a distance.

- **Revenge:** Did you do something bad to the demon? The demon will take revenge. Did you do something bad to the demon's evoker? The demon will take revenge. Did you step on the wrong crack in the sidewalk? You get the idea.

Meet the Gang

Demons are always ugly. They love to frighten you with their looks, even before doing anything substantial. And they're quite a diverse bunch:

- **Alyda** (*The Unnamable*): A constantly pissed off, tall, white-haired creature with brownish skin and a sense of humor worse than a platoon of Nazis.

- **Azazel** (*Fallen*): A pure spirit who moves through bodies of people or animals. He is sadistic, left-handed, and likes to sing—most recently "Time Is on My Side" by the Rolling Stones. The next time around, he may be singing songs by 'NSync . . . which will be *really* scary.

- **Betelgeuse** (*Beetlejuice*): A filthy man with white hair, a black-and-white suit, and a sexual appetite rivaling Australia in size. Just say his name three times and you've got company. Betelgeuse specializes in scaring away the living (known as bio-exorcism). If people are scared by ghosts, why shouldn't ghosts scared by people? So just call Betelgeuse. **Best Defense:** Say his name three times. You can send him back the same way he came.

- ***Candyman:*** Demon in the ghetto. (see entry)

- **Cenobites:** Demons into bondage. (see entry)

- **The Collector** (*Tales from the Crypt Presents: Demon Knight*): A seductive good-looking bald man with a mood swing every five seconds. The Collector can create as many demons as he wants, stabbing his hand and causing a puddle of blood to appear on the ground. The puddle will produce one demon. More puddles, more demons. In the beginning, the demons had seven keys to control the power of the cosmos. God scattered the keys, now the demons want 'em back. The special key works only if the demons have seven aligned stars in the sky (evidently, as it was in the beginning) and seven souls to grab. These are you and half a dozen of your friends. **Best Defense:** Spit sacred blood on its face. The demon will yell, scream, and curse . . . but dissolve.

- **The Djinn** (*Wishmaster* series): A bizarre-looking guy with dark skin and a talent for seeing and granting the dark side of any wish.

- **He Who Walks Behind the Rows** (*Children of the Corn*): And that's pretty much all he does, most of the time. Occasionally, he shakes the earth, moves the clouds, and makes the corn part. Just for fun. But when he's hungry, you must feed him 19-year-old victims. If you have a shortage of teenagers, anyone else will do fine. **Best Defense:** Burn the cornfield. Chances are that He Who Walks Behind the Rows will burn, too.

- **The Imp:** "I'm a demon in a bowling trophy, baby . . ." (see entry)

- **Freddy Krueger:** Sharp-clawed, handsomeness-challenged dream marauder. (see entry)

- ***The Leprechaun:*** Irish bloke, chockful o' blarney. (see entry)

- ***Pumpkinhead:*** Goulish gourd for hire. (see entry)

- **The Tall Man:** Pallid giant always playing with his balls. (see entry)

- **Umoia Omube** (*Curse III: Blood Sacrifice*): A humanoid fish that comes from the sea. It has a large mouth, two fishy hands, and apparently a breathing problem when out of the water. It smells like rotten fish, so you know when it's around. Didn't you pay your respects to the family who'd lost a child? The demon will be called by the spirit of the child to take revenge. **Best Defense:** Burn up the place where the demon is—twice. The first time it won't work, the second time it will. Don't ask why, we haven't figured it out either.

How to Kill or at Least Get Rid of Them

One of the toughest tasks you may face in your whole life. But it's not impossible . . .

- **Bless It:** Your best defense is offense. Give the demon the thing it desires the least, and you'll make it go away for good . . . or until the next sequel.

- **Trap It:** Seal the demon in a small container, where it'll lose all of its powers, and be preserved for future generations to enjoy.

- **Wish It Away:** According to the demons, their job is granting you any wish. So ask for them to go back where they belong. It's an offer they can't refuse.

- **Kill Everyone in Sight:** So the demon won't find a body to possess. No, no, wait: if you do that, he'll get exactly what he wants. So, let's think . . . we'll have to get back to you.

What to Do if You Meet One

Don't let the demon seduce you. Easy money, easy love, easy life . . . demons can turn you upside down and inside out; there is always a second (if not a third) meaning to what they promise. Build your own success. May be harder, but so much better!

Candyman

Classification: the occult / demons / *Cenobitus honeybeeum*

Footage:

1992, *Candyman* by Bernard Rose
1995, *Candyman: Farewell to the Flesh* by Bill Condon
1999, *Candyman: Day of the Dead* by Tury Meyer

The Skinny: Hellraiser in the 'hood.

Quotable: "I hear you're lookin' for Candyman, bitch. Well, you found him."

Habitat: In the mirrors of Chicago's Cabrini Green housing project, New Orleans, and Los Angeles.

Origin: In 1890, gifted African-American painter Daniel Robitaille was commissioned to paint a portrait of a landowner's daughter. When Daniel knocked her up, the landowner had Daniel's arm chopped off, then had honey poured on the poor man's face, prompting thousands of bees to sting him while the people chanted his name five times. Before dying, Daniel checked his puffy face in his lover's mirror, and somehow his spirit got trapped inside the glass. But let's not dwell on the past, shall we?

A hundred years later a dim-witted graduate student studying urban legends wanted to demonstrate that Candyman was merely a myth. The legend said that if you stand in front of a mirror and say "Candyman" five times, he'll come out of the mirror and kill you. The dim-witted graduate student actually performed the chant, Candyman actually appeared, and after the first inning the score was Candyman: 1, Dim-witted Graduate Student: O.

"What? Is it the hook? I also have a toothbrush attachment . . ."

Gramercy Pictures/Shooting Star

Identification: Candyman is a tall black man with a fur trench coat and a pretentious Gothic manner about him. His face is clean-shaven and his hair short. He loves bees (occasionally he has a few thousand underneath his coat) and has a large, sharp hook where his right hand used to be.

Cravings: "They will say that I have shed innocent blood. What's blood for if not for shedding? With my hook for a hand I'll split you from your groin to your gullet." Straight to the point, eh? But Candyman also needs us to believe in him. And lastly, he just wants companionship in his hell. He'll entice you with offers like, "Believe in me, be my victim," or, "The pain, I can assure you, will be exquisite." And heck, if you're into that sort of thing, who are we to stop you?

Behavior: Candyman appears right behind you, sometimes right in front of you, sometimes right through you (c/o his hook). He will either: (a) kill you instantly, (b) kill someone close to you, or (c) invite you to "the other side," to join his spooky world of death. If you refuse to come with, he'll revert to options (a) and (b). He has superhuman strength, can communicate with you telepathically, and doesn't cast an image on videotape. Candyman can fly, rise out of water, and vanish into thin air.

Danger: Only if you're dumb enough to try to prove to your friends that Candyman doesn't exist. Let the demon sleep inside the mirror. Reflect upon it for a bit . . .

How to Kill Him: Forget turning your back to the mirror and saying "Namydnac" five times—it won't work. Try stabbing him with a fiery stake. We're not sure if it'll be lethal; he'll sure scream a lot, though. One of the best options is getting your hands on the original mirror that belonged to Daniel Robitaille's lover. As soon as you've got it, smash it. This action frees the soul of the Candyman, whose image will freeze, crystallize, and explode. Or explode, freeze, and crystallize. Or crystallize, explode, and freeze. Who cares, as long as he's gone?

Yet the very, very best option is to "destroy the good" (since "evil cannot exist without good"). This means destroying his paintings, which were "good." But ultimately you must "destroy the myth" by attributing Candyman's carnage to a mere mortal, effectively taking away his power . . . until the next sequel, that is.

What to Do if You Meet Him: Since the sparing of your life is already a lost cause at this point, taunt him about Betelguese. After all, you only have to say Betelguese's name *three* times to bring him, and you don't even need a mirror. What is Candyman, anyway—some kind of production-line reject?

Current Status: He should be gone, but sooner or later some idiot will try to impress his friends and family in front of a mirror. Only then will we know for sure.

Body Count: 30 people and 1 dog; 21 other people were allegedly also victims of Candyman, but this has never been confirmed.

Cenobites

Classification: the occult / demons / *Demonus sadomasochistia*

Footage:

1987, *Hellraiser* by Clive Barker
1988, *Hellbound: Hellraiser II* by Tony Randel
1992, *Hellraiser III: Hell on Earth* by Anthony Hickox
1996, *Hellraiser: Bloodline* by Alan Smithee (Kevin Yagher)
2000, *Hellraiser: Inferno* by Scott Derrickson

The Skinny: Pain-loving demons who come when you solve a Rubik's cube.

Quotable: "I am pain!"

Habitat: Hell, sometimes Earth, and now even *SPACE*!

Origin: A few centuries ago a master carpenter created the most challenging puzzle in the world: a golden box which ended up becoming a gateway to hell. In 1921, Captain Elliott Spencer found this box in India. He had been told the box was the key to unbelievable pleasure. Unfortunately, what Captain Spencer experienced was unbearable pain, as he was quickly transformed into a pincushion. Through time, he found that he truly *enjoyed* this pain and became the leader of a sect of sadomasochists called the Cenobites, who roam hell waiting for other immensely curious schmucks to solve the puzzle box so that they can recruit new blood—literally.

Identification: Pinhead is a bald guy with a couple dozen pins stuck into his head, like the reverse of a porcupine. Other Cenobites have similarly gruesome appearances: one is fat and lumpy with sunglasses, another has a pierced face, one has no eyes and a chattering jaw. And Cenobites never smile. You get the picture. Not the kind of folks you want to invite over for tea.

Cravings: Cenobites thrive on suffering and are willing to spend eternity exploring your flesh. Sounds like a hoot, eh?

Behavior: The Cenobites like to give and receive pain. Just like Regis Philbin. Due to their endless patience, they're not particularly aggressive and move very calmly. However, they are quite persistent in their recruiting.

Danger: If you solve the puzzle box, it's like inviting them to a never-ending dinner party. And you're the dinner. No one escapes once they've entered the Cenobites' own private hell (or heaven, depending upon your taste).

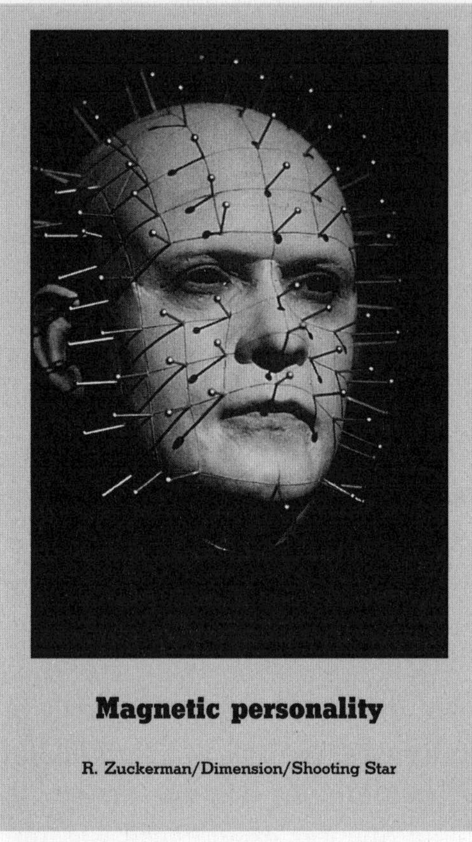

Magnetic personality

R. Zuckerman/Dimension/Shooting Star

How to Destroy Them: Cenobites aren't mortal, which makes killing them a moot point. However, depriving them of suffering and pain might make them a little more vulnerable. The best thing to do seems to be to remind them of their human past. It will get them thinking, and while they're distracted, you might be able to slip away. The key word here is *might.*

What to Do if You Meet One: Because they view pain as pleasure, their idea of a warm welcome is a barrage of fishhooks ripping at your flesh. And this is only your reward for solving the puzzle. If you happen to run into them and *haven't* solved the puzzle, you're off the hooks. So to speak.

Current Status: Still roaming, still hurting . . . now even in space, where no one can hear you scream with delight.

Body Count: 26 people, 1 robot, 1 disco, and 1 dove.

The Imp

Classification: the occult / demons / *Makingyournightmares cometruibus*

Footage:

1988, *Sorority Babes in the Slimeball Bowl-O-Rama* by David DeCoteau

The Skinny: Make a wish, such as "I wish I won't die tonight." The Imp may listen to you. Or not.

Quotable: "Uh, it's hard, isn't it? So much to wish for and only one wish!"

Habitat: Plaza Camino, a mall in a small American town.

Origin: In 1956, Dave McCade, a way-below-average bowler, decided to use black magic to evoke an imp so that he could become a good bowler and also take care of some personal business. To the Imp, "taking care of Dave's personal business" meant "ripping the guts out of the people who were bothering poor Dave." When the bodies started piling up, Dave ended up trapping the Imp inside a trophy—just before being sent to the gas chamber for the Imp's deeds. So, since 1956, the Imp had been trapped in the trophy. What could possibly go wrong?

Identification: The Imp is a small ghoul with pointy ears, a long face, an oval mouth with lots of teeth, dark eyes, and graspy hands. Its color is brown gray, and its voice is deep and warm.

Cravings: To bother people with its magical powers.

Behavior: If freed from the vessel in which it's trapped (let's say, for instance, that a sorority initiation rite involves someone clumsy stealing a trophy . . .), the Imp lures everybody into its one-wish-per-person routine, making you see things that you really desire: gold, gorgeous women, glamorous dresses. But it's only a facade. Its real purpose is to torment people, because it's an imp . . . and, well, that's what imps do. It can't help itself ("I have to do this!"). Unfortunately, if you turn your back to the Imp, it'll turn some demonic creations against you—so one way or another, someone's gonna be sorry.

Danger: Despite its small size (less than two feet tall), its powers are tremendous, and among these are the ability to seal up a place with deadly energy (so that you can't get in or out) and turning people into demons. Both of which can put a really sour spin on a party.

How to Kill It: You can't. It may be possible to make the Imp use its magic against itself, but nobody knows how to pull this particular trick off. But we have seen that if you trap the creature in a small container, it loses all its powers. "Why?" you may ask. "Not a clue," we say. But it worked for 30 years, so we assume it works without too much thought.

What to Do if You Meet Him: Don't listen to him. No matter how enthralling his offers may sound, always keep in mind that it's an evil trick!

Current Status: Alive and probably well, trapped inside a tobacco tin, waiting for someone to set him free again.

Body Count: 8 people: 4 were turned into demons and killed, 4 were killed by the demons.

Freddy Krueger

Classification: the occult / demons / *Facejobius desperatlyneedius*

Footage:

1984, *A Nightmare on Elm Street* by Wes Craven
1986, *A Nightmare on Elm Street 2: Freddy's Revenge* by Jack Sholder
1987, *A Nightmare on Elm Street 3: Dream Warriors* by Chuck Russell
1988, *A Nightmare on Elm Street 4: The Dream Master* by Renny Harlin
1989, *A Nightmare on Elm Street 5: The Dream Child* by Stephen Hopkins
1992, *Freddy's Death: The Final Nightmare* by Rachel Talalay
1994, *Wes Craven's New Nightmare* by Wes Craven

The Skinny: Evil doesn't die. Frequently, it doesn't sleep, either.

Quotable: "One, two, Freddy's coming for you. Three, four, better lock your door. Five, six, grab a crucifix. Seven, eight, gonna stay up late. Nine, ten, never sleep again."

Habitat: Your nightmares.

Origin: An affable bunch of teenage friends suddenly start to dream about this mean guy with a hat and a glove with razors. Soon the teens begin to die, care of the glove. After much paranoia, a girl finds out that this guy was once a child molester who'd been burned up by a group of angry parents. So Freddy had come back to complete his job, executing the children of Elm Street.

Identification: A thin man with his body and face covered by thousands of burns; Freddy wears a dirty red-and-green-striped pullover, dark brown pants, boots, a fedora hat, and a glove with four razor-sharp blades, one for each finger. But Freddy is a master of disguise: he can turn into a waiter, a maid, a nurse, a telephone, a motorbike . . . whatever the heck he likes!

Cravings: He scares and kills, that's about it. But one time he ate a "dead head pizza" . . .

Behavior: Springing into teenagers' dreams, trying to scare them to death. Every now and then Freddy decides to leave the dream world and hang around the real one. When he gets real gutsy, Freddy jumps out of the script to terrorize the actors and creators of the *Nightmare* series.

Danger: If Freddy kills you in the dream world, you die in the real world as well. Having all your dreams fulfilled doesn't sound so hot anymore, does it?

How to Kill Him: As Freddy is a dream, it should be enough just to turn your back on him, taking away all his energy. But, Freddy *is* Freddy, after all, so this doesn't always work. But remember: he has a bit of an Oedipus complex, so talking about his mother works almost every time. And fire *always* works. It caused his original death and still has great power over him.

What to Do if You Meet Him: Remember that if you meet him you are most likely in a dream, and in a dream *anything* is possible! Unfortunately, Freddy knows this as well. The trick is making the dream work for *you*, not him.

Current Status: He shows up in your subconscious whenever he feels like it. Enjoy!

Body Count: 31

"I'll ask you one last time: where'd you put the damned Clearasil?!!"

New Line/Shooting Star

Leprechaun

Classification: the occult / demons / *Notascutes asyodas*

Footage:

1993, *Leprechaun* by Mark Jones
1994, *Leprechaun 2* by Rodman Flender
1995, *Leprechaun 3* by Brian Trenchard-Smith
1997, *Leprechaun 4: In Space* by Brian Trenchard-Smith
2000, *Leprechaun in the Hood* by Brian Trenchard-Smith

The Skinny: Just in case you were feeling "lucky" . . . here's a little guy who'll change your mind.

Quotable: "Small though I am, mighty is my spirit when bloody battle calls. Come at me with what you will. Shoot me, stab me, kill me a hundred ways. Still I fight on. I am eternal as the sun, I am a thousand demons from Hell. Death and damage is my game, agony is my name!"

Born: March 17, 5 B.C.

Turf: Little Irish villages, big American villages, Las Vegas, the hood, and now, inevitably . . . outer space!

Biography: Once upon a time, the Leprechaun showed up to follow some wise guy who stole his gold. Another time, the Leprechaun came back after 1,000 years to fulfill a curse: he had to marry the descendant of a man who tried to trap him (you know, family matters). Yet another time, he was turned into a statue thanks to a cheap medallion. Once the medallion was removed, the little goblin was on the loose again. The Leprechaun then appeared on the remote planet of Ithacon, where he planned to marry the daughter of the King of Dominia. Pretty busy schedule for a gnome, eh?

Appearance: The Leprechaun is a two-foot-tall goblin dressed in green. He wears a little hat, little shoes with golden buckles, and green-and-white socks. His wrinkled face can use a lift and a haircut. He has clasping hands (with a life of their own if severed from the body), evil eyes, and a big mouth—which speaks with a thick Irish brogue.

Cravings: "I want me gold!" Actually, the Leprechaun wants *any* gold. His power generates from ancient coins, but he's a total sucker for any other kind of gold (rings, coins, bracelets). He loves eating potatoes and puffing his pipe, and being entertained by women he has turned into love-zombies. He really loves drinking, and he really, really loves polishing shoes. And he really, really, really loves counting his gold over and over again. Ultimately, he wants to be the king of the universe. Think big, they say.

Behavior: The Leprechaun has telekinetic powers, can turn invisible, can imitate any voice, is a shapeshifter as well as a master of illusions. Once he's free to walk around, he grows stronger and stronger. Extremely spiteful, he doesn't hesitate to bite, scratch, or break necks to nullify whoever bothers him. These little elves are extremely territorial and can't tolerate the intrusion of another leprechaun in their domain. This will always lead to a fight. "Leprechaun fight, leprechaun fight!!!"

Danger: Reportedly one of the elves of Satan, so forget the Lucky Charms. If you take away his gold, you'll be granted one wish per coin. But the Leprechaun won't let you get away easily. Also, he really hates it if you make fun of him. In either case, he feels compelled to kill you. Beware: if the Leprechaun bites you, you'll slowly turn into an elf yourself (and the Leprechaun is very alluring in a Darth Vader–Luke Skywalker way. The only difference? You'll eat potatoes instead of ruling the universe). You'll need a lot of strength not to fall into the trap—but it's worth it to keep from becoming a leprechaun yourself. And, very important: never steal his gold flute! You see, the flute has hypnotic powers and makes everyone love your music, no matter how crappy and awful it is. The Leprechaun will want his flute back . . . *badly.*

How to Kill Him: The only thing that kills a leprechaun is a freshly plucked four-leaf clover. It has to touch the body of the elf, but it's better if you shove it into his mouth. Like fairies, he can be harmed by wrought iron, but it's a little harder to make him eat a big old gate than a tiny little leaf. You can seal him inside a box, placing a cloverleaf on the lid. But you know that old saying, "A leprechaun and the four-leaf clover on the top of his crate are soon parted." . . . All right, it's not an old saying, but that's what happens. You can also send him into space. He'll blow up.

What to Do if You Meet Him: Bake a load of potatoes and toss him some shoes. But avoid sneakers: he can't shine 'em. You can also pass him a joint with four-leaf weed in it. You'll knock him out cold . . . for a while.

Current Status: Gone, but always ready to come back. This time as the king of rap . . . hey, it worked for Vanilla Ice, didn't it?

Body Count: 27 people and 2 fingers. He also turned a man into a spider by altering his DNA . . . don't ask (or, see Creations/Biologically Engineered).

Pumpkinhead

Classification: the occult / demons / *Thisisnot whatlinusawaits*

Footage:

1988, *Pumpkinhead* by Stan Winston
1994, *Pumpkinhead II: Blood Wings* by Jeff Burr

The Skinny: A myth is a myth no longer: it kills, haunts, and makes delicious pies for Thanksgiving.

Quotable: "Bolted doors, and windows barred, guard dogs prowling in the yard won't protect in your bed; nothing will from Pumpkinhead."

Habitat: Small towns. And deep in American folklore.

Origin: Pumpkinhead is a demon looking for vengeance—either yours or its own. The first time we met it, it was because of a storekeeper whose son was killed by a gang of bikers. Using some of his own blood and some of his kid's, and the spell of the old witch Haggis, the man evoked the demon to seek revenge. The second time, it was because a bunch of thrill-seeking kids recited a magic spell over the graveyard of Tommy (Pumpkinhead's son, no less) and . . . well, you know how these things go.

Appearance: Pumpkinhead is a very tall humanoid figure, with two pumpkin arms, a pumpkin torso, a pumpkin tail, and two pumpkin legs. It has two long, sharp pumpkin hands and a pumpkin head with two white pumpkin eyes. The creature's extremely strong. Also, it walks around going "RRARR!"

Cravings: Revenge is its nourishment.

Behavior: Pumpkinhead generally walks in the woods looking for people who have to die. Since the demon is driven by the blood it has received, it'll go after the people who bother the blood donor. When Pumpkinhead grabs a victim, it mutilates, twists heads, snaps in two, rips arms and legs off like the petals of a daisy, cuts hair till it reaches the stomach, and stuff like that.

Danger: If someone once said, "I'll get you back!" then don't sleep near a forest, especially if rumor has it that a witch is living somewhere in that very same forest.

How to Kill It: Once Pumpkinhead has started, there's nothing you can do to stop it. But if you're the one who gave the blood to invoke it, whatever happens to you happens to the demon. So, if you kill yourself, you kill Pumpkinhead. Sadly enough, your suicide will be necessary.

If Pumpkinhead's looking for its own vengeance, once it has closed the loop, it lets you kill it. Miss Osie, its guardian, had a necklace with a small bag on it, which seemed quite valuable to Pumpkinhead, but we're not told what's inside. Look for Miss Osie and ask her. And do let us know, please.

What to Do if You Meet It: Mind your own business, don't kill anyone, and live happily ever after.

Current Status: Gone, but its body lies somewhere at the bottom of a well. And Miss Osie still holds the spell.

Body Count: 15 people; and 1 man had to be killed in order to stop the demon.

The Tall Man . . .

Classification: the occult / demons / *Demonicus anemicus*

Footage:

1979, *Phantasm* by Don Coscarelli
1988, *Phantasm 2* by Don Coscarelli
1994, *Phantasm III: Lord of the Dead* by Don Coscarelli
1998, *Phantasm: Oblivion* (a.k.a. *Phantasm IV: Infinity*) by Don Coscarelli

The Skinny: There's a tall man. A dark, sinister, tall man. Scaaaary.

Quotable: "Don't believe everything you see . . . Seeing is easy. Understanding, well, it takes a little more time."

Habitat: Sinister-looking funeral homes, like the ones in Morningside Graveyard, Perigord, Holtsville, and Boulton, Oregon. Also Death Valley.

Origin: His former name was Jebediah Morningside, and he was a disturbed undertaker who wanted to find answers: What happens when we die? Where do we go? Why is there always a missing sock after you wash your clothes? Anyway, he somehow managed to build a passage to connect him to other dimensions. His quest is anything but easy, so the Tall Man has to pop out of nowhere, generally "nesting" in the funeral home of your hometown. Although he never appreciates *your* business, you are *his* business.

Identification: The Tall Man is the antithesis of "chubby": he's thin, thinner, and thinnest. Always dressed in black, he never cracks a smile, talks only if forced to, and always seems to move in slow motion. But this doesn't make him less dangerous (on the other hand, if he's driving his hearse, he thinks he's Mario Andretti). The Tall Man can regenerate parts of his body if sawn off, and his blood is a yellow goo. The Tall Man's favorite tool—and guardian—is the silver sphere (see below).

Cravings: The Tall Man needs bodies. According to a person who's been turned into a sphere, he "amasses an army to conquer dimensions, worlds unknown."

Behavior: Every funeral home where the Tall Man works has a bi-dimensional door that allows him to reach different places. The Tall Man fills his new homes with an army of flying spheres that he produces himself, stealing the brains of people and shrinking them into the spheres. At the same time he's found this strange red-skied desert place (a planet? a place in the future? hell?), where he runs a small business that we don't know about. Anyway, because of the gravity and the atmosphere of this mysterious place, the workers have to be midgets. At least, this is what we're told.

And here's a way he found to kill two birds (and several gazillion people) with one stone: the shrinking of the brain has a side effect, which is the shrinking of the whole body of the brain donor. Again, our mole told us that "the dwarf creatures are the bypass of the process, left with only the vestigial part of the cerebral cortex. They act on instinct and impulse. He compacts the corpse, amputates the mind, and encases it. He then turns their bodies into drones and their minds into killers."

That's why the guy runs a funeral home: he has a lot of bodies, and if there's not enough, he digs them up from the graveyard. And if that's not enough, he picks from among the townfolk. The Tall Man uses the spheres not only to kill people but also to open gates to the other dimension.

Oh, one last thing: he doesn't like the cold.

Danger: The Tall Man wants to kill you or to transform you into one of his servants or even into one of his spheres, if not both. So he follows you. Either that, or he sends his midgets. However, he needs you in one piece. Furthermore, if he really likes you, he'll plant one of his spheres in your head, to better control you. If you amputate his hands, they turn into small teethy monsters, again aiming at your brain.

How to Kill Him: The Tall Man is quite invulnerable: you can drop him into a hole and seal it with a boulder, but he'll come back. You can inject acid into his body, but he'll come back. You can hang him high, but he'll come back. You can blow him up, but he'll come back. You can freeze him to pieces (to find that he has a sphere in his skull), but he'll come back. So forget it.

What to Do if You Meet Him: If you notice that your town's live population has quickly diminished, and strange Jawa-like midgets are roaming around, it's a good time to consider taking that job in Greenland. If you're face-to-face with him, prime a grenade: since he wants his victims in one piece, he might let you go. *Might* let you go. Buy him an ice cream.

Current Status: The Tall Man is still alive, halfway between his place and ours, ready to come back at the first opportunity.

Body Count: The Tall Man's enthusiasm in using either live or dead bodies for his purposes makes the counting quite hard; he definitely dwarfed 74 people and killed and resurrected more than 5 people. Certainly, there are a lot more in the same situation. He ran over a dog, too.

. . . and the Silver Sphere

Classification: the occult / the possessed / objects / *Forkballim minddrillicus*

Identification: A chrome ball five inches in diameter, with a shrunken human brain inside. It can produce hooks, saws, drills, laser beams, and even an eye to check you out. The sphere flies about five to six feet from the ground. It comes with a lifetime warranty and a free 30-day trial. If you're not completely satisfied (and if you're still alive), return the sphere to the Tall Man for a full refund. Or for a first-class funeral.

Behavior: It flies around, usually aiming for your forehead; if it lands, two safety hooks keep it steady while a drill performs a quick lobotomy. The spheres are either kept in a box over an altar or all together on the ceiling of a funeral home. The Tall Man uses the spheres not only to kill people but also to open the gate to other dimensions.

Danger: If the silver sphere wants to kill you, it follows you. Or it might follow you home and then signal to its master. Occasionally (once in a blue moon), the sphere traps a friendly brain, so it can be on your side, or at least try to stall the Tall Man for a while. Not common.

How to Kill Them: The silver sphere can be destroyed with a rifle. You need good aim, because it flies fast. A sledgehammer may help, or a nunchaku. The best is a tuning fork, the one you use to tune your guitar, *probably* because it resembles the passage fork. But that's another music.

What to Do if You Meet Them: Move fast and erratically, because it takes them a long time to slow down and turn. Wear Rollerblades. Remember that the Tall Man can activate or deactivate a sphere simply by looking at it. It's a great chance for him to pull a prank on you.

Current Status: The spheres are still there, and according to our informer, "There are thousands."

Body Count: The silver spheres have reportedly killed 5 people, 2 hands, 1 ear, 4 doors, and 1 rat.

The Possessed

You are all my children . . .
Freddy Krueger in *A Nightmare on Elm Street Part 2: Freddy's Revenge*

The devil or other evil spirits can possess anything they like: a person, a car, a doll, even Tom Arnold (the only logical explanation why he agreed to star in *Carpool*). Needless to say, the possessed do things they wouldn't ordinarily do—like terrorize your lily-white ass.

Behavior & Skills

The possessed are not entirely conscious of what they're doing. Someone else is pulling the strings.

- **ESP (or Lucky Guess?):** No matter where you hide, the possessed will find you. Proof positive that they've got higher (or lower) powers working in their favor.

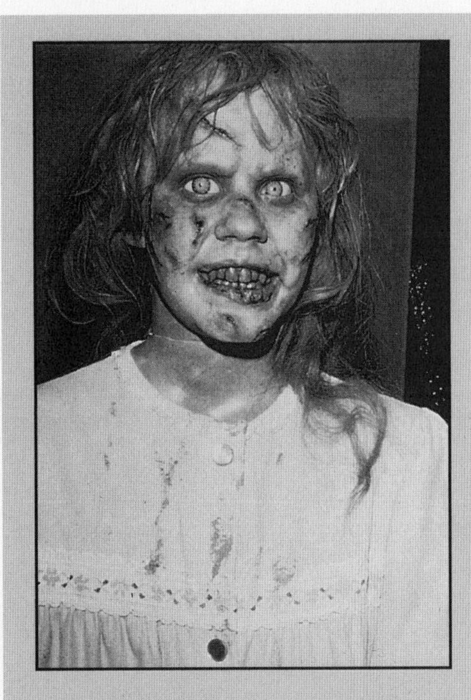

First to be weeded out in the Claudia Schiffer Look-alike Contest.

S.S. Archives/Shooting Star

- **Invulnerability:** You can kill the creature, and kill it, and kill it, and kill it, and kill it, and kill it, and kill it, and kill it, and kill it . . . it'll always stand right back up and fight even harder (Michael Myers and Jason Voorhees).

- **Seemingly Running All by Themselves:** Dominant feature of possessed machines, such as *The Car, Christine,* or *The Mangler.*

Spotting Possession

The possessed (like other nouns) are persons, places, or things that once were normal and ordinary looking, but are now abnormal—yet still very frequently ordinary looking. Here's a partial roster of the possessed we've spotted:

• **Chucky** (*Child's Play* series): Dangerously disagreable doll. (see entry)

• ***Der Golem:*** Man-sized statue made with clay which obeys its evil creator. **Best Defense:** Remove the medallion and the Golem will swoon into a pile of clay. Or remove the first letter of the word written on its forehead—*emet* which means "truth," leaving *met,* which means "death," and therefore relief.

• ***The Mangler:*** Hardley-Watson "model 6" steam ironing machine, packed with gears, chains, and wheels and puffing hot steam. But the Mangler doesn't just iron sheets. It has a thing for flesh, too.

• **Oil slick** (*Creepshow 2*): Moving oil slick with an appetite for bathers.

• **Silver spheres:** "Goodness gracious, great balls of ire!"(see entry for the Tall Man in the Demons section)

• **Sutter Cane Books** (*In the Mouth of Madness*): Hardcover or paperback, with the name "Sutter Cane" written on the cover. Carefully written to drive you crazy.

• **Toulon's dolls** (*Puppetmaster*): Living dolls created in 1939 by a mystical puppeteer. Deadly little action figures that move by themselves but are still selling better than "Jar Jar Binks" at Toys "R" Us. **Best Defense**: Pointless.

• **Wax statues** (*Waxwork*): Representing the most popular movie monsters—the Wolfman, Dracula, Audrey II, the living dead, and so on. If a wax statue kills you, you become a wax statue as well. And with every 18 (6 + 6 + 6, get it?) souls taken, the possessed becomes a flesh-and-blood creature that can head out into the world to kill some more. **Best Defense:** Let the sunshine strike them. They'll melt in a lake of ooze, worms, and cockroaches.

VEHICLES

• ***The Car:*** Large black sedan with a powerful engine and a treacherous horn. Its black windshield doesn't let you see the driver, but don't bother—there is none. Its favorite pastime is running over people while obnoxiously honking its horn.

• ***Christine:*** She'll drive you up the wall . . . or through it. (see entry)

• ***The Sleeping Car:*** A former derailed train coach turned into an apartment. Previously occupied by a serial killer (of course) whose spirit has stayed behind to have a little fun. **Best Defense:** Stay out and/or blow it up.

• **Michael Myers:** Relentless is too mild a word. (see entry)

• **Regan MacNeil** (*The Exorcist*): A nice little girl whose head spins like a merry-go-round. She also speaks in a low, rumbling voice and vomits on priests for amusement. Other than that, she's an absolute doll. **Best Defense:** Exorcism, baby.

• **Jack Torrance:** Solves cabin fever with an axe. (see entry)

• **Jason Voorhees:** Solves everything with an axe, or whatever's handy. (see entry)

How to Kill Them

Tricky business: very often, killing the possessed doesn't mean killing the possessor. You can stop the possessor for a while, but stay alert: sooner or later it'll be showtime again.

• **Explosives:** They'll erase *The Car* from the earth and stall Jason for a while.

• **Usually You Can't:** So don't waste your time.

• **Exorcism:** It works, but the devil is smart, and he'll try everything to trick you. Assuming, of course, that you are able to convince the Church to authorize an exorcism in the first place. And while we're at it, what would happen with a possessed Muslim? Does the Church cover that, too? Ah, questions . . .

Michael Myers

Classification: the occult / the possessed / *Kirkus afterjamieleecurtis*

Footage:

1978, *Halloween* by John Carpenter
1981, *Halloween II* by Rick Rosenthal
1988, *Halloween 4: The Return of Michael Myers* by Dwight H. Little
1989, *Halloween 5: The Revenge of Michael Myers* by Dominique Othenin-Girard

1995, *Halloween: The Curse of Michael Myers* by Joe Chappelle
1998, *Halloween H20: Twenty Years Later* by Steve Miner

The Skinny: A stalker who just won't die. He must have some help from below . . .

Quotable: "A man wouldn't do that." "This is not a man."

Born: 1957.

Stomping Grounds: Haddonfield, Illinois; Summer Glen, California; or anywhere he can slash.

Biography: October 31, 1963, little Michael grabbed a kitchen knife and used it to inform his sister of his desire to become an only child. When the Myerses found the massacre, they locked little Mikey in a mental institution—but he escaped 15 years later. And came back home.

"Hello . . . I'm Michael. *Knife* to meet you. Ha-ha, just a little on-the-job humor to lighten things up . . ."

Compass International/Shooting Star

Identification: The quintessential bogeymen, Michael is a tall man dressed in black, always wearing a white, unexpressive Captain Kirk mask (under which is hidden his *real* unexpressive face). He loves knives, daggers, axes, pitchforks, hairpins . . . any sharp thing he can find. And he doesn't utter a single word . . . ever.

Cravings: Killing. Michael kills you if you are in his path. Michael kills you if you are not in his path. Michael doesn't listen to reason, he just kills you, no matter who you are or why you're there. After twenty years of activity as a mad slasher, Michael is still after his sister. Not the one he slashed, of course—the other one, who was only two when Michael showed the world for the first time what he was really good at.

As regards feeding his body, Michael doesn't eat much: his only known snack consisted of a dog. Not a hot dog . . . a *real* dog.

Behavior: He goes around killing young couples (usually the men first), starting at his family's old house in Haddonfield, Illinois, but then wandering here and there seeking out more victims (he knows how to drive perfectly well, even if he spent 15 years in an asylum starting at the age of six). Once he has a knife, Michael is a happy man. And he is dying to use that knife. And his victims are dying because he is dying to use that knife.

Fun Fact: Michael always walks, while all of his victims run away like Ben Johnson; but no matter what, Michael catches up and even precedes the person.

How to Kill Him: You'd like to know how, wouldn't you? Us, too. Sam Loomis, the doctor who wanted to erase Michael from the face of the earth, has tried everything: shooting him, setting him on fire, running over him with a truck, blowing him up. Nothing. Michael's always back, angry, armed, and dangerous. Much like Robert Downey, Jr.

What to Do if You Meet Him: Wave good-bye and catch the first Concorde to Sydney, Australia.

Current Status: Beheaded by his own sister. But he'll be back, sooner or later.

Body Count: 75 people and 4 dogs.

Jack Torrance

Classification: the occult / the possessed / *Nicholsoni offthedeependus*

Footage:
1980, *The Shining* by Stanley Kubrick

The Skinny: Writer gets cabin fever, loses control of mind, then gets ax-happy.

Quotable: "Darling! Light of my life! I'm not gonna hurt you. You didn't let me finish my sentence. I said, I'm not gonna hurt ya. I'm just gonna bash your brains in. I'm gonna bash 'em right the f*@% in!"

Stomping Grounds: The Overlook Hotel in the Colorado Rockies.

Origin: Jack, a novelist with more alcohol than blood in his veins, decides to baby-sit the Overlook Hotel all through the winter with his wife and kid, just to have a peaceful place to write his next novel. Then the Torrance family finds a large group of uninvited guests (read "ghosts") who spoil the family vacation a little by talking Jack into horrific atrocities.

Oh, by the way, his son Danny can "shine," an uncommon capacity to see not so clearly both the past and the future. He sees the ghosts, too, and channels his clairvoyant perceptions about his father through his little finger. Throw in a mousy wife thinner than spaghetti, and you have quite the colorful family.

Identification: He could be Jack Nicholson's twin brother—just a little more normal and without sunglasses.

Hobbies: He walks through the hotel corridors talking to himself, waving his arms, and meeting ghosts. When he types, the only line he puts on paper (thousands and thousand of times) is "All work and no play make Jack a dull boy." Every now and then Jack uses the ax to chop up the hotel's woodwork. Once in a while he decides to exterminate his family—or is it really Jack making the decisions?

How to Kill Him: Jack is just a man; you can shoot him, stab him, poison him. But the best of the best is to have him spend the night in a blizzard. After that, you can sell him off as an ice sculpture.

What to Do if You Run into Him: Don't disturb him when he's writing. In fact, don't disturb him at all, which is pretty hard with someone already so disturbed.

Current Status: Dead, but probably still milling through the Overlook Hotel with his ghostly friends from the roaring twenties.

Body Count: 1 person and 1 door.

Jason Voorhees

Classification: the occult / the possessed / *Hockeymaskus wontgiveupum*

Footage:

1980, *Friday the 13th* by Sean S. Cunningham
1981, *Friday the 13th Part 2* by Steve Miner
1982, *Friday the 13th Part 3* by Steve Miner
1984, *Friday the 13th: The Final Chapter* by Joseph Zito
1985, *Friday the 13th Part V: A New Beginning* by Danny Steinmann
1986, *Friday the 13th Part VI: Jason Lives* by Tom McLoughlin
1988, *Friday the 13th Part VII: The New Blood* by John Carl Buechler
1989, *Friday the 13th Part VIII: Jason Takes Manhattan* by Rob Hedden
1993, *Jason Goes to Hell: The Final Friday* by Adam Marcus
2001, *Jason X* by Jim Isaac

The Skinny: Dead Man Walking . . . and killing.

Quotable: "Jesus Christmas! Holy Jesus God damn! Holy Jesus jumping Christmas sh*$!"

Born: On Friday the 13th in 1946.

Stomping Grounds: Crystal Lake and Manhattan and now, inevitably . . . outer space!

Origin: Summer of 1957: Jason drowned at Crystal Lake Summer Camp. His counselors were too busy making out to hear his muffled cries. Summer 1980: a group of sexually active teenagers were hired to reopen the camp, which had long been closed. Ignoring the advice of the village loony, they got themselves into many compromising positions. Especially the horizontal position. In all cases, this position became perpetual after a deadly visit. Since then, Crystal Lake has been given the inviting nickname "Camp Blood."

Identification: The first time he appeared, Jason was a gruesome monster-child: deformed face, protruding teeth, crossed eyes. The second time he appeared, he must have been hitting the gym, because he was a big gorilla, and wore a bag on his head. Eventually, the bag was exchanged for a hockey mask, which is now his trademark.

"This is going to hurt me more than it hurts you. NOT."

S.S. Archives/Shooting Star

In the future, he'll be a little more cyber-cool, but his core will be the same. Jason never talks and always walks. Yet no one can figure out how he always reaches the hiding place first.

Cravings: Horny teenagers and anyone else he runs into.

Behavior: He usually carries machetes, knives, axes, chainsaws—anything he can find in the local hardware store. And he always stalks playing his creepy theme, which goes "ch ch ch, ah ah ah . . ." If you hear it, skip town quick or you're toast.

How to Destroy Him: They've shot him, hanged him, drowned him, bathed him in acid, blown him to bits—and nothing works. Or actually, it *seems* to work, but Jason is *always* back, each time angrier than before. It is believed that only a Voorhees can kill a Voorhees, so just call up Jason's family and ask for a favor. But Jason might end up possessing the body of that Voorhees in order to continue his quest. So when you make your phone call, be sure to mention that it's a *big* favor.

What to Do if You Meet Him: *He* meets *you.* And then you meet your maker. Pretend to be his mother, and he'll be distracted for a while. But not for long.

Current Status: He'll appear in the year 2455. Which means about 1,300 *Friday the 13th*s to go. Oh, joy. Oh, bliss.

Body Count: 135 people, 1 dog, and 1 boom box.

Christine

Classification: the occult / the possessed / *Antideus machina*

Footage:

1983, *Christine* by John Carpenter

The Skinny: Evil car takes revenge on its owner's enemies, all the while retaining that "Turtle Wax shine."

Quotable: ". . . watch what you call my car. She's real sensitive."

Manufactured: December 1957.

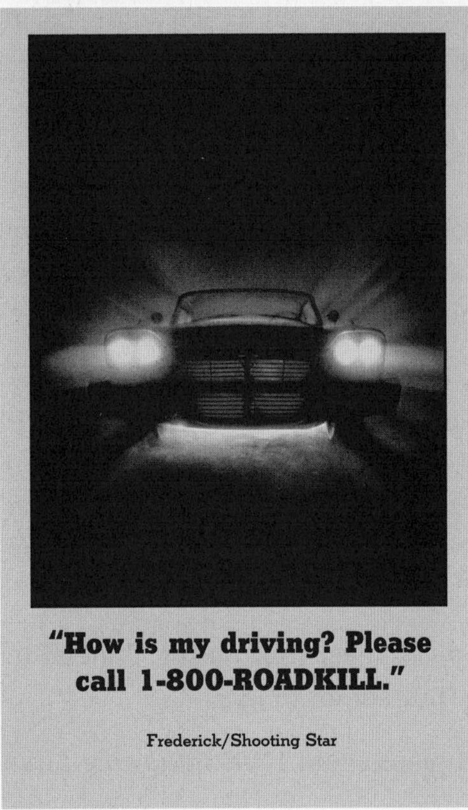

"How is my driving? Please call 1-800-ROADKILL."

Frederick/Shooting Star

Stomping Grounds: The streets of America.

Origin: While she was first being assembled at the factory, she slammed her hood on the arm of a mechanic, severing his hand. But we have no idea what she had against the guy. Later the same day she killed the factory's production manager for good measure.

Identification: Shiny red 1957 Plymouth Fury, white top, perfect inside and out, runs well, no salvage, vintage radio. Yep, Christine is a real beauty, but only when she's loved. At one point one of her owners couldn't afford the upkeep, so Christine was rotting away in the middle of a yard: rusty, dirty, and surrounded by waist-high grass. In 1978, Christine's newest owner restored her glorious sheen.

Cravings: Gas, love, and revenge.

Behavior: She makes her owners fall in love with her. *Deeply* in love, to the ends of the earth and back, surpassing all significant others, friends, and family. Christine requites this love by getting even with her owners' enemies.

Danger: She drives herself with a lead foot, often into the torsos of pedestrians. And because she doesn't seem to mind hurting herself, hiding behind thin walls doesn't help.

How to Destroy Her: Christine has this annoying habit of regenerating herself, which might be good for her owner's insurance premiums, but not for your health. If you smash her, she simply slinks into the shadows, and after a few seconds—and the sound of crinkling metal—*voilà*, she's ba-a-a-ack: brand-new and ready to rev, race, and kill again. Most recently, someone smashed her as flat as a pancake, but we can't be so sure it worked.

What to Do if You Meet Her: For starters, try not to scrape the tip of your key along her side door. But seriously, you have to get to where she can't reach you. Unlike the smart folks who have failed to evade her by running down the middle of the street, you've gotta get your butt inside a thick concrete building, into a helicopter, or even on a cruise ship if possible.

Current Status: Squashed into a small cube at a Rockbridge, California, junkyard in December 1978, but current whereabouts unknown. So if you're in the market for a '57 Fury, resist the temptation.

Body Count: 10 people and 1 hand.

Chucky

Classification: the occult / the possessed / *Gijoes myass*

Footage:

1988, *Child's Play* by Tom Holland
1990, *Child's Play 2* by John Lafia
1991, *Child's Play 3: Look Who's Stalking* by Jack Bender
1998, *Bride of Chucky* by Ronny Yu

The Skinny: Serial-killer doll gets mean and nasty with just about everyone.

Quotable: "Don't f#@& with the Chuck!"

Stomping Grounds: Toy stores; homes; military academies.

Origin: Your average serial killer (in this case Charles Lee Ray, the "Lake Shore Strangler") is taught by your average voodoo man how to transfer an average soul into an average doll. The serial killer performs this trick just before his average death, and the average doll (Chucky) is then sold to the average kid who becomes involved in your average "my doll is alive and nobody will believe me until they start to drop like flies, then it'll be too late" story.

Identification: The Chucky doll comes in a box, is 30 to 35 inches tall, with red hair, friendly eyes, and a smile. It wears blue overalls over a sweatshirt, and red and white sneakers. Chucky speaks with a lovable voice—using prerecorded lines—but sometimes it uses the voice of a serial killer, which is not a delight for the ears. The Teletubbies are better for educational purposes.

Cravings: Chucky likes to kill, but its ultimate goal is to find a new body in which to reincarnate and walk the earth as a man again. Chucky is also after an amulet, the Heart of Damballa, which is necessary in order to transfer souls into human bodies. Eventually he'd like to create an army of perverse dolls like himself.

Behavior: Chucky pretends to be a kid's best friend and whenever you aren't paying any attention, the doll pitter-patters over and gets you with a rolling pin, a scalpel, a knife, a razor . . . or else it bites you. Sometimes Chucky doesn't require batteries (which were included anyway), and it tirelessly chases you everywhere. Charles Lee Ray had a very bad temper, and it seems to have gotten worse once inside the doll. Chucky follows you, particularly if you're a body that it is interested in for its reincarnation.

Danger: If you're a kid, beware! Your new best friend might stab you just to check your blood type. If you're related to a kid, beware! Chucky doesn't split hairs—stomp on his feet, and he'll massacre you. If you don't know any kids and aren't even related to one, beware! There could always be a Chucky doll with your name written on it.

Not to mention that it recently teamed up with a soul mate—another doll, possessed by the soul of Tiffany, Charles Lee's former girlfriend. And the duo is more explosive than nitro and glycerin.

How to Kill It: "To the heart, Ramon!" Since Chucky is slowly turning himself into a living creature, his heart is the most vulnerable spot. You can try to blow his head up with a pump, make him walk into a huge fan, or riddle its body with a load of bullets. But history tells us that Chucky is not in a hurry. He'll wait for the next available chance . . .

What to Do if You Meet It: Suggest your kid buy another toy.

Current Status: Dead (perhaps), but his son is still around.

Body Count: 24 people, 1 killed because Chucky replaced blanks with live rounds; 2 cars, 2 dolls; 2 more people were killed by Tiffany, and 1 by Chucky's son.

"Yes, in fact, I *do* work for Supercuts . . . how'd you know?"

Universal/ Shooting Star

Haunted Places

Purgatory's over—you go to hell!

Nell in *The Haunting*

Origins

Houses, hotels, buildings . . . if they're haunted, here's why:

- **Trapped Ghosts:** New tenants move into an old house, which has been the scene of horrible murders. One of its former residents has gone berserk and has exterminated his or her family (*The Amityville Horror, The Haunting, The Shining*), then has committed suicide; that's the standard. The building has absorbed all the evil energy.

- **Burial Ground:** The house has been built on a graveyard (*Poltergeist, Amityville II: The Possession*). Corpses hate when that happens.

- **Gates Between Dimensions:** The building is a passageway between different dimensions (*Inferno, House*), and many creatures use it whenever they feel like it. The bad news is that the same creatures refuse to split the rent with you.

- **Place Offered to Satan:** It'll contain many wax statues, as well as time doors to fantasy worlds (*Waxwork*).

Cravings & Behavior

So many haunted places, so few needs:

- **The Living Must Leave:** Whoever enters one of these properties has to flee as soon as possible. Not necessarily alive. The houses will use all the tricks in the book to scare people away: rattling furniture, sinister squeaking, sudden hallucinations, bugs from the walls, mud slides, red-eyed pigs . . . nothing will be left out.

- **The Others Want Rest:** The houses hate to be bothered by newcomers, but sometimes they chase one special victim through the years, even if the victim moves from one place to another. Only when that particular person is taken care of will the house rest. In order to track the target, the house may send one ghost on patrol (the *Poltergeist* series) or use an object that was in the house: a lamp (*Amityville 4: The Evil Escapes*) or a mirror (*Amityville: A New Generation, The Boogey Man*).

- **Souls:** If the house is a *Waxwork*, it'll need souls to bring the monster statues to life.

How to Neutralize Them

This is going to be a little more complicated than vacuuming.

- **Destroy the Place:** This doesn't work every time, but it'll stall the evil for a while. Unfortunately, sooner or later it will return.

- **Bless the Ground:** It provides a barrier between whoever lives under the house and the house itself. Again, whoever lives underneath is quite smart and usually able to find a loophole to get back to haunting you as soon as possible.

- **Find the Gate and Step into It:** This one requires courage. First, locate the place in the house that's used as a passage. Second, dive into it. You'll create a state of confusion that will give you time enough to do your business, like to recoup one abducted member of your family. But when the house recoils, it'll become nastier.

- **Don't Take No Crap:** Stand up to it and refuse to give in. This option takes some guts (*The Haunting*).

What to Do if You Move into One

Check the classified section of your newspaper twice, then . . .

- **Move Out!**

Locations

A few places where one can find a haunted house (that is, if one really wants to):

- **Alcatraz:** The prison has been chosen by a moody ghost to make the usual mayhem. Talk about your "trapped spirit" *(Slaughterhouse Rock).*

- **Berkshire Hills, Massachusetts:** Hill House is host to Dr. David Marrow's underhanded psychological study of fear, which turns real when the house's former owner gets personal with one of the study's subjects (*The Haunting*).

- **Chicago:** Among the pools, computer-controlled elevators, and impressive apartments, a state-of-the-art skyscraper houses a bunch of ghosts who give the renters a hard time (*Poltergeist III*).

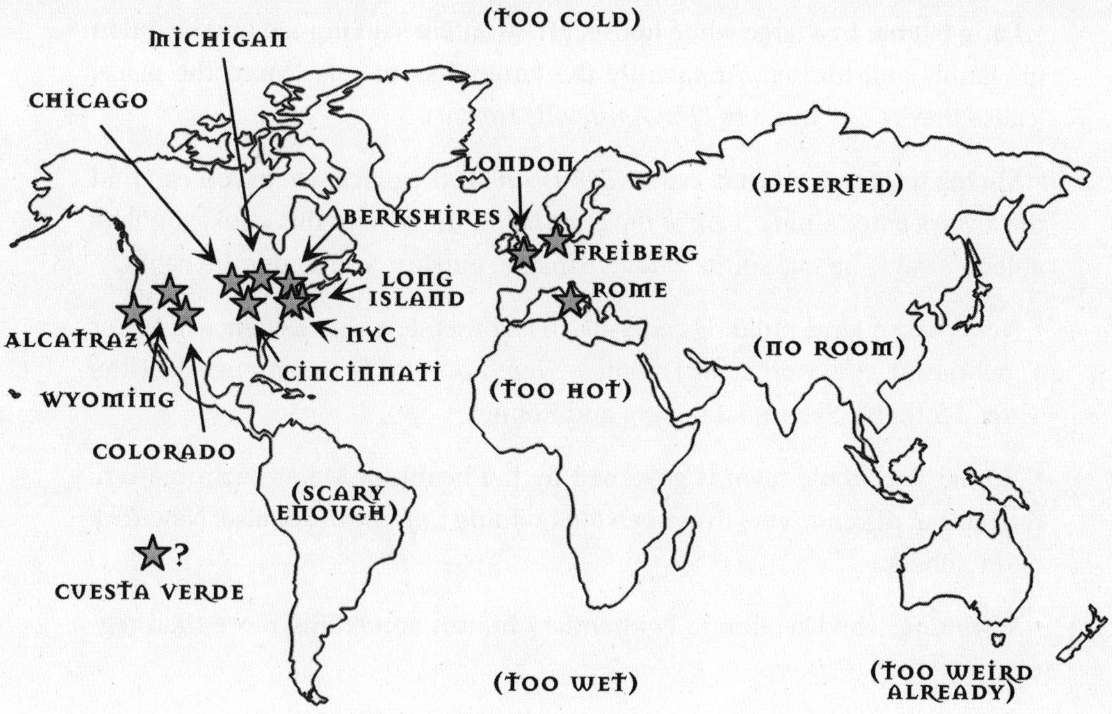

IT'S A HAUNTED WORLD, AFTER ALL!

- **Cincinnati:** A brick house is the turf for numerous ghosts, including Vietnam Vets (*House*), as well as a door through to other places and times (*House II*).

- **Colorado:** Among breathtaking mountain scenery, you can find the AAA-recommended Overlook Hotel, with all the comforts and amenities: over a hundred suites, a great lounge, a haunted room (#237), and several ghosts (*The Shining*).

- **Cuesta Verde:** Phase one of a new residential complex has been built over a graveyard. The real-estate developer has moved the tombstones, but he "forgot" to do the same with the bodies (*Poltergeist*). Now the rent is due.

- **Freiberg:** Here you can find Mater Suspiriorum, the Mother of Sighs. She's the eldest one of the Three Mothers (a.k.a. Death) and she lives in a modern house (*Inferno*). (See also: New York and Rome.)

- **London:** At 55 Lodovico Street you'll find a house that holds what remains of a man who's ready to come back if you feed him fresh blood (*Hellraiser*).

  Unfortunately, this process will also open a door to hell. It all happens on the second floor, if you must know.

• **Long Island:** In a large white house, Mr. Montelli's lid flipped and he did in his family and himself. Apparently the family has merely leased the place, 'cause they're still in there (*The Amityville Horror*).

• **Michigan:** A secluded log cabin (*Evil Dead*) is the place where you can find the always entertaining *Book of the Dead.* With the help of this book, you'll be able to awake the evil spirits who live inside, outside, and under the cabin.

• **New York:** A large building conceals, in its basement, the residence of Mater Tenebrarum, the Mother of Darkness (*Inferno*). She is the youngest of the Three Mothers. (See also: Freiberg and Rome.)

• **Rome:** The whole town is governed by the beautiful Mater Lachrimarum, the Mother of Tears, who lives in an old building (*Inferno*). (See also: New York and Freiberg.)

• **Wyoming:** The Creedmore Penitentiary houses something more than regular prisoners (*Prison*).

In Conclusion, a Little Bit of Advice: If a bizarre gentleman offers you $1 million to spend one night in a house on haunted hill, and on the invitation it says "Terror. Humiliation. Perhaps even murder," do yourself a favor and go to the movies.

Sorcerers and Warlocks

Illusions are trickery. Magicians do it for real.

Valentin in *Lord of Illusions*

Sorcerers and warlocks are the real deal, baby. These chaps know how to get jiggy with powerful potions and conjurations and they don't fool around (well, okay, a little bit, but who doesn't?). The intimidating feats they perform can change your whole perspective on who's in charge—God or someone else.

The vast majority of people trafficking in magic are evil. They are greedy. They want to control others. They like the power. And if you get in their way, heaven help you.

Habitat

- **Magic Clubs:** Hanging around the fledglings just to show off and boost their egos.

- **Godforsaken Out-of-the-Way Places:** Where they (and, in rare cases, their entourage) can live free of the confines of polite society and cast spells involving extreme weather and loud explosions without disturbing the neighbors.

- **Private Dwellings:** Usually with dank dens and altars hidden behind a more normal-looking apartment or house facade.

Identification

With the exception of a few sorcerers who lived in the past, "modern" sorcerers have a pretty updated look.

- **The Pentagram Killer** (*The First Power*), **Conal Cochran** (*Halloween III: Season of the Witch*), **Joseph Curven** (*The Haunted Palace*), **Tommy, Roger, their mother**, and **Grandpa** (*Hack-O-Lantern*), **Philip Swann** and **Nix** (*Lord of Illusions*), **Horace Pinker** (*Shocker*), and the ***Warlock*** all look like ordinary human beings with a darker side.

- **Lo Pan** (*Big Trouble in Little China*) is an ancient Asian man with white hair and a beard, but he can easily turn into a young Asian man with black hair and a beard. And a ray of light coming out his mouth and eyes.

- **Ulrich** is an old-fashioned sorcerer, with theatrical mannerisms and all the clichés of the part. But he's good at his job (*Dragonslayer*).

Special Skills

- **Commanding the Elements:** It's great for outdoor parties, especially if that day it's sprinkling. Invite Ulrich and he'll take care of the weather.
- **Flying Around:** One of the abilities of the *Warlock* and Philip Swann.
- **Telekinetic Powers:** Moving objects and people at will.
- **Cursing:** If you burn them you'll have this promise: you and your town will undergo great suffering. Oh, and they may come back, as well (*The Haunted Palace*).
- **Killing All the Children:** Using special masks that will turn a kid's head into a box of snakes, literally speaking. This is Conal Cochran's dream, an offering to the planet.
- **Murdering the World:** Nix believes this to be his full-time job. And he's working really hard to accomplish the task.
- **Moving Through Electrical Cables:** To permanently switch you off.
- **Organizing a Cult:** This is Nix's part-time job. He calls disciples and orders them to cleanse the world. And they obey.
- **Entering Your Mind:** To drive you crazy, making you see things. Another specialty of Nix.
- **Surviving the Electric Chair:** If you're bad, your prayers will be answered (*Shocker*).

How to Kill Them

Black magicians are "the real McCoy," and they can "do stuff." These people deal directly with the darker side of life, they have influential friendships in the realm of shadows, some of them know Satan personally—they spend the holidays together. Maybe you can neutralize them for a while, you can run away from them, you can trick them . . . but they'll always come back, more wicked and evil than ever. It all depends on the box office.

What to Do if You Meet One

Whatever you do, DO NOT interrupt any magical ceremony, whether a voodoo hootenanny or a satanist shindig. This is a big no-no.

Witches

We're the weirdos, mister.

Nancy in *The Craft*

A witch is a woman who deals with Satan himself. She offers him gifts, and Satan gives her back supernatural powers. Fair and square. Witches are touched by the Evil Hand: they know things, they move in the background, they mind their own business. They help you only if you ask for it, but you have to pay a high price (and witches don't accept Visa, MasterCard, or American Express).

Habitat

Witches like lonely locations as well as busy places.

- **The Shack:** The witch who lives alone prefers a small house made with wood and stones. The house is filthy, dark, with a jumbo cauldron in the fireplace: this is where the witch prepares her potions. By the way: she does make *an awful lot* of potions.

- **The Castle:** Every now and again we find a rich, noble queen who also has become a witch. Or a witch who also has become a rich, noble queen. Take your pick.

- **The Modern Building:** A school (*Suspiria*), a hotel (*The Witches*), or a nice quaint house (*The Witches of Eastwick*).

Identification

- **The Look:** The witch can change her look at will, or simply make you see what she likes you to see: to your eyes she could be a gorgeous young woman, while in reality she looks like a cross between a DeSoto and Jamie Farr. Evil witches look ugly, and they may appear like really, really old woman—we're talking a few centuries at least—but only *apparently* weak and fragile (*Pumpkinhead II: Blood Wings*). Don't be fooled. Every now and again witches are vain, so they change their aspect and appear as gorgeous women. But most witches are bald and have pointy noses (*The Witches*) and their skin constantly itches. Witches can wear lifelike masks of ordinary women over their ugly, rotten, and grotesque faces. One witch had no fewer than six breasts (*Necrop-*

olis), which she used to feed some ghouls with a fluid obtained from human souls. Not exactly "mother's milk."

• **Voice:** A witch is very cold and plain if she's talking to someone who's not a member of her coven. But when two or more witches chatter, they modulate their voices with such variety that not even Celine Dion (thank God) is able to reproduce it. During the night a witch snores as if she had a beehive shoved up her nose (*Suspiria*).

• **Clothing:** Some witches dress in dark colors and heavy clothes (*Suspiria*), some dress very alluringly (*The Guardian*), and some go for the statuesque and regal look (*Snow White and the Seven Dwarfs*). Witches have square feet, which they mask with square shoes. OK, it's an awful disguise, but they hope nobody notices.

Cravings

• **Kids:** They love kids. They chase kids. They eat kids. Or sometimes they suck away from kids their life power: the kids die of old age while the witches grow younger and younger. The more children consumed, the longer a witch's life.

• **Souls:** Same purpose as kids: the more souls the witch sucks in through the victim's forehead, the longer she'll live.

• **Revenge:** A witch casts a spell on you because you've humiliated or damaged her—or someone close to her.

• **Power:** Every so often you find a witch who wishes to control everything, with her power, wealth, and influence. The more she gets, the more she wants. Yes, that's right: Leona Helmsley is, in fact, a witch.

Behavior

SCHEDULE

• **On the Night of the Full Moon:** Witches get together every full moon, in a party under the stars known as Sabbath. They dance, jump up and down, scream a lot, and eventually make their trade with Satan. Occasionally, you'll find a quartet of witches, and in this case they form a small organization in which every witch is one corner: North, South, East, West—or earth, air, fire, and water.

• **The Town Anniversary:** Very common in those little towns that were once witch-infested. On the 100th, 200th, and 300th birthdays of the town, it's not rare to see a bunch of female newcomers: they arrive and go ballistic on the whole village.

TRICKS OF THE TRADE

• **Superhuman Strength:** A witch can move almost any weight and resist unbearable assaults (*Suspiria, The Guardian, The Witch*).

• **Smelling a Child's Presence:** They're so aroused by kids that they can sniff their presence from a distance (*Hocus Pocus, The Witches*).

• **Levitating, Walking on Water, Changing the Colors of Things:** Pretty good gimmicks, especially if you are invited to a "hidden talent contest" (*The Craft*).

• **Healing Themselves:** A witch can mend her own body. And she doesn't pay HMO fees (*The Craft*).

• **Using a "Familiar":** A familiar is an animal, such as a black cat or a dog (*Play Dead*), or else a zombie they bring back from the grave to do their bidding (*Hocus Pocus*).

SOMEONE IS A WITCH IF . . .

• **She Flies on a Broom (or Even a Vacuum Cleaner):** The most obvious clue you might stumble upon. A true witch rides with the broomcorn in front, not aerodynamically situated behind her.

• **She Casts a Spell on You:** If you have an argument with an old woman and the next day you wake up turned into a pig . . . well then, congratulations. You've met the witch of the village. Next time think twice before arguing with someone you don't know.

• **She Hates Garlic:** Like vampires, witches are not garlic-friendly. Garlic is a blood purifier and can wipe away any sorcery from your body.

Danger

MAGICAL POWERS

• **Hypnosis:** A witch charms one or more kids—even the whole town's kids, by singing a sinister lullaby. Once in the witch's mansion, the kids are lost. Hypnosis works on adults, too.

• **Resurrecting the Dead:** This is the trick they use in order to access places where they can't go, such as a graveyard. Zombie familiars will do their bidding, and even if they are destroyed, witches can just resurrect replacements.

• **Making Demons Walk the Earth:** Must be their idea of a good time. Also it's one of the things they have to do in order to keep Satan at bay.

How to Destroy Them

A witch is vulnerable, but a hard target.

• **Blades or Pointy Objects:** If you manage to get close enough to a witch, stab her in the neck with a pointy object—such as the plume of a peacock statue; not every witch owns one, but if she does, that'll do it.

• **Blessed Ground:** Drag a witch onto hallowed ground, such as a graveyard or a church: she will be turned into a statue—and a very ugly one.

• **Drop a Whole House on Her:** You'll kill her and make her body vanish.

• **Fire:** Fire cleans, consumes, destroys everything in its path. Witches definitely don't like fire. They don't even smoke.

• **Sunlight:** If a magic spell has brought back one or more witches, you have to wait for the sunlight. If the witch is hit by the light before taking the life force from the children, she will explode.

• **Water:** Toss a bucket of water at the witch; she'll melt. Or toss the witch into a river, preferably with a bag of stones attached to her. She'll drown.

• **BONUS TRACK #1:** If you're dealing with a young witch who's not totally in control of the power she's invoked, then this formula will apply: "whatever a witch sends out, she will get back times three." In a nutshell, it means that the witch will suffer a bigger punishment than the one she's dealt to her victims. If you're lucky, the punishment will get her before she gets you. But don't count on it.

• **BONUS TRACK #2:** Sometimes, the spirit a witch invokes may turn the invoker crazy. The witch ends up in the loony bin, and we live happily ever after.

• **BONUS TRACK #3:** Once a witch is dead, ding dong, the spells that she cast fade away, granting freedom to her victims.

What to Do if You Meet One

Don't have any of the weapons mentioned above? Try one of these tricks:

- **Shoot Them:** You won't kill them, but you'll stop them for a while.
- **Beat Them:** Again, just a stopgap.
- **Trick Them:** This only works if the witch you're dealing with has just been resurrected from a few centuries ago: she's not familiar with progress. You can scare her using a Zippo lighter and call yourself the Lord of Fire, and stuff like that. Again, this will stop the witch only for a while.
- **The Best:** "Only a circle of salt can protect thy victims from thy power." All witches loathe salt. This is the tip that Satan himself wrote in a witch spellbook. Hey, if it works, what the hell!

In Conclusion, a Little Bit of Advice: Stay away from the town of Burkittsville (formerly Blair), Maryland, no matter what. If you want to do a documentary, do it on the puppy dogs in your backyard.

Telekinetics

This is screwball beyond belief!

Lieutenant Parker in *Shocker*

Telekinetics are folks who can move objects with their minds and change others' thoughts at will. Which seems like a great gift if you're trying to get ahead in life. But for some reason it tends to make a person really unhappy, either because it makes him feel like an outsider, or because he eventually realizes that the gift was from Uncle Satan, and it's he who is holding the remote.

No one really knows how a person becomes telekinetic in the first place. Truth is, the telekinetics don't usually know either. But these are very special people with amazing powers, and they can pull off miracles before your very eyes. If they don't pull your eyes out of their sockets first . . .

Identification

Telekinetics look fairly plain for the most part. But when they get worked up, they start to look and act downright demonic, and there's just no reasoning with them. It's better to find them out when they're in their "wow, isn't this cool . . . I can bend spoons!" phase. Then you can pretend to have contracted leprosy and move to Hawaii.

- **Carrie White** (see entry), **Rachel Lang** (*The Rage: Carrie 2*), **Robin Sandza** (*The Fury*), and **John Morlar** (*The Medusa Touch*) look like ordinary folks.

- ***Patrick*** is a man sent into a coma by a stupid accident. But his brain is still fully functional.

- **Jan Compton** (*The Brain That Wouldn't Die*) is a gorgeous woman who constantly wears a white cap. Oh yeah . . . and she doesn't have a body attached to her head. Only a neck.

Special Skills

These folks can use their minds to perform household chores. But they also have a little fun every now and again.

- **Ignition, Blast Off:** When a telekinetic's eyes open wide, something bad is about to happen; usually, it's a fire or a big explosion (*Carrie, The Rage: Carrie*

2, Firestarter, The Fury, Patrick). So, beware. And get ready for one smokin' barbecue.

- **Mechanically Inclined:** Machines are very simple things and can easily be controlled by the telekinetic mind. So they can flip cars (*Carrie*), cause merry-go-rounds to speed up and break out of their gears (*The Fury*), or make planes crash (*The Medusa Touch*).

- **Hacking into Your Mainframe:** Telekinetics can read your thoughts like a billboard and then bend them to make you do things against your will, such as falling off a bike (*Carrie*), destroying a lab (*The Brain That Wouldn't Die*), jumping out of a window (*The Medusa Touch*), or watching an entire season of *Rugrats*.

- **Naughty, Naughty:** If you do them wrong, telekinetics will make you pay for it. The more egregious the wrongdoing, the more extreme the payback.

- **Currently Under Observation:** Evidently, telekinesis is now being studied in a lab at Princeton University (*The Rage: Carrie 2*). Shows that all our hard-earned tax dollars aren't being pissed away on the FBI's *X-Files*.

How to Kill Them

This is almost impossible. Telekinetics can read your mind and know your moves even before you think of them. Best thing is to surreptitiously get them steaming mad and watch them spin out of control until they destroy themselves. Sure beats bingo on a Saturday night.

What to Do if You Meet One

When you see a person perform an amazing feat which you think strays from the path of reality, just smile pleasantly and walk away. Never ask, "How did you do that?" or "What kind of freak are you, anyway?" Unless you're stupid enough to want to find out.

Carrie White

Classification: the occult / black magic / telekinetics / *Telekinesis teenrageous*

Footage:
1976, *Carrie* by Brian De Palma

Born: September 21, 1963.

The Skinny: Outcast teenage girl gets pissed, kills all with telekinetic powers.

Quotable: "They're all gonna laugh at you!"

Stomping Grounds: High school.

Biography: Carrie was the only child of Margaret and Ralph White, but Mr. White supposedly kicked the bucket before his daughter's arrival. Margaret, a religious nut, gave birth to Carrie in her own bedroom, cutting the umbilical cord all by herself (how disgusting!). Then she kept Carrie shielded from the evils of the world for the next 15 years by telling her that people would only make fun of her. This was her idea of motherly affection.

"Does anybody have a Handi Wipe?"

S.S. Archives/Shooting Star

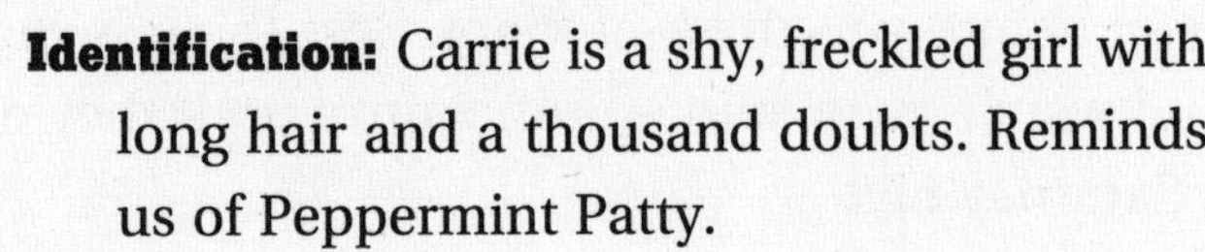

Identification: Carrie is a shy, freckled girl with long hair and a thousand doubts. Reminds us of Peppermint Patty.

Cravings: Fitting in. When your mom never tells you about the birds and the bees, it's a lot harder not to get stung. After getting stung one too many times, she wants revenge.

Behavior: She uses her telekinetic powers mostly as a shield to protect herself against people who make fun of her; she also destroys inanimate objects to vent her frustration. But Carrie can be quite lethal; for instance, she destroyed an entire prom, barricading all the doors and making the student body fly here, there, and everywhere.

Danger: Basically a nice girl, Carrie becomes vicious only after experiencing the true horrors of high school. Then she becomes a telekinetic Charles Bronson.

How to Kill Her: Like any other human. But she'll destroy herself after regretting her misdeeds.

What to Do if You Meet Her: Try to become her not-so-close friend. Being on her good side is a decided advantage.

Current Status: Sucked into the ground on May 28, 1979, at about 2:00 A.M. But Carrie is always ready to come back and haunt our dreams.

Body Count: Almost an entire prom (73 people), 2 people in a car, and 1 overbearing parent.

SIGNS THAT YOU'RE IN A HORROR MOVIE

It's not always easy for you to tell that you're in a horror movie. But there are some telltale signs that can put you on the right track. Such as . . .

- Nobody believes what you're saying.
- You're invited to an unsupervised party where the alcohol flows, there's so much smoke that it seems you're in a Paula Abdul video, and one by one all your friends start to disappear.
- The light suddenly goes off while you're in your apartment, laundry room, pool, gym, or locker room.
- Every radio or TV is turned off as soon as there's some breaking news about escaped patients or prisoners.
- A complete stranger asks you to have sex "away from it all"—in a forest or on the beach at night.
- Your significant other asks you to have sex "away from it all"—in a forest or on the beach at night.
- TV stations start to air old black-and-white horror movies, like *The Thing* or *Frankenstein*, in continuing rotation.
- An old man on a bicycle rides through town at night yelling, "You're all gonna die!"
- Your camp counselor tells you a scary tale around the fire. Nobody believes the tale, and all your friends mock it . . . until someone, wearing a stupid rubber mask, jumps out of the darkness to startle everybody. Keep your eye on the prankster: chances are that he or she won't see the light of the following morning.
- Your parents decide to reveal a horrible secret about someone who died when they were young. Of course, Mom and Dad had formerly vowed to "take this secret with them to the grave."
- It's the 100th anniversary of a terrible massacre in your town, and suddenly dark clouds are approaching.
- You go out on a boat and the engine dies. Somebody says, "It's some seaweed!"
- While checking for a noise, someone says, "Relax: it was only a cat!"
- The phone rings late at night or early in the morning, but nobody is on the line. And if someone with a raspy voice is there, it's usually worse. But if they try to get you to switch long-distance companies again, you're in a nightmare of your own.

The Undead

You talk about him as if he were a human being.
That part of him died years ago.

Dr. Sam Louis in *Halloween 4: The Return of Michael Myers*

Ghosts

They're he-e-e-re!

Carol Anne Freeling in *Poltergeist*

Origins & Habitat

Ghosts come about because something that shouldn't have happened has happened and someone has kicked the bucket. At the check-in point for the afterlife, ghosts lose their way and come back to Earth. They are tormented creatures who don't have a clue how to snap the tie that binds them to this undead realm, or even how to get back their luggage from check-in.

Ghosts live everywhere: nice new houses, spooky old houses, modern skyscrapers . . . not to mention the air all around us. Ghosts can be stationary (living in the same place for a long time, because of a curse or because the rent is cheap), they can invade a place for a while (if they find a door in that place, or if there's an anniversary of an important event), or they can follow a specific person because they feel connected with him or her.

Identification

It's hard to see a ghost; sometimes it's even harder to tell if you're dealing with one.

- **Joseph Carmichael** (*The Changeling*): A crippled, dark-haired kid who was an influential man's son. He's trapped inside a large house in Seattle, waiting for revenge.

- **Eva Galli** (*Ghost Story*): A beautiful woman who seduces you and, just as you're about to score, changes into the most repulsive creature you've ever seen. Usually you die from a stroke. What a way to go.

• **Dirty Red-Eyed Sailors** (*The Fog*): They move together, hiding in a large cloud of fog. A long time ago they were shipwrecked and murdered near the town of Antonio Bay. They vowed to return 100 years later. And guess what day it is?

• **Flying Globes of Light** (*Poltergeist*): Different shapes and sizes, glowing and lighting up your living room. And you can't use the clapper to turn them off.

• **Giant Worms** (*From Beyond*): They're amazingly ugly and filled with teeth.

• **The Soul Collector** (*The Frighteners*): A Grim Reaper wannabe, usually without a scythe, but wearing a long, brown cape and a big hood over its head. He engraves a number on the forehead of his next victim before taking him or her. He just wants to keep his collection neat and tidy.

• **Reverend Henry Kane** (*Poltergeist II*): A sinister minister with connections in the afterlife. Not good to confess your sins to this padre.

Cravings

You can see right through them (literally).

• **Drawn by the Force:** They're attracted by the life force of the living: the life force means life and memories to them; something that they desire but can't have anymore. Rats!

• **Loose Ends:** They have some unfinished business on Earth, and they cut a deal which allows them to try to finish it. In this case, they want you to listen to them—otherwise they'll get angry.

• **Retribution:** They want revenge for an injustice that has been committed in the past. This is the worst kind.

• **Rebirth:** They want a child in whom they can live again (*Ghostbusters II*).

• **Relatives:** They still want to see their friends and family.

• **A Good Old-fashioned Fright:** They want to scare you. And they're pretty darn good at that.

Behavior & Specialties

Ghosts have nothing to lose and everything to gain.

• **Who Died?:** They're dead but they don't know they're gone. Nobody told them. They didn't ask, either.

• **Getting Lost:** They're lost. Apparently, the afterlife isn't well mapped.

• **Playing Peekaboo:** They roam the space around us, and as soon as we can see them, they can see us.

• **Major-league Klutzes:** Many were movers in their prior lives, because it seems they spend all of their new lives breaking delicate things or sliding tables across floors (*The Changeling, Poltergeist*).

• **Camera Shy:** Some of them don't cast a reflection in the mirror. Or appear on film, either.

• **Chilling Out:** They suddenly lower the temperature of the room they're in. Doesn't matter if you have a thermostat or a space heater, it'll get so cold that you'll find yourself saying, "Hey, it's cold in here!" (*The Sixth Sense, Stir of Echoes*). If it's not a ghost, it's probably El Niño.

• **Shapeshifting:** Some can appear as they were before dying and as they are now after a few decades underground (*Ghost Story*).

How to Kill Them

If you establish contact with them, ask what they want, then you'll probably be able to satisfy their needs. And usually once a ghost has finished its business on Earth, it is free to go to its final destination. Usually.

Unless you decide to induce your own death, do your business soul to soul with the evil ghost and finally be resurrected before any brain damage becomes irreversible. It's not an easy task, especially because your time "on the other side" is really short (*The Frighteners*).

What to Do if You Meet One

• **Just Listen:** Maybe they have to tell you something, maybe they're trying to lead you to some part of the house you live in, maybe they want to use you as their new emissary. They'll be grateful. Perhaps.

• **The Resonator:** It's an interesting machine that allows you to see the creatures that live around us and that come *From Beyond*. Unfortunately, these creatures can see us as well, and their first idea is to chomp our heads off.

• **Who You Gonna Call?:** (212) 555-2368. It's the *Ghostbusters*' direct phone line, open 24 hours a day, seven days a week.

Resurrected

"Why doesn't he have a heartbeat?"
". . . Maybe it takes a while."
Jeff and Drew in *Pet Sematary II*

The resurrected are former living creatures who have come back from the grave. There might be more than one reason for this return: someone could have found a magic spell (either engraved on a sarcophagus or hidden on a heavy-metal album), or a person has been buried in hallowed ground (like a Micmac Indian cemetery), or the dead being was merely tired of living in hell and broke the chain of damnation to come back. It may sound confusing, but the resurrected are among the most confused creatures that you'll ever meet: many of them don't know why they're back or for what purpose, so they wander around, taking wild guesses.

Identification

Resurrections may look pretty rotten, almost like zombies, but they have an extra sparkle in their eyes that makes them unique. But no less dangerous.

They all start out fine, but as time goes by, their flesh deteriorates and they literally fall apart. Unless they're able to gain some vital energy from their victims. The ***mummies*** *all look the same: bandages, bandages, and more bandages. (see entry)*

- **Matt Cordell** (*Maniac Cop*): NYC cop goes beyond the call of duty . . . and beyond retirement.

- **Sammi Curr** (*Trick or Treat*): Dead heavy-metal star comes back with a little help from his fans.

- **Gus Gilbert** (*Pet Sematary II*): Former cop with a twisted sense of justice likes to skin rabbits. He also has an appetite like Pavarotti, but the rigor mortis keeps him slim and trim.

- **Renee Hallow** (*Pet Sematary II*): Former actress returns as bad ("cruel") actress.

- **Headless Horseman:** Just like it sounds. (see entry)

- **Mary Lou Maloney** (*Prom Night II* and *III*): Former prom queen returns looking for love.

• **George Stark** (*The Dark Half*): Writer's pseudonym gets "killed" by the real author, then the pseudonym decides to "kill" the real author.

Cravings

• **Cleaning Up the City:** It's not an easy job, but somebody's got to do it. They want to pull up the bad roots, no matter if the resurrected is a bad root himself (*Maniac Cop, The Dark Half*).

• **Getting Even:** Did you do something to the resurrected, either before or after the resurrection? Well, you'll have to pay for it.

• **Going Back Home:** Memories . . . a resurrected's first thought is to come back home to loved ones. Usually to kill them (*Pet Sematary*).

• **Living Again:** Same desire as many ghosts, with the sole difference that the resurrected is not just ectoplasm, but putrid flesh and bones.

• **Whatever Their Master Wants:** If the resurrected has been brought back to Earth by someone, the two are connected (oftentimes telepathically). The resurrection has to obey its master's voice.

Behavior

• **Anger:** For some strange reason, every resurrected comes back as an evil creature.

• **Playing with You:** The younger the resurrected, the more playful he or she is. Sadly, "toys" for a resurrected includes things like scalpels and other sharp objects. Not a barrel of fun.

How to Kill Them

They've already gone to the final place and back, so they're used to it.

• **Bullet to the Head:** It works pretty much every time.

• **Fire:** It melts the body of the resurrected. Quite disgusting and slower than the bullet, but it does the job.

• **Electric Cable in the Mouth:** This is hard, but if you happen to be in a room with an electric cable cut in two, then shove the cable down the mouth of your enemy, and bingo, bango, you'll fry the guy.

• **Lethal Injection:** This is probably the hardest of them all, especially since the resurrection will protest all the way through. Use earplugs so you won't hear your enemy screaming, "It's not fair! It's not fair!" and you'll go home happy about a job well done.

- **Sacrifice a Human Soul:** It takes this and a whole lot more to send Mary Lou Maloney back to hell. But it's a start.

What to Do if You Meet One

Resurrected males are grumpy and vicious. Resurrected females are sexy and vicious. With very few exceptions, they don't like you. Best thing to do: step aside, let them come through, and forget about the whole thing. And don't play heavy-metal records backward.

About Animals . . .

There's this pet cemetery in Ludlow, Maine, behind which there's a larger one, the Micmac Indians' ancient burial ground. And if you bury a dead body in it, it'll come back. Someone tried with an animal: first a cat, Churchill (*Pet Sematary*), which came back smelly, nasty, cold, with yellow eyes and the bad habit of scaring the crap out of people. Later on, it was a dog, Zowie (*Pet Sematary II*) who came back. Now it seems that both the animals are gone for good. But you never know: if your pet smells bad, think twice before getting too close.

Headless Horseman

Classification: undead / resurrected / *Migraineus curedforeverum*

Footage:

1999, *Sleepy Hollow* by Tim Burton

The Skinny: Violent horseman who always aims for the head.

Quotable: "Watch your head."

Habitat: The town of Sleepy Hollow (north of New York City); the Tree of the Dead by the Horseman's grave, which is a gateway between two worlds—ours and hell.

Origin: In 1799, during the American Revolution, a carnage-loving Hessian mercenary was captured, summarily killed, and, for good measure, beheaded. His body and head were buried in the same tomb (stupid!!) in the western woods, "a haunted place where brave men will not venture." He was later brought back to our world by unpopular request, lack of skull notwithstanding.

Identification: How many headless horsemen have you seen? Well, one's more than enough, we can assure you, and if you see him, you'll recognize him at once: tall (but a little shy of his former stature), sinister, and headless (but of course); wearing dark garments and always brandishing a sword. In order to avoid running into trees, he uses a horse that has its own head intact.

Cravings: He kills people with his sword, then "kidnaps" the heads.

Behavior: Before his entrance, fires extinguish, flocks of sheep run amok, bolts of lightning cross the sky . . . he must spend a fortune on special effects. Anyway, he swoops in and is instantly after his assigned victim. Once he finds him or her, he swings his sword and *pop!* goes the victim's head. The Horseman then places the head inside the tree of the dead, a tree that also happens to bleed if you chop at it. Creepy, eh?

Danger: Whoever has the Horseman's skull controls him. So, if you're on the bad side of whoever stole the Horseman's cranium, you're basically SOL. The Horseman will find and shishkebab you with ease.

How to Get Rid of Him: The smartest trick is to get a hold of his pilfered skull and give it back to him: the Headless Dude will become human again, and therefore mortal. Also, he'll be sucked into the tree, down into hell, and vanish forever. Hopefully.

What to Do if You Meet Him: Run into a sacred area, like a graveyard or a church. He won't follow you there. But don't underestimate him: even without a head, he can think of a thousand of ways to outsmart you. Oh, also please refrain from cracking silly jokes like, "Quit while you're *ahead*," and the like. It seems that his sense of humor was also located in the missing noggin.

Current Status: He's been sent back. And his horse along with him.

Body Count: 11 people, 1 unborn child, presumably 1 kid; 1 ladder, 1 window, and several expensive props and sets.

Mummies

He . . . he went for a little walk!

Ralph Norton in *The Mummy*

Habitat

- **Egypt:** Ancient or modern (tombs, underground temples, or lost cities like Hamunaptra, City of the Dead, lost mostly because nobody was able to pronounce its name correctly, and moved away).

- **England:** Museums, private homes.

- **America:** Mapleton, Massachusetts, the Louisiana Bayou; Marin County, California.

Curses, Foiled Again!

It all started a long, long, long, long time ago: guy met gal, forbidden love ensued, gal died, guy tried to resurrect her, high priests got mad, guy got mummified—it was always the same old story. There were a few exceptions, of curse.

Here's how a few VIPs turned into walking toilet-tissue displays:

- **High Priest Imhotep** (*The Mummy*): In order to resurrect his dead beloved Princess Anck-es-en-amon, a.k.a. Anck-Su-Namum, and to give her a much simpler name like "Maggie," he stole the Scroll of Thoth. The priest got caught, probably because he pranced around Isis's temple yelling, "I got the Scroll of Thoth! I got the Scroll of Thoth!" He was then mummified while still alive, buried in a secret place, and the key was thrown away. A slightly different version has Imhotep using the Black Book of the Dead (instead of the scroll); he was still a pain in the neck.

- **Queen Kara** (*The Awakening*): After killing thousands just for the heck of it, she was buried alive with a spell on her: she would be reborn as the daughter of someone who, wandering the desert, would trip into the gigantic portal to the temple where poor Kara had been buried 4,000 years earlier. So if you're planning to go to Egypt and you're expecting a child, don't wander around the desert.

- **3,000-Year-Old Prince Kharis** (*The Mummy's Hand, The Mummy's Tomb, The Mummy's Ghost, The Mummy's Curse*): Kharis used the sacred tana leaves in order to resurrect his dead beloved Princess Ananka, but this provoked Isis, the goddess of life. You know how prissy the gods are about their personal belongings. Especially their sacred tana leaves. So Kharis was captured, his tongue cut off, and his body gift-wrapped and buried alive in a site known only to the Arkhon priests. As the secret location became no longer secret, the priests moved Kharis close to Ananka's tomb. Trying to make it up to him, the gods granted him immortality. A little too late for that, though.

- **4,000-Year-Old High Priest Kharis** (*The Mummy*, 1959): In an attempt to revive his love, Princess Ananka, he stole the Scroll of Life and got busted. As a punishment, his tongue was ripped out, and he was embalmed alive, with the curse to guard the tomb of the princess. Also, the heavy mascara he was wearing was taken away from him and given to Cher. The priest was furious, especially because a thousand years later another Kharis came into the spotlight and suffered the same fate, and this created a confusion when the two went to claim Social Security benefits.

- **Pharaoh Ra-Antef** (*The Curse of the Mummy's Tomb*): He was butchered by his brother Be, and as a unique segment of our "mummy history," he was buried dead. Be entombed his bro along with a medallion that held the secret of immortality. Evidently Be was not very bright.

- **Pharaoh Safirama** (*Dawn of the Mummy*): A mean and evil ruler died and was entombed with a lot of gold and other ostentatious displays of his wealth. If anybody were to steal any of the gold, Safirama would be resurrected and get back his gold through the will of Osiris. It's not clear why Osiris didn't just mind her own business, but we suppose this is just how ancient Egypt worked.

- **Queen Tera** (*Bram Stoker's The Mummy*): She was a beautiful princess, if you skip the fact that she had seven fingers on her right hand. She was the only one in her school able to count to twelve without using any toes, though. She was killed by a priest because of her popularity with the masses. To get back at the priest, Tera's dying breath cursed everything in the room where she was killed. Either that, or she ate sixty garlic pizzas before being slain.

- **Klaris** (*Abbott and Costello Meet the Mummy*), **Popoca** (*The Aztec Mummy*), and **Prem** (*The Mummy's Shroud*): These were probably just buff guys who showed up at the wrong moment in the ceremony, got mummified randomly, and were then used as protectors of hidden treasures.

Identification

The Mummies all tend to look the same, which makes it extremely difficult for you to determine which one you're facing . . . as if that mattered.

- **Face:** Almost constantly overbandaged, as if coming out of plastic surgery. The mouth is outside the bandages most of the time. If wearing no bandages, the mummy's face looks like Dick Clark with no makeup.

- **The Reincarnated Face:** Bizarre, with glow-in-the-dark eyes and skin so wrinkled that the very sight of it would make Oil of Olay stock jump through the roof.

- **Body:** Its rotten body is a human figure—not always properly working, though. As time goes by, it grows stronger and more functional.

- **Scent:** The mummy is accompanied by a characteristic smell, mainly b.o. and "meal," which was used as an embalming agent. So if you smell this awful stench, it's either a mummy or a Frenchman.

Cravings

- **Tana-Leaf Tea:** It's the Mummy's cup of tea. For real. These leaves grew in central Africa on a now extinct bush. An infusion made with tana leaves will lure the mummy from wherever it is, as well as cause an awful lot of smoke.

- **The Scroll of Thoth/The Black Book of the Dead:** Precious documents with a spell used by the goddess Isis to raise Osiris from the dead.

- **The Sacred Medallion:** It's a symbol that gives sustenance to the Mummy. It also tells where the tomb of the rich Princess Ara is located.

- **Jewels:** If you steal the treasures that belonged to the mummy-to-be, chances are it'll want you to give them back—no questions asked (well, it can't talk!).

- **Rats, Scarabs, and Other Bugs:** Mummies gotta eat, too!

- **Devouring Whoever Profanes the Treasures:** Frequently the Mummy has been placed as a guard of immense treasures or annoying princesses. And its job is to protect them until the end of time. Which turns out to be very boring if nobody desecrates the tomb.

- **Kidnapping Beautiful Women Who Remind the Mummy of Its Ancient Lover:** Just hope your face doesn't ring any bells.

• **Superhuman Strength:** The Mummy is really quite strong for someone 3,000 years old.

• **Invulnerable to Conventional Weapons:** Tough old geezers at that!

• **Walking, Limping:** The Mummy moves extremely slowly. But sometimes it forgets and walks at a quick pace. Sometimes it drags one foot, just to add a little pizzazz.

• **Burning Flesh with Just a Touch:** Thanks to the green goo that oozes from its bandages (*Dawn of the Mummy*).

• **Inducing Pain/Death at a Distance:** The Mummy can control your mind and heart, causing impressive scars on your body or even death by shock.

• **Inducing You to Do Something Odd:** The Mummy can control your brain, too, making you act really strange. The mummy can also read your secret ATM PIN number.

• **Reincarnation:** Often the Mummy leaves instructions.

• **Remote Control:** Mummies can be controlled by their masters.

• **Calling for Help:** The Mummy can bring wall carvings to life to help with the terror.

• **Transformation:** Turning into a bat, a spider, or sand (*Wrestling Woman vs. the Aztec Mummy, The Mummy*).

• **Looking for Love:** It seems that the mummies were all students of the powerful pharaoh Viag Ra, who taught them the art of love after many many years of life.

• **Speaking Fluent English:** Remarkably enough, even if born, raised, killed, and resurrected in ancient Egypt, many mummies are able to speak perfect English with only a slight accent, like Omar Sharif. But less charming. And less broke.

Danger

First of all, it seems that Egyptians are not allowed to dig up their own dead—that's why they need help from the outside. If an Egyptian guy approaches you with this request, ask yourself, "Why should I dig up an old corpse to please this sinister fellow?" Or if someone tells you that entering the tomb of this or that god could be "the most important discovery since Tutankhamen," pack and leave.

Once resurrected, the mummy has the habit of incurring *Hamdie*, or bringing along with it the 10 plagues of Egypt, so get ready to face swarms of locusts or other insects, water turned into blood, sudden eclipses, meteor showers . . . that kind of stuff.

If you encounter a baleful priest who tries to con you into getting a special injection of fluid made with tana leaves, you'll become immortal. Which sounds very cool. But wait until you hear the catch: you'll become a mummy yourself (*The Mummy's Ghost*).

How to Destroy Your Mummy

- **The Princess Routine:** Try to look like an ancient princess and call to the goddess Isis, who will hopefully pulverize the Mummy before the Mummy pulverizes you.

- **Hocus-Pocus:** If you find the right incantation, you can disintegrate the monster (but you have to learn ancient Egyptian, first, for the correct pronunciation).

- **Try the Gold Book:** If the Black Book of the Dead can resurrect a corpse, the Gold Book can send it back. The bad news is that not only do they not come in paperback, there's only one copy available on the planet.

- **Give It Up:** Simply give the Mummy what it wants, whether it's jewels, medallions, or other knickknacks.

- **Fire, Explosives:** An extreme cure, which doesn't always work that well. Nevertheless, the Mummy seems to be afraid of fire. Thousands of bullets are recommended, too. Or a small dose of TNT. Or a not-so-small dose of TNT.

- **Best of the Best:** Make a whole building collapse on it. Or else lead it to a small swamp, and get the Mummy to walk into it.

What to Do if You Meet a Mummy

Don't show any fear. Oftentimes, mummies are more scared than we are. Oh, no, wait; that's koala bears. All right, never mind.

- **Kitty Power:** Mummies are afraid of cats, because they're the guardians of the underworld. It sort of reminds them that they're dead and they have to go back. Or else they're allergic.

- **Whip Out Your Holy Symbol:** If face-to-face, show the corpse a star of David: the mummy will think you're a Jew and make you its servant. Which ain't as cool as it sounds.

If you want to see a real mummy, go to the British Museum. Just don't read any of the hieroglyphics out loud.

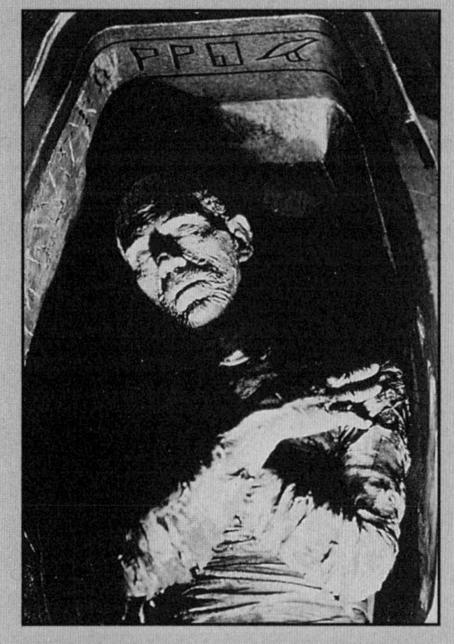

"Mmmph . . . hit the snooze bar again . . . just five more months and I'll get up . . . "

S.S. Archives/Shooting Star

Current Status

All in all, waiting for some other nimwad to say the magic spell one more time.

Body Count

- **3,000-year-old Kharis:** 14 people, 1 is left in a state of shock; 2 fences, 1 wall, 1 museum room, and part of an ancient monastery.
- **Queen Tera:** 7 people, 1 eye, and 1 rat.
- **Queen Kara:** 6 people and 1 statue.
- **Imhotep (the New and Improved One):** 4 people.
- **4,000-year-old Kharis:** 3 people, 2 doors, and 1 window.
- **Imhotep:** 3 people and 1 dog.
- **Klaris:** 0.

Zombies

When there's no more room in hell, the dead will walk the earth.

Peter in *Dawn of the Dead*

Origins

There are two main groups of zombies:

- **The Voodoo Zombie:** This is a person, not necessarily a dead one, who belongs entirely to a priest or a sorcerer. The person becomes no more than a silent robot who executes the master's orders.

- **The Living Dead:** This kind of zombie comes back from the grave for many reasons. It might be the result of a scientific experiment gone wrong; it could have been enticed by a polluted environment, or by a sick alien plan to use dead men against the human race. And, of course, there's the zombie who comes back from the grave for no reason at all.

Habitat

- **Haiti:** Inhabiting this area is a prerogative of the voodoo zombie, where the sorcerers assemble their little armies of big, bulky former human beings. If you take our advice, change the route of your next vacation—unless you like the Marilyn Manson look.

- **In Town:** This is the turf of all other zombies; there's more food (us, that is) in town. According to Dr. Logan, an expert in zombology, the rate of living dead to humans is 400,000 to 1. There goes the neighborhood.

- **Polluted Rivers:** This is a fine place to hide a corpse, particularly if you want to have it come back as an "almost" living creature. Nowadays it isn't hard to find a river with the requisite characteristics.

- **Sewers:** Used by the army to hide unpopular experiments, like an attempt to eliminate the homeless in a radical way. If the trick works, fine; if it doesn't, oh well: let's simply conceal the whole thing, with a classified name (*C.H.U.D.*, for instance), either in the sewers or in . . .

• **Military Warehouses:** Another place where you can find your living dead, canned and ready to serve: you only have to open the barrel, and *voilà!*

Identification

THE VOODOO ZOMBIE

• **Face & Skin:** The skin of this zombie is exactly like it was when the body was free from the magic. One thing for sure, no matter where the body comes from, this zombie has a stone face that betrays no emotion. It would be an excellent poker player.

• **Wardrobe:** This zombie is poorly dressed; the priest doesn't give it an allowance, so it can't fall into the Gap.

THE LIVING DEAD

• **Face & Skin:** This zombie (formerly "ghoul") has dug its way right through the ground: that's why it doesn't look very healthy. You can meet either gray, bluish, or green zombies, and even some in an advanced state of decomposition.

• **Wardrobe:** Zombies which move in large groups are crumpled and dirty, with a poor wardrobe: they seem not to pay attention to fashion. On the other hand, solitary zombies pay a lot of attention to their outfits, and like to be trendy.

Cravings

• **Human Flesh (Warm):** This is the preferred treat for the largest number of the living dead; they come after us, open their mouths, and bite. Arms, legs, heads, hands, hips, anywhere is fine (for them). After all, you are what they eat. But they're not "cannibals" because they don't eat each other, and to their eyes we're not of the same species. Well, to our eyes, they aren't, either. But it's pointless trying to explain this to a zombie. It has no patience.

• **Fun Fact:** They're *constantly* hungry.

• **Unfortunate Side Effect:** You die.

• **Really Unfortunate Side Effect:** If the zombies don't completely tear you apart, you come back as a hungry zombie yourself. And so on, and so on, like a chain letter.

• **Brains:** A specific need of the army-generated living dead (*The Return of the Living Dead*); they want brains either because, according to the zombies, "it makes the pain of being dead go away," or because, according to scientists, "they draw energy from the neurons to survive." We don't know who's right; we only know that if a zombie bites its way into your brain through your skull, it's no fun at all.

- **Killing People/Revenge:** Some zombies are ill-tempered just because; so they kill people with different techniques: they crack them in two, they twist necks, they strangle . . . But there's another wave of zombies which generally operate alone: these are the zombies who have some unfinished business on earth and come back to take care of it. Work, work, work.

- **Love:** Love never dies, someone used to say. And love is the power that moves mountains, clears the skies, crosses the oceans, rinses the socks, and makes Mariah Carey sing. And love makes you say, *"My Boyfriend's Back."* Get a life. Or a death.

Behavior

PROWLING

- **Slow, Stumbling:** The living dead have spent some time underground, so it's quite natural for them to have what is called "rigor mortis": a rigid body, some trouble coordinating their steps, but an unshakable energy which makes them walk, and walk, and walk. This kind of walk is also practiced by the voodoo zombies.

- **Running Like Hell:** The zombies who've been reanimated by a gas called *trioxine* (manufactured by Darrow Chemicals) say the hell with rigor mortis and run like the U.S. Olympic team. Pay attention to these zombies, because they are really a pain in the neck. Not only figuratively speaking.

- **Dancing:** In rare cases, you can bring a corpse partially to life, or at least make it sensitive to music. As long as a band is playing, your zombie will move toward the thing it cared for the most when it was alive.

LANGUAGE

Zombies don't talk to each other; but there's excitement when they spot some food, so frequently they communicate their enthusiasm:

- **Moans, Grunting:** Many zombies aren't well-mannered creatures, but then again what do you expect?

• **Need Work:** Some voodoo zombies connect with their masters, repeating what he or she says or thinks. However, a zombie's vocal apparatus is as numb as its body, so forget about a James Earl Jones kind of voice and think of Barney from *The Simpsons.*

• **Talking Quite Well, Thank You:** Again, trioxine does the miracle, and its zombies properly master language. But not only trioxine-created zombies talk; generally speaking, every zombie who's back to finish some stuff up will be able to talk. But they can absolutely nag you to death.

• **Silent:** The voodoo zombie, the unluckiest among all the zombies, usually doesn't even have the gift of the spoken word; it prowls speechlessly. You can hit it on the big toe with a hammer and watch it try to scream. It's great fun at parties.

WHY THEY GO WHERE THEY GO

• **Instinct:** Zombies led by instinct go back to where their memories take them. It could be a house, a mall, or simply along the street. They seem quite lazy: wherever one goes, the others follow. This is easier for them—no annoying discussions about "whose choice of restaurant."

• **Acting on Purpose:** Zombies with an attitude. They know exactly what they're doing, they have a perfect idea where to go and who to hassle.

FOLLOW THE NOISE

It's especially common for the instinctive zombies to be attracted by noise; if you make the mistake of drawing one, in less than 60 seconds you'll be surrounded by a whole bunch.

Danger

Ninety-nine times out of a hundred, the living dead are hostile creatures, so you have to think fast.

• **High (They Want to Eat):** If you see a crowd of living dead flocking toward you, don't waste time. Spin on your heels and dart away: you're in their path as well as their menu.

• **Still High (They Want to Kill):** Same as above, with the only difference being that they won't eat you. They just want to kill you. That's all.

• **It Depends on the Priest:** Don't mess with the priest, and you'll live long and prosper. Mess with the priest, and tell us where to send the flowers.

• **Zero:** A few zombies aren't interested in human flesh; they still kill, but this is incidental. Clue: the zombie who walks alone and talks has a bark worse than its bite. Usually.

• **Good News:** Carnivorous zombies can be domesticated (it's going to be a long and difficult road, but they can really learn how to work for you).

• **Bad News:** Because of the above, they can also figure out how to use a gun.

How to Dispose of Them

THE VOODOO ZOMBIE

• **Kill It:** Not only does the voodoo zombie look like a nerd—the way it's pushed around by its master and can't talk—but you can also kill it quite easily.

• **Destroy the Symbol That Keeps It Alive:** To end the magic and free the poor man. Quite often it's enough to demolish the object the priest uses to give the zombie its energy. It's even better to demolish the priest. The result will be the same, but the risk of being turned into one of the walking dead will drastically plummet.

THE LIVING DEAD

• **Disconnect the Head from the Body:** The largest number of living dead are switched to the "off position" as soon as their brains are destroyed. You can shoot, pierce, saw, smash, cut, drill, slice, trim, squeeze, pulverize, separate, snip, mash, crash, stab, poke, carve, detach, or ax the head of any zombie you find. Pick your favorite verb and be our guest.

• **Chop Them Up:** Use a chainsaw, a lawn mower, knives, poles, any blade or utensil. If this doesn't stop them, they'll still come after you—but only one piece at a time. It shouldn't be that hard to outsmart a leg or a nose.

• **Electrical Shock:** You fry them up and solve the problem of being eaten alive. And if you're not too fussy, you can enjoy a little barbecue with your friends.

• **Fire:** Not every zombie can be eliminated with fire, but if you persist, sooner or later you'll consume them. There's a little problem with the trioxine zombies: the smoke generated from the combustion will bring other corpses back to life. And it'll turn you into one of the living dead, too. But only after a lot of pain . . .

• **Blow Them to Pieces:** A little extreme, but pretty effective. You need at least a grenade launcher.

• **Nuke 'Em:** Maybe a little drastic, but with a little bomb you take care of the zombies. And the living. And the houses. And the towns. And part of the country.

• **Don't Feed Them:** Some zombies are still subject to biological decay; like a vampire, if the zombie doesn't eat, it'll rot and consequently turn into ashes.

• **You Can't:** Unfortunately, there are a couple of tough species that are indestructible. And if you bump into them you're really jinxed!

What to Do if You Meet Them

First of all consider moving, maybe to a tropical island (avoid Haiti, though). Then you might want to try one of these suggestions:

• **Run As Fast As You Can:** This is still the best thing to do. It *almost* never fails.

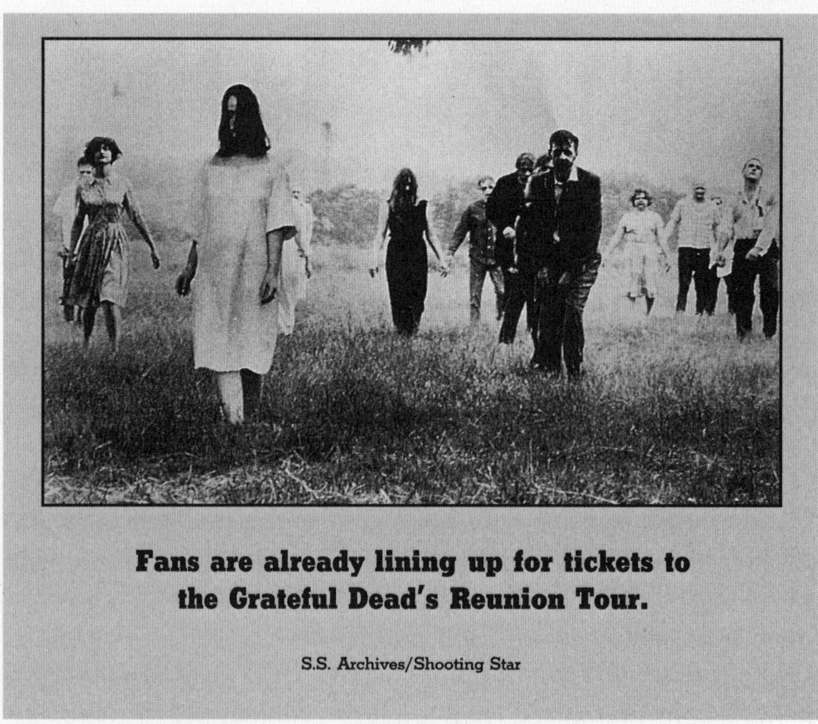

Fans are already lining up for tickets to the Grateful Dead's Reunion Tour.

S.S. Archives/Shooting Star

- **Push Them Over:** If you're dealing with slow-moving zombies, try to push one of them; highly unstable, it'll fall among the others, creating a domino effect that you can smartly use while applying the first suggestion in this list.

- **Organize Wrestling Matches:** Do this only with the slow-moving zombies: you ain't gonna kill 'em, but at least you'll have some fun. Watch out for their teeth, or restrain them with a muffler.

Stopgap measures

- **Use CO_2 or Another Freezing Element:** This paralyzes the living dead forever, as long as the temperature of their surroundings remains low enough to keep the ice from melting. Send a delegation of zombies to the North Pole, it may work.

- **Tranquilizers:** We know it sounds stupid, but there's a breed of zombies that originated from zingaia, the bite of a mutated red monkey (*Simian raticus*) from Sumatra. Believe it or not, you can force these zombies to behave if you give them lots of sedatives. But *a lot.*

Vampires

The strength of the vampire is that people will not believe in him.

Dr. Abraham Van Helsing in *Dracula*

Origins

Vampires have been around for as long as anyone can remember. The most infamous bloodsucker dynasty sprang up in Transylvania in 1462, courtesy of Count Vlad, later known as Dracula. But there have been many other families, in places such as ancient Egypt, Paris, and Central America. Despite their differences, they all have one thing in common: they're cursed, not blessed. They are painfully aware of this and seem to want to take it out on the rest of us.

- **The Sacred Point of View:** The Church poses an interesting theory. Prague, 1311: Jan Valek was born. He became a priest and turned against the Church. After his capture, he was tried for heresy and burned at stake. But before that, they exorcised him, because it was believed that he was possessed. Something went wrong (can you actually think of an exorcism where things went smoothly?), and Valek was turned into a dead body who "lives on" or, if you like, the first vampire.

Habitat

Because of the vampire population explosion, it has become necessary for them to seek out a variety of haunts:

- **The Spooky Castle:** It screams "Beware of Vampire," but certainly creates the proper mood.

- **The Big City:** Advantages: more food, less conspicuous, vibrant nightlife, screaming victims less likely to cause panic. Disadvantage: more likely to be invited to appear on *Celebrity Death Match*.

- **Abandoned Buildings, Campers, Caves, the Beach:** For the mobile vampire, who doesn't feel the need to settle down, any place will do—seaside resorts (*The Lost Boys*), or even Winnebagos (*Near Dark*).

APPEARANCE

The old-school bloodsucker looked like royalty, while most modern vampires look like drug addicts:

- **Face:** Almost every vampire has prominent canines (with the exception of Nosferatu's incisors), but only shows them when preparing to attack or when getting overemotional. They also have very pale skin and eyes which can change color.

- **Duds:** The classic vampire is the most elegant, wearing tuxedos, dark capes, or expensive Armani suits (*Bram Stoker's Dracula*). Modern vampires tend to go casual: leather jackets, jeans, shirts—practical wash-'n-wear stuff.

AVOIDING HORROR IN EVERYDAY LIFE

You can't be too careful. No matter how alert you are, in order to survive, there still are a few things you should keep in mind. So, here is a list of big no-nos.

Activities to Avoid

- Swimming by yourself in the moonlight.
- Trespassing on a witch's property.
- Digging graves for former serial killers.
- Investigating strange noises in the basement or the attic.
- Following bloody footsteps or trails through a creepy house.
- Daring to sleep in the lonely house on the hill.
- Reading spells from ancient books.

Places to Avoid

- The laundry room in the basement (especially the one with the flickering light).
- Old warehouses (especially the ones with flickering lights).
- Deserted cabins in the forest (especially the ones with flickering lights *and* broken swings in the back).
- A camp that has been dubbed "Camp Blood" or something equally enticing.
- Anywhere near a graveyard, and who cares if your friends call you "chicken."

"The Disposable Person" . . . Don't Be This Guy!

- The single person on a camping trip.
- The one who tries to warn everybody about the terrible menace.
- The first one who reaches a glowing meteor that has just landed "behind those trees."
- The rebel son of a police officer, sheriff, or army officer.
- "The jolly good fellow," "the prankster," or "the one who doesn't believe in monsters."
- "The sidekick," *no matter what*—even if the hero is your best friend.

• **I See Your True Colors Shining Through:** When some modern vampires reveal their inner beauty, they turn into creatures which only vaguely resemble the human form. The "real" vampire is a grotesque being with colored skin, the face of an animal, and long hands and nails. Its body undergoes a complete transformation into part bat, part snake, and part Kathy Lee Gifford.

TELLTALE SIGNS

You don't need to be Columbo to figure out if someone is a vampire:

• **I Love the NightLife, I Got to Boogie:** Though a few are immune or only slightly bothered by sunlight, vampires generally prefer the dark.

• **Vampires Have Many Faces:** They can transform into an animal (bat, rat, wolf, reptile), a dense mist, or even into another person (*Vampire in Brooklyn*).

• **The Mirror Has No Faces:** Most vampires have no reflection in a mirror. Which makes shaving much more difficult.

• **Media Exposure:** Vampires can't be photographed, but can, in fact, be audiotaped (*Interview with the Vampire*).

• **I Wanna Live Forever:** Vampires have no pulse and are never sick. Makes for cheap health insurance. They also don't age, as long as they drink fresh blood on a regular basis. But some vampires age one year per decade (*My Best Friend Is a Vampire*).

Cravings

Vampires need blood, otherwise they'll perish; or, like a car without a battery, they simply won't start.

• **Blood Types:** It used to be that the blood needed to be human, straight from the body. But some vampires give a sense of "humanity" to their miserable lives by sparing humans and drinking preserved blood, which comes in easy-to-store plasma bags (*Nadja*), or feeding on fake blood produced by a synthesizing plant (*Sundown: The Vampire in Retreat*) or even animal blood—but strictly for survival.

• **Cannibalism:** Sometimes vampires can feed a member of their species with their own blood. This can't go on forever, but it's a nice option in case of an emergency.

SCHEDULE

- **At Night:** Vampires prowl almost exclusively at night.

- **During the Day:** Most vampires sleep during the day, usually inside comfortable coffins. Some are really picky and will only sleep in their own coffin. Athletic vampires hang from the tops of caves like bats, while others sleep underwater with their lungs floating on the surface (*Children of the Night*). Ultimately, they'll take any place out of the sun.

- **Round the Clock:** A few vampires can endure sunlight; some with lessened powers (*Bram Stoker's Dracula*), some with normal powers (*The Addiction*), some with Stefanie Powers (Robert Wagner). And some vampires use sunblock SPF 100 in order to avoid getting fried (*Blade, Sundown: The Vampire in Retreat*).

ABILITIES

Vampires have special abilities that distinguish them from human beings:

- **Superhuman Strength:** As if they were on supernatural steroids. They can easily scale walls, levitate, or even fly (either in human or bat form).

- **Quick Movement:** Faster than the human eye—so they can play obnoxious tricks on you like rearranging the furniture just as you're about to sit down.

- **Heightened Senses:** Night vision and acute hearing—so you can't gossip behind their backs.

ALMOST HUMAN–ALMOST

Sometimes flickerings of their past humanity still infiltrate their behavior:

- **Inner Conflict:** Some vampires experience constant conflict between their human and vampire natures. They are also quite prone to mood swings.

- **Twinkletoes:** Vampires enjoy dancing, especially in front of large audiences.

- **Birds Do It, Bees Do It . . . :** Besides creating new vampires from their bites, vampires can also reproduce just like us. The child can either be a full vampire, which is what usually happens with the firstborn, or else a half vampire who needs to be awakened to its destiny.

PREDATORY ACTIVITIES

Vampires draw blood from the bodies of their victims; the classic vampire is neat and leaves two small holes from the bite. Modern vampires have become more ravenous and sloppy. The victim's fate depends upon the mood of the vampire:

- **Dying:** This occurs either because the vampire has drained all the blood from your body, or else snapped your neck to keep you from coming back.

- **Becoming a Vampire:** In many cases, after one bite you're already a vampire; or you might need to be fed vampire's blood—which occurs after you've been taken to the brink of death.

- **Or, Worse Yet, Becoming a Vampire's Slave:** To help during the daylight hours. They can force you to do it with hypnotism, or by feeding you a few drops of their blood. From this moment on you become an insect-eating ghoul. But look at the bright side: insects are chock full o' protein!

MAGICAL POWERS

- **Hypnosis:** And afterward you don't remember anything.

- **Walking Through Walls:** But only if they really need to.

- **Shapeshifting:** Projecting their image elsewhere.

- **Telekinesis:** Causing explosions, moving stuff all over the place.

- **Fire:** Some vampires can produce fire from their bare hands or with just a glance.

- **Look Out, Finger Soldiers!:** In Romania, there was a vampire who had the unique ability to break off the tips of his fingers in order to create miniature helper ghouls (*Subspecies*) which were less dangerous than annoying.

BIG NO-NOS

- **Don't Invite Them In:** A few polite vampires need to be *invited* into your house. The problem is that if you're dumb enough to invite them in, the methods of killing them mentioned below become utterly ineffective. BIG mistake.

- **Religious Discussions with Vampires:** Obvious, no?

- **Intimacy:** Try, no matter how sexy the vampire you are facing, *not* to get involved romantically with him or her. Human relationships are bad enough. The undead can persecute you for centuries to come.

How to Destroy Them

The vampire is an immortal creature. "Immortal" being a relative term. There are in fact many, many ways to get rid of those pesky vampires:

- **Sunshine, on My Shoulders:** The gentle morning light causes the creature to be consumed in a smoldering fire which leaves an ugly stain on your carpet. And Ray•Bans won't protect them.

- **Ye Olde Stake Through the Heart:** A wooden stake, or pretty much anything hard enough to pierce the vampire's body.

- **Crucifix:** Almost all vampires fear crucifixes, even if they try to trick you with lines like, "You must have faith in order for that to work!" or "I'm a Muslim vampire." Don't pay any attention.

- **Garlic:** Serve Italian food.

- **Holy Water, Communion Hosts, Rosary Beads, and Other Holy Relics:** Effective as well.

- **Off With 'Is 'Ead!:** This works because you sever the central nervous system. A shotgun blast to the neck usually achieves the same effect. And it's great fun watching a vampire's body stumbling around looking for its head.

VAMPIRE SLAUGHTER:
EFFECTIVE METHODS

METHOD Maybe Give It a Shot Surefire

Beheading

Crucifix

Garlic

Holy Water

Stake

Sunlight

• **Torch the SOB:** Although a few seem immune, vampires are not great fans of fire.

• **The Van Helsing Remedy:** A stake through the heart, decapitation, and then a purification with fire. It's best to be thorough.

What to Do if You Meet Them

Don't have any of the weapons mentioned above? Try one of these tricks:

• **Shoot Them:** Not lethal (unless to the neck), but at least it can distract the vampire for a few moments.

• **Slit the Throat:** Stops them for a while but not the definitive solution.

• **Get Me to the Church:** Not a vampire's favorite public place.

• **Tell the Vampires to Go Away:** Try this, no matter how stupid it sounds. Tell—don't ask—tell the vampires to go away. They may just leave. Worth a shot.

So, *You've* Turned into a Vampire: Now, What?

If you or your friends are able to kill the head vampire, all the people who were vampirized will turn back to normal. But it's not going to be an easy task. Most of these old bats have been the head vampire for centuries. In any case, there's another solution: you could transfuse human blood into the vampirized body. It will return to normal . . . except for the inevitable emotional scarring.

Count Dracula

Classification: the undead / vampires / *Vampiribus grandaddy-o*

Footage:

1931, *Dracula* by Tod Browning
1943, *Son of Dracula* by Robert Siodmak
1958, *Horror of Dracula* by Terence Fisher

1974, *Andy Warhol's Dracula* by Paul Morrisey
1979, *Dracula* by John Badham
1987, *The Monster Squad* by Fred Dekker
1992, *Bram Stoker's Dracula* by Francis Ford Coppola
1995, *Dracula: Dead and Loving It* by Mel Brooks
. . . and the list goes on and on.

The Skinny: The most popular vampire of all time.

Quotable: "Children of the night. What a music they make."

Born: 1462.

Stomping Grounds: Transylvania, London, and other places.

"Now for the big splash in my spring-summer collection, I present to you: the cape . . . with a splash of color!"

S.S. Archives/Shooting Star

Origin: Count Dracula used to live in Transylvania, if the term "live" can be used in this case—because, after all, Dracula is one of the living dead. He owned a castle in the country, but since his was the classic small town, people began to yakkety-yak behind his back. So he had to leave.

Identification: Depends upon your historical era and his mood at the time. Most often Dracula appears as a very elegant man, pale, thin, and sporting two pointy canine teeth (but only since the 1950s). He can easily turn into a bat, a wolf, or a bunch of mice. Dracula can also turn into a ugly bald creature (resembling Michael Jackson following that infamous Pepsi commercial) or pretty much anything he wants.

Cravings: Gallons of fresh blood.

Behavior: He's definitely a night person—sunlight in most cases can kill him. He is always looking for a snack; which means that after a while a fresh crew of vampires will crowd your town.

Danger: If your name happens to be Van Helsing, no problemo! Otherwise, you could meet Count Dracula while dancing, after sunset, looking for new take-out drinks (preferably young women). But this doesn't mean that you are safe if you're male. Dracula's female converts will go after you if the Count doesn't pay his own visit.

How to Kill Him: Probably the most vulnerable creature ever to grace the silver screen; you can stab him with a sharp pole made with white ash, give him some garlic, touch him with a blessed crucifix (but you *must* have faith, otherwise the crucifix is powerless), have him drink holy water, or overexpose him to sunlight.

What to Do if You Meet Him: Don't let on that you know who he is. Just play dumb. Unless he's being blatant about his identity. In which case tell him you're ordained. Maybe he'll stay away. Maybe not.

Current Status: Dead and getting tired of it.

Body Count: Unfathomable, but he *usually* doesn't kill.

APPENDIX 1

Monster Taxonomy

Bold-faced entries appear in the book.

Aliens

PARASITES
Alien
Andromeda Strain
The Creeping Unknown
The Creeps (*Night of the Creeps*)
The Green Slime
The Hidden
Lunar Fungus (*Mutiny in Outer Space*)
Robert Heinlein's The Puppet Masters
Strangers *(Dark City)*
John Carpenter's The Thing
Yog—Monster from Space

DOPPELGÄNGERS
Spencer Armacost (*The Astronaut's Wife*)
The Arrival
The Astounding She-Monster
Body Snatchers
The Borrower
The Brain from Planet Arous
Children of the Damned
Edgar *(Men in Black*)
Exter (*This Island Earth*)
The Faculty
I Married a Monster from Outer Space
Invasion of the Bee Girls
Invisible Invaders
It Came from Outer Space
King Koopa (*Super Mario Bros.*)
Lord Crumb (*Bad Taste*)
Sam Phillips (*Xtro*)
Ra (*Stargate*)
Sil *(Species)*
They Live

METEOR-RELATED
Alien Dead
***The Blob* (1958, 1972)**
The Deadly Spawn
Die, Monster, Die!
Happy Toyz Truck *(Maximum Overdrive)*
Meteor Monster
The Monolith Monsters
Jones Ruhk (*The Invisible Ray*)
They Came from Beyond Space
Track of the Moon Beast
Triffids (*The Day of the Triffids*)
Jordy Verrill (*Creepshow*)
Steven West (*The Incredible Melting Man*)
Nahum Witly (*The Farm*)

MARTIANS
The Angry Red Planet
The Day Mars Invaded Earth
Devil Girls from Mars
Five Million Years from Earth
Invaders from Mars
Invasion of the Saucer Men
It! The Terror from Beyond Space
Mars Attacks!
Mars Needs Women
Queen of Blood
Red Planet Mars
Rocketship X-M
Santa Claus Conquers the Martians
Space Master X-7
Spaced Invaders
Species II
War of the Worlds

MEANIES
The Adventures of Buckaroo Banzai
The Beast with a Million Eyes
The Crawling Eye
The Creeping Unknown
The Dark
Dalek (*Dr. Who and the Daleks*)
Dogora the Space Monster
Earth vs. the Flying Saucers
Eros, Tanna (*Plan 9 from Outer Space*)
Extraterrestrial *(ID4)*
Fire Maidens of Outer Space

The Giant Claw
Giant Cucumber (*It Conquered the World*)
Id Monster (*Forbidden Planet*)
Invasion of the Star Creatures
Killers from Space
Klendathu Bugs *(Starship Troopers)*
Krites *(Critters)*
Kronos
Liquid Sky
Ming the Merciless (*Flash Gordon*)
The Mysterians
Pet Monster (*TerrorVision*)
Space Spiders (*Lost in Space*)
Starship Invasion
Strange Invaders
Tod (*Mom and Dad Save the World*)
The 27th Day
Venusian Androids (*Target Earth*)
Ymir (*20 Million Miles from Earth*)
Zoa Lord (*The Guyver*)

PREDATORS
The Atomic Submarine
Dr. Frank-N-Furter (*The Rocky Horror Picture Show*)
Gigantic Flytrap (*Bad Channels*)
Killer Klowns from Outer Space
Liquid Sky
Nocturnal Flying Aliens *(Pitch Black)*
Predator
Teenagers from Outer Space
The Thing from Another World

Beasts

ANIMALS
Anaconda
Asian Crocodiles *(Lake Placid)*
Barracuda
The Birds
Cockroaches (*Creepshow*)
Cujo
Ella (*Monkey Shines*)
Frogs
Grizzly
Kingdom of the Spiders
Mako: the Jaws of Death
Mamba
Orca
Razorback
Sharks *(Jaws)*
Spiders (*Arachnophobia*)
Stanley
Willard's Mice (*Willard, Ben*)

PLANTS
Audrey II *(Little Shop of Horrors)*
The Day of the Triffids
Ju-Ju (*The Woman Eater*)
Man-Eating Plants (*The Angry Red Planet*)
The Navy vs. the Night Monsters
Tabonga (*From Hell It Came*)
The Thing from Another World
Tree (*Poltergeist*)
Tree (*The Wizard of Oz*)
The Unknown Terror
The Woods (*Evil Dead*)

PREHISTORIC
Carnosaur
The Crater Lake Monster
Creature from the Black Lagoon
Cro-Magnon Caveman (*Memorial Valley Massacre*)
Dinosaurs!
Dinosaurs (*Jurassic Park*)
Dinosaurs (*The Land That Time Forgot*)
Eegah
Gigantis, the Fire Monster
Graboids *(Tremors)*
Invisible Dinosaur (*Sound of Horror*)
Slokantropus (*Schlock*)
Theodore Rex
Trog
Valley of Gwangy

UNDISCOVERED
WEREWOLVES
American Werewolves *(in London, Paris)*
The Beast Must Die!
The Curse of the Werewolf
House of Dracula
The Howling
The Howling III: the Marsupials
My Mom Is a Werewolf
Larry Talbot *(The Wolf Man)*
Teen Wolf
The Werewolf
Werewolf of London
Wolf

YETI AND SASQUATCHES
Anthropoid X (*The Abominable Snowman of the Himalayas*)
Bigfoot
Creature from the Black Lake
Curse of the Bigfoot
Half Human
Harry *(Harry and the Hendersons)*
The Legend of Boggy Creek
Man Beast
The Mysterious Monster
Night of the Howling Beast
Night of the Demon
The Snow Creature
Utah (*The Mighty Pecking Man*)
Yeti

DRAGONS
Dragonslayer
Dragonheart
Pete's Dragon
The Sword and the Dragon
Willow

UNIQUE DISCOVERIES
Akua (*Demon of Paradise*)
Aylmer (*Brain Damage*)
The Black Scorpion
Bug
Creature from the Deep (*Deepstar Six*)
Earth vs. the Spider
Fluffy (*Creepshow*)
Gamera the Invincible
Gargantuas (*War of the Gargantuas*)
Giant Archaea Ottoia (*Deep Rising*)
Giant Cockroaches (*The Applegates*)
The Giant Gila Monster
Giant Octopus (*Tentacles*)
The Giant Spider Invasion
Giant Squid (*20,000 Leagues Under the Sea*)
Godzilla (1956, 1998)
Gorgo
Gremlins
King Kong
Monster in the Closet
Mighty Joe Young (1949, 1998)
Q
Orangutan Gargantua (*Africa Screams*)
Phantoms
Rana: The Legend of Shadow Lake
Rodan
Shriekers *(Tremors 2: Aftershocks)*
Spasms

Titano the Superape
Varan, the Unbelievable

Creations

MACHINES

Computers

Brainscan
Colossus (*The Forbin Project*)
Edgar (*Electric Dreams*)
HAL 9000 *(2001: A Space Odyssey)*
Master Control Program (*Tron*)
Proteus IV (The Demon Seed)
Skynet (*Terminator* series)
The Ultimate Computer (*Superman III*)

Robots

Evil Bill & Ted (*Bill & Ted's Bogus Journey*)
Gog
Gort (*The Day the Earth Stood Still*)
Gunslinger *(Westworld)*
Hector (*Saturn 3*)
Killbots *(Chopping Mall)*
Killer Robots (*Moon Trap*)
Mark 13 (*Hardware*)
Maximilian *(The Black Hole)*
Sentinel Robots (*Halloween III: Season of the Witch*)
Sentinel Spider Robots (*Runaway*)
Terminator T-1000 *(Terminator 2: Judgment Day)*

Cyborgs

Cyborg
Cyborg 2087
Max 404 (*Android*)
Jobe Smith (*The Lawnmower Man*)
Replicants *(Blade Runner)*
Terminator T-101 *(Terminator* series)
Universal Soldiers

BIOLOGICALLY ENGINEERED

"Aquatica" Mako Sharks *(Deep Blue Sea)*
Bats
The Blob (1988)
Blue Ribbon Teens (*Disturbing Behavior*)
The Brain that Wouldn't Die
Cobra Man (*SSSSSSS*)
The Colossus of New York
Creature with the Atom Brain
Dead Kids
Dinosaurs *(Jurassic Park* series)
Eve, Sil (*Species* series)
Frankenstein's Monster
Jack Frost
Jack Griffin *(The Invisible Man)*
Dr. Jekyll and Mr. Hyde
The Killer Shrews
Konga
Kothoga (*The Relic*)
Leviathan
The Lift
Max (*Man's Best Friend*)
Judas Breed Cockroaches *(Mimic)*
Mind Ripper
Mutants (*Forbidden World*)
Night of the Lepus
The Outsiders *(Watchers)*
Parasite
Piranha
Reanimated corpses (*Re-Animator* series)
Scorpion Man (*Leprechaun 4: in Space*)
Jobe Smith *(The Lawnmower Man)*
Professor Steiner (*The Projected Man*)
Dr. Hank Symen *(Habitat)*
Syngenor
Tarantula

MUTANTS

Human

"Its" *(It's Alive!* series)
Cathy and John Beck (*The Bat People*)
Charles Brady (*Sleepwalkers*)
The Brood
Cat People
C.H.U.D.
***The Fly* (1958, 1986)**
Mutated Man (*The Day the World Ended*)
Octaman
Patrick Ross (*Species II*)
Society
Scanners

Animal

Alligator
Bug
Cemetery Creature (*Graveyard Shift*)
Deadly Eyes
The Deadly Mantis
Empire of the Ants
Giant Animals (*Food of the Gods*)
The Giant Gila Monster
Gojira
The Horror of Party Beach
Humanoids from the Deep
Katahadis *(Prophecy)*
Of Unknown Origin
The Phantom from 10,000 Leagues
***Piranha* (1978, 1981)**
Slugs

Nuclear Contamination

The Amazing Colossal Man
Attack of the Crab Monsters
Attack of the Giant Leeches
The Beast from 20,000 Fathoms
The Crawling Hand
The Deadly Mantis
Dogs
Empire of the Ants
The Giant Behemoth
Giant Crustacean (*Island Claws*)
Giant Crustacean (*Island of Terror*)
Giant Grasshoppers (*Beginning of the End*)
Godzilla
Gojira
The Hideous Sun Demon
The Horror of Party Beach
Invasion of the Bee Girls
It Came from Beneath the Sea
The Magnetic Monster
Monster from Green Hell
Monster from the Ocean Floor
Monster That Challenged the World
Octaman
The Phantom from 10,000 Leagues
Radiation Creature (*Day the World Ended*)
Rodan
The Slime People
Tarantula
Them!
X the Unknown
The War of the Gargantuas

Psychopaths

ALTER EGOS

Norman Bates *(Psycho)*
Bobbi *(Dressed to Kill)*
Carter Nix (*Raising Cain*)
Dr. Jekyll and Mr. Hyde
Corky Withers (*Magic*)

THE GIFTED
Dr. Decker (*Nightbreed*)
Hannibal Lecter *(Manhunter, The Silence of the Lambs)*
Patrick
Dr. Anton Phibes *(The Abominable Dr. Phibes)*
Dr. Evan Rendell, Jr. *(Dr. Giggles)*

THE OBSESSED
Angela Baker *(Sleepaway Camp)*
Jerry Blake (*Stepfather*)
Kris Bolin (*The Temp*)
Billy Caldwell *(Silent Night, Deadly Night)*
Ricky Caldwell *(Silent Night, Deadly Night II* and *III)*
Hedra Carlson (*Single White Female*)
Nick Cavanaugh (*Boxing Helena*)
Pete Davis (*Unlawful Entry*)
Chip Douglas (*The Cable Guy*)
Diesel Truck *(Duel)*
Alex Forrest (*Fatal Attraction*)
Darian Forrester (*The Crush*)
Ruben Goetz (*Copycat*)
Jane Hudson (*What Ever Happened to Baby Jane?*)
Mark Lewis (*Peeping Tom*)
Manny (*The Fan*)
David McCall (*Fear*)
Peter Neal (*Tenebrae*)
Hugie Warriner (*Dead Calm*)
Annie Wilkes *(Misery)*

RELIGIOUS ZEALOTS
Children of the Corn
John Doe (*Se7en*)
Krug (*Last House on the Left*)
Nick & Lily Laemle (*Parents*)
Mommy and Daddy *(The People Under the Stairs)*
Horace Pinker (*Shocker*)

THE VENGEFUL
Belial *(Basket Case)*
Brenda (*Urban Legend*)
Max Cady (*Cape Fear*)
Erik *(The Phantom of the Opera)*
Peyton Flanders (*The Hand That Rocks the Cradle*)
Freaks
Alex Hammond (*Prom Night*)
Carter Hayes (*Pacific Heights*)
Jennifer "Jenny" Hill (*I Spit on Your Grave*)
Edward Lionheart (*Theater of Blood*)
Scream series killers
Scuba Diver (*Amsterdamned*)
Myles Sheffield (*Bloodmoon*)
Mrs. Voorhees (*Friday the 13th*)
Benjamin Willis (*I Know What You Did Last Summer* series)

STALKERS
Henry—Portrait of a Serial Killer
Jack the Ripper
The Knoxes *(Natural Born Killers)*
Leatherface *(The Texas Chainsaw Massacre)*
Pluto *(The Hills Have Eyes)*
John Ryder *(The Hitcher)*
Gunther Stryker (*The Funhouse*)

The Supernatural

THE OCCULT

THE DEVIL
Amityville 3D
The Chosen
Louis Cyphre (*Angel Heart*)
Leland Gaunt (*Needful Things*)
John Milton *(The Devil's Advocate)*
976-EVIL
Pazooso (*The Exorcist*)
Damien Thorn *(The Omen)*
Daryl Van Horne (*Witches of Eastwick*)

DEMONS
Alyda (*The Unnamable*)
Azazel (*Fallen*)
Betelgeuse (*Beetlejuice*)
Candyman
Cenobites *(Hellraiser)*
The Collector (*Tales from the Crypt: Demon Knight*)
Djinn (*The Wishmaster*)
He Who Walks Behind the Rows (*Children of the Corn*)
The Imp *(Sorority Babes in the Slimeball Bowl-O-Rama)*
Freddy Krueger *(Nightmare on Elm Street)*
Leprechaun
Lo Pan (*Big Trouble in Little China*)
Pumpkinhead
The Tall Man *(Phantasm)*
Umoia Omube (*Curse III: Blood Sacrifice*)

THE POSSESSED
Regan MacNeil (*The Exorcist*)
Michael Myers *(Halloween)*
Jack Torrance *(The Shining)*
Jason Voorhees *(Friday the 13th* series)
Churchill (*Pet Sematary*)
Greta (*Play Dead*)
Zowie (*Pet Sematary II*)
The Ambulance
The Car
Christine
The Mangler
The Sleeping Car
Books by Sutter Cane (*In the Mouth of Madness*)
Chucky *(Child's Play* series)
Der Golem
Oil Slick, The (*Creepshow 2*)
The Silver Sphere *(Phantasm)*
Toulon's Doll (*Puppetmaster*)
Wax monster statues (*Waxwork*)

HAUNTED PLACES
Alcatraz Prison (*Slaughterhouse Rock*)
The Boogey Man's house
A Chicago skyscraper (*Poltergeist III*)
The Cotton family's house (*Hellraiser*)
Cuesta Verde residences (*Poltergeist*)
Hill House (*The Haunting*)
House
House on Haunted Hill
Inferno houses
Long Island House (*The Amityville Horror*)
The Overlook Hotel (*The Shining*)
A Michigan cabin (*Evil Dead*)

SORCERERS AND WARLOCKS
Conal Cochran (*Halloween III*)
Joseph Curven (*The Haunted Palace*)
The Hack-O-Lantern family of sorcerers
Lo Pan (*Big Trouble in Little China*)
Nix (*Lord of Illusions*)
Pentagram Killer (*The First Power*)
Horace Pinker (*Shocker*)
Philip Swann (*Lord of Illusions*)
Ulrich (*Dragonslayer*)
Warlock

Witches
The Blair Witch Project
Madame Blanc, Miss Tanner (*Suspiria*)
The Craft witches
Mrs. Ernst (*The Witches*)
Eva (*Necropolis*)
Eva (*Play Dead*)
Camilla Grander (*The Guardian*)
Queen Grimelde (*Snow White and the Seven Dwarfs*)
Hocus Pocus witches
Mary (*The Witch*)
Miss Osle (*Pumpkinhead II: Blood Wings*)
The Wicked Witch of the West (*The Wizard of Oz*)

Telekinetics
Jan Compton (*Brain That Wouldn't Die*)
Rachel Lang (*The Rage: Carrie 2*)
Charlie McGee (*Firestarter*)
John Morlar (*The Medusa Touch*)
Patrick
Robin Sandza (*The Fury*)
Carrie White (*Carrie*)

THE UNDEAD

Ghosts
Johnny Bartlett (*The Frighteners*)
Joseph Carmichael (*The Changeling*)
Dead Sailors (*The Fog*)
From Beyond ghosts
Eva Galli (*Ghost Story*)
Rev. Henry Kane (*Poltergeist II, III*)
Cuesta Verde ghosts (*Poltergeist*)

The Resurrected
Matt Cordell (*Maniac Cop*)
Gage Creed (*Pet Sematary*)
Sammi Curr (*Trick or Treat*)
Gus Gilbert (*Pet Sematary II*)
Headless Horseman (*Sleepy Hollow*)
Klaris (*Africa Screams*)
Mary Lou Mahoney (*Prom Night II, III*)
The Mummy
George Stark (*The Dark Half*)

Zombies
Dead Alive
Jessica Holland (*I Walked with a Zombie*)
I Was a Teenage Zombie
My Boyfriend's Back
Night of the Living Dead series
The Plague of the Zombies
Return of the Living Dead series
Sugar Hill zombies
White Zombie

Vampires
The Addiction
Blade vampires
Children of the Night
Dracula
From Dusk Till Dawn vampires
Interview with the Vampire
John Carpenter's Vampires
The Lost Boys
Lothos (*Buffy the Vampire Slayer*)
Marie (*Innocent Blood*)
Maximillian (*Vampire in Brooklyn*)
My Best Friend Is a Vampire
Nadja
Near Dark vampires
Nosferatu
Sundown: The Vampire in Retreat
Vampyr

APPENDIX 2

Recommended Study

The *HMSG* Movie List

v-video l-laserdisc d-dvd (*at the time of print*)

Abbott & Costello Meet Dr. Jekyll and Mr. Hyde (1953) by Charles Lamont *[v, l, d]*

Bud Abbott, Lou Costello, Boris Karloff, Craig Stevens *Hey, Abboooott! There's a guy who's changing his face! Who's on first?*

Abbott & Costello Meet Frankenstein (1948) by Charles T. Barton *[v, l, d]*

Bud Abbott, Lou Costello, Bela Lugosi, Lon Chaney, Jr., Glenn Strange *Hey, Aboooottt! There's a guy who claims to be a vampire and another a monster! Who's on second?*

Abbott & Costello Meet the Mummy (1955) by Charles Lamont *[v, l, d]*

Bud Abbott, Lou Costello, Marie Windsor, Michael Ansara *Hey, Abboooott! There's a guy all wrapped up in paper tissue! Who's on third?*

The Abominable Dr. Phibes (1971) by Robert Fuest *[v, l, d]*

Vincent Price, Joseph Cotten, Peter Jeffrey, Hugh Griffith, Terry-Thomas *A man seeks vengeance among the doctors who didn't save his wife: 10 doctors, 10 plagues of Egypt; you do the math.*

The Addiction (1995) by Abel Ferrara *[v, l]*

Lili Taylor, Annabella Sciorra, Kathryn Erbe, Christopher Walken *A woman is bitten by a New York vampire and becomes worse than a drug addict.*

The Adventures of Buckaroo Banzai Across the Eighth Dimension (1984) by W. D. Richter *[v, l]*

Peter Weller, John Lithgow, Ellen Barkin, Jeff Goldblum, Christopher Lloyd *It's the story of a surgeon rock singer physicist car driver government troubleshooter hero. Do you need anything else?*

Africa Screams (1949) by Charles Barton *[v, l]*

Bud Abbott, Lou Costello, Hillary Brooke, Max Baer *Hey, Abboooot! We're on safari with a giant gorilla! Naturally!*

Alien (1979) by Ridley Scott *[v, l, d]*

Tom Skerritt, Sigourney Weaver, John Hurt, Ian Holm, Harry Dean Stanton, Yaphet Kotto, Veronica Cartwright *Seven people are trapped in a spaceship with the angriest, meanest, most pissed-off extraterrestrial ever seen.*

Alien³ (1992) by David Fincher *[v, l, d]*

Sigourney Weaver, Charles S. Dutton, Charles Dance, Paul McGann, Brian Glover *The aliens are still the same, while this time Ripley is bold and bald.*

Alien Dead (1980) by Fred Olen Ray *[v]*

Buster Crabbe, Ray Roberts, Linda Lewis, Mike Bonavia *A meteor crashes in a Florida swamp and brings back the dead from the grave. You can't imagine the excitement.*

Alien Resurrection (1997) by Jean-Pierre Juneut *[v, l, d]*

Sigourney Weaver, Wynona Rider, Dominique Pinon, Ron Perlman, Gary Dourdan *Still fighting aliens, still dropping like flies. And we find out the aliens can swim underwater.*

Aliens (1986) by James Cameron *[v, l, d]*
Sigourney Weaver, Carrie Henn, Michael Biehn, Paul Reiser, Lance Henriksen, Bill Paxton *Ripley, who fought the first alien, has to go on an alien-infested planet for payback.*

Alligator (1980) by Lewis Teague *[v]*
Robert Forster, Robin Riker, Michael Gazzo, Perry Lang, Henry Silva *A giant alligator survives for a while in the sewer, then pops out for a little bit of fun.*

Alligator II: The Mutation (1988) by John Hess *[v, l]*
Joseph Bologna, Dee Wallace Stone, Richard Lynch, Woody Brown *Another giant alligator survives for a while in the sewer, then pops out for a little bit of fun.*

The Amazing Colossal Man (1957) by Bert I. Gordon *[v]*
Glenn Langan, Cathy Downs, James Seay, Larry Thor *An army officer is exposed to radiation, grows to over 60 feet, and attacks Las Vegas.*

The Ambulance (1990) by Larry Cohen *[v, l]*
Eric Roberts, James Earl Jones, Megan Gallagher, Richard Bright *Victims of the streets of New York jump on an ambulance and vanish. A man tries to find out where they're taken.*

An American Werewolf in London (1981) by John Landis *[v, l, d]*
David Naughton, Griffin Dunne, Jenny Agutter, John Woodvine, Brian Glover *An American tourist is attacked by a werewolf while in Great Britain. The results are devastating.*

An American Werewolf in Paris (1997) by Anthony Waller *[v, l, d]*
Tom Everett Scott, Julie Delpy, Vince Vieluf, Phil Buckman, Julie Bowen *An American tourist is attacked by a werewolf while in France. The results are devastating.*

The Amityville Horror (1979) by Stuart Rosenberg *[v, l, d]*
James Brolin, Margot Kidder, Rod Steiger *A young couple buy a possessed house and it takes them more than the first mortgage payment to figure it out.*

Amityville II: The Possession (1982) by Damiano Damiani *[v, l]*
James Olson, Rutanya Alda, Burt Young, Jack Magner *What actually happened inside the Long Island house that now is possessed? Do you really wanna know?*

Amityville 3D (1983) by Richard Fleischer *[v, l]*
Tony Roberts, Tess Harper, Robert Joy, Candy Clark *An investigator tries to unveil what (if anything) is hiding in the house.*

Amityville 4: The Evil Escapes (1989) by Sandor Stern *[v]*
Patty Duke, Jane Wyatt, Frederic Lehne, Norman Lloyd *Nothing new under the sun. Not to mention under the roof of the house.*

Amityville 1992: It's About Time (1992) by Tony Randel *[v, l]*
Stephen Macht, Shawn Weatherly, Megan Ward, Dick Miller *The chaos started because of a mantel clock belonging a child killer from the 15th century. It took six movies to figure that out.*

Amityville: A New Generation (1993) by John Murlowski *[v, l]*
Ross Patridge, Julia Nickson-Soul, Lala Sloatman, David Naughton *A mirror from the original house holds evil spirits inside, and wherever it's placed, it kindly helps you die.*

The Amityville Curse (1990) by Tom Berry *[v]*
Kim Coates, Dawna Wightman, David Stain *Oh, why bother?*

Amsterdamned (1988) by Dick Maas *[v, l]*
Huub Stapel, Monique Van de Ven, Serge-Henre Valcke, Hidde Maas, other actors with funny-sounding names *A scuba diver patrols the Amsterdam channels and randomly picks people to be slashed.*

Anaconda (1997) by Luis Llosa *[v, l, d]*
Jennifer Lopez, Ice Cube, Jon Voight, Eric Stoltz, Jonathan Hyde *There's this big slimy creature who's sneaky and lethal. It's Jon Voight. Oh, and there's a snake, too.*

Android (1982) by Aaron Lipstadt *[v, l]*
Klaus Kinski, Don Opper, Brie Howard, Norbert Weisser *A faithful android learns that he's about to be "put to sleep."*

The Andromeda Strain (1971) by Robert Wise *[v, l, d]*
Arthur Hill, David Wayne, James Olson, Kate Reid *A pool of scientists engage in a battle against time to stop a virus from outer space.*

Andy Warhol's Dracula (1974) by Paul Morrissey
Undo Kier, Dalila di Lazzaro, Monique Van Vooren, Joe Dallesandra *Sex, orgies, promiscuity . . . oh yeah, and dracula, too.*

Angel Heart (1987) by Alan Parker *[v, l, d]*
Mickey Rourke, Lisa Bonet, Charlotte Rampling, Robert De Niro *A private eye has to locate a mysterious figure at the request of the even more mysterious Louis Cyphre.*

The Angry Red Planet (1959) by Ib Melchior *[v]*
Gerald Mohr, Nora Hayden, Les Tremayne, Jack Kruschen *The first Earth expedition to Mars is not received by the welcome wagon. Actually, the Martians kick butt!*

The Applegates / Meet the Applegates (1991) by Michael Lehman *[v, l]*
Ed Begley, Jr., Stockard Channing, Dabney Coleman, Bobby Jacoby, Cami Cooper *Giant Brazilian cock-*

roaches assume the identity of a family and move to American suburbia.

Arachnophobia (1990) by Frank Marshall *[v, l, d]*
Jeff Daniels, Julian Sands, Harley Jane Kozak, Brian McNamara, John Goodman *A new, deadly breed of spider invades a small town, and nobody knows what to do to stop them.*

The Arrival (1996) by David Twohy *[v, l, d]*
Charlie Sheen, Ron Silver, Lindsay Crouse, Teri Polo *A race of aliens needs our planet to be warmer in order to colonize it. But somebody discovers the naughty plan . . .*

The Astounding She-Monster (1958) by Ronnie Ashcroft *[v, d]*
Robert Clarke, Kenne Duncan, Shirley Kilpatrick *A female alien can kill simply by touching you. As if this weren't enough, she lands in the middle of a kidnapping.*

The Astronaut's Wife (1999) by Rand Ravich *[v, d]*
Johnny Depp, Charlize Theron, Joe Morton, Clea DuVall, Donna Murphy, Nick Cassavetes *Astronauts get beaned by some space debris and start listening to a lot of radio.*

The Atomic Submarine (1959) by Spencer Bennet *[v]*
Arthur Franz, Dick Foran, Brett Halsey, Tom Conway *Looking for the cause of strange energy coming from the ice caps, a submarine finds no less than a flying saucer.*

Attack of the Crab Monsters (1957) by Roger Corman *[v]*
Richard Garland, Pamela Duncan, Russell Johnson, Leslie Bradley *A pool of scientists is trapped on a shrinking island which houses giant brain-eating crabs.*

Attack of the Giant Leeches / The Giant Leeches (1959) by Bernard L. Kowalski *[v, d]*
Ken Clark, Yvette Vickers, Jan Shepard, Michael Emmet *A swamp is infested by giant leeches which truly love human blood.*

Bad Channels (1992) by Ted Nicolaou *[v, l]*
Paul Hipp, Martha Quinn, Aaron Lustig, Ian Patrick Williams *A DJ is taken hostage in his radio station by an alien who steals people by shrinking them and trapping then in glasses.*

Bad Taste (1988) by Peter Jackson *[v, l]*
Peter Jackson, Pete O'Herne, Mike Minett, Terry Potter *A whole town is crowded with humanoid aliens who want to use us as food for their intergalactic fast-food chain.*

Barracuda / The Lucifer Project (1978) by Harry Kerwin *[v]*
Wayne-David Crawford, Jason Evers, Bert Freed, Roberta Leighton *This time it's the barracuda's turn to be contaminated, visit some beaches, and pick off a few swimmers.*

Basket Case (1982) by Frank Henenlotter *[v, l, d]*
Kevin Van Hentenryck, Terri Susan Smith, Beverly Bonner, Robert Vogel *Former Siamese twins (one normal, the other deformed) are looking for the barbaric doctors who separated them. It's payback time!*

Basket Case 2 (1990) by Frank Henenlotter *[v, l]*
Kevin Van Hentenryck, Annie Ross, Jason Evers, Kathryn Meisle *Belial and his brother are back—but this time jealousy is their worst enemy: Belial finds love.*

Basket Case 3: the Progeny (1992) by Frank Henenlotter *[v, l]*
Kevin Van Hentenryck, Annie Ross, Gil Roper, Tina Louise Hilbert, Dan Biggers *Belial and his lovely wife give birth to a bucket of little Belials. Somebody wants to steal them, but freaks don't forgive.*

Bat People (1974) by Jerry Jameson *[v]*
Stewart Moss, Marianne McAndrew, Michael Pataki, Paul Carr *During their honeymoon, a couple is attacked by bats. The husband is bitten. Not much of a honeymoon after that.*

Bats (1999) by Louis Morneau *[v, d]*
Lou Diamond Phillips, Dina Meyer, Bob Gunton, León *They're bats, they're hungry for human flesh. Add it up.*

The Beast from 20,000 Fathoms (1953) by Eugene Lourie *[v, l]*
Paul Christian, Paula Raymond, Cecil Kellaway, Kenneth Tobey, Lee Van Cleef *After an atomic blast, a dinosaur is awakened and it's very grumpy.*

The Beast Must Die! (1974) by Paul Annett *[v, l]*
Calvin Lockhart, Peter Cushing, Charles Gray, Marlene Clark *A millionaire invites several guests for a thrilling weekend in his mansion: the man knows one of his guests is a werewolf.*

The Beast with a Million Eyes (1956) by David Kramarsky
Paul Birch, Lorna Thayer *An alien, whose sole purpose is to bring hate and malice everywhere, lands close to a farm and starts doing his job.*

Beetlejuice (1988) by Tim Burton *[v, l, d]*
Michael Keaton, Alec Baldwin, Geena Davis, Jeffrey Jones, Catherine O'Hara, Winona Ryder *A newly dead couple calls a bio-exorcist to get rid of certain people. Then they have to get rid of the bio-exorcist.*

Beginning of the End (1957) by Norman Taurog *[v]*
Brian Donlevy, Robert Walker, Beverly Tyler, Audrey Totter *Atomic radiation damages both people and the environment, so you could have giant grasshoppers at your next picnic.*

Beware! The Blob / Son of Blob (1972) by Larry Hagman *[v, d]*
Robert Walker, Richard Stahl, Godfrey Cambridge, Carol Lynley, Larry Hagman, Dick Van Patten *For no particular reason, the Blob (part of it) has been kept in a small container which is, naturally, opened.*

Bigfoot (1987) by Danny Huston *[v]*
Colleen Dewhurst, James Sloyan, Gracie Harrison,

Joseph Maher *Your average anthropologist is on the trail of the Sasquatch. Guess what? He finds it!*

Big Trouble in Little China (1986) by John Carpenter *[v, l]*

Kurt Russell, Kim Cattrall, Dennis Dun, James Hong *A gang of Oriental thugs kidnaps a green-eyed woman to offer her as a gift to an ancient sorcerer.*

Bill & Ted's Bogus Journey (1991) by Peter Hewitt *[v, l]*

Keanu Reeves, Alex Winter, William Sadler, Joss Ackland, George Carlin *Two California dudes travel through time and space, ending up in hell and heaven—and also end up fighting with evil doppelgänger robots.*

The Birds (1963) by Alfred Hitchcock *[v, l, d]*

Rod Taylor, Tippy Hedren, Jessica Tandy, Suzanne Pleshette *A small sea town is attacked by a swarm of mean birds. Eye-popping everywhere.*

The Black Hole (1979) by Gary Nelson *[v, l, d]*

Maximillian Shell, Anthony Perkins, Robert Forster, Joseph Bottoms, Yvette Mimieux, Ernest Borgnine *A starship finds another starship "parked" on the edge of a black hole. Its captain is a madman with vicious robots.*

The Black Scorpion (1957) by Edward Ludwig *[v]*

Richard Denning, Carlos Rivas, Mara Corday, Mario Navarro *Mexico: a volcano erupts and a gigantic scorpion follows. Neat-o.*

Blade (1998) by Stephen Norrington *[v, l, d]*

Wesley Snipes, Stephen Dorff, Kris Kristofferson, N'Bushe Wright, Donal Logue *Part man, part vampire, he fights like a bat but kills like a samurai. He needs instructions, because he's messed up.*

Blade Runner (1982) by Ridley Scott *[v, l, d]*

Harrison Ford, Rutger Hauer, Sean Young, Edward James Olmos, Daryl Hannah *In the 21st Century a special police unit chases replicants to destroy them. The replicants ain't happy.*

The Blair Witch Project (1999) by Daniel Myrick & Eduardo Sanchez *[v, d]*

Heather Donahue, Michael Williams, Joshua Leonard *Three real students get lost in the woods while filming a make-believe documentary on a fake witch. Or three make-believe students get lost for real while filming a fake documentary on a witch. Whatever.*

The Blob (1952) by Irwin S. Yeaworth, Jr. *[v, l, d]*

Steve McQueen, Aneta Corseant, Earl Rowe, Olin Hamlin *Red goo pops out of a meteor and starts gulping innocent people in a small village.*

The Blob (1988) by Chuck Russell *[v, l, d]*

Kevin Dillon, Shawnee Smith, Donovan Leitch, Ricky Paul Goldin *Pink goo pops out of a meteor and starts gulping innocent people in a small village.*

Blood for Dracula (1974) by Paul Morrisey *[v, l]*

Joe Dallesandro, Udo Kier, Arno Juerning, Maxime McKendry *The Count has to move from Transylvania to Italy in order to find virgin blood. It won't be an easy task.*

Bloodmoon (1982) by Alec Mills *[v, l]*

Leon Lissek, Christine Amor, Ian Patrick Williams, Helen Thomson *Young couples' eyes and fingers vanish from an Australian school. Clues point to the only suspect.*

Body Snatchers (1994) by Abel Ferrara *[v, l, d]*

Gabrielle Anwar, Meg Tilly, Forrest Whitaker, Terry Kinney *The body snatchers snatch bodies on a military base, but somebody doesn't want to be snatched. Conflict.*

The Boogey Man / The Boogeyman (1980) by Ulli Lommel *[v]*

Suzanna Love, Ron James, Nicholas Love, John Carradine *A broken mirror induces some people to kill, others to die.*

Boogeyman 2 / Boogeyman II (1982) by Bruce Starr *[v]*

Suzanna Love, Ulli Lommel, Shannah Hall *A broken mirror induces boring deaths everywhere.*

The Borrower (1989) by John McNaughton *[v, l]*

Rae Dawn Chong, Antonio Fargas, Don Gordon, Tom Towles *An alien falls to Earth and, in order to survive, needs to replace his head with human heads.*

Boxing Helena (1993) by Jennifer Chambers Lynch *[v, l]*

Julian Sands, Sherilyn Fenn, Bill Paxton, Art Garfunkel *A surgeon is so obsessed with his ex that, after a car crash, he amputates her arms and legs to make himself indispensable.*

Brain Damage (1988) by Frank Henenlotter *[v, d]*

Rick Herbst, Gordon MacDonald, Jennifer Lowry, Theo Barnes *A young kid adopts a parasite which gives him a powerful drug in exchange for fresh brains.*

The Brain from Planet Arous (1958) by Nathan Juran *[v, l]*

John Agar, Joyce Meadows, Robert Fuller, Henry Travis *An alien invader takes over a scientist's brain . . . and his dog's, waiting to conquer the world.*

Brainscan (1994) by John Flynn *[v, l]*

Edward Furlong, Frank Langella, T. Rider-Smith, Amy Hargreaves *A video game hosted by the vicious Trickster turns out to be a little too real: whoever you kill in the game dies for real.*

The Brain That Wouldn't Die (1963) by Joseph Green *[v, d]*

Herb (Jason) Evers, Virginia Leith, Adele Lamont, Leslie Daniel *While seeking the perfect body, a scientist keeps alive his wife's head, a head with telekinetic powers, no less.*

Bram Stoker's Dracula (1992) by Francis Ford Coppola *[v, l, d]*

Gary Oldman, Anthony Hopkins, Winona Ryder, Keanu Reeves, Richard E. Grant, Cary Elwes *The story of the popular Count Vlad as never told before.*

Bram Stoker's The Mummy (1997) by Jeffrey Obrow *[v, l, d]*

Louis Gossett, Jr., Amy Locane, Eric Lutes, Mack Lindsay-Chapman, Richard Karn *A female mummy is resurrected so that she can kill a lot of people just for the heck of it.*

Bride of Chucky (1998) by Ronny Yu *[v, l, d]*

Jennifer Tilly, Brad Dourif, Katherine Heigl, Nick Stabile, John Ritter, Alexis Arquette *Chucky has a wife this time, but he ain't settling down, oh no. Now they kill in stereo.*

Bride of Frankenstein (1935) by James Whale *[v, l, d]*

Boris Karloff, Colin Clive, Valerie Hobson, Ernest Thesiger *The mad scientist is lured into creating a companion for his monster (who didn't die in the fire like we thought).*

Bride of Re-Animator (1990) by Brian Yuzna *[v, l, d]*

Jeffrey Combs, Bruce Abbott, Claude Earl Jones, Fabiana Udenio *The mad scientist is lured into creating a companion for himself, while toying with so many body parts you can't imagine.*

The Brood (1979) by David Cronenberg *[v, l]*

Oliver Reed, Samantha Eggar, Art Hindle, Cindy Hinds *A woman is in therapy, allegedly because everyone she hates is being killed by strange kids armed with mallets.*

Bug (1975) by Jeannot Szwarc *[v]*

Bradford Dillman, Joanna Miles, Richard Gilliland, Jamie Smith Jackson *An earthquake opens up a crack in the ground, unleashing an undiscovered breed of insects capable of setting things on fire.*

The Cable Guy (1996) by Ben Stiller *[v, l, d]*

Jim Carrey, Matthew Broderick, Leslie Mann, George Segal *A young man realizes too late that the cable guy he called is a psychopath who delivers more than 57 channels.*

Candyman (1992) by Bernard Rose *[v, l, d]*

Virginia Madsen, Tony Todd, Xander Berkeley, Kasi Lemmons *A legend says that a killer lives in a mirror and you can call him—but at your own risk. Guess what happens here?*

Candyman: Farewell to the Flesh (1995) by Bill Condon *[v, l]*

Tony Todd, Kelly Rowan, Timothy Carhart, Veronica Cartwright *The man with the hook is back, this time in New Orleans, right in time for Mardi Gras.*

Candyman: Day of the Dead (1999) by Tury Meyer *[v, l, d]*

Tony Todd, Donna D'Errico, Wade Andrew Williams, Nick Corri *The man with the hook is back again, in Los Angeles, for the Dies of Muertos. Oh, the joy!*

Cape Fear (1991) by Martin Scorsese *[v, l]*

Robert De Niro, Nick Nolte, Jessica Lange, Juliette Lewis, Joe Don Baker *A convict comes out of jail with one purpose: to destroy the lawyer who let him go to the slammer.*

The Car (1977) by Elliott Silverstein *[v, l, d]*

James Brolin, Kathleen Lloyd, John Marley, Ronny Cox *A black sedan roars down the streets of a small town, often placing pedestrians between its tires and the asphalt.*

Carnosaur (1993) by Adam Simon *[v, l, d]*

Diane Ladd, Raphael Sbarge, Jennifer Runyon, Harrison Page *A geneticist creates a new species of dinosaurs which pop out from virus-infected chicken eggs.*

Carnosaur 2 (1994) by Louis Morneau *[v, l, d]*

John Savage, Cliff DeYoung, Arabella Holzbog, Ryan Thomas Johnson *A secret government installation is mined, both with dynamite and small dinosaurs.*

Carnosaur 3: Primal Species (1996) by Jonathan Winfrey *[v, l, d]*

Scott Valentine, Janet Gunn, Rick Dean, Rodger Halstead *A group of terrorists kidnap the little dinosaurs, but they soon find out it was a big mistake.*

Carrie (1976) by Brian De Palma *[v, l, d]*

Sissy Spacek, Piper Laurie, William Katt, John Travolta, Amy Irving, Nancy Allen *The freckled, nerdish little girl from high school is back, and this time she's mad!*

Cat People (1942) by Jacques Torneur *[v, l]*

Simone Simon, Kent Smith, Jane Randolph, Jack Holt *A Serbian woman houses a deep secret inside her body: she's a pussy . . . cat.*

Cat People (1982) by Paul Schrader *[v, l, d]*

Nastassia Kinski, Malcolm McDowell, John Heard, Annette O'Toole, Ed Begley, Jr. *Brother and sister are the last of the cat people: they can turn into black panthers whenever excited.*

The Changeling (1980) by Peter Medak *[v, l, d]*

George C. Scott, Trish Van Devere, John Russell, Melvyn Douglas *A composer rents a huge mansion to relax, but the previous tenant (a child's ghost) doesn't seem to want to move.*

Children of the Corn (1984) by Fritz Kiersch *[v, l, d]*

Peter Horton, Linda Hamilton, R. G. Armstrong, John Franklin *A young couple stop in a town to find out all the adults are gone. But the kids are there, and they're not too friendly.*

Children of the Corn II: The Final Sacrifice (1992) by David F. Price *[v, l]*

Terence Knox, Paul Scherrer, Rosalind Allen, Christie Clark *The children are moving in on another town, but the idea of erasing the adults is still on their minds.*

Children of the Corn III: Urban Harvest (1994) by James D. R. Hickox *[v, l]*

Daniel Cerney, Ron Melendez, Mari Morrow, Duke Stroud *Two Amish kids are sent to Chicago; here, one of them uses a lot to recreate his corn field to worship evil.*

Children of the Corn IV: The Gathering (1996) by Greg Spence *[v, l]*
Naomi Watts, Brent Jennings, Jaime Renee Smith, William Windom, Karen Black *Fourth chapter of the Children's neverending story: here almost every kid in town is hit by a dangerous fever... with a purpose.*

Children of the Corn V: Field of Terror (1998) by Ethan Wiley *[v, l]*
Stacy Galina, Alexis Arquette, Ahmet Zappa, Greg Vaughan, Adam Wylie, Eva Mendez, Fred Williamson, David Carradine *The children are back, still worshiping the devil and milking the same cow.*

Children of the Corn 666: Isaac's Return (1999) by Kari Skogland *[v, d]*
Nancy Allen, Natalie Ramsey, Paul Popowich, Alix Koromzay, John Patrick White, John Franklin *Isaac cracks corn and I don't care, Isaac cracks corn and I don't care....*

Children of the Damned (1964) by Anton Leader *[v, l]*
Ian Hendry, Alan Badel, Barbara Ferris, Patrick White *The silver-haired kids are back, trying once again to rule the Earth. They're no Rugrats.*

Children of the Night (1992) by Tony Randel *[v]*
Peter DeLuise, Karen Black, Ami Dolenz, Maya McLaughlin, Garrett Morris *Vampires who sleep underwater (with their lungs floating on the surface) take over a small town.*

Child's Play (1988) by Tom Holland *[v, l, d]*
Brad Dourif, Catherine Hicks, Alex Vincent, Chris Sarandon *A killer knows how to transfer his spirit into a talking doll—which becomes a talking and killing doll.*

Child's Play 2 (1990) by John Lafia *[v, l, d]*
Brad Dourif, Alex Vincent, Jenny Agutter, Gerrit Graham *The talking and killing doll is a die hard, so it comes back for another serving.*

Child's Play 3: Look Who's Stalking (1991) by Jack Bender *[v, l, d]*
Brad Dourif, Justin Whalin, Perrey Reeves, Jeremy Sylvers *The doll is back, and this time it wants a body in order to come back as a man: so it goes to military school.*

Chopping Mall / Killbots (1986) by Jim Wynorski *[v]*
Kelli Maroney, Tony O'Dell, Suzee Slater, Russell Todd, Paul Bartel *Four couples sneak into a shopping center the night a lightning bolt hits the computer and the surveillance robots run amuck.*

The Chosen / Holocaust 2000 (1978) by Alberto DeMartino *[v]*
Kirk Douglas, Agostina Belli, Simon Ward, Anthony Quayle *The executive of a power plant realizes his son is the Antichrist and wants to nuke the world with the plant.*

Christine (1983) by John Carpenter *[v, l, d]*
Keith Gordon, John Stockwell, Alexandra Paul, Robert Prosky, Harry Dean Stanton *A nerdy kid falls for a '58 Plymouth—and vice versa. But the car ain't the Love Bug: this one is b-b-bad to the bone.*

C.H.U.D. (1984) by Douglas Cheek *[v, l, d]*
John Heard, Daniel Stern, Christopher Curry, Kim Greist, John Goodman *An underground toxic waste disposal unfortunately affects many homeless people who live in the sewer: they become cannibals.*

C.H.U.D. 2: Bud the Chud (1989) by David Irving *[v, l]*
Brian Robbins, Bill Calvert, Gerrit Graham, Robert Vaughn *Two students accidentally resurrect a C.H.U.D., who runs free in their small town, biting and transforming a bunch of people.*

Colossus of New York (1958) by Eugene Lourie
John Baragrey, Mala Powers, Otto Kruger, Robert Hutton *A doctor implants the brain of his dead son into the head of a gigantic robot. Something bad is bound to happen.*

Copycat (1995) by John Amiel *[v, l, d]*
Sigourney Weaver, Holly Hunter, Dermot Mulroney, Harry Connick, Jr. *A woman psychiatrist who was attacked by a psychopath is asked by a detective for help: there's a copycat on the loose.*

The Craft (1996) by Andrew Fleming *[v, l, d]*
Robin Tunney, Fairuza Balk, Neve Campbell, Rachel True, Skeet Ulrich *Three young witches find a fourth, who, if in the group, will give them unlimited power. But they make her angry...*

The Crater Lake Monster (1977) by William R. Stomberg *[v]*
Richard Cardella, Glenn Roberts, Mark Siegel, Kacey Cobb *A small dinosaur pops out of a lake and uses people as munchies.*

The Crawling Eye (1958) by Quentin Lawrence *[v, l, d]*
Forrest Tucker, Laurence Payne, Janet Munro, Jennifer Jayne *A stationary cloud hides a group of mean aliens who—guess what?—want to take over the world.*

The Crawling Hand (1963) by Herbert L. Strock *[v, l]*
Alan Hale, Jr., Rod Lauren, Richard Arlen, Peter Breck *A kid turns into a killer zombie after finding the hand of an astronaut.*

Creature from the Black Lagoon (1954) by Jack Arnold *[v, l, d]*
Richard Carlson, Julie Adams, Richard Denning, Antonio Moreno, Whit Bissell, Ricou Browning *An expedition in the Amazon accidentally bumps into the Gill Man, a prehistoric guy in a rubber suit who is fascinated by sex.*

The Creature Walks Among Us (1956) by Jack Arnold *[v, l]*
Jeff Morrow, Rex Reason, Leigh Snowden, Gregg Palmer, Ricou Browning *Scientists give the Gill Man*

a pair of lungs, but what makes him mad is the ridiculous pajamas they dress him in.

Creature with the Atom Brain (1955) by Edward L. Cahn

Richard Denning, Angela Stevens, Gregory Gaye, Tristnam Coffin *A scientist brings back the dead thanks to an atomic device, then the newly created zombies are used as gangsters.*

The Creeping Unknown / The Quatermass Experiment (1956) by Val Guest *[v, l]*

Brian Donlevy, Margia Dean, Jack Warner, Richard Wordsworth *An astronaut comes back to Earth infected by a parasite which turns him into a deadly creature.*

Creepshow (1982) by George A. Romero *[v, l, d]*

Hal Holbrook, Adrienne Barbeau, Fritz Weaver, Leslie Nielsen, E. G. Marshall, Ed Harris, Stephen King *Five entertaining horror episodes based on a comic book and "sewn together" by a sixth story of voodoo revenge.*

Creepshow 2 (1987) by Michael Gornick *[v, l]*

Lois Chiles, George Kennedy, Dorothy Lamour, Tom Savini *Three less entertaining horror episodes based on a comic book and "sewn together" by a fourth toon story of plant revenge.*

Critters (1986) by Stephen Herek *[v, l]*

Dee Wallace Stone, M. Emmet Walsh, Billy Green Bush, Scott Grimes, Billy Zane *A bunch of malevolent gobble-it-all aliens land on Earth and wreak havoc until the space police come to the rescue.*

Critters 2: The Main Course (1988) by Mick Garris *[v, l]*

Scott Grimes, Liane Curtis, Don Opper, Barry Corbin *The aliens are back and hungrier: this time they're trying to take over a whole town. The space police are still after them.*

Critters 3 (1991) by Kristine Peterson *[v, l]*

Aimee Brooks, John Calvin, Katherine Cortez, Leonardo DiCaprio *The space rodents take over a building—à la* Die Hard.

Critters 4 (1992) by Rupert Harvey *[v, l]*

Don Opper, Brad Dourif, Paul Whitthorne, Angela Bassett *This time the aliens menace the crew of a starship. At least this time they remain in space.*

The Crush (1993) by Alan Shapiro *[v, l]*

Cary Elwes, Alicia Silverstone, Jennifer Rubin, Amber Benson *A young woman becomes obsessed with a journalist. Really, really, really, really, really obsessed.*

Cujo (1983) by Lewis Teague *[v, l, d]*

Dee Wallace Stone, Daniel Hugh-Kelly, Danny Pintauro, Ed Lauter *A slobbering St. Bernard becomes a slobbering rabid killer St. Bernard.*

Curse III: Blood Sacrifice (1990) by Sean Barton *[v]*

Christopher Lee, Jenilee Harrison, Henry Cele *The rule is simple: do not stop any voodoo ceremonies. If you do, then accept the consequences.*

Curse of Frankenstein (1957) by Terence Fisher *[v]*

Peter Cushing, Christopher Lee, Hazel Court, Robert Urquhart *Victor Frankenstein gets so obsessed with his creature that he is a mad mad scientist.*

Curse of the Cat People (1944) by Gunther von Fritsch, Robert Wise *[v, l]*

Simone Simon, Kent Smith, Jane Randolph, Elizabeth Russell *A little girl is chased by her father's first wife's vision. Could she be another entity . . . ?*

Curse of the Fly (1965) by Don Sharp

Brian Donlevy, Carole Gray, George Baker, Michael Graham *A man escaped from an institution ends up in another one: the family who's trying to use the teleporter.*

The Curse of the Mummy's Tomb (1964) by Michael Carreras

Terence Morgan, Ronald Howard, Fred Clark, Jeanne Ronald *A mummy is on the loose in Victorian London. The mummy's brother (!) is among the people fighting the thing.*

The Curse of the Werewolf (1960) by Terence Fisher *[v, l]*

Oliver Reed, Clifford Evand, Yvonne Romain, Catherine Feller, Anthony Dawson *A werewolf is the result of human depravity, but nevertheless, is still a werewolf.*

Cyborg (1989) by Albert Pyun *[v, l]*

Jean-Claude Van Damme, Deborah Richter, Vincent Klyn, Alex Daniels *In the not-so-distant future, a cyborg (guess who?) enjoys punishing people by beating the living hell out of them.*

Cyborg 2087 (1966) by Franklin Adreon

Michael Rennie, Wendell Corey, Eduard Franz, Karen Steele *Cyborgs from the future are sent back in time in order to change the present.*

Damien: The Omen II / The Omen 2 (1978) by Don Taylor *[v, l, d]*

William Holden, Lee Grant, Lew Ayres, Robert Foxworth, Jonathan Scott-Taylor, Lance Henriksen *Damien goes to military school, and people start to drop like flies.*

The Dark / The Mutilator (1979) by John Cardos *[v]*

William Devane, Cathy Lee Crosby, Richard Jaeckel, Keenan Wynn, Casey Kasem *An alien has laser eyes and head-ripping hands. The police are after the creature, but heads will roll before they catch it.*

Dark City (1998) by Alex Proyas *[v, l, d]*

Rufus Sewell, William Hurt, Kiefer Sutherland, Jennifer Connelly, Richard O'Brien *It's always night in a strange town that seems to be changing all the time—and has a few of its inhabitants flying around.*

The Dark Half (1993) by George A. Romero *[v, l, d]*

Timothy Hutton, Amy Madigan, Michael Rooker, Julie Harris, Robert Joy *A writer decides to "kill" his commercial pseudonym. Evidently, the pseudonym has something to say about that.*

Daughter of Dr. Jekyll (1957) by Edgar G. Ulmer *[v]*

John Agar, Gloria Talbott, Arthur Shields, John Dierkes *Somebody steals Dr. Jekyll's secret formula and haunts the scientist's daughter, who believes she's a monster herself.*

Dawn of the Dead / Zombie (1978) by George A. Romero *[v, l, d]*
David Emge, Ken Foree, Gaylen Ross, Scott H. Reiniger, Tom Savini *And the next day, over the towns four of the survivors find a cozy shelter in a mall. But the zombies are still there.*

The Day Mars Invaded Earth (1962) by Maury Dexter
Kent Taylor, Marie Windsor, William Mims, Betty Beals *These Martians are doppelgängers and they replace the family of a scientist, while trying to conquer the world.*

Day of the Dead (1985) by George A. Romero *[v, l, d]*
Lori Cardille, Terry Alexander, Joe Pilato, Jarlath Conroy *And the next day, zombies take over the world: a few people live underground, trying to domesticate the zombies. Good luck.*

The Day of the Triffids (1963) by Steve Sekely *[v, l]*
Howard Keel, Nicole Maurey, Janette Scott, Kieron Moore *After a meteor shower, part of the population is blind, part of the plants are carnivorous.*

The Day the Earth Stood Still (1951) by Robert Wise *[v, l]*
Michael Rennie, Patricia Neal, Hugh Marlowe, Sam Jaffe *An alien comes to Earth to bring an antinuclear warning. Not everybody agrees, though.*

Day the World Ended (1956) by Roger Corman *[v]*
Richard Denning, Lori Nelson, Adele Jergens, Mike Connors *A monster generated by radiation attacks the human race.*

Dead Calm (1989) by Phillip Noyce *[v, l, d]*
Sam Neill, Nicole Kidman, Billy Zane *Never pick up hitchhikers. Even if they're on a lifeboat heading toward your yacht.*

Dead Heat (1988) by Mark Goldblatt *[v, l]*
Joe Piscopo, Treat Williams, Lindsay Frost, Darren McGavin, Vincent Price *A dead cop has 12 hours to find out, with the help of his partner, who killed him and how he's sort of come back to life.*

Dead Kids / Strange Behavior (1981) by Michael Laughlin *[v]*
Michael Murphy, Louise Fletcher, Dan Shor, Fiona Lewis *While a doctor conducts a few experiments on students, the town is invaded by killer zombies. Coincidence?*

Deadly Eyes / The Rats (1982) by Robert Clouse *[v]*
Sam Groom, Sara Botsford, Scatman Crothers, Lisa Langlois *The town is invaded by mice. The minor snag is that they're as large as Dobermans and twice as mean.*

The Deadly Mantis (1957) by Nathan Juran *[v, l]*
Craig Stevens, William Hopper, Alix Talton, Donald Randolph *New York City receives an illegal alien: it's a praying mantis the size of a jumbo jet.*

The Dead Zone (1983) by David Cronenberg *[v, l, d]*
Christopher Walken, Brooke Adams, Tom Skerritt, Martin Sheen, Herbert Lom *After a five-year coma, a man wakes up with a special, unwanted gift: he can see the future.*

Deep Blue Sea (1999) by Renny Harlin *[v, l, d]*
Samuel L. Jackson, Saffron Burrows, Thomas Jane, LL Cool J, Jacqueline McKenzie *Experiments on shark brain cells cause sharks to grow smarter and meaner. Oops.*

Deep Rising (1998) by Stephen Sommers *[v, l, d]*
Treat Williams, Famke Janssen, Anthony Heald, Kevin J. O'Connor, Wes Studi *A group of terrorists hijack a yacht exactly when a never-before-seen monster from the bottom of the sea visits.*

DeepStar Six (1989) by Sean S. Cunningham *[v, l]*
Taurean Blacque, Nancy Everhard, Greg Evigan, Miguel Ferrer, Matt McCoy *An underwater explosion caused by an underwater base awakens an underwater monster. Underwater deaths follow.*

Demon of Paradise (1987) by Cirio H. Santiago *[v]*
Kathryn Witt, William Steis, Leslie Huntly, Laura Banks *Hawaii: rumor has it there's a creature "from the Triassic era" that captures and skins people. Well, they're not just rumors.*

The Demon Seed (1977) by Donald Cammell *[v, l]*
Julie Christie, Fritz Weaver, Gerrit Graham, Berry Kroeger *A woman all alone in a house controlled by a computer finds that her electronic housekeeper wants a son.*

Destroy All Monsters! (1968) by Inoshiro Honda *[v, d]*
Akira Kubo, Jun Tazaki, Yoshio Tsuchiya, Kyoto Ai *All of the Japanese monsters are held prisoner on a very large island. Yeah, sure, they'll stay quiet.*

Devil Girls from Mars (1954) by David MacDonald *[v]*
Patricia Laffan, Hugh McDermott, Hazel Court, Adrienne Corri *They're devilish, they're girls, and they're coming from Mars straight to England. Isn't this enough?*

The Devil's Advocate (1997) by Taylor Hackford *[v, l, d]*
Al Pacino, Keanu Reeves, Charlize Theron, Judith Ivey, Craig T. Nelson *A very good lawyer from Florida with a lousy southern accent reaches the Big Apple . . . and the gates of hell.*

Die, Monster, Die! (1965) by Daniel Haller *[v]*
Boris Karloff, Nick Adams, Suzan Farmer, Patrick Magee *A meteor lands too close to a farm, and most of all too close to a farmer.*

Dinosaurus! (1960) by Irvin S. Yeaworth, Jr. *[v, d]*
Ward Ramsey, Paul Lukather, Kristina Hanson, Alan Roberts *A caveman and two dinosaurs come back to life on a tropical island. Hey, it could happen!*

Disturbing Behavior (1998) by David Nutter *[v, l, d]*
James Marsden, Katie Holmes, Nick Stahl, Bruce Greenwood, William Sadler *An upgrade to make the "perfect" students causes more damage than Windows 2000.*

Dr. Black, Mr. Hyde (1976) by William Crain *[v]*
Rosalind Cash, Stu Gilliam, Bernie Casey, Marie O'Henry *An African-American Jekyll turns into a Caucasian Hyde and goes on a rampage.*

Dr. Giggles (1992) by Manny Coto *[v, l, d]*
Larry Drake, Holly Marie Combs, Glenn Quinn, Keith Diamond *An alleged doctor escapes from a loony bin and begins to cure unwilling people "his way."*

Dr. Jekyll and Mr. Hyde (1920) by John S. Robertson *[v, l]*
John Barrymore, Martha Mansfield, Brandon Hurst, Charles Lane *Good-natured Dr. Jekyll screws up and becomes ill-natured Mr. Hyde. Silent movie.*

Dr. Jekyll and Mr. Hyde (1932) by Rouben Mamoulian *[v, l]*
Fredric March, Miriam Hopkins, Halliwell Hobbes, Rose Hobart *Good-natured Dr. Jekyll screws up and becomes ill-natured Hyde. But this time he talks.*

Dr. Jekyll and Mr. Hyde (1941) by Victor Fleming *[v, l]*
Spencer Tracy, Ingrid Bergman, Lana Turner, Donald Crisp *Good-natured Dr. Jekyll screws up and becomes ill-natured Hyde. Ho-hum.*

Dr. Jekyll and Sister Hyde (1972) by Roy Ward Baker *[v]*
Ralph Bates, Martine Beswick, Gerald Sim *Same stuff, with one twist: it's not "mister," it's "sister." Get it? Ha-ha.*

Dr. Phibes Rises Again! (1972) by Robert Fuest *[v, l ,d]*
Vincent Price, Robert Quarry, Peter Cushing, Beryl Reid, Terry-Thomas *Sequel to* The Abominable Dr. P, *the sad doctor is still trying to reunite with his dead wife. Soon . . .*

Dr. Who and the Daleks (1965) by Gordon Fleming *[v]*
Peter Cushing, Roy Castle, Jennie Linden, Roberta Tovey *Dr. Who and his elite friends meet the Daleks, very obnoxious robots with a penchant for annihilating the human race.*

Dogora the Space Monster (1964) by Inoshiro Honda *[v]*
Yoko Fujiama, Yuno Tanzan, Dan Yuma, Naomi Fleur *An oversized amoeba lands in a swamp and starts eating coal and diamonds. Interesting alimentary habits.*

Dogs (1976) by Burt Brickenroff *[v]*
David McCallum, Sandra McCabe, George Wyner *A nuclear accelerator near a campus makes the dogs kill everyone and get a (pe)degree.*

Dracula (1931) by Tod Browning *[v, l, d]*
Bela Lugosi, Helen Chandler, David Manners, Dwight Frye *Count Vlad steps into the "Goth" scene and dominates it, even without his trademark fangs.*

Dracula (1979) by John Badham *[v, l, d]*
Frank Langella, Laurence Olivier, Kate Nelligan, Donald Pleasence *Count Vlad comes back (in color) and appears much more explicitly than his predecessor.*

Dracula: Dead and Loving It (1995) by Mel Brooks *[v, l]*
Leslie Nielsen, Peter MacNicol, Steve Weber, Amy Yasbeck, Mel Brooks *Count Vlad steps into the "Goth" scene, trips, falls, and (for once) we laugh at him.*

Dragonheart (1996) by Rob Cohen *[v, l, d]*
Dennis Quaid, David Thewlis, Pete Postlethwaite, Dina Meyer, Julie Christie, voice of Sean Connery *A hunter wants to kill every single dragon in order to vindicate an old betrayal. But the last dragon changes his mind . . .*

Dragonslayer (1981) by Matthew Robbins *[v, l]*
Peter MacNicol, Caitlin Clarke, Ralph Richardson, John Hallam *A young apprentice sorcerer takes on the task of killing a malevolent dragon. Not your average walk in the park.*

Dressed to Kill (1980) by Brian De Palma *[v, l]*
Angie Dickinson, Michael Caine, Nancy Allen, Keith Gordon *The patient of a psychiatrist is doing to gorgeous women what Buffy does to vampires.*

Duel (1971) by Steven Spielberg *[v, l]*
Dennis Weaver, Eddie Firestone, Jacqueline Scott, Lou Frizzel *A salesman makes one mistake: he outruns a truck. And now the truck is after him. On the road again . . .*

Earth vs. the Flying Saucers (1956) by Fred F. Sears *[v, l]*
Hugh Marlowe, Joan Taylor, Donald Curtis, Morris Ankrum *Oh, a bunch of flying saucers enter our atmosphere and cause some trouble, but in the end we kind of win.*

Earth vs. the Spider (1958) by Bert I. Gordon *[v]*
Ed Kemmer, June Kenny, Geene Persson, Gene Roth *If you capture and allegedly kill one very large spider, do not put it on display in your high school.*

Edge of Sanity (1989) by Gérard Kikoine *[v, l]*
Anthony Perkins, Glynis Barber, Sarah Maur-Thorp, David Lodge *This could have been titled* Dr. Jekyll & Jack the Ripper, *because that describes exactly what happens.*

Eegah (1962) by Nicholas Merriwether (Arch W. Hall, Sr.) *[v, d]*
Arch W. Hall, Jr., Richard Kiel, Marilyn Manning, William Waters (Arch W. Hall, Sr.) *A towering caveman pops out of nowhere and falls in love with a blond woman who screams all day long. Dreadful songs, too.*

Electric Dreams (1984) by Steve Barron *[v, l]*

Lenny Von Dohlen, Virginia Madsen, Maxwell Caulfield, voice of Bud Cort. *Your average 20th-century triangle: a boy, a girl, and a computer. And the last one is really jealous.*

The Emperor and the Golem (Cisaruv pekar, pekaruv cisar) (1951) by Martin Fric
Jan Werich, Natasa Gollová, Frantisek Cerny, Jirí Plachy, Bohus Záhorsky, Zdenek Stepánek, Frantisek Filipovsky *An angry emperor, a case of mistaken identity, and of course . . . a Golem. Fun for the whole family.*

Empire of the Ants (1977) by Bert I. Gordon *[v]*
Joan Collins, Robert Lansing, Albert Salmi, Robert Pine *Take some ants, add a pinch of radioactivity, and* voilà*! You'll have giant ants vs. people.*

The Evil Dead (1983) by Sam Raimi *[v, l, d]*
Bruce Campbell, Ellen Sandweiss, Betsy Baker, Hal Delrich, Sarah York *Five kids spend the night in a log cabin and get almost thoroughly possessed by a spirit which lives in the nearby forest.*

Evil Dead 2: Dead by Dawn (1987) by Sam Raimi *[v, l, d]*
Bruce Campbell, Sarah Berry, Dan Hicks, Kassie Wesley *Another log cabin vacation and another thorough possession thanks to a spirit which still lives in the nearby forest.*

The Exorcist (1973) by William Friedkin *[v, l, d]*
Ellen Burstyn, Max von Sydow, Linda Blair, Jason Miller, Lee J. Cobb *A 12-year-old girl is possessed by the devil and as of today keeps scaring audiences across the world.*

Exorcist II: the Heretic (1977) by John Boorman *[v, l, d]*
Richard Burton, Linda Blair, Louise Fletcher, Kitty Wynn, James Earl Jones *The devil on the rebound. All of these actors have been in much better movies. Pass on this one.*

The Exorcist III (1990) by William Peter Blatty *[v, l, d]*
George C. Scott, Ed Flanders, Brad Dourif, Jason Miller *A police inspector slowly finds out that a series of murders are linked together and to a certain Mr. Devil . . .*

Fallen (1999) by Gregory Hoblit *[v, l, d]*
Denzel Washington, John Goodman, Donald Sutherland, Embeth Davidtz, James Gandolfini *A cop is haunted by a demon whose main purpose is to bring about the end of civilization. Evidently, it's a common pastime among demons.*

The Fan (1996) by Tony Scott *[v, l, d]*
Robert De Niro, Wesley Snipes, Ellen Barkin, John Leguizamo, Benicio Del Toro, Patti D'Arbanville, Chris Mulkey *A baseball star meets his #1 fan. But he can't get rid of him that easily.*

The Farm (1987) by David Keith *[v]*
Wil Wheaton, Claude Akins, Cooper Huckabee, John Schneider *A meteorite lands very close to a farm, and everybody gets an overdose of radiation and begins to kill.*

Fatal Attraction (1987) by Adrian Lyne *[v, l, d]*
Michael Douglas, Glenn Close, Anne Archer, Ellen Hamilton Latzen, Stuart Pankin *One fling can ruin a man's life (as well as his wife's, son's . . .).*

Fear (1996) by James Foley *[v, d]*
Mark Wahlberg, Reese Witherspoon, William L. Petersen, Amy Brenneman, Alyssa Milano, Christopher Gray, Gary Riley *Love is a many-splendored thing—even if your lover is so obsessed with you that he destroys anything keeping you apart.*

The Final Conflict (1981) by Graham Baker *[v, l, d]*
Sam Neill, Rossano Brazzi, Don Gordon, Lisa Harrow *Damien is a grown-up now, and he's ready to fight a reborn Jesus.*

Fire Maidens of Outer Space (1955) by Cy Roth *[v]*
Anthony Dexter, Susan Shaw, Paul Carpenter, Harry Fowler, Sydney Tafler *On one of Jupiter's moons lives a race of Fire Maidens in desperate need of human company.*

Firestarter (1984) by Mark L. Lester *[v, l, d]*
David Keith, Drew Barrymore, George C. Scott, Martin Sheen, Heather Locklear *A little girl can generate fire at will. Very useful for camping, she's tracked down by some "evil guys" who want to study her.*

The First Power (1990) by Robert Resnikoff *[v, l]*
Lou Diamond Phillips, Tracy Griffith, Jeff Kober, Mykel T. Williamson *A chase between a cop and the spirit of an executed devil worshiper who can't stop killing.*

Five Million Years to Earth (1968) by Roy Ward Baker
James Donald, Barbara Shelley, Andrew Keir, Julian Glover *A very large spacecraft is found underneath London. The aliens are still effective, even after all this time.*

Flash Gordon (1980) by Mike Hodges *[v, l, d]*
Sam J. Jones, Melody Anderson, Topol, Max von Sydow, Ornella Muti *The superhero who has no superpowers faces his archenemy, Ming. And the battle is scored by no less than Queen.*

The Fly (1958) by Kurt Neumann *[v, l, d]*
Al (David) Hedison, Patricia Owens, Vincent Price, Herbert Marshall *Is teleportation possible? Well, technically, yes. But be sure to be alone in the chamber, otherwise . . . "Help meeee!"*

The Fly (1986) by David Cronenberg *[v, l, d]*
Jeff Goldblum, Geena Davis, John Getz, Joy Boushel *Is teleportation possible? Oh, yes. But again, check your telepod or you'll become a new creature.*

The Fly II (1989) by Chris Walas *[v, l, d]*
Eric Stoltz, Daphne Zuniga, Lee Richardson, John Getz *The son of the scientist who tried teleportation is a superhuman waiting to turn into a large fly.*

The Fog (1980) by John Carpenter *[v, l]*
Adrienne Barbeau, Jamie Lee Curtis, Hal Holbrook, Janet Leigh *The 100-year-old curse about the fog,*

the dead sailors, and other scary stuff proves to be true. And a village pays the consequences.

Food of the Gods (1976) by Burt I. Gordon *[v]*
Marjoe Gortner, Ralph Meeker, Pamela Franklin, Ida Lupino *Oozing white goo makes animals bigger. Doesn't that sound like the perfect recipe for disaster?*

Forbidden Planet (1956) by Fred McLeod Wilcox *[v, l, d]*
Walter Pidgeon, Leslie Nielsen, Anne Francis, Warren Stevens *A spacecrew lands on a planet which is home to the Id Monster—an alien with a poor sense of humor.*

Forbidden World (1982) by Allan Holzman *[v, l]*
Jesse Vint, June Chadwick, Dawn Dunlap, Linden Chiles *The crew of a spacecraft accidentally bump into an alien which chases, bites, and causes mutations to its prey.*

The Forbin Project (1970) by Joseph Sargent *[v]*
Eric Braeden, Susan Clark, Gordon Pinsent, William Schallert *One of the most sophisticated computers is so sophisticated that it tries to kill everyone who gets to the keyboard.*

Frankenstein (1910) by J. Searle Dawley
Charles Ogle *The first "on-screen" attempt to create a monster. Silent.*

Frankenstein (1931) by James Whale *[v, l, d]*
Colin Clive, Mae Clarke, John Boles, Boris Karloff *It's alive! It's alive, it's alive, it's alive! . . .*

Frankenstein Meets the Wolf Man (1943) by Roy W. Neill *[v, l]*
Lon Chaney, Jr., Bela Lugosi, Lionel Atwill, Ilona Massey *There's room for only one of these treacherous monsters . . . the fight is nasty and gruesome.*

Frankenstein 70 (1958) by Howard W. Kotch *[v]*
Boris Karloff, Tom Duggan, Donald Barry, Jana Lund *A descendant of the original Frankenstein wants to keep up with Grandpa's experiment—and of course, he succeeds!*

Frankenstein Unbound (1990) by Roger Corman *[v, l]*
John Hurt, Raul Julia, Bridget Fonda, Nick Brimble, Jason Patric *From the 21st century to the past, a not-so-mad scientist gets the bug of recreating life.*

Freaks (1932) by Tod Browning *[v, l]*
Wallace Ford, Olga Baclanova, Harry Earles, Daisy Earles, Leila Hyams *All of the circus freaks find out that the real weirdos are the people around them. It's payback time.*

Freddy's Death: the Final Nightmare (1991) by Rachel Talalay *[v, l, d]*
Robert Englund, Lisa Zane, Shon Greenblatt, Lezlie Deane, Ricky Dean Logna *Tracking the origin of Mr. Krueger, we get acquainted with his offspring . . . and we enter his mind.*

Friday the 13th (1980) by Sean S. Cunningham *[v, l, d]*
Betsy Palmer, Adrienne King, Harry Crosby, Kevin Bacon *Camp Crystal Lake is open again after a "bloody" past. But the bodies start to pile up . . .*

Friday the 13th: The Final Chapter (1984) by Joseph Zito *[v, l, d]*
Crispin Glover, Kimberly Beck, Barbara Howard, E. Erich Anderson *Do you really believe it's the final chapter? Get real! Oh, by the way: 13 deaths in this flick.*

Friday the 13th Part 2 (1981) by Steve Miner *[v, l, d]*
Betsy Palmer, Amy Steel, John Furey, Adrienne King *The camp is still open, the campers are still numerous, the body count higher.*

Friday the 13th Part 3 (1982) by Steve Miner *[v, l, d]*
Dana Kimmell, Paul Kratka, Tracie Savage, Jeffrey Rogers *Pretty much the same, only this time in 3-D: demented, delusional, and disappointing.*

Friday the 13th Part V: A New Beginning (1985) by Danny Steinmann *[v, l]*
John Shepard, Melanie Kinnaman, Shavar Ross, Richard Young *Oh, why bother? Here there's not even Jason!*

Friday the 13th Part VI: Jason Lives (1986) by Tom McLoughlin *[v, l]*
Thom Mathews, Jennifer Cooke, David Kagan, Renee Jones *Tell us something we don't know.*

Friday the 13th Part VII: The New Blood (1988) by John Carl Buechler *[v, l]*
Lar Park Lincoln, Terry Kiser, Susan Blu, Kevin Blair *Blah, blah, blah.*

Friday the 13th Part VIII: Jason Takes Manhattan (1989) by Rob Hedden *[v, l]*
Jensen Daggett, Kane Hodder, Peter Mark Richman, Scott Reeves *Yadda, yadda, yadda.*

The Frighteners (1996) by Peter Jackson *[v, l, d]*
Michael J. Fox, Trini Alvarado, Peter Dobson, John Astin, Jeffrey Combs *A sensitive person follows a serial killer who was devastating when he was alive. Now that he's dead, he's a bitch.*

Frogs (1972) by George McGowan *[v, d]*
Ray Milland, Sam Elliott, Joan Van Ark *We think that the title gives away who the killers are in this movie, which takes place on an island on July 4th.*

From Beyond (1986) by Stuart Gordon *[v, l]*
Jeffrey Combs, Barbara Crampton, Ted Sorel, Ken Foree *If you've ever wondered, yes, there are ghosts floating in the air around us. But they're mean and ferocious.*

From Hell It Came (1957) by Dan Milner
Tod Andrews, Tina Carver, Linda Watkins, John McNamara *A Native American, who at the time of this movie was still called an "Indian," is killed and buried, but a walking tree vindicates him.*

The Funhouse (1981) by Tobe Hooper *[v, l, d]*
Elizabeth Berridge, Cooper Huckabee, Miles Chapin, Largo Woodruff *The funhouse of a carnival is as scary as it looks . . . and even more!*

The Fury (1978) by Brian De Palma *[v, l]*
Kirk Douglas, John Cassavetes, Carrie Snodgress, Amy Irving, Charles Durning *The Secret Service wants to use a kid whose telekinetic powers are greater than his dad's. But the kid doesn't like the situation.*
Futureworld (1976) by Richard T. Heffron *[v, l]*
Peter Fonda, Blythe Danner, Arthur Hill, Yul Brynner *The ultimate amusement park offers emotion, joy . . . and death to the guests. Sequel to* Westworld.
Gamera, Guardian of the Universe (1997) by Shusuke Kaneko *[v, d]*
Tsuyoski Ihara, Akira Onodera, Ayoko Fujitani, Shinobu Nakayama *A new, improved, but still crappy-looking, flying, rotating, fire-farting turtle lands on Japan and wreaks havoc.*
Gamera, the Invincible (1965) by Noriaky Yuasi *[v]*
Brian Donlevy, Albert Dekker, John Baragrey *A flying, rotating, fire-farting turtle lands on Japan and wreaks havoc.*
Ghostbusters (1984) by Ivan Reitman *[v, l, d]*
Bill Murray, Dan Aykroyd, Harold Ramis, Sigourney Weaver, Rick Moranis *If there's something strange in your neighborhood, who you gonna call . . . ?*
Ghostbusters II (1989) by Ivan Reitman *[v, l, d]*
Bill Murray, Dan Aykroyd, Harold Ramis, Sigourney Weaver, Rick Moranis *If there's still something strange in your neighborhood, who you gonna call . . . ?*
Ghost Story (1981) by John Irvin *[v, l, d]*
Fred Astaire, Melvyn Douglas, Douglas Fairbanks, Jr., John Houseman *Four friends who hide a terrible secret crack up when the ghost of the terrible secret pays them a visit.*
The Giant Behemoth (1959) by Eugene Lourie
Gene Evans, Andre Morell, John Turner, Leigh Madison *A radioactive dinosaur attacks London and ruins the queen's tea.*
The Giant Claw (1957) by Fred F. Sears *[v]*
Jeff Morrow, Mara Corday, Morris Ankrum, Edgar Barrier *The largest puppet vaguely shaped like a bird attacks towns. The army fights back.*
The Giant Gila Monster (1959) by Ray Kellog *[v, l, d]*
Don Sullivan, Lisa Simone, Shug Fisher, Jerry Cortwright *It's giant, it's from Gila, and it's a monster. Isn't this enough?*
The Giant Spider Invasion (1975) by Bill Rebane *[v]*
Steve Brodie, Barbara Hale, Leslie Parrish, Alan Hale *It's giant, it's—oh, well, you get the picture anyway. Creepy crawlers.*
Gigantis, the Fire Monster (1959) by Motoyoshi, Hugo Grimaldi *[v]*
Hiroshi Koizumi, Setsuko Makayama *Godzilla-wannabe.*
Gnaw: Food of the Gods II (1989) by Damian Lee *[v]*
Paul Coufos, Lisa Schrage, Jackie Burroughs, Colin Fox *Some lab rats consume a strange substance and become very, very large.*
Godzilla (Gojira) (1954) by Inoshiro Honda *[v, l, d]*
Takashi Shimura, Raymond Burr, Mamoto Kochi, Akira Takarada *Extremely large, extremely vicious radioactive lizard attacks Tokyo.*
Godzilla (1998) by Roland Emmerich *[v, l, d]*
Matthew Broderick, Jean Reno, Maria Pitillo, Hank Azaria, Kevin Dunn *Extremely large, extremely pregnant, extremely vicious radioactive lizard attacks New York.*
Gog (1954) by Herbert L. Strock
Richard Egan, Constance Dowling, Herbert Marshall, John Wengraf *A scientific plant is cursed with mysterious deaths. Could the responsible party be a robot run amuck?*
Der Golem, Wie Er in Die Welt Kam (1920) by Paul Wegener
Albert Steinruck, Paul Wegener, Lydia Salmonova, Ernst Beutsch *Clay-made statue comes alive and executes its master's will.*
Gorgo (1954) by Eugene Louirè *[v, l, d]*
Bill Travers, William Sylvester, Vincent Winter *An English ship finds a prehistoric lizard walking on the ocean floor. But it's not alone, and London will pay the price.*
Graveyard Shift (1990) by Ralph S. Singleton *[v, l]*
David Andrews, Kelly Wolf, Stephen Macht, Brad Dourif *The workers of a mill start to disappear one by one. Maybe the responsible party is this thirty-foot-long bat.*
The Green Slime (1969) by Kinij Fukasaku *[v]*
Robert Horton, Richard Jaeckel, Luciana Paluzzi, Burt Widom *Green slime grows when it touches human blood. Don't ask.*
Gremlins (1984) by Joe Dante *[v, l, d]*
Zach Galligan, Phoebe Cates, Hoyt Axton, Frances Lee McCain, Dick Miller *A kid can't see his fuzzy pet as a treacherous menace to humanity.*
Gremlins 2: the New Batch (1990) by Joe Dante *[v, l, d]*
Zach Galligan, Phoebe Cates, John Glover, Robert Prosky, Dick Miller *The same kid still can't see his fuzzy pet as a treacherous menace to humanity.*
Grizzly (1976) by William Girdler *[v, d]*
Christopher George, Joe Dorsey, Joan McCall, Sandra Dorsey *The vacation of a group of campers takes a ride in the dumpster when a ferocious bear slices everyone it finds.*
The Guardian (1990) by William Friedkin *[v, l]*
Jenny Seagrove, Dwier Brown, Carey Lowell, Brad Hall *The "I-have-a-perfect-resume" Nanny forgot to put that she's also a witch. Hey, it could happen.*
The Guyver (1992) by Screaming Mad George, Steve Wang *[v, l]*
Mark Hamill, Vivian Wu, Jack Armstrong, David Gale *While everyone else can turn into a large hideous evil monster, a man turns into a large hideous good monster.*
Habitat (1997) by Renee Daalder *[v, l, d]*
Alice Krige, Balthazar, Tcheky Karyo, Kenneth Welsh

Scientist turns his house into a green house, then himself into a cloud of pollen.

Hack-O-Lantern (a.k.a. "Halloween Night") (1987) by Emilio Miraglia and Jag Mundhra *[v]*

Hy Pyke, Gregory Scott Cummins, Katina Garner, Carla Baron, Jeff Brown, Patricia Christie, Michael Potts, Larry Coven *A whole family worship Satan. And they are awful neighbors, too.*

Halloween (1978) by John Carpenter *[v, l, d]*

Jamie Lee Curtis, Donald Pleasence, Nancy Loomis, P. J. Soles, Charles Cyphers *First appearance of Michael Myers. And he's scary as Hell!*

Halloween II (1981) by Rick Rosenthal *[v, l, d]*

Jamie Lee Curtis, Donald Pleasence, Jeffrey Kramer, Charles Cyphers, Lance Guest *Second appearance of Michael Myers. Still scary, and on his way to becoming a myth.*

Halloween III: Season of the Witch (1983) by Tommy Lee Wallace *[v, l, d]*

Tom Atkins, Stacey Nelkin, Dan O'Herlihy, Ralph Strait *Michael Myers's path is jeopardized by this strange story of a sorcerer who wants to kill almost every kid on Halloween. Cool.*

Halloween 4: the Return of Michael Myers (1988) by Dwight H. Little *[v, l, d]*

Donald Pleasence, Ellie Cornell, Danielle Harris, Michael Pataki *Michael Myers is back and with a new set of knives. The path is paved with gold (and blood).*

Halloween 5: the Revenge of Michael Myers (1989) by Dominique Othenin-Girard *[v, l, d]*

Donald Pleasence, Ellie Cornell, Danielle Harris, Don Shanks *Still good ol' Michael, doing what he does best.*

Halloween: The Curse of Michael Myers (1995) by Joe Chappelle *[v, l, d]*

Donald Pleasence, Mitchell Ryan, Marianne Hagan, Leo Geter *Michael is still around, slicing and dicing.*

Halloween H20 (1998) by Steve Miner *[v, l, d]*

Jamie Lee Curtis, Adam Arkin, Michelle Williams, Adam Hann-Byrd, Jodi Lyn O'Keefe, Janet Leigh, Josh Hartnett, L. L. Cool J. *Michael and his older sister are reunited, but she doesn't "feel so good."*

The Hand That Rocks the Cradle (1992) by Curtis Hanson *[v, l]*

Annabella Sciorra, Rebecca De Mornay, Matt McCoy, Ernie Hudson *She's mad, angry, and seeking revenge: she's the Nanny from hell (or thereabouts).*

Hannibal (2001) by Ridley Scott

Anthony Hopkins, Julianne Moore, Gary Oldman, Giancarlo Giannini *Hannibal goes to Italy.*

Hardware (1990) by Richard Stanley *[v, l]*

Dylan McDermott, Stacy Travis, John Lynch, Iggy Pop *Very violent story of a man who finds some robot parts that don't want to be shelved—and they resume their mission: kill!*

Harry and the Hendersons (1987) by William Dear *[v, l]*

John Lithgow, Melinda Dillon, Margaret Langrick, Joshua Rudoy *A sasquatch is found and "adopted" by a family.*

The Haunted Palace (1963) by Roger Corman *[v, l]*

Vincent Price, Debra Paget, Lon Chaney, Jr., Frank Maxwell *Don't you hate when you move into a castle that is under an evil spell and the entire town is populated by mutants?*

The Haunting (1999) by Jan de Bont *[v, l, d]*

Liam Neeson, Catherine Zeta-Jones, Lili Taylor, Owen Wilson, Marian Seldes, Bruce Dern, Virginia Madsen *Underhanded psychologist conducts study on fear in a "haunted" house. Soon, the joke's on him.*

Hellbound: Hellraiser II (1988) by Tony Randel *[v, l, d]*

Ashley Laurence, Claire Higgins, Kenneth Cranham, Imogen Boorman *The gates of Hell are opened once again by the puzzle box. If you're looking for trouble, you've found it.*

Hell High (1984) by Douglas Grossman *[v, d]*

Christopher Stryker, Christopher Cousins, Millie Prezioso, Jason Bill *Your average little girl who witnessed some sex and caused a double death has grown up and is ready to pop again.*

Hello Mary Lou: Prom Night 2 (1987) by Bruce Pittman *[v, l]*

Michael Ironside, Wendy Lyon, Justin Louis, Lisa Schrage *The prom queen who died while being crowned comes back to school for a little fun. Beware . . .*

Hellraiser (1987) by Clive Barker *[v, l, d]*

Andrew Robinson, Clare Higgins, Ashley Laurence, Sean Chapman *Pleasure and pain: do they coincide? Well, this flick tells you.*

Hellraiser III: Hell on Earth (1992) by Anthony Hickox *[v, l]*

Doug Bradley, Terry Farrell, Kevin Bernhardt, Paula Marshall, Ken Karpenter *Pinhead and other cenobites are back on Earth, looking for disciples.*

Hellraiser: Bloodline (1996) by Alan Smithee (Kevin Yagher) *[v, l, d]*

Bruce Ramsey, Valentina Vargas, Doug Bradley, Kim Myers *The story of the cenobites, from ancient times to space.*

Hellraiser: Inferno (2000) by Scott Derrikson *[v, d]*

Craig Sheffer, Doug Bradley, Carmen Argenziano, Ian Barford *What is the puzzle box? Where did it come from? And why can't you leave it alone, stupid?!*

Henry: Portrait of a Serial Killer (1990) by John McNaughton *[v, l, d]*

Michael Rooker, Tom Towles, Tracy Arnold *A serial killer who kills at random and with different styles. Creepy and disturbing.*

The Hidden (1987) by Jack Sholder *[v, l, d]*

Michael Nouri, Kyle MacLachlan, Ed O'Ross, Clu Gulager *Cop and special (very special) agent follow the steps of an astute alien who loves cars, drugs and rock'n'roll.*

The Hidden 2 (1994) by Seth Pinsker *[v]*
Raphael Sbarge, Kate Hodge, Jovin Montanaro, Christopher Murphy *Oh, well . . . our alien started out so well, but here he takes a turn for nowhere-land.*

The Hideous Sun Demon (1959) by Robert Clarke *[v, d]*
Robert Clarke, Patricia Manning, Nan Peterson, Patrick Whyte *Doctor finds himself in trouble whenever hit by sunlight: he turns into a large lizard.*

The Hills Have Eyes (1977) by Wes Craven *[v]*
Susan Lanier, Robert Houston, Martin Speer, Dee Wallace Stone, Michael Berryman *Your average middle-class American family meet your not-so-average mutated cannibalistic brutal family who live in the desert.*

The Hills Have Eyes Part 2 (1984) by Wes Craven *[v]*
Michael Berryman, Kevin Blair, John Joe Bob Briggs Bloom, Janus Blythe *Round 2.*

The Hitcher (1986) by Robert Harmon *[v, l, d]*
C. Thomas Howell, Rutger Hauer, Jennifer Jason Leigh, Jeffrey DeMunn *Don't pick up hitchhikers. Just don't. Or you'll meet John Ryder—and you positively won't like him.*

Hocus Pocus (1993) by Kenny Ortega *[v, l]*
Bette Midler, Kathy Najimy, Sarah Jessica Parker, Thora Birch, Doug Jones *Three witches come back to their town on Halloween night after 300 years.*

Horror of Dracula (1958) by Terence Fisher *[v, l]*
Peter Cushing, Christopher Lee, Michael Gough, Melissa Stribling *Another match for Dracula & Van Helsing. Everyone wins, everyone loses.*

The Horror of Party Beach (1964) by Del Tenney
John Scott, Alice Lyon, Allen Laurel, Eulabelle Moore *Weird!!! Ghoulish atomic beasts who live off warm, human blood!*

House (1986) by Steve Miner *[v, l, d]*
William Katt, George Wendt, Richard Moll, Kay Lenz *A writer with writer's block moves into a haunted house and is chased by ghosts.*

House II (1987) by Ethan Wiley *[v, l, d]*
John Ratzenberger, Arye Gross, Royal Dano, Bill Maher *There's a room in the house which leads to a prehistoric world, to the old west, to very different ghost places . . . Uh . . .*

House of Dracula (1945) by Erle C. Kenton *[v, l]*
Lon Chaney, Jr., Martha O'Driscoll, John Carradine, Lionell Atwill *A doctor tries to cure the monsters (Dracula, Frankenstein's Creature, The Wolfman), but it's not an easy task.*

House of Frankenstein (1944) by Erle C. Kenton *[v, l]*
Boris Karloff, J. Carrol Naish, Lon Chaney, Jr., John Carradine *A couple of escapees hide in a Chamber of Horrors—and nothing goes right.*

House on Haunted Hill (1999) by William Malone *[v, d]*
Geoffrey Rush, Famke Janssen, Taye Diggs, Ali Larter, Bridgette Wilson, Peter Gallagher, Chris Kattan *Who wants to be a millionaire? Spend one night in this house and, if you aren't killed, mauled, absorbed by the walls, electrocuted, or decapitated, you'll get one million dollars the next morning.*

The Howling (1981) by Joe Dante *[v, l]*
Dee Wallace Stone, Patrick Macnee, Dennis Dugan, Christopher Stone *A whole village in the mountains houses a terrible secret. A secret that has fangs, hair, and howls at the moon.*

The Howling III: The Marsupials (1987) by Philippe Mora *[v, l]*
Barry Otto, Imogen Annesley, Dasha Blahova, Max Fairchild *An Australian werewolf comes to town and becomes an actress in horror movies—but she's the real horror.*

Humanoids from the Deep (1980) by Barbara Peetrie *[v, l, d]*
Doug McClure, Ann Turkel, Vic Morrow, Cindy Weintraub *Hormone aimed at salmon growth has a side effect: it causes prehistoric fish to develop legs and a taste for murder and rape.*

Humanoids from the Deep (1996) by Jeff Yonis *[v, l]*
Robert Carradine, Emma Samms, Mark Rolston, Justin Walker, Danielle Weeks, Clint Howard, Barry Nolan, Joey Chang *An army experiment to create the perfect amphibian soldier goes wrong and here we go again.*

I Know What You Did Last Summer (1997) by Jim Gillespie *[v, l, d]*
Jennifer Love Hewitt, Sarah Michelle Gellar, Ryan Philippe, Freddie Prinze, Jr., Muse Watson *Four kids kill (believe they killed?) a fisherman. One year later, they're attacked by a man with a hook and a slicker.*

I Married a Monster from Outer Space (1959) by Gene Fowler, Jr. *[v]*
Tom Tyron, Gloria Talbott, Robert Ivers, Peter Baldwin *A few days before her marriage, a young woman notices her soon-to-be husband isn't her husband anymore.*

I, Monster (1972) by Stephen Weeks
Christopher Lee, Peter Cushing, Mike Raven, Richard Hurndall *Jekyll-Hyde kind of story.*

The Incredible Melting Man (1978) by William Sachs *[v, d]*
Alex Rebar, Burr DeBenning, Myron Healey, Michael Aldredge *An astronaut survives contamination which turns his body into a melting goo.*

Independence Day (1996) by Roland Emmerich *[v, l, d]*
Will Smith, Jeff Goldblum, Bill Pullman, Randy

Quaid *Aliens on big starships take Earth by storm—literally. But we fight back.*

Inferno (1980) by Dario Argento *[v, d]*

Leigh McCloskey, Eleonora Giorgi, Daria Nicolodi, Gabriele Lavia *New York, Freiberg, Rome: the Three Infernal Mothers live in pretty darned expensive penthouses.*

Innocent Blood (1992) by John Landis *[v, l, d]*

Anne Parillaud, Anthony LaPaglia, Robert Loggia, David Proval, Don Rickles *A French vampire sinks her teeth into a Mafia boss—and creates a race of vampires who make you an offer you can't refuse.*

Interview with the Vampire (1994) by Neil Jordan *[v, l, d]*

Tom Cruise, Brad Pitt, Kirsten Dunst, Christian Slater, Antonio Banderas *The curse of being a vampire is explained here by an expert: Luis, who's been a batman for more than 200 years.*

In the Mouth of Madness (1995) by John Carpenter *[v, l, d]*

Sam Neill, Jurgen Prochnow, Charlton Heston, David Warner *The mysterious disappearance of a best selling writer opens a door to a realm of nightmares.*

Invaders from Mars (1953) by William Cameron Menzies *[v, l]*

Helena Carter, Arthur Franz, Jimmy Hunt, Leif Erickson *Doppelgänger aliens take over a whole town. Is it a dream, is it real or is it Memorex?*

Invasion of the Bee Girls (1973) by Denis Sanders *[v]*

Victoria Vetri, William Smith, Anitra Ford, Cliff Osmond *Women turn into a savage race of sex-hungry creatures.*

Invasion of the Body Snatchers (1956) by Don Siegel *[v, l, d]*

Kevin McCarthy, Dana Wynter, Carolyn Jones, King Donovan *You fools! You're in danger! Can't you see? They're after all of us! They're here already! You're next! You're next! You're next!...*

Invasion of the Body Snatchers (1978) by Philip Kaufman *[v, l, d]*

Donald Sutherland, Brooke Adams, Veronica Cartwright, Leonard Nimoy, Jeff Goldblum *See above. This time it's in color.*

Invasion of the Saucer Men (1957) by Edward L. Kahn *[v]*

Steve Terrell, Gloria Castillo, Frank Gorshin, Raymond Hatton *Aliens take it out on cars instead of on humanity. For the moment we're safe.*

Invasion of the Star Creatures (1962) by Bruno VeSota *[v]*

Frankie Ray, Robert Ball, Dolores Reed, Gloria Victor, Jim Almanzer, Anton Arnold, Lenore Bond *Two alien women attempt to conquer Earth with an army of vegetables.*

Invisible Invaders (1959) by Edward L. Kahn

John Agar, Jean Byron, Robert Hutton, Philip Tonge *They're coming from the moon and they hide in caves. Slowly but increasingly, they take over men.*

The Invisible Man (1933) by Jack Arnold *[v, l, d]*

Claude Rains, Gloria Stuart, Dudley Digges, William Harrigan *Scientist becomes, in no particular order, invisible and crazy.*

Island Claws (1980) by Hernan Cardenas *[v]*

Robert Lansing, Steve Hanks, Nita Talbot, Barry Nelson *Nuclear reactor spillage mutates crabs. Or were they mutated already? Who knows? Who cares?*

Island of Terror (1966) by Terence Fisher *[v]*

Peter Cushing, Edward Judd, Carole Gray, Niall MacGinnis *Team of researchers cause a horrid mutation and pay the consequences.*

I Spit on Your Grave (1977) by Mier Zarchi *[v, l, d]*

Camille Keaton, Eron Tabor, Richard Pace, Anthony Nichols, Gunter Kleeman *A young woman is repeatedly raped by four men. After a moment of panic, she works her terrible revenge.*

I Still Know What You Did Last Summer (1998) by Danny Cannon *[v, l, d]*

Jennifer Love Hewitt, Freddie Prinze, Jr., Brandy Norwood, Mekhi Phifer, Muse Watson, Bill Cobbs, Matthew Settle *Two of the four kids are still alive and still attacked by a man with a hook and a slicker.*

It Came from Beneath the Sea (1955) by Robert Gordon *[v, l]*

Kenneth Tobey, Faith Domergue, Donald Curtis, Ian Keith *Large six-tentacled octopus emerges from the Pacific and attacks San Francisco.*

It Came from Outer Space (1953) by Jack Arnold *[v, l]*

Richard Carlson, Barbara Rush, Charles Drake, Russell Johnson *A spacecraft crash-lands in the desert. To make the necessary repairs, the aliens assume the identity of townfolk.*

It Conquered the World (1956) by Roger Corman *[v]*

Peter Graves, Beverly Garland, Lee Van Cleef, Sally Fraser *Treacherous cucumber creature threatens the world—or at least a dozen people.*

It's Alive (1974) by Larry Cohen *[v]*

John P. Ryan, Sharon Farrell, Andrew Duggan, Guy Stockwell *Pollution and the like causes the birth of a new, malevolent, and deformed race of babies, who kill and kill and kill...*

It's Alive 2: It Lives Again (1978) by Larry Cohen *[v]*

Frederic Forrest, Kathleen Lloyd, John P. Ryan, Andrew Duggan *... and kill and kill and kill...*

It's Alive 3: Island of the Alive (1987) by Larry Cohen *[v]*

Michael Moriarty, Karen Black, Laurene Landon, Gerrit Graham *... and kill and kill and kill. But this time, they're full-sized adults.*

It! The Terror from Beyond Space (1958) by Edward L. Kahn *[v, d]*

Marshall Thompson, Shawn Smith, Kim Spalding,

Ann Doran *The capsule of a second mission to Mars comes back with the sole survivor from the first mission—and something else . . .*

Jack Frost (1996) by Michael Cooney *[v]*

Scott MacDonald, Chris Aliport, Stephen Mendel, F. William Parker *A criminal is melted with genetic acid and becomes a killer icicle-throwing snowman.*

Jason Goes to Hell: The Final Friday (1993) by Adam Marcus *[v, l]*

Kane Hodder, John D. LeMay, Karu Keegan, Steven Williams *Sure, sure.*

Jason X (2001) by Jim Isaac

Kane Hodder, Peter Mensah, Melyssa Ade, Chuck Campbell *Jason is back . . . actually, he's forward: he's in space!*

Jaws (1975) by Steven Spielberg *[v, l, d]*

Roy Scheider, Robert Shaw, Richard Dreyfuss, Lorraine Gary, Murray Hamilton *A giant shark takes a vacation on Amity island, gulping people here and there.*

Jaws 2 (1978) by Jeannot Szwarc *[v, l]*

Roy Scheider, Lorraine Gary, Murray Hamilton, Joseph Mascolo *Another giant shark gets too close to the beach: the local sheriff steps into the arena and gets all wet.*

Jaws 3 / Jaws 3D (1983) by Joe Alves *[v, l]*

Dennis Quaid, Bess Armstrong, Louis Gossett, Jr., Simon MacCorkindale *Not one, but two sharks go on a sightseeing tour in a waterpark.*

Jaws: the Revenge (1987) by Joseph Sargent *[v, l, d]*

Lorraine Gary, Michael Caine, Mario Van Peebles, Lance Guest *Again, the umpteenth shark tries to ruin the vacation of a widow, but it just ends up ruining the movie for the audience.*

Jekyll and Hyde . . . Together Again (1982) by Jerry Belson *[v]*

Mark Blankfield, Bess Armstrong, Krista Errickson, Tim Thomerson *Sex and drugs in the life of one of the most popular horror icons.*

Jurassic Park (1993) by Steven Spielberg *[v, l, d]*

Sam Neill, Laura Dern, Jeff Goldblum, Richard Attenborough, Bob Peck, Martin Ferrero *To add pizzazz to a theme park, an eccentric billionaire clones dinosaurs. What could possibly go wrong?*

Killer Klowns from Outer Space (1988) by Stephen Chiodo *[v, l]*

Grant Cramer, Suzanne Snyder, John Vernon, John Allen Nelson *One of the strangest yet most lethal invasions America has ever experienced.*

Killers from Space (1954) by W. Lee Wilder *[v, d]*

Peter Graves, James Seay, Steve Pendleton, Barbara Bestar *A dead scientist is resurrected by aliens in order to get information on atomic destruction.*

The Killer Shrews (1959) by Ray Kellog *[v, d]*

James Best, Ingrid Goude, Ken Curtis, Baruch Lumet *They are shrews, and they kill. Satisfied?*

Kingdom of the Spiders (1977) by John Cardos *[v]*

William Shatner, Tiffany Bolling, Woody Strode, Lieux Dressler *Arizona is about to be leveled by a very large tarantula invasion.*

King Kong (1933) by Merian C. Cooper and Ernest B. Schoedsack *[v, l]*

Fay Wray, Robert Armstrong, Bruce Cabot, Frank Reicher *Oversized gorilla is captured and shipped to New York, where it escapes, climbs the Empire State Building, and plunges to its death.*

King Kong (1976) by John Guillermin *[v, l, d]*

Jeff Bridges, Charles Grodin, Jessica Lange, René Auberjonois *Oversized gorilla is captured and shipped to New York, where it escapes, climbs the World Trade Center and plunges to its death.*

King Kong Escapes (1968) by Inoshiro Honda *[v]*

Rhodes Reason, Mie Hama, Linda Miller, Akira Takarada *Kong goes to Japan!*

King Kong Lives (1986) by John Guillermin *[v, l]*

Brian Kerwin, Linda Hamilton, John Ashton, Peter Michael Goetz *Kong didn't die by falling from the World Trade Center: it just needs a heart transplant and . . . oh, never mind.*

King Kong vs. Godzilla (1963) by Thomas Montgomery and Inoshiro Honda *[v, d]*

Michael Keith, James Yagi, Tadao Takashima, Mie Hama *Um . . .*

Konga (1961) by John Lemont *[v, d]*

Michael Gough, Margo Johns, Jess Conrad, Claire Gordon *A tiny problem occurs when a scientist, instead of creating something useful, enlarges a chimpanzee with a death wish.*

Kronos (1957) by Kurt Neumann *[v, l]*

Jeff Morrow, Barbara Lawrence, John Emery, George O'Hanlon *A robot can absorb Earth's energy and bring destruction.*

Lake Placid (1999) by Steve Miner *[v, d]*

Bill Pullman, Bridget Fonda, Oliver Platt, Betty White *A lake in Maine is infested with Asian crocodiles. Don't ask, and enjoy their meal.*

The Land That Time Forgot (1975) by Kevin Connor *[v]*

Doug McClure, John McEnery, Susan Penhaligon, Keith Barron *A submarine crew finds a strange land where dinosaurs are still walking around.*

Last House on the Left (1972) by Wes Craven *[v, l]*

David Hess, Lucu Grantham, Sandra Cassel, Mark Sheffler *Two young women who were savagely raped take their revenge. Inside the last house on the left.*

The Lawnmower Man (1992) by Brett Leonard *[v, l, d]*

Jeff Fahey, Pierce Brosnan, Jenny Wright, Mark Bringleson *An experiment in mind expansion takes a wrong turn when a below-average-intelligence grass cutter receives the deluxe treatment.*

Lawnmower Man 2: Jobe's War (1995) by Farhad Mann *[v, l, d]*

Patrick Bergin, Matt Frewer, Austin O'Brien, Ely Pouget *Upgrade of the previous movie.*

Leatherface: The Texas Chainsaw Massacre III (1989) by Jeff Burr *[v, l]*
Kate Hodge, William Butler, Ken Foree, Tom Hudson *The man with the saw is back, in a shiny new adventure not really very related to the previous two.*

Leprechaun (1993) by Mark Jones *[v, l, d]*
Warwick Davis, Jennifer Aniston, Ken Olandt, Mark Holton *Don't steal a pot of gold, otherwise you'll have a small potato-eating, shoe-shining, gold-keeping imp chasing and killing you.*

Leprechaun 2 (1994) by Rodman Flender *[v, l, d]*
Warwick Davis, Sandy Baron, Adam Biesk, James Lancaster, Clint Howard *Didn't you hear us? DO NOT steal a pot of gold!!!*

Leprechaun 3 (1995) by Brian Trenchard-Smith *[v, l]*
Warwick Davis, John Gatins, Michael Callan, Caroline Williams *What part of "do not steal a pot of gold" is unclear to you? Even being in Vegas doesn't justify your actions.*

Leprechaun 4: In Space (1996) by Brian Trenchard-Smith *[v, l]*
Warwick Davis, Rebekah Carlton, Brent Jasmer, Debbie Dunning *Oh, never mind!*

Leprechaun in the Hood (2000) by Rob Spera *[v, d]*
Warwick Davis, Ice-T, A. T. Montgomery, Rashaan Nall, Red Grant *Just what part of "Oh, never mind!" did you not understand?*

Leviathan (1989) by George Pan Cosmatos *[v, l, d]*
Peter Weller, Ernie Hudson, Hector Elizondo, Amanda Pays, Richard Crenna *An underwater station houses a competent crew and a multiform bloodthirsty creature that just doesn't want to go away.*

The Lift (1983) by Dick Maas *[v, l]*
Huub Stapel, Willeke Van Ammelroy, Josine Van Dalsum, Pret Romer *State-of-the-art elevator is controlled by a real brain with an attitude: first floor, decapitation; second floor, strangulation; third floor . . .*

Link (1986) by Richard Franklin *[v, d]*
Elisabeth Shue, Terence Stamp, Steven Pinner, Richard Garnett *Lab monkey does not very kind things to cats and dogs, and even less kind things to human beings.*

Liquid Sky (1983) by Slava Tsukerman *[v, l, d]*
Anne Carlisle, Paula E. Sheppard, Susan Doukas, Otto Von Wernherr *UFO passes over Manhattan and the aliens get strangely interested in drugs.*

Little Shop of Horrors (1968) by Roger Corman *[v, l, d]*
Jackie Joseph, Jonathan Haze, Mel Welles, Dick Miller *In the small flower shop just around the corner, a plant attracts clients . . . literally.*

Little Shop of Horrors (1986) by Frank Oz *[v, l, d]*
Rick Moranis, Ellen Greene, Vincent Gardenia, Steve Martin *In the small flower shop just around the corner, a plant sings, and attracts clients . . . literally.*

Lord of Illusions (1995) by Clive Barker *[v, l, d]*
Scott Bakula, Famke Janssen, Kevin J. O'Connor, Daniel von Bargen *Stage magic vs. real magic. The hand is quicker than the eye. Especially if chopped off and thrown out of a window.*

The Lost Boys (1987) by Joel Schumacher *[v, l, d]*
Jason Patric, Kiefer Sutherland, Corey Haim, Jami Gertz, Dianne Wiest *Cool, new Gothic vampires terrorize a small village in old-fashioned style. But still effectively.*

Lost in Space (1998) by Stephen Hopkins *[v, l, d]*
William Hurt, Matt LeBlanc, Gary Oldman, Mimi Rogers, Heather Graham *Family Robinson take off toward the planet Alpha Prime, but take the wrong exit at the space highway and become the title.*

The Lost World: Jurassic Park (1997) by Steven Spielberg *[v, l, d]*
Jeff Goldblum, Julianne Moore, Vince Vaughn, Arliss Howard, Pete Postlethwaite *Remember the cloned dinosaurs? Well, they're still alive and kickin' and headed toward San Diego. Move over, Shamu.*

Magic (1978) by Richard Attenborough *[v, l]*
Anthony Hopkins, Ann-Margret, Burgess Meredith, Ed Lauter *A ventriloquist is subdued by his own dummy. But the dummy is the ventriloquist.*

The Magnetic Monster (1953) by Curt Siodmak
Richard Carlson, King Donovan, Jean Byron, Byron Foulger *Don't steal an isotope that loves to absorb energy and grow to impossible dimensions. It tends to ruin your Sunday night.*

Mako: the Jaws of Death (1976) by William Grefe *[v]*
Richard Jaeckel, Jennifer Bishop, Harold Sakata, John Chandler *If you get a special protector symbol, you can swim with sharks and ask them to do dirty deeds for you.*

Mamba (1989) by Mario Orfini
Trudie Styler, Gregg Henry *To "reconcile" with his ex-wife, an electronic genius locks the woman in her own house and places a poisonous snake in her care.*

The Mangler (1995) by Tobe Hooper *[v, l]*
Robert Englund, Ted Levine, Daniel Matmor, Vanessa Pike *A laundry machine is possessed by the devil, but it needs a few offerings every now and again to guarantee wealth to the cleaners.*

Manhunter (1986) by Michael Mann *[v, l, d]*
William L. Petersen, Kim Greist, Joan Allen, Brian Cox *An FBI agent needs the help of a psychokiller in order to track another serial killer. First time for Dr. Hannibal Lecter on screen.*

Maniac Cop (1988) by William Lustig *[v, l, d]*
Tom Atkins, Bruce Campbell, Laurene Landon, Richard Roundtree *New York Cop gets killed but somehow comes back to honor his badge. Well, maybe now he's a little too extreme.*

Maniac Cop 2 (1990) by William Lustig *[v, l, d]*
Robert Davi, Claudia Christian, Michael Lerner, Bruce Campbell *Round 2.*

Maniac Cop 3 (1993) by William Lustig, Joel Soisson *[v, l]*
Robert Z'Dar, Robert Davi, Gretchen Becker, Paul Gleason *Round 3? You kidding?*

Man's Best Friend (1994) by John Lafia *[v, l]*
Ally Sheedy, Lance Henriksen, Frederic Lehne, Robert Costanzo *A DNA-spliced dog is on the loose and (of course) its brain is highly unstable. So, beware of the dog!*

Mars Attacks! (1996) by Tim Burton *[v, l, d]*
Jack Nicholson, Pierce Brosnan, Michael J. Fox, Glenn Close, Sarah Jessica Parker, Rod Steiger *Tiny little Martians land on Earth and destroy whatever is in front of them. Will humanity survive?*

Mars Needs Women (1968) by Larry Buchanan *[v]*
Tommy Kirk, Yvonne Craig, Byron Lord, Roger Ready *The title says it all.*

Mary Reilly (1996) by Stephen Frears *[v, l]*
Julia Roberts, John Malkovich, George Cole, Michael Gambon *Dr. Jekyll's maid's story. She had to clean up after Mr. Hyde's mess.*

Mary Shelley's Frankenstein (1994) by Kenneth Branagh *[v, l]*
Kenneth Branagh, Robert De Niro, Helena Bonham Carter, Tom Hulce *One of the most faithful recreations of a creature's recreation. "Are you talkin' to me, little girl?"*

Maximum Overdrive (1986) by Stephen King *[v, l, d]*
Emilio Estevez, Pat Hingle, Laura Harrington, Christopher Murny *The machines rebel against mankind. Mostly, it's just a bunch of trucks, but the result is lame.*

The Medusa Touch (1978) by Jack Gold *[v]*
Richard Burton, Lino Ventura, Lee Remick, Harry Andrews *Psychiatrist tries to stop her telekinetic patient—with little if no success at all.*

Memorial Valley Masacre (1988) by Robert C. Huges *[v]*
John Kerry, Mark Mears, Lesa Lee, Cameron Mitchell *A caveman wrecks the reopening of a valley park. He runs, kills, hotwires cars, uses bulldozers . . . Huh?*

MIB: Men in Black (1997) by Barry Sonnenfeld *[v, l, d]*
Tommy Lee Jones, Will Smith, Linda Fiorentino, Vincent D'Onofrio, Rip Torn *The aliens are among us! Hey, according to the Men in Black, they've almost always been among us. So, why bother?*

Mighty Joe Young (1949) by Ernest B. Schoedsack *[v, l]*
Terry Moore, Ben Johnson, Robert Armstrong, Joseph Young *An oversized gorilla is brought to civilization and put into an act. The animal (duh) will rebel.*

Mighty Joe Young (1998) by Ron Underwood *[v, l, d]*
Bill Paxton, Charlize Theron, Rade Serbedzija, Regina King, Peter Firth, Naveen Andrews, David Paymer, Robert Wisdom *Update of the previous story, same result.*

Mimic (1997) by *Guillermo Del Toro [v, l, d]*
Mira Sorvino, Jeremy Northam, Alexander Goodwin, Giancarlo Giannini *Breed of cockroaches invades New York's underground tunnels and steals subway passengers.*

Misery (1990) by Rob Reiner *[v, l, d]*
James Caan, Kathy Bates, Lauren Bacall, Richard Farnsworth *Very successful writer has an accident and is rescued by his #1 fan. Who also happens to be a wacko.*

Mission to Mars (2000) by Brian De Palma *[v, d]*
Gary Sinise, Don Cheadle, Connie Nielsen, Jerry O'Connell, Kim Delaney, Tim Robbins The year is 2020. Guess where NASA is sending a mission?

Mom and Dad Save the World (1992) by Greg Beeman *[v, l]*
Teri Garr, Jeffrey Jones, Jon Lovitz, Thalmus Rasulala, Eric Idle *The idiot ruler of a planet of idiots is about to blow up Earth, but he falls in love with an earthling and beams her up to his planet.*

Monkey Shines: An Experiment in Fear (1988) by George A. Romero *[v, l, d]*
Jason Beghe, John Pankow, Kate McNeil, Chistine Forrest *Lab monkey addicted to a special drug develops a love for murder and kidnaping.*

The Monolith Monsters (1957) by John Sherwood *[v]*
Lola Albright, Grant Williams, Les Tremayne, Trevor Bardette *Meteorite fragments, if wet, become fierce slow-walking creatures.*

Monster from Green Hell (1957) by Kenneth Crane *[v]*
Jim Davis, Robert E. Griffin, Barbara Turner, Joel Fluellen *A space experiment involving wasps generates a lethal mutation in Africa(!).*

The Monster from the Ocean Floor (1954) by Wyott Ordung *[v]*
Anne Kimball, Stuart Wade, Wyott Ordung *Monstrously dull squid is chased by a submarine which has nothing better to do.*

Monster High (1989) by Rüdiger Poe *[v]*
Dean Iandoli, Diana Frank, David Marriott, Robert M. Lind, Sean Haines *An invasion from space is defeated by a basketball game. Kind of like Michael Jordan's* Space Jam, *but much much worse.*

Monster in the Closet (1986) by Bob Dahlin *[v]*
Donald Grant, Denise DuBarry, Claude Akins, Howard Duff, Henry Gibson *A new species of large, brown monsters pop out of every closet in town. Stay alert.*

The Monster Squad (1987) by Fred Dekker *[v, l]*
Andre Gower, Robby Kiger, Stephen Macht, Duncan

Regehr, Tom Noonan *Dracula & Co. are in town, and a gang of kids are ready to face them. Almost.*

The Monster That Challenged the World (1957) by Arnol Laven *[v]*

Tim Holt, Audrey Dalton, Hans Conried, Casey Adams *There's a new race of sea slugs (mutated, of course) that threatens humanity and ultimately, the world.*

Moontrap (1989) by Robert Dyke *[v, l]*

Walter Koenig, Bruce Campbell, Ligh Lombardi, Robert Kurcz *Alien devices are accidentally set in motion, and turn a moon base into a moon trap!*

The Mummy (1932) by Karl Freund *[v, l, d]*

Boris Karloff, Zita Johann, David Manners, Edward Van Sloan *A very scary mummy is brought back to life and tries to take it out on the desecrators.*

The Mummy (1959) by Terence Fisher *[v, l]*

Peter Cushing, Christopher Lee, Felix Aylmer, Yvonne Furneaux *Another very scary mummy is brought back to life and tries to take it out on the desecrators.*

The Mummy (1999) by Stephen Sommers *[v, d]*

Brendan Fraser, Rachel Weisz, Arnold Vosloo, Kevin J. O'Connor *A new, computer-improved very scary mummy is brought back to life and tries to take it out on the desecrators.*

The Mummy's Curse (1944) by Leslie Goodwins *[v]*

Lon Chaney, Jr., Peter Coe, Virginia Christine, Kay Harding *Final chapter in the story of the mummy Kharis. Probably.*

The Mummy's Ghost (1944) by Reginald LeBorg *[v]*

Lon Chaney, Jr., John Carradine, Ramsay Ames, Robert Lowery *The limping mummy Kharis is on the prowl one more time (this time being the third).*

The Mummy's Hand (1940) by Christy Cabanne *[v]*

Dick Foran, Wallace Ford, Peggy Moran, Cecil Kellaway *Kharis is resurrected for the first time, and it limps its way through mayhem and killing.*

The Mummy's Shroud (1967) by John Gilling *[d]*

Andre Morell, John Phillips, David Buck, Elizabeth Sellars *Mummy #1 and mummy #2 wreak havoc in Britain.*

The Mummy's Tomb (1942) by Harold Young *[v]*

Lon Chaney, Jr., Dick Foran, John Hubbard, Elyse Knox *Second turn of Kharis, which has a different face but still the same energy and killing wish.*

Mutiny in Outer Space (1965) by Hugo Grimaldi

William Leslie, Dolores Faith, Pamela Curran, Richard Garland *On their way back home, a space crew gets attacked by a parasite.*

My Best Friend Is a Vampire (1988) by Jimmy Huston *[v]*

Robert Sean Leonard, Evan Mirand, Cheryl Pollak, René Auberjonois *Two high-school buddies stumble upon a slight problem: one of them has been turned into a vampire.*

My Boyfriend's Back (1993) by Bob Balaban *[v, l]*

Andrew Lowery, Traci Lind, Danny Zorn, Edward Herrmann *Killed kid comes back to bring his live date to the prom.*

My Mom's a Werewolf (1988) by Michael Fischa *[v, l]*

Susan Blakely, John Saxon, Katrina Caspary, John Schuck *A woman gets bitten by a handsome lycanthrope and turns into one herself. Understandable apprehension on the part of her husband.*

The Mysterians (1959) by Inoshiro Honda *[v]*

Kenji Sahara, Yumi Shirakawa, Momoto Kochi, Akihiko Hirata *Landing on Earth after the death of their planet, the Mysterians take possession of a lake and of almost all the women.*

Nadja (1995) by Michael Almereyda *[v, l, d]*

Elina Lowensohn, Suzy Amis, Galaxy Craze, Peter Fonda *Dracula and Van Helsing's heirs meet in modern-day New York. What are the odds of them bumping into each other?*

Natural Born Killers (1994) by Oliver Stone *[v, l, d]*

Woody Harrelson, Robert Downey, Jr., Juliette Lewis, Tommy Lee Jones *The life and times of a couple of killers who believe they're "natural born" killers. If they aren't, they at least do a very good job at it.*

The Navy vs. the Night Monster (1966) by Michael Hoey

Mamie Van Doren, Anthony Eisley, Pamela Mason, Bill Gray *Large and mean flesh-eating trees attack people. The navy (???) intervenes.*

Near Dark (1987) by Kathryn Bigelow *[v, l]*

Adrian Pasdar, Jenny Wright, Bill Paxton, Jenette Goldstein, Lance Henriksen *A group of vampires live inside shacks and vans, and some of them fall in love and get burned (by all means).*

Needful Things (1993) by Fraser Heston *[v, l, d]*

Ed Harris, Bonnie Bedelia, Max Von Sydow, Amanda Plummer, J. T. Walsh *Mr. Gaunt opens a store in a little village and slowly turns half of the townspeople against the other half. Devilish!*

Nightbreed (1990) by Clive Barker *[v, l]*

Craig Sheffer, Anne Bobby, David Cronenberg, Charles Haid *A special kid is brought into Median, a town filled with monsters, while a crazy psycho kills to and fro.*

A Nightmare on Elm Street (1984) by Wes Craven *[v, l, d]*

John Saxon, Heather Langenkamp, Ronee Blakley, Robert Englund, Amanda Wyss *The spirit of a dead child molester invades the dreams of a bunch of kids whom he didn't molest.*

A Nightmare on Elm Street 2: Freddy's Revenge (1986) by Jack Sholder *[v, l, d]*

Mark Patton, Hope Lange, Clu Gulager, Robert Englund, Kim Myers *Freddy and his glove are back, in the same house where he found his second temporary death.*

A Nightmare on Elm Street 3: Dream Warriors (1987) by Chuck Russell *[v, l, d]*

Patricia Arquette, Robert Englund, Heather Langenkamp, Craig Wasson *Ready for some more? Freddy sure is!*

A Nightmare on Elm Street 4: the Dream Master (1988) by Renny Harlin *[v, l, d]*

Robert Englund, Rodney Eastman, Danny Hassel, Andras Jones *And another helping for big bad voodoo Freddy.*

A Nightmare on Elm Street 5: the Dream Child (1989) by Stephen Hopkins *[v, l, d]*

Robert Englund, Lisa Wilcox, Kelly Jo Minter, Danny Hassel *Freddy has a baby boy. Or not. Anyway, he's still mean and evil.*

Night of the Creeps (1986) by Fred Dekker *[v, l]*

Jason Lively, Jill Whitlow, Tom Atkins, Steve Marshall *Straight from space, in a lab near you, a bunch of aggressive brain-eating slugs invade your school.*

Night of the Lepus (1972) by William Claxton

Stuart Whitman, Janet Leigh, Rory Calhoun, DeForest Kelley *Treacherous (!) hoppity-hop bunny rabbits become giant and carnivorous.*

Night of the Living Dead (1968) by George A. Romero *[v, l, d]*

Judith O'Dea, Duane Jones, Karl Hardman, Marilyn Eastman *They're dead . . . but they're living! And they're coming after you (at a very slow pace).*

Night of the Living Dead (1990) by Tom Savini *[v, l, d]*

Tony Todd, Patricia Tallman, Tom Towles, William Butler *They're dead . . . but they're living! And they're coming after you (at a very slow pace), but this time in color.*

976-EVIL (1988) by Robert Englund *[v, l]*

Stephen Geoffreys, Jim Metzler, Maria Rubell, Sandy Dennis *"Horrorscope" phone line turns out to be a little too intense, and the bill to pay is not only financial.*

976-EVIL 2: The Astral Factor (1991) by Jim Wynorski *[v]*

Debbie James, René Assa, Patrick O'Bryan, Phil McKeon, Leslie Ryan, Rod McCary, Paul Coufos, Brigitte Nielsen *Please hang up and try again.*

Nosferatu, Eine Symphonie des Grauens (1922) by F. W. Murnau *[v, l, d]*

Max Schreck, Alexander Granach, Gustav von Wagenheim, Greta Schroeder *Tall, bald, skinny: one of the most frightening vampires in history.*

Nosferatu (1979) by Werner Herzog *[v, l, d]*

Klaus Kinski, Isabelle Adjani, Bruno Ganz, Roland Topor *A retelling of the same story of the nondead.*

Octaman (1971) by Harry Essex *[v]*

Kerwin Mathews, Pier Angeli, Jeff Morrow, Jerry Guardino *Part man, part beast, all tentacles: it's Octaman!*

Of Unknown Origin (1983) by George P. Cosmatos *[v]*

Peter Weller, Jennifer Dale, Lawrence Dane, Kenneth Welsh *Man vs. beast. In this case, a very large female rat with a mind way above average.*

The Omen (1976) by Richard Donner *[v, l, d]*

Gregory Peck, Lee Remick, Harvey Stephens, Billie Whitelaw *A very wealthy politician adopts a kid who is all smiles, cheer and—oh, yeah—is the son of the devil.*

Orca (1977) by Michael Anderson *[v, l]*

Richard Harris, Charlotte Rampling, Will Sampson, Robert Carradine *After a giant shark, a giant octopus, a giant flock of barracudas, a giant swarm of piranhas . . . oh, don't bother.*

Pacific Heights (1990) by John Schlesinger *[v, l]*

Melanie Griffith, Matthew Modine, Michael Keaton, Mako *What do you do if your neighbor is a nutcase?*

Parasite (1982) by Charles Band *[v, l, d]*

Robert Gualdini, Demi Moore, Luca Bercovici, James Davidson *Scientist who creates a new parasite (is there a market for this kind of stuff?) runs away when his creation gets under his skin.*

Parents (1989) by Bob Balaban *[v, l, d]*

Randy Quaid, Mary Beth Hurt, Bryan Madorsky, Sandy Dennis *Are the two smiling parents of little Michael really cannibals, or . . . ?*

Patrick (1977) by Richard Franklin *[v]*

Susan Penhaligon, Robert Helpann, Rod Mullinar, Julia Blake *A kid slips into a coma after a car crash, and looks for revenge courtesy of his newly acquired paranormal powers.*

Peeping Tom (1960) by Michael Powell *[v, l, d]*

Karl-Heinz Boehm, Moira Shearer, Anna Massey, Maxine Audley *A seriously disturbed young photographer captures models on film as he kills them.*

The People Under the Stairs (1991) by Wes Craven *[v, l]*

Everett McGill, Wendy Robie, Brandon Adams, Ving Rhames *Bizarre couple keep an army of kids hidden in the basement, and are looking for more.*

Pete's Dragon (1977) by Don Chaffey *[v, l]*

Helen Reddy, Jim Dale, Mickey Rooney, Red Buttons, Shelley Winters *An orphan's best friend is a dragon that can fly and turn invisible.*

Pet Sematary (1989) by Mary Lambert *[v, l, d]*

Dale Midkiff, Fred Gwynne, Denise Crosby, Blaze Berdahl *Tragedy strikes the Creed family when little Gage dies. But luckily(?), an ancient Indian burial ground can bring him back. Evil.*

Pet Sematary 2 (1992) by Mary Lambert *[v, l]*

Anthony Edwards, Edward Furlong, Clancy Brown, Jared Rushton *The son of an actress is so obsessed with his mom that when she dies, he buries her in the same evil place as the last movie.*

Phantasm (1979) by Don Coscarelli *[v, l, d]*

Michael Baldwin, Bill Thornbury,

Reggie Bannister, Kathy Lester, Angus Scrimm *A truly bizarre science-fiction horror fantasy: flying steel balls, killer dwarfs, other dimensions . . .*

Phantasm 2 (1988) by Don Coscarelli *[v, l]*

James LeGros, Reggie Bannister, Angus Scrimm,

Paula Irvine *More of the same, almost incomprehensible gory stuff.*

Phantasm III: Lord of the Dead (1994) by Don Coscarelli *[v, l]*

Reggie Bannister, A. Michael Baldwin, Bill Thornbury, Angus Scrimm *And more.*

Phantasm: Oblivion / Phantasm IV: Infinity (1998) by Don Coscarelli *[v, l, d]*

Reggie Bannister, A. Michael Baldwin, Kathy Lester, Angus Scrimm *And just when you thought that it was over, more!*

The Phantom of Paris (1931) by John S. Robertson *[v, l, d]*

John Gilbert, Leila Hyams, Lewis Stone, Jean Hersholt *A magician is accused of murder. Is he the person responsible? Loosely based on* The Phantom of the Opera.

The Phantom of the Opera (1925) by Rupert Julian *[v, l, d]*

Lon Chaney, Sr., Norman Kerry, Mary Philbin, Arthur Edmund Carewe *Who is the kidnapper of beautiful singers inside the opera house? What is his purpose? And why do chandeliers keep falling?*

The Phantom of the Opera (1943) by Arthur Lubin *[v, l, d]*

Nelson Eddy, Susanna Foster, Claude Rains, Edgar Barrier *Remake of the previous story, pretty much the same. Chandelier included.*

The Phantom of the Opera (1962) by Terence Fisher *[v, l]*

Herbert Lom, Heather Sears, Thorley Walters, Edward DeSouza *"Chandeliers keep falling on my head . . ."*

The Phantom of the Opera (1989) by Dwight H. Little *[v, l]*

Robert Englund, Jill Schoelen, Alex Hyde-White, Bill Nighy *And more, and more—but this time the phantom skins his victims.*

Phantom of the Opera (1998) by Dario Argento *[v, d]*

Julian Sands, Asia Argento, Andrea Di Stefano, Nadia Rinaldi *Same old, same old.*

The Phantom of the Paradise (1974) by Brian De Palma *[v, l]*

Paul Williams, William Finley, Jessica Harper, George Memmoli *Great rock version of the previous four movies.*

Phantoms (1998) by Joe Chappelle *[v, l, d]*

Peter O'Toole, Rose McGowan, Joanna Going, Liev Schreiber, Ben Affleck *Ancient creature absorbs an entire village (and who knows how many else). But this time someone tries to fight back.*

Piranha (1978) by Joe Dante *[v, d]*

Bradford Dillman, Heather Menzies, Kevin McCarthy, Keenan Wynn, Barbara Steele, Dick Miller *Riverside summer camp gets infested with voracious fish, the result of an experiment to create an even more vicious piranha for 'Nam.*

Piranha (1995) by Scott Levy *[v, l]*

Alexandra Paul, William Katt, Soleil Moon Frye, Monte Markham *Like Gus Van Sant's* Psycho, *a shot-by-shot remake of the previous movie. And like Gus's* Psycho, *this also sucks.*

Piranha II: the Spawning (1981) by James Cameron *[v, l]*

Tricia O'Neil, Steve Marachuck, Lance Henriksen, Ricky Paul *New and improved voracious piranhas can now fly!*

Pitch Black (2000) by David Twohy *[v, d]*

Vin Diesel, Radha Mitchell, Cole Hauser, Keith David *A planet happens to experience a total eclipse every 23 years. And a few deadly creatures start to roam the surface. Can you imagine how hungry they might be?*

Plan 9 from Outer Space (1956) by Ed Wood *[v, l, d]*

Bela Lugosi, Tor Johnson, Lyle Talbot, Vampira *Hardly believable aliens intimidate the earthlings and plan to resurrect the dead in a classic bad, bad, bad, bad, bad, bad movie.*

Poltergeist (1982) by Tobe Hooper *[v, l, d]*

JoBeth Williams, Craig T. Nelson, Beatrice Straight, Heather O'Rourke, Zelda Rubinstein *Ghosts invade a suburban home and kidnap a little girl via TV set. Spooky.*

Poltergeist II (1986) by Brian Gibson *[v, l, d]*

Craig T. Nelson, JoBeth Williams, Heather O'Rourke, Will Sampson, Zelda Rubinstein *Other ghosts, same unlucky little girl.*

Poltergeist III (1988) by Gary Sherman *[v, l]*

Tom Skerritt, Nancy Allen, Heather O'Rourke, Lara Flynn Boyle *Once again, different ghosts, but the little girl is still the same.*

Predator (1987) by John McTiernan *[v, l, d]*

Arnold Schwarzenegger, Carl Weathers, Bill Duke, Jesse Ventura, Shane Black *A commando and some extremely well-trained soldiers face an almost invisible alien who loves games. Especially if it wins them.*

Predator 2 (1990) by Stephen Hopkins *[v, l]*

Danny Glover, Gary Busey, Ruben Blades, Maria Conchita Alonso, Robert Davi *In futuristic 1997 Los Angeles, another invisible alien lands and interferes with the already hectic life of a cop.*

Prison (1988) by Renny Harlin *[v, l]*

Lane Smith, Viggo Mortensen, Chelsea Field, Lincoln Kirkpatrick *A prison houses evil guys and the ghost of a criminal who was executed a few decades earlier in the same place. Revenge.*

The Projected Man (1967) by Ian Curteis

Bryant Halliday, Mary Peach, Norman Woodland, Ronald Allen *No flies here, just a scientist who tries his version of teleportation, and simply disfigures himself, becoming an angel of death.*

Prom Night (1980) by Paul Lynch *[v, l, d]*

Jamie Lee Curtis, Leslie Nielsen, Casey Stevens,

Eddie Benton *A kid who witnessed the death of a little girl is now grown up.*

Prom Night III: The Last Kiss (1989) by Ron Oliver, Peter Simpson *[v, l]*

Tim Conlon, Cyndy Preston, Courtney Taylor, David Stratton *The former* Prom Night *queen Mary Lou is back, looking for sex and murder. Sequel to* Hello Mary Lou, *blah blah.*

Prom Night 4 (1991) by Clay Borris *[v]*

Nikki DeBoer, Alden Kane, Joy Tanner, Alle Ghadban *A priest vows to save sluts and whores, but he becomes your average serial killer who keep kids under siege in their house.*

Prophecy (1979) by John Frankenheimer *[v]*

Talia Shire, Robert Foxworth, Armand Assante, Victoria Racimo *Once a bear, now a towering mosaic of several animals, a ruthless creature terrorizes and kills people in the woods.*

Psycho (1960) by Alfred Hitchcock *[v, l, d]*

Anthony Perkins, Janet Leigh, Vera Miles, John Gavin, John McIntire, Martin Balsam *A boy, his mother, their motel, the shower . . . the best.*

Psycho (1998) by Gus Van Sant *[v, l, d]*

Vince Vaughn, Anne Heche, Julianne Moore, Robert Forster *A boy, his mom, their motel, the shower . . . but why?*

Psycho II (1983) by Richard Franklin *[v, l, d]*

Claudia Bryar, Anthony Perkins, Vera Miles, Meg Tilly *Norman Bates is back, 22 years later. Is he sane? Is he crazy? We'd bet on the second option.*

Psycho III (1986) by Anthony Perkins *[v, l, d]*

Anthony Perkins, Diana Scarwid, Jeff Fahey, Roberta Maxwell *The Bates Motel is once again open and ready to accept new customers . . . forever.*

Psycho IV: the Beginning (1990) by Mick Garris *[v]*

Anthony Perkins, Henry Thomas, Olivia Hussey, C. C. H. Pounder *What was poor Norman's adolescence like? Well, here you have all the answers.*

Pumpkinhead (1988) by Stan Winston *[v, l, d]*

Lance Henriksen, John DiAquino, Kerry Remsen, Matthew Hurley *Devastated by the death of his son, a father evokes the most terrible and ancient demon to seek revenge. He'll partially succeed.*

Pumpkinhead II: Blood Wings (1994) by Jeff Burr *[v, l]*

Ami Dolenz, Andrew Robinson, Kane Hodder, R. A. Mihailoff *A group of teens looking for some fun first run over an old witch, then bring the son of a demon back to life.*

Puppetmaster (1989) by David Schmoeller *[v, l, d]*

Paul Le Mat, Jimmie F. Skaggs, Irene Miracle, Robyn Frates *A hotel is crammed with malignant puppets with an intelligence of their own.*

The Puppet Masters (1994) by Stuart Orme *[v, l]*

Donald Sutherland, Eric Tahl, Julie Warner, David Keith *A UFO crash-lands near a town. Little by little, all the folks are controlled by the aliens who camp out on the people's shoulders.*

Q (1982) by Larry Cohen *[v, l, d]*

David Carradine, Michael Moriarty, Richard Roundtree, Candy Clark, John Capodice *Probably evoked by worshipers, probably just landed in New York, a winged serpent creates chaos in the town that never sleeps.*

Queen of Blood (1966) by Curtis Harrington *[v, l]*

John Saxon, Basil Rathbone, Judi Meredith, Dennis Hopper *A space vampire is found and, since nobody can think anything better to do with it, is brought to Earth.*

Raising Cain (1992) by Brian De Palma *[v, l, d]*

John Lithgow, Lolita Davidovich, Steven Bauer, Frances Sternhagen *Carter Nix may or may not have a twin brother who's nasty, heartless, and mean. Oh, and who's also a killer.*

Rana: The Legend of Shadow Lake (1975) by Bill Rebane *[v]*

Paul Callaway, Richard Lange, Glenn Scherer, Brad Ellingson, Karen McDiarmid, Alan Ross, Julie Wheaton *Is it true that the lake down the road houses a mysterious creature, or is it just a myth?*

Razorback (1984) by Russell Mulcahy *[v, l]*

Gregory Harrison, Bill Kerr, Arkie Whiteley, Judy Morris *Australian village is terrorized by an abnormally large razorback that attacks both kangaroos and humans.*

Re-Animator (1985) by Stuart Gordon *[v, l, d]*

Jeffrey Combs, David Gale, Robert Sampson, Gerry Black *Scientist creates a fluid to resurrect dead tissue. But his house becomes a freak show.*

Red Planet Mars (1952) by Harry Horner *[v]*

Peter Graves, Andrea King, Marvin Miller, Herbert Berghof *And what if Mars were inhabited by none other than God?*

The Relic (1996) by Peter Hyams *[v, l, d]*

Penelope Ann Miller, Tom Sizemore, Linda Hunt, James Withmore *The opening of an exhibit on superstition is demolished by a flesh-eating mutation. Talk about being jinxed.*

The Return of the Fly (1959) by Edward L. Bernds *[v, l, d]*

Vincent Price, Brett Halsey, David Frankham, John Sutton *The son of the careless doctor who tried teleportation follows in his dad's footsteps. And becomes a man-fly himself.*

The Return of the Living Dead (1985) by Dan O'Bannon *[v, l]*

Clu Gulager, James Karen, Linnea Quigley, Don Calfa *What if the living dead depicted in Romero's movies wasn't just a fluke, but was caused by an experiment gone awry?*

The Return of the Living Dead III (1993) by Brian Yuzna *[v, l]*

Mindy Clarke, J. Trevor Edmond, Kent McCord, Basil Wallace *You can use trioxin to generate carnivorous living dead, or to bring back your dead girlfriend as a carnivorous fiancée.*

The Return of the Living Dead, Part 2 (1988) by Ken Wiederhorn *[v, l]*

Dana Ashbrook, Marsha Dietlein, Philip Bruns, James Karen *A contaminated living dead is cremated but its contagious smoke lands on a graveyard, and . . . use your imagination.*

Revenge of the Creature (1955) by Jack Arnold *[v, l]*

John Agar, Lori Nelson, John Bromfield, John Wood *The Gill Man is captured and kept (for a very short time) in a sea park. Then it escapes.*

Rocketship X-M (1950) by Kurt Neumann *[v, l, d]*

Lloyd Bridges, Osa Massen. Hugh O'Brian, John Emery *A spaceship to the moon shifts a little and becomes a spaceship to Mars.*

The Rocky Horror Picture Show (1975) by Jim Sharman *[v, l, d]*

Tim Curry, Susan Sarandon, Barry Bostwick, Little Nell, Richard O'Brien *Fantasy-musical about a crazy scientist who creates monsters and wears high heels.*

Rodan (1957) by Inoshiro Honda *[v, l]*

Kenji Sawara, Yumi Shirakawa, Akihiko Hirata, Akio Kobori *This time the monster on the loose that terrifies Tokyo is a large pterodactyl.*

Rosemary's Baby (1968) by Roman Polanski *[v, l, d]*

Mia Farrow, John Cassavetes, Ruth Gordon, Sidney Blackmer *Would you dare, in order to build an exceptional career, to sell the soul of your son to Satan?*

Runaway (1984) by Michael Crichton *[v, l, d]*

Tom Selleck, Cynthia Rhodes, Gene Simmons, Kirstie Alley *A cop's specialty is tracking and neutralizing misbehaving robots. It's not an easy job, but somebody's got to do it.*

Santa Claus Conquers the Martians (1964) by Nicholas Webster

John Call, Leonard Hicks, Vincent Beck, Donna Conforti *To bring joy and happiness to the red planet, the Martians kidnap Santa Claus.*

Saturn 3 (1980) by Stanley Donen *[v, l, d]*

Farrah Fawcett, Kirk Douglas, Harvey Keitel, Douglas Lambert *Space station accepts a strange man and his robot Hector, which will turn out to be a sexual harasser.*

Scanner Cop (1994) by Pierre David *[v, l]*

Daniel Quinn, Darlanne Fluegel, Richard Grove, Mark Rolston *Character of the title uses his superpowers to track a man whose job consists of telling other people to kill scanners. Boomerang.*

Scanners (1981) by David Cronenberg [v, l]

Stephen Lack, Jennifer O'Neill, Patrick McGoohan, Lawrence Dane, Michael Ironside *The side effect of a drug given to pregnant women causes the children to come into this world as telekinetics.*

Scanners II: The New Order (1991) by Christian Duguay [v, l]

David Hewlett, Deborah Raffin, Yvan Ponton, Isabelle Mejias *There's an attempt to trap all of the scanners—but how can you succeed in a plan with people who can read your mind?*

Scanners III: The Takeover (1992) by Christian Duguay [v, l]

Liliana Komorowska, Valerie Valois, Daniel Pilon, Collin Fox *A new drug helps the scanners, but turns them into evil creatures with ESP powers. Not good.*

Scanners: The Showdown / Scanner Cop II: Volkin's Revenge (1994) by Steve Barnett [v]

Daniel Quinn, Patrick Kilpatrick, Khrystyne Haje, Stephen Mendel *Final chapter (as of today) of the battle between good scanners and bad scanners.*

Schlock (1971) by John Landis *[v, d]*

Saul Kahan, Joseph Piantadosi, Eliza Garrett, John Landis *A group of teens discover a missing link: not a monkey, not a man, but a possible menace to humanity. Or maybe not.*

Scream (1996) by Wes Craven *[v, l, d]*

Neve Campbell, David Arquette, Courteney Cox, Skeet Ulrich, Matthew Lillard *A small community (and in particular one young woman) is terrorized by a wily killer wearing a wonderfully scary mask.*

Scream 2 (1997) by Wes Craven *[v, l, d]*

Neve Campbell, David Arquette, Courteney Cox, Jerry O'Connell, Jada Pinkett *Two years after the events narrated in the first chapter, young Sidney is frightened once again by a sort of copycat.*

Scream 3 (2000) by Wes Craven *[v, d]*

David Arquette, Neve Campbell, Courteney Cox Arquette, Scott Foley, Lance Henriksen *Here we go again, Sidney! Do you like scary sequels?*

Se7en (1995) by David Fincher *[v, l, d]*

Brad Pitt, Morgan Freeman, Gwyneth Paltrow, Kevin Spacey *Seven deadly sins, seven murders carefully planned by the twisted mind of a psychopath. Will he score?*

The Sea Serpent (1986) by Gregory Greens *[v]*

Timothy Bottoms, Taryn Power, Jared Martin, Ray Milland *Wrongfully accused of being responsible for the death of his crew, a man looks and finds the truth: there is a large sea serpent!*

The Shining (1980) by Stanley Kubrick *[v, l, d]*

Jack Nicholson, Shelley Duvall, Danny Lloyd, Scatman Crothers *The family of a writer attempt to spend a whole winter in a hotel which doesn't look very ordinary. What about room 236 . . . ?*

Shocker (1989) by Wes Craven *[v, l, d]*

Michael Murphy, Peter Berg, Cami Cooper, Mitch Pileggi *A serial killer is fried in the chair, but thanks to his ritualistic praying, he comes back as an electrical serial killer.*

The Silence of the Lambs (1990) by Jonathan Demme *[v, l, d]*

Jodie Foster, Anthony Hopkins, Scott Glenn, Ted Levine, Brooke Smith *FBI agent asks again for the help of a cannibalistic serial killer in order to track down another madman. Chilling.*

Silent Night, Deadly Night (1984) by Charles E. Sellier, Jr. *[v, l]*

Lilyan Chauvan, Gilmer McCormick, Robert Brian Wilson, Linnea Quigley *Little Billy sees his parents being killed by a thief dressed as Santa. Years later they dress him as Santa. Will his lid flip?*

Silent Night, Deadly Night II (1986) by Lee Harry *[v, l, d]*

Eric Freeman, James L. Newman, Elizabeth Cayton, Jean Miller *Little Ricky (Billy's little brother) sees his brother as Santa being killed. Is this family cursed!*

Silent Night, Deadly Night III (1989) by Monte Hellman *[v, l]*

Robert Culp, Richard Beymer, Bill Moseley, Samantha Scully *Same little brother, but with a different face and a pot on his head. Nevertheless, he's still pretty good at killing.*

Silent Night, Deadly Night 5: The Toy Maker (1991) by Martin Kitrosser *[v]*

Mickey Rooney, Jane Higginson, William Thone, Tracy Fraim *A toymaker has a new series of toys: they keep killing, and killing . . .*

Silver Bullet (1985) by Daniel Attias *[v, l]*

Corey Haim, Gary Busey, Megan Follows, Everett McGill *There's a new werewolf in town, and he's not friendly. Can he be stopped?*

Single White Female (1992) by Barbet Schroeder *[v, l]*

Bridget Fonda, Jennifer Jason Leigh, Steven Weber, Peter Friedman *Always double-check the references of your new roommates. You never know . . .*

The Sixth Sense (1999) by M. Night Shamalayan *[v, l, d]*

Bruce Willis, Haley Joel Osment, Toni Collette *A kid can see dead people. The problem is that dead people can see the kid.*

Slaughterhouse Rock (1987) by Dimitri Logothetis *[v, l]*

Nicholas Celozzi, Tom Reilly, Donna Denton, Hope Marie *The ghost of a dead singer appears in a dream of a teen and asks him to go to Alcatraz to kill the evil and free the singer's soul.*

Sleepaway Camp (1983) by Robert Hiltzik *[v, d]*

Mike Kellin, Katherine Kamhi, Paul DeAngelo, Jonathan Tierston *The orphan of a disturbed couple of parents, a little boy is sent to camp—and the bodies start to pile up.*

Sleepaway Camp 2: Unhappy Campers (1988) by Michael A. Simpson *[v]*

Pamela Springsteen, Renee Estevez, Brian Patrick Clarke, Walter Gotell *Angela is back, and still going to the summer camp—and the bodies continue piling up.*

Sleepaway Camp 3: Teenage Wasteland (1988) by Michael A. Simpson *[v]*

Pamela Springsteen, Tracy Griffith, Mark Oliver, Kim Wall *Angela comes back one more time to a summer camp—and the bodies just keep on piling up.*

The Sleeping Car (1989) by Douglas Curtis *[v]*

David Naughton, Judy Aranson, Jeff Conaway, Kevin McCarthy *Yes, there is a ghost living in this train car turned into an apartment. Why do you ask?*

Stephen King's Sleepwalkers (1992) by Mick Garris *[v, l]*

Brian Krause, Madchen Amick, Alice Krige, Jim Haynie *The last two descendants of a feline race don't want to end the race.*

Sleepy Hollow (1999) by Tim Burton *[v, d]*

Johnny Depp, Christina Ricci, Miranda Richardson, Michael Gambon, Casper Van Dien, Jeffrey Jones *The classic tale brought to gory life . . . or a reasonable facsimile.*

The Slime People (1962) by Robert Hutton *[v]*

Robert Hutton, Les Tremayne, Susan Hart, Robert Burton *Los Angeles is invaded by a group of human lizards who walk in the fog and kill in the fog, too.*

Slugs (1987) by J. Piquer Simon *[d]*

Michael Garfield, Kim Terry, Philip Machale *Cannibalistic slugs invade the country and the towns, and eat their meals.*

Snow White and the Seven Dwarfs (1937) by Ben Sharpsteen *[v, l]*

Adriana Caselotti, Harry Stockwell, Lucille LaVerne, Scotty Mattraw *Heigh-ho, heigh-ho . . . Yes, it's a cartoon. But the witch is one of the scariest ever seen.*

Society (1989) by Brian Yuzna *[v, l]*

Billy Warlock, Devin Devasquez, Evan Richards *Teenager goes to the psychiatrist because he believes he's hallucinating about his mutant family. Boy, could he have saved a bundle!*

Son of Dracula (1943) by Robert Siodmak *[v, l]*

Lon Chaney, Jr., Evelyn Ankers, Frank Craven, Robert Paige *A descendant of the popular Count reaches America and starts to make disciples.*

Sorority Babe in the Slimeball Bowl-O-Rama (1987) by David DeCoteau *[v, d]*

Linnea Quigley, Brinke Stevens, Andras Jones, John Wildman *An imp who lived for a long time inside of a bowling trophy is freed. And it doesn't waste any time gettin' busy.*

Sound of Horror (1964) by Jose Antonio Nieves-Conde

James Philbrook, Arturo Fernandez, Soledad Miranda, Ingrid Pitt *This is the story of an invisible dinosaur. How they determined it was an invisible dinosaur and not an elephant is a mystery.*

Spaced Invaders (1990) by Patrick Read Johnson *[v, l]*

Douglas Barr, Royal Dano, Ariana Richards, Kevin Thompson *Aliens misunderstand a broadcast of Orson Welles's radio drama and think the invasion they planned is taking place on Earth.*

Space Master X-7 (1958) by Edward Bernds *[v, d]*
Bill Williams, Robert Ellis, Lyn Thomas, Paul Frees *Space fungus is brought to Earth from a satellite, and contamination is just around the corner.*

Spasms (1982) by William Fruet *[v]*
Peter Fonda, Oliver Reed, Kerrie Keane, Al Waxman *A rich man is telepathically linked to a giant blue snake which ends up on the loose in San Diego.*

Species (1995) by Roger Donaldson *[v, l, d]*
Ben Kingsley, Michael Madsen, Alfred Molina, Forest Whitaker, Natasha Henstridge *Human DNA + alien DNA. What could possibly go wrong? Everything.*

Species II (1998) by Peter Medak *[v, l, d]*
Michael Madsen, Ernie Hudson, Natasha Henstridge *They have the sexiest alien in history and they keep her in a plastic bubble watching* The Dukes of Hazzard.

SSSSSSS (1973) by Bernard L. Kowalski *[v]*
Strother Martin, Dirk Benedict, Heather Menzies, Richard B. Shull *A scientist maintains that snakes will rule the world. So he wants to change humanity into reptiles. His lawyer is one step ahead.*

Stanley (1972) by William Grefe *[v]*
Chris Robinson, Alex Rocco, Susan Carroll, Steve Alaimo *The best friend of a former soldier is a rattlesnake. Go figure his enemies . . .*

Starship Invasions (1977) by Ed Hunt *[v]*
Robert Vaughn, Christopher Lee, Daniel Pilon, Helen Shaver *A battle between "good" aliens and "evil" aliens ends up involving us for some reason.*

Starship Troopers (1997) by Paul Verhoeven *[v, l, d]*
Casper Van Dien, Michael Ironside, Neil Patrick Harris, Clancy Brown *There's a planet crowded with nasty spiders, and we must destroy them all. It's doable, but splatter is just around the corner.*

The Stepfather (1989) by Jeff Burr *[v, l]*
Terry O'Quinn, Meg Foster, Caroline Williams, Jonathan Brandis *A man gets married, massacres his new family, gets married again, massacres his new family . . .*

The Stepfather 2 (1987) by Joseph Ruben *[v, l]*
Terry O'Quinn, Shelley Hack, Jill Schoelen, Stephen Shellan *. . . gets married again, massacres his new family, gets married again, massacres his new family . . .*

Stir of Echoes (1999) by David Koepp *[v, d]*
Kevin Bacon, Kathryn Erbe, Illeana Douglas, Kevin Dunn *Another kid can see dead people. But his dad is pretty screwed up, too.*

Strange Invaders (1983) by Michael Laughlin *[v]*
Paul Le Mat, Nancy Allen, Diana Scarwid, Michael Lerner *A new race of body snatchers touch ground in a small midwestern town.*

Sundown: The Vampire in Retreat (1991) by Anthony Hickox *[v]*
David Carradine, Bruce Campbell, Deborah Foreman, Dana Ashbrook *A village in the desert is populated by vampires who produce their own synthetic blood. But you can smell rebellion in the air . . .*

Superman III (1983) by Richard Lester *[v, l]*
Christopher Reeve, Richard Pryor, Annette O'Toole, Jackie Cooper *The man of steel faces a very rich man and his terrible supercomputer.*

Suspiria (1977) by Dario Argento *[v, l]*
Jessica Harper, Joan Bennett, Alida Valli, Udo Kier *A ballet school is actually a facade made with chicken wire and corrugated metal that masks a witch hideout.*

The Sword and the Dragon (1956) by Alexander Ptushko *[v]*
Boris Andreyer, Andrei Abrikosov *A young warrior faces dragon after dragon after dragon with his sword.*

Syngenor (1990) by George Elanjian, Jr. *[v]*
Starr Andreef, Mitchell Laurence, David Gale, Charles Lucia *Another bad experiment goes wrong: a humanoid lizard bursts into the basement of an industrial building and kills.*

Tales from the Crypt Presents: Demon Knight (1995) by Ernest Dickerson *[v, l, d]*
Billy Zane, William Sadler, Jada Pinkett, Brenda Bakke *Good vs. evil, the final match (for the moment). Creepy and interesting, it involves even the blood of Christ as a weapon.*

Tarantula (1955) by Jack Arnold *[v, l]*
Leo G. Carroll, John Agar, Mara Corday, Nestor Paiva *Scientist, spider, lab . . . can you guess who's gonna get the super-size treatment?*

Target Earth! (1954) by Sherman Rose *[v]*
Richard Denning, Virginia Grey, Kathleen Crowley, Richard Reeves *Robots from space are after us. Help, help!*

Teenagers from Outer Space (1959) by Tom Graeff *[v, d]*
Tom Graeff, Dawn Anderson, Harvey B. Dunn, Bryant Grant *A race of obnoxious Hanson look-alikes invade Earth to find companions as well as food for their pet monster.*

Teen Wolf (1985) by Rod Daniel *[v, l]*
Michael J. Fox, James Hampton, Scott Paulin, Susan Ursiti *A kid discovers that he's linked to his family's werewolf past.*

The Temp (1993) by Tom Holland *[v, l]*
Timothy Hutton, Lara Flynn Boyle, Faye Dunaway, Dwight Shultz *Sexual harassment and beyond on the job: and your office will never be the same.*

Tenebrae (1982) by Dario Argento *[v, l, d]*
Anthony Franciosa, Daria Nicolodi, Giuliano Gemma, John Saxon *A killer imitates what he reads in the books of a popular writer. Could there be a link . . . ?*

Tentacles (1977) by Oliver Hellman (Ovidio Assonitis) *[v]*

John Huston, Shelley Winters, Henry Fonda, Bo Hopkins *Giant octopus gets too close to the shore and people start to vanish. Of course, nobody believes the "giant octopus" theory.*

The Terminator (1984) by James Cameron *[v, l, d]*

Arnold Schwarzenegger, Linda Hamilton, Michael Biehn, Paul Winfield *A robot is sent from the future to kill the mother of the man who will be the leader of the future rebellion against machines.*

Terminator 2: Judgment Day (1991) by James Cameron *[v, l, d]*

Arnold Schwarzenegger, Linda Hamilton, Edward Furlong, Robert Patrick *A robot is sent from the future to protect the mother and the man who will be the leader of the future rebellion against machines.*

TerrorVision (1986) by Ted Nicolau *[v]*

Gerrit Graham, Mary Woronov, Diane Franklin, Bert Ramsen *Thanks to a satellite dish, a family "receives" a monster from space. But the TV set is too narrow for the beast.*

The Texas Chain Saw Massacre (1974) by Tobe Hooper *[v, l, d]*

Marilyn Burns, Allen Danzinger, Paul A. Partain, William Vail *There's a family who live in a secluded house decorated with bones and human leather. They definitely are NOT normal.*

The Texas Chainsaw Massacre 2 (1986) by Tobe Hooper *[v, l, d]*

Dennis Hopper, Caroline Williams, Bill Jahnson, Jim Siedow *The family is back, with a whole new set of chainsaws.*

Theater of Blood (1973) by Douglas Hickox *[v, l]*

Vincent Price, Diana Rigg, Ian Hendry, Robert Morley *An actor believes the critics have a thing against him, so he shows them he has a thing against them, too.*

Them! (1954) by Gordon Douglas *[v, l]*

James Withmore, Edmund Gwenn, Fess Parker, James Arness *Only giant ants.*

Theodore Rex (1995) by Jonathan Betuel *[v, l]*

Whoopi Goldberg, Armin Mueller-Stahl, Richard Roundtree, Juliet Landau *Buddy buddy kind of movie, with one African-American female cop and one eight-foot-tall T-Rex(!).*

They Live (1988) by John Carpenter *[v, l, d]*

Roddy Piper, Keith David, Meg Foster, George Flower, Peter Jason *Thanks to a special pair of glasses, a couple of friends discover the truth behind consumerism. It's all an alien conspiracy!*

The Thing (1982) by John Carpenter *[v, l, d]*

Kurt Russell, Wilford Brimley, T. K., Carter, Richard Masur *A spacecraft lands in Antarctica, and when the pilot is awakened the day sours for everybody.*

The Thing from Another World (1951) by Christian Nyby *[v, l]*

James Arness, Kenneth Tobey, Margaret Sheridan, Dewey Martin *After being defrosted, a carrot man terrorizes a polar base. Watch the sky!*

This Island Earth (1955) by Joseph M. Newman *[v, l, d]*

Jeff Morrow, Faith Domergue, Rex Reason, Russell Johnson *To defend their planet, some aliens kidnap two scientists from Earth to get some help.*

Track of the Moon Beast (1976) by Richard Ashe *[v]*

Chase Cordell, Donna Leigh Drake, Gregorio Sala, Patrick Wright *If a fragment of a meteor gets under your skin, chances are you'll become a hideous monster.*

Tremors (1990) by Ron Underwood *[v, l, d]*

Kevin Bacon, Fred Ward, Finn Carter, Michael Gross, Reba McEntire *Underground worms attack a small village in Nevada. The battle commences.*

Tremors 2: Aftershocks (1996) by S. S. Wilson *[v, l, d]*

Fred Ward, Michael Gross, Helen Shaver, Christopher Gartin *Underground worms "evolve" into aboveground killers. The battle continues.*

Trick or Treat (1986) by Charles Martin Smith *[v]*

Tony Fields, Marc Price, Ozzy Osborne, Gene Simmons *Remember all that jazz about playing a heavy-metal album backward to listen to satanic messages? Well, don't try it.*

Trog (1970) by Freddie Francis *[v]*

Joan Crawford, Michael Gough, Kim Braden, David Griffin *A missing link is found and lost.*

Tron (1982) by Steven Lisberger *[v, l, d]*

Jeff Bridges, Bruce Boxleitner, David Warner, Cindy Morgan *A computer whiz is sucked into a program and has to play video games from the inside. It's a matter of life or death.*

20 Million Miles from Earth (1957) by Nathan Juran *[v, l]*

William Hopper, Joan Taylor, Frank Puglia, John Zaremba *Venusian creature is on the loose, this time in Rome. It kills people and eats pizza.*

2001: A Space Odyssey (1968) by Stanley Kubrick *[v, l, d]*

Keir Dullea, William Sylvester, Gary Lockwood, Daniel Richter, Douglas Rain *The evolution of mankind, from beast, to space traveler, to victim of machines, to a newborn baby. Perhaps.*

20,000 Leagues Under the Sea (1954) by Richard Fleisher *[v, l]*

Kirk Douglas, James Mason, Peter Lorre, Paul Lukas *Captain Nemo and his futuristic submarine attack ships and terrorize towns.*

The 27th Day (1957) by William Asher

Gene Barry, Valerie French, Arnold Moss, George Voskovec *Aliens test humankind by giving us an interesting but tempting device.*

Twisted Brain (1974) by Larry N. Stouffer *[v]*
Pat Cardi, Rosie Holotik, John Niland, Austin Stroker *Teen version of "Jekyll and Hyde" story. Nothing really new under the sun.*

Universal Soldiers (1992) by Roland Emmerich *[v, l, d]*
Jean-Claude Van Damme, Dolph Lundgren, Ally Walker, Ed O'Ross *Using the cadavers of GIs, the government wants to build perfect cyborgs trained to kill and virtually unstoppable.*

The Unknown Terror (1957) by Charles Marquis Warren
John Howard, Paul Richards, May Wynn, Mala Powers *Fungus parasite finds a cozy environment among a crew of scientists working in South America.*

Unlawful Entry (1992) by Jonathan Kaplan *[v, l]*
Kurt Russell, Ray Liotta, Madeleine Stowe, Roger E. Mosley *Hired to make an apartment burglar-proof, a good cop becomes bad cop, obsessed with the wife of the homeowner.*

The Unnamable (1988) by Jean-Paul Ouellette *[v, l]*
Charles King, Mark Kinsey Stephenson, Alexandra Durrell, Laura Albert *After more than 200 years, a creature still lives inside the same old house, where a few students play "dare to spend the night."*

The Unnamable 2: The Statement of Randolph Carter (1992) by Jean-Paul Ouellette *[v, l]*
Mark Kinsey Stephenson, John Rhys-Davies, David Warner, Julie Strain *After more than 204 years, a creature still lives inside the same house, but this time she's freed from her demonic body for a while.*

Urban Legend (1999) by Jamie Blanks *[v, d]*
Jared Leto, Alicia Witt, Rebecca Gayheart, Joshua Jackson, Natasha Gregson Wagner, Robert Englund *A killer uses modern folklore to stage strange murders. Pretty fun, especially because you know how every story already ends: you die!!*

Valley of Gwangy (1969) by James O'Connolly *[v, l]*
James Franciscus, Gila Golan, Richard Carlson, Laurence Naismith *Cowboys find a valley with living dinosaurs. Hi-ho stegosaurus!*

Vampire in Brooklyn (1995) by Wes Craven *[v, l]*
Eddie Murphy, Angela Bassett, Kadeem Hardison, Allen Payne *Vampire Maximillian reaches Brooklyn looking for the last descendant of his race. She's a woman, and she's a cop.*

Vampires (1999) by John Carpenter *[v, d]*
James Woods, Daniel Baldwin, Sheryl Lee, Thomas Ian Griffith, Maximillian Schell *Mercenaries kill vampires for a living. Vampires kill mercenaries for a dying.*

Varan, the Unbelievable (1961) by Inoshiro Honda, Jerry Baerwitz *[v]*
Myron Healey, Tsuruko Kobayashi, Kozo Nomura, Ayumi Sonoda *Can you believe Varan? Probably not. It looks like a reptile, but they say it's a squirrel. Oh well . . .*

Village of the Damned (1960) by Wolf Rilla *[v, l]*
George Sanders, Barbara Shelley, Martin Stephens, Laurence Naismith *Some 10 children are born in England. They are eager to learn, especially how to destroy us.*

Village of the Damned (1995) by John Carpenter *[v, l, d]*
Christopher Reeve, Kirstie Alley, Linda Kozlowski, Mark Hamill *Once again, 10 children are born—in America this time—but they hate humans and want to kill us all.*

Warlock (1991) by Steve Miner *[v, l, d]*
Richard E. Grant, Julian Sands, Lori Singer, Mary Woronov *A warlock who escaped execution 300 years ago comes to Los Angeles and looks for a book to unravel the entire universe.*

Warlock: The Armageddon (1993) by Anthony Hickox *[v, l]*
Julian Sands, Chris Young, Paula Marshall, Steve Kahan *Now the warlock is after a few stones which, when all together, will open the gates of hell. He can't make up his mind.*

War of the Gargantuas (1966) by Inoshiro Honda *[v]*
Russ Tamblyn, Kumi Mizuno, Kipp Hamilton, Yu Fujiki *Two giants, one green and evil, one brown and less evil, menace Tokyo.*

War of the Worlds (1953) by Byron Haskin *[v, l, d]*
Gene Barry, Ann Robinson, Les Tremayne, Lewis Martin *Martians land on Earth disguised as meteors, and level everything to the ground, foregoing any attempt to communicate.*

Watchers (1986) by Jon Hess *[v, l]*
Corey Haim, Barbara Williams, Michael Ironside, Lala *Two lab experiments escape: one is a super-intelligent dog; the other one is a deformed killing machine. They hate each other.*

Watchers II (1990) by Thierry Notz *[v, l]*
Marc Singer, Tracy Scoggins, Tom Poster, Jonathan Farwell *Sequel-remake of the previous flick.*

Watchers 3 (1994) by Jeremy Stanford *[v, l]*
Wings Hauser, Gregory Scott Cummins, Daryl Roach, John K. Linton *Sequel-remake of the previous sequel-remake. Simply set in the jungle to add something new.*

Watchers Reborn (1998) by John Carl Buelcher *[v]*
Mark Hamill, Lou Rawls, Gary Collins, Lloyd Garroway, Kane Hodder, Floyd Levine, Stephen Macht, Lisa Wilcox *Sequel-remake of the previous sequel-remake of the previous sequel-remake. Oh.*

Waxwork (1988) by Anthony Hickox *[v, l]*
Zach Galligan, Deborah Foreman, Michelle Johnson, Dana Ashbrook *Wax statues in a museum come to life and plan to take over the world.*

Waxwork 2: Lost in Time (1991) by Anthony Hickox *[v, l]*
Zach Galligan, Alexander Godunov, Bruce Campbell, Michael Des Barres *A wax museum has a door*

that leads into other times, with one thing in common: you die.

Werewolf of London (1935) by Stuart Walker *[v, l]*
Henry Hull, Warner Oland, Valerie Hobson, Lester Matthews *While in Tibet searching for the remedy for lycanthropy, a man is attacked by a werewolf and becomes one himself. In London.*

Wes Craven's New Nightmare (1994) by Wes Craven *[v, l, d]*
Robert Englund, Heather Langenkamp, Miko Hughes, David Newsom, John Saxon, Freddy Krueger *What if Freddy gets sick and tired of being portrayed on screen, and jumps out of the written page for real?*

Westworld (1973) by Michael Crichton *[v, l, d]*
Yul Brynner, Richard Benjamin, James Brolin, Dick Van Patten *Delos is the most sophisticated theme park, where you can play, have sex, and even kill robots. One day they kill back.*

What Ever Happened to Baby Jane? (1962) by Robert Aldrich *[v, l, d]*
Bette Davis, Joan Crawford, Victor Buono, Anna Lee *Two sisters hate each other, but one is in a wheelchair, while the other is crazy.*

Willard (1971) by Daniel Mann *[v, l]*
Bruce Davison, Ernest Borgnine, Elsa Lanchester, Sandra Locke *A timid orphan takes his revenge when he befriends and trains a bunch of rats who "take care of problems" for him.*

Willow (1988) by Ron Howard *[v, l]*
Val Kilmer, Warwick Davis, Jean Marsh, Joanne Whalley *The quest for retrieving a child who will help fight an evil queen. Dragons, transformations, magic, and adventure.*

The Wishmaster (1997) by Robert Kurtzman *[v, l, d]*
Tammy Lauren, Andrew Divoff, Robert Englund, Chris Lemmon *An evil genie grants wishes to everyone... but from his twisted, eerie point of view.*

The Wishmaster 2: Evil Never Dies (1999) by Jack Sholder *[v, d]*
Andrew Divoff, Paul Johansson, Holly Fields, Bokeem Woodbine, Carlos Leon, Christopher Boyer *One more time!*

The Witches (1990) by Nicolas Roeg *[v, l, d]*
Anjelica Huston, Mai Zetterling, Jasen Fisher, Rowan Atkinson *A witch convention is ruined by a couple of kids who will soon be turned into mice.*

The Witches of Eastwick (1987) by George Miller *[v, l, d]*
Jack Nicholson, Cher, Michelle Pfeiffer, Susan Sarandon *The devil incarnates into a seductive man who finds a place in three women's hearts. But the women aren't ordinary chicks.*

The Wizard of Oz (1939) by Victor Fleming *[v, l, d]*
Judy Garland, Margaret Hamilton, Ray Bolger, Jack Haley, Bert Lahr *We fly from Kansas to Oz... don't tell us we have to tell you the story of this movie.*

Wolf (1994) by Mike Nichols *[v, l, d]*
Jack Nicholson, Michelle Pfeiffer, James Spader, Kate Nelligan *A book editor is bitten by a werewolf and becomes one himself, sort of forever.*

The Wolf Man (1941) by George Waggoner *[v, l, d]*
Lon Chaney, Jr., Claude Rains, Maria Ouspenskaya, Ralph Bellamy *Chubby Larry Talbot is bitten by a werewolf and becomes one himself. What's worse, he knows about it.*

The Woman Eater (1959) by Terence Young *[v, d]*
Stewart Granger, Edwige Feuillère, Ronald Squire, Mary Jerrold *Amazonian plant is kept alive by a scientist who feeds it with women parts.*

Wrestling Women vs. the Aztec Mummy (1959) by René Cardona, Sr.
Lorena Velasguez, Armando Silvestre *With a title like this, who needs a story?*

X the Unknown (1956) by Leslie Norman *[v, d]*
Dean Jagger, Leo McKern, William Lucas, Edward Chapman *A radioactive mud surfaces on Earth and melts anyone who's too close.*

Xtro (1983) by Harry Bromley Davenport *[v, l]*
Philip Sayer, Bernice Stegers, Danny Brainin, Simon Nash, Maryam D'Abo *A man is abducted by aliens and sent back three years later—but he's become a vicious creature with a passion for killing.*

Xtro II: the Second Encounter (1991) by Harry Bromley Davenport *[v, l]*
Jan-Michael Vincent, Paul Koslo, Tara Buckman, Jano Fradson *Surprise! This movie is not sequel to the previous one. Yeah, there is an alien and stuff, but everybody and everything runs amuck.*

Xtro: Watch the Skies (Xtro 3) (1995) by Harry Bromley Davenport *[v]*
Sal Landi, Jim Hanks, Robert Culp, Andrew Divoff *Don't ever kill the mate of an alien, especially if it's marooned on a desert island—and you're around.*

Yeti (1977) by Frank Kramer (Gianfranco Parolini) *[v]*
Phoenix Grant, Mimmo Crao, Jim Sullivan, Tony Kendall *An abominable snowman is defrosted and brought to town. Guess what? It destroys everything.*

Yog—Monster from Space (1971) by Inoshiro Honda *[v]*
Akira Kubo, Yoshio Tsuchiya *A space amoeba lands on Earth and "possesses" a few of the sea creatures, sending them on a killing rampage.*

APPENDIX 3

Here's how the body counts of the monsters covered in the HMSG *stack up:*

Monster	People	Animals	Active?
1. *Aliens*	*191*	*1*	*?*
2. Jason Voorhees (*Friday the 13th* series)	*124*	*1*	*Yes*
3. Jack Griffin (*The Invisible Man)*	*122*	*0*	*No*
4. *Killer Klowns from Outer Space*	*120+*	*1*	*?*
5. The Tall Man (*Phantasm* series)	*79+*	*1*	*?*
6. *Carrie* White	*76*	*0*	*No*
7. Lord Crumb & His Army (*Bad Taste)*	*75+*	*0*	*No*
8. Michael Myers (*Halloween* series)	*75*	*4*	*Yes*
9. The Knoxes (*Natural Born Killers)*	*74+*	*?*	*Yes*
10. *Children of the Corn*	*72+*	*1*	*Yes?*
11. Damien Thorn (*The Omen* series)	*62+*	*0*	*No*
12. *The Blob*	*51*	*6*	*Yes*
13. Horace Pinker (*Shocker)*	*50+*	*100+*	*No*
14. The "its" (*It's Alive* series)	*45*	*2*	*Yes*
15. Angela Baker (*Sleepaway Camp* series)	*45*	*0*	*Yes*
16. *The Hidden*	*42*	*2*	*?*
17. *The Outsiders*	*41+*	*2*	*No*
18. Johnny Bartlett (*The Frighteners)*	*40*	*0*	*No*
19. *Predator*	*37*	*0*	*Yes*
20. Freddy Krueger (*A Nightmare on Elm Street* series)	*31*	*0*	*Yes*
21. *Candyman*	*30*	*1*	*?*
22. *Alligators*	*27*	*1*	*No*
23. *Terminator* T-101	*27*	*0*	*No*
24. The Dinosaurs (*Jurassic Park)*	*26+*	*3*	*Yes*

Monster	People	Animals	Active?
25. The Cenobites (*Hellraiser)*	*26*	*1*	*No*
26. Giant Animals (*Food of the Gods* series)	*25+*	*0*	*Yes*
27. Chucky (*Child's Play)*	*24 (+1)*	*0*	*No?*
28. Dr. Evan Rendall (*Dr. Giggles)*	*24*	*0*	*No*
29. Ricky Caldwell (*Silent Night, Deadly Night II* and *III)*	*21*	*0*	*?*
30. *Maximum Overdrive* Machines	*20+*	*1*	*?*
31. *976-EVIL*	*19 (+2)*	*1*	*?*
32. Great White Shark (*Jaws* series)	*19*	*2*	*No*
33. The *Leprechaun*	*19*	*0*	*?*
34. John Ryder (*The Hitcher)*	*19*	*0*	*No*
35. *John Carpenter's The Thing*	*17*	*3*	*?*
36. Cro-Magnon Caveman (*Memorial Valley Massacre)*	*16*	*3*	*Yes*
37. *Night of the Creeps*	*16*	*2*	*Yes*
38. Graboids (*Tremors* series)	*16*	*2*	*No*
39. *Piranha*—Flying	*16*	*?*	*No?*
40. Belial (*Basket Case* series)	*16*	*0*	*Yes*
41. Hannibal Lecter (*Manhunter, The Silence of the Lambs)*	*16*	*0*	*Yes*
42. Akúa (*Demon of Paradise)*	*16*	*0*	*?*
43. *Pumpkinhead*	*16*	*0*	*?*
44. Myles Sheffield (*Bloodmoon)*	*16*	*0*	*No?*
45. *Humanoids from the Deep* (1976)	*15+*	*9*	*Yes*
46. Francis Dollarhyde, a.k.a. "The Tooth Fairy" (*Manhunter)*	*15*	*0*	*No*
47. Dr. Anton Phibes (*The Abominable Dr. Phibes* series)	*14*	*0*	*Yes*
48. Sil (*Species)*	*14*	*0*	*Yes*
49. Kharis (*The Mummy* series)	*14*	*0*	*?*
50. Kothoga (*The Relic)*	*13*	*1*	*No*
51. Headless Horseman (*Sleepy Hollow)*	*12+*	*0*	*No*
52. Mary Lou Mahoney (*Prom Night II* and *III)*	*12*	*0*	*?*
53. *Leviathan*	*11+*	*0*	*No*
54. Monster Pet (*TerrorVision)*	*11*	*0*	*Yes*
55. *Trucks*	*11*	*0*	*Yes*
56. Giant Octopus (*Tentacles)*	*11*	*0*	*No*
57. Ben & the Rats (*Willard)*	*10+*	*0*	*Yes*
58. Draco (*Dragonheart)*	*10+*	*0*	*No*
59. *Bats*	*10*	*6*	*Yes*
60. Krites (*Critters* series)	*10*	*5+*	*No?*
61. Ted Wornakis (*Psycho Cop)*	*10*	*1*	*Yes*
62. *Christine*	*10*	*0*	*Yes*
63. Sam Harper (*Uncle Sam)*	*10*	*0*	*No*
64. Peter Neal (*Tenebrae)*	*10*	*0*	*No*
65. Nix (*The Lord of Illusions)*	*10*	*0*	*No*
66. George Stark (*The Dark Half)*	*10*	*0*	*No*
67. Pamela Voorhees (*Friday the 13th)*	*10*	*0*	*No*
68. *The Creature from the Black Lagoon*	*9*	*2*	*No*
69. *The Borrower*	*9*	*1*	*Yes*
70. Brenda (*Urban Legend)*	*9*	*1*	*Yes*
71. *The Sea Serpent*	*9*	*?*	*Yes*
72. Killbots (*Chopping Mall)*	*9*	*0*	*No?*
73. *Humanoids from the Deep* (1996)	*8+*	*1*	*Yes*
74. Nocturnal Flying Aliens (*Pitch Black)*	*8+*	*0*	*Yes*
75. *Grizzly*	*8*	*2*	*No*
76. *Frogs*	*8*	*0*	*Yes*

Monster	People	Animals	Active?
77. Imp (*Sorority Babes in the Slimeball Bowl-O-Rama)*	*8*	*0*	*Yes*
78. Billy Caldwell (*Silent Night, Deadly Night)*	*8*	*0*	*No*
79. Jame Gumb, a.k.a. "Buffalo Bill" (*The Silence of the Lambs)*	*8*	*0*	*No*
80. Spiders (*Arachnophobia)*	*7*	*100+*	*No*
81. "Aquatica" Mako Sharks (*Deep Blue Sea)*	*7*	*2*	*No*
82. Queen Tera (*Bram Stoker's The Mummy)*	*7*	*1*	*?*
83. Cemetery Creature (*Graveyard Shift)*	*7*	*1*	*No*
84. David Kessler (*An American Werewolf in London)*	*7*	*1*	*No*
85. Psycho Scuba Diver (*Amsterdamned)*	*7*	*1*	*No*
86. Terminator T-1000 (*Terminator 2: Judgment Day)*	*7*	*1*	*No*
87. Father Jonas (*Prom Night IV: Deliver Us from Evil)*	*7*	*0*	*?*
88. Peter Neil (*Tenebrae)*	*7*	*0*	*No*
89. *Deep Star Six* Creature	*6(+4)*	*0*	*No*
90. Max (*Man's Best Friend)*	*6*	*2*	*No*
91. *Orca*	*6*	*0*	*Yes*
92. Queen Kara (*The Awakening)*	*6*	*0*	*Yes*
93. Benjamin Willis (*I Know What You Did Last Summer* series)	*6*	*0*	*Yes*
94. Blake and the Ghosts (*The Fog)*	*6*	*0*	*?*
95. Aylmer (*Brain Damage)*	*6*	*0*	*No*
96. Daryl Revock (*Scanners)*	*6*	*0*	*No*
97. Annie Wilkes (*Misery)*	*6*	*0*	*No*
98. *The Mangler*	*5(+4)*	*0*	*Yes*
99. Eggar's Mother (*The Final Terror)*	*5*	*20+*	*No*
100. *Anaconda*	*5*	*2*	*Yes*
101. *Octaman*	*5*	*1*	*?*
102. Silver Spheres (*Phantasm* series)	*5*	*1*	*?*
103. Hugie Warriner (*Dead Calm)*	*5*	*1*	*No*
104. *Hack-O-Lantern* Cult	*5*	*0*	*Yes*
105. *House on Haunted Hill*	*5*	*0*	*Yes*
106. Dr. Hank Symen (*Habitat)*	*5*	*0*	*Yes*
107. Umoia Omube (*Curse III: Blood Sacrifice)*	*5*	*0*	*Yes*
108. John Doe (*Se7en)*	*5*	*0*	*No*
109. Edgar (*MIB: Men in Black)*	*5*	*0*	*No*
110. Alex Hammond (*Prom Night)*	*5*	*0*	*No*
111. Pino Petto (*Silent Night, Deadly Night V: The Toy Maker)*	*5*	*0*	*No*
112. Azazel (*Fallen)*	*4+*	*0*	*Yes*
113. *The Birds*	*4+*	*0*	*Yes*
114. *Razorback*	*4*	*800+*	*No*
115. Oil Slick (*Creepshow II)*	*4*	*1*	*Yes*
116. *Gremlins*	*4*	*0*	*Yes*
117. Jennifer "Jenny" Hills (*I Spit on Your Grave)*	*4*	*0*	*Yes*
118. *Xtro*	*4*	*0*	*Yes*
119. Cristiano Berti (*Tenebrae)*	*4*	*0*	*No*
120. HAL 9000 (*2001: A Space Odyssey)*	*4*	*0*	*No*
121. *Stanley*	*4*	*0*	*No*
122. Gunther Stryker (*The Funhouse)*	*4*	*0*	*No*
123. Larry Talbot (*The Wolf Man* series)	*4*	*0*	*No*
124. *The Brood*	*4*	*0*	*?*
125. The Collectors (*Tales from the Crypt: Demon Knight)*	*4*	*0*	*?*
126. Gus Gilbert (*Pet Sematary II)*	*3*	*20+*	*No*
127. Witches (*The Craft)*	*3*	*7*	*Yes*
128. *Lake Placid* Crocodiles	*3*	*3+*	*Yes*

Monster	People	Animals	Active?
129. Andy McDermott (*An American Werewolf in Paris)*	*3*	*1*	*Yes*
130. Imhotep (*The Mummy* 1932)	*3*	*1*	*No*
131. Carter Nix and . . . (*Raising Cain)*	*3*	*0*	*Yes*
132. Riff Raff (*The Rocky Horror Picture Show)*	*3*	*0*	*Yes*
133. Strangers (*Dark City)*	*3*	*0*	*Yes*
134. Kharis (*The Mummy* 1959)	*3*	*0*	*?*
135. *Yog—Monster from Space*	*3*	*0*	*?*
136. *Cujo*	*3*	*0*	*No*
137. *Patrick*	*3*	*0*	*No*
138. John Milton (*The Devil's Advocate)*	*2(+2)*	*0*	*Yes*
139. Charles Brady (*Stephen King's Sleepwalkers*)	*2*	*20+*	*No*
140. Mary Brady (*Stephen King's Sleepwalkers*)	*2*	*20+*	*No*
141. *The Thing from Another World*	*2*	*4*	*No*
142. Blue Ribbon Teens (*Disturbing Behavior)*	*2*	*0*	*Yes*
143. Spencer Armacost/Gooey Alien (*The Astronaut's Wife)*	*2*	*0*	*Yes*
144. Hill House (*The Haunting)*	*2*	*0*	*No?*
145. Maximillian (*The Black Hole)*	*2*	*0*	*No?*
146. Cage Greed (*Pet Sematary)*	*2*	*0*	*No*
147. Gunslinger (*Westworld* series)	*2*	*0*	*No*
148. Happy Toyz Truck (*Maximum Overdrive)*	*2*	*0*	*No*
149. Shriekers (*Tremors 2: Aftershocks)*	*2*	*0*	*No*
150. Zowie (*Pet Sematary 2)*	*1*	*2*	*No*
151. Audrey II (*Little Shop of Horrors)*	*1*	*0*	*Yes*
152. Bobbi (*Dressed to Kill)*	*1*	*0*	*Yes*
153. Proteus IV (*The Demon Seed)*	*1*	*0*	*Yes*
154. Jack Torrance (*The Shining)*	*1*	*0*	*?*
155. Dr. Frank-N-Furter (*The Rocky Horror Picture Show)*	*1*	*0*	*No*
156. Renee Hallow (*Pet Sematary 2)*	*1*	*0*	*No*
157. *Eegah*	*0*	*1*	*No*
158. Ernie "Chip" Douglas (*The Cable Guy)*	*0*	*0*	*Yes*
159. Klaris (*Abbott & Costello Meet the Mummy)*	*0*	*0*	*No*